ADEPT INITIATE

THE IMPERIAL ADEPT PREQUEL

NATHAN TUDOR

ADEPT INITIATE

NATHAN TUDOR

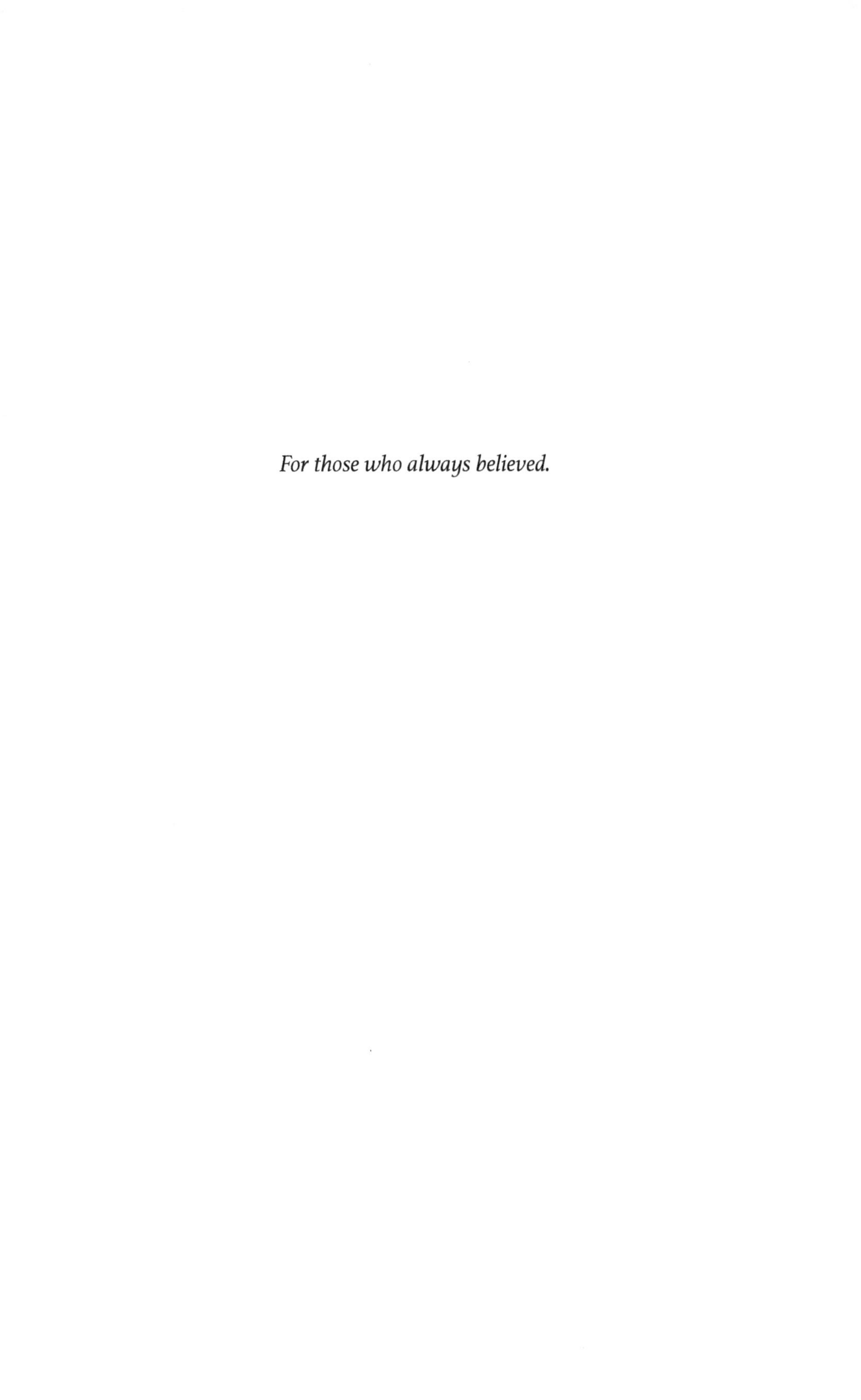

For those who always believed.

CONTENTS

PART I

STRANGERS

1

THIRTY SILVER

THE MOON WAS HIGH, and the air was cold in Shugrith, the Jewel of the Sands.

Rebbaelah passed the threading needle through her little brother's ripped tunic. Despite some vigorous scrubbing in the river earlier, the dark stain of blood persisted.

He had gotten into a fight. Again, the other boys had been bigger than him. Three to one. He'd fought them anyway.

Thank the Four, she'd been near enough to hear the commotion and put a stop to things. Putting a stop to things had involved breaking one of the boys' noses, which her mother said was wrong. No woman should have a reputation for violence, for interfering in the affairs of men. Someday she would have to find a husband, and that sort of reputation boded ill for a woman's prospects.

Well, that was a problem for the future. And if the Four didn't want her to fight on her little brother's behalf, they could have made her shorter. If she had to bear the jeers of boys calling her a giant, she might as well put her height to use.

Her brother *was* upset about it, she knew. That bothered her more. But again, what was she to do? Their father died nearly three years ago. And if their mother wasn't going to do anything, it fell to Rebbaelah.

Many things fell to Rebbaelah. Sewing up the torn clothes. Cooking what meager meals they could manage. Buying the ingredients for those meals, which inevitably involved a great deal of haggling.

The folks at the market only haggled for her own sake. She knew that much. Some days it irked her, knowing that they had such pity for her family. But at least they put on the show of treating her like any other customer instead of just giving her a lower price from the outset.

Her eyes stung. She blinked it away, turned her attention back to the sewing. It was nearly finished. Her brother had fallen asleep already, tired from his afternoon dust-up. She was tired too, but there were still chores to be done.

Footsteps by the door. She recognized her mother's tread. Fast, but not stumbling. She was sober then. Good—maybe she would be able to prepare the leaven for tomorrow after all. That would ease Rebbaelah's burden for the night.

The door opened slowly. Rebbaelah looked up, frowning.

Iverah beyt'Avadh had lost much since her husband's death. Peace, stability, happiness. But years, she had lost far more years than the passage of time merited. In the three years since her husband's death, she seemed to have aged a decade. Her hair was limp and lifeless, her eyes haunted. Always her lips tugged mournful grooves down her face. Even the merriment of drink abated her little—there was no merriment in wine, only temporary obliteration.

"Is your brother asleep?" she whispered, still standing in the doorway.

Rebbaelah nodded. "He is. He was in a fight earlier. He got hurt." From the corner of her eye, she watched for any reaction.

Today, Iverah must have felt more maternal than most, because she actually seemed wounded by the news. For a moment, Rebbaelah almost thought she was going to go check on him. But still, she stood in the doorway.

"Well," she said, venting a sigh, "I think we should surprise him. Get him...get him a treat for tomorrow."

Rebbaelah's fingers stopped their needlework. Now she looked at her mother head-on, not bothering to hide her confusion. "A treat."

Iverah swallowed, nodded her head again and again. "Lelah told me her landlord's fig grove ripened early. The workers are going to harvest tomorrow. If we go tonight..."

Rebbaelah nodded slowly. The law in Talynis allowed for such things. Technically, the impoverished were not to take their share until *after* the owner had gone through and harvested the first pass, but if you were sparing in how much you took, Lelah's landlord didn't care.

"I didn't know Lelah still talked to you."

Iverah flinched. "She's worried for us. She's still a good friend."

Rebbaelah didn't feel bad about how that had stung, not anymore at least. Maybe that meant she was a wicked daughter, but if the gods had any displeasure with her, it couldn't be much worse than what she already had to bear.

Still, figs were figs. A welcome change from the barley loaves they subsisted on every day. And they *were* her brother's favorite.

"Let me finish sewing this and then we can go."

"No, we should go now," said Iverah. "While the moon is still high. Before the wind kicks up."

Rebbaelah bit her tongue. Sacred verses about the virtue of obedient children rolled through her mind. Funny how the priests always taught those so readily, but held off on reciting anything that adjured parents.

"Yes, mother," she whispered, setting aside the tunic.

Iverah seemed relieved, and she even went to pick up her basket on her own instead of waiting for Rebbaelah to get it.

Rebbaelah padded to the cot in the corner of the room where her little brother lay snoozing beneath a threadbare blanket. Gently, she pressed a small kiss to his temple. His features twitched, and he mumbled something. He seemed to be dreaming.

She stood, picked up her basket, and followed her mother out the door.

THE FIG GROVE was not far outside the gates. Shugrith was not the capital of Talynis, but it may have been the best place to live. Once, Rebbaelah's father had told her that in other *maiir* people had to walk half an hour to find crops for picking. Shugrith was a place of plenty, though, well-watered and green.

They made the walk even faster than normal. Ordinarily, Rebbaelah led the way, ensuring Iverah didn't drag her feet. Tonight though, her mother set the pace.

She found herself watching her mother, observing how she moved. The determination of her steps. The way her eyes stayed fixed forward. How her chin stayed high instead of drooping down to her chest.

Her mother looked...*herself* again.

Rebbaelah swallowed.

Don't get excited. Don't hope. It won't last.

Iverah noticed she was watching and actually offered a frail smile. The expression looked foreign on her face, like the muscle memory had been forgotten and reconstructed.

Something sparked in Rebbaelah's heart.

Maybe the gods were giving her something after all. Years after they had taken her father, years of silence—now maybe they were finally attending to her.

Maybe they were giving her mother back.

She stood straighter, hurrying to match her mother's stride.

They said nothing on the way, and Rebbaelah was glad for it. Even seeing this sort of purpose was enough. Words were too danger-ous, too liable to bring something wrong. She didn't trust herself to speak, and she didn't want to hear anything from her mother, not yet.

But if this really was a step in the right direction...

She imagined her brother waking up tomorrow, eyes bright as he took in the fresh figs. One of his teeth had fallen out last week, so he would chew on the left side.

She smiled, and felt surprised when she realized it.

One good night, one good morning. Even if that was all she got, it would be something. And it would represent the possibility of more.

The grove was planted alongside one of Shugrith's rivers. It wasn't the biggest in the *maiir*, but it did produce the sweetest figs, famous throughout the city.

So Rebbaelah frowned at the lack of any night watchmen. "Where's Lelah's husband? Doesn't he watch the grove this close to harvest?"

"He's probably just taking a nap somewhere. Maybe we'll see him further in."

Rebbaelah bit her lip, but followed as her mother stepped between the trees. They had walked about a minute before she spotted a tree easy enough to pick from. Setting her basket down, she jumped, grabbing hold of the branch near the trunk and setting her foot, and levered herself up.

Eagerly, she took hold of the nearest fig and squeezed it with her finger and thumb. Then she frowned. "Not ripe."

She reached for another, but Iverah snapped, "Not there. I told you, Lelah told me where they ripened."

Rebbaelah scowled as she dropped back to earth. "No, you said Lelah told you the figs ripened early."

"Well, the whole grove doesn't turn at once, girl. Now stop climbing trees and follow me—they're toward the other end."

Muttering to herself, Rebbaelah set the basket on her hip and trudged after her mother.

"It's fine," she grumbled. "Don't let it ruin things. Focus on the figs."

And she did. She looked up, taking in the trees as they went. The shapes of the leaves, their color. The size and number of the fruits hanging from their boughs.

And she slowed.

Fruits ripened at different times—there were always the firstfruits of the seasonal harvest—but *this* early? Some of these looked like they wouldn't turn for another two weeks at the soonest.

And then she lowered her gaze.

She was alone.

"Mother?" she called, hesitantly. "Mother, I can't see you."

A rustling at her side. She turned.

"Mo—"

The gag came between her teeth in a flash. She screamed to no avail. She dropped the basket, punching wildly, but bigger, rougher hands clamped down on her wrists, twisting her arms behind her.

Rebbaelah thrashed and kicked like a wild animal in a snare. All the while, she screamed against the gag, feeling her throat go raw. Thick rope fastened her wrists, and a sharp blow to the hip buckled her to her knees.

"Play nice or I cut your throat, girl."

Rebbaelah went still, eyes widening. The breath at her ear was hot, and she caught a sour whiff of it. Whiskers tickled her ear as the man spoke.

Not just one man—two. The one speaking, holding her at the shoulders, and another one standing a few feet away. This second one wore boots—fine boots—with an equally fine overcoat and glittering rings on his fingers. His neat black beard came to a point, and his eyes were half-lidded as he spoke. "Didn't say she'd be so feisty."

Her mother answered. "Well, she works hard. She's strong. That's good, isn't it?"

Rebbaelah screwed her eyes shut. Tears were spilling now.

So that's what was happening.

She tasted bile, and she thought of the gods. The gods who she had actually considered for a moment were returning something they had taken,

However many times I cursed you, I send again twice over. All four of you!

The finely dressed man stroked his trimmed beard. "Sure, sure. Look at me, girl."

She didn't. He grabbed her hair, twisting her head toward his voice. She groaned against the gag, new tears prickling at her eyes.

"Look or I'll cut off your eyelids."

That was a lie. He was a slaver—he had to be. He wouldn't want his goods damaged.

But it hurt, so she obeyed.

He took her chin in his fingers, turning her face this way and that. This close, he smelled of cheap oils. The tunic beneath his overcoat was roughspun, not smooth and tailored.

He shrugged. "She's pretty enough."

"And a virgin," her mother offered.

Rebbaelah's stomach turned. It had been one thing when her mother was drunk, or angry, or a sobbing mess—but to hear her talking about her like *merchandise*.

She might have lost her stomach if she'd had enough in there to lose.

The slaver hummed. "All right. The agreed upon fee then." He reached inside his coat and withdrew a purse clinking with coin. "Thirty silver."

Iverah snatched it away, holding it close to her chest.

You should be holding me *like that*. Rebbaelah thrashed again. The slaver rewarded her with a swift backhanded slap.

"Come along, girl. We're behind schedule. And don't run—your hands are tied to Damez there."

She chanced a glimpse over her shoulder, and sure enough, the rope cinching her wrists was looped around the man's waist. He offered her a nasty grin as she shoved her forward.

She stumbled, and he kicked her in the ribs.

"None of that," bellowed Damez. "We know all the tricks. Up."

He kicked again before she even had a chance to comply, then hauled her up by the rope. Her hands were tingling by now, nearly void of feeling.

As they took her away, Rebbaelah threw one glance back. Her mother was counting through the purse. By chance, she peered up from the bag and locked eyes with Rebbaelah.

'*I hate you*,' she tried to say, but the gag muffled it into almost animalistic groaning.

Something flickered across Iverah's face. Pain maybe. Anger. And then she turned her back.

Damez shoved Rebbaelah again. This time, she didn't lose her footing. But she couldn't see through the tears, and so Damez roughly tugged her back into line as she meandered forward.

Once they cleared the fig grove, they tossed her into a cart. Her shoulder hit the rough wood and continued to ache as the cart trundled along. She lay there, staring up at silent, uncaring stars that continued turning in their courses, indifferent to what transpired on the earth. She lay there sobbing, unable to scream.

2

THE WANDERING GOD

REBBAELAH STUMBLED THROUGH THE SAND. The sweltering sun beat down overhead, baking the crown of her skull. The heat of the chains and manacles had grown so great that the slaver had ordered Damez to wrap cloth around their hands, lest the metal burn their skin.

Their travels were lengthy, always at the times when they were least likely to encounter anyone else. Everyone in the line, after all, was Talynisti. Were they to be found, the force of the law would be harsh and swift.

So they traveled in the hottest part of the day, when the sand burned underfoot and the air cracked lips. They traveled in the darkest part of the night, when the cold stripped the body's warmth away, right down to the bone. The day drained them of all energy; the night forbade them proper rest. And as they walked further and further from the city of Shugrith, toward the *maiir*'s edge, the climate turned more and more extreme.

The slaver, his name was Baranzir. He spoke to his crew in Zarushan, so many of his words were lost on Rebbaelah. But now and then, he would address them in Karellan. Usually he gave orders, and if they disobeyed his orders, then Damez would mete out some form of punishment.

Not all the other slaves—and she had already taken to thinking of herself as such, after so few days—could understand Karellan, and so one who could was expected to translate. Sometimes Rebbaelah did that. Other times, her tongue was so swollen and her throat so parched that she just let Damez' rod bring compliance to the confused slaves. She felt bad about that the first time she had let it happen. By the fourth or fifth time, she just didn't think of it anymore. All she could think of was her thirst.

And her thirst was great. She had never left the *maiir* before, but by the terrain, by the thinness and the rarity of water, she could only guess they were almost into the desert proper. How did Baranzir plan to cross? Did he have one of the Mithallkiym as a guide? Or would he stick by the better known ways, risking discovery of his crimes?

Such thoughts came, such thoughts went. Always, the thirst remained. She would watch the camels traipsing along. Beautiful creatures—stoic, stolid, unharmed by the brutal sandwhip winds or the paucity of hydration.

Baranzir had little need for water, certainly. He had numerous waterskins. Wineskins too, Rebbaelah guessed, based on how boisterous he became in the night. Some evenings she could hear him and his woman in their little tent, laughing, arguing sometimes. She started to have waking dreams of slipping her restraints and bursting into that tent, stealing Baranzir's knife and killing him. Him and all his horrible allies. The woman. Damez. The archer who kept a keen eye on them at every moment.

She prayed the gods would give her such a chance, even if it were the last thing she got in this life. She asked they forgive her for her imprecations and curses against heaven, that they let her do this one good thing by freeing these people.

But day by day, she stopped caring for the gods' help, and she stopped caring about any lofty goals of freedom. She just wanted to stop the thirst. She wanted to bathe. She wanted to eat an actual meal instead of a stale, burnt morsel of bread.

But what was she to do? Always she was bound. Walking, the

chains. Sleeping, the chains. They were given no privacy to relieve themselves. To Baranzir, they were no different from livestock.

The train approached a frail stream. Rebbaelah could smell it on the wind—faint, but unmistakable. The scent of water had become the only glimmer of goodness in her world.

Baranzir barked something to his accomplices, and the train began to slow. Rebbaelah's heart soared.

"Drink up!" bellowed the slaver. "Won't get water like this for quite some time."

Damez began leading his camel to the stream, tugging the chain along. Then, Baranzir called out again in Zarushan, and Damez stopped. Rebbaelah stared vacantly as he spoke. Water. All she wanted was water. Why make them wait any longer?

And then Damez began moving down the chain with a key, unshackling them.

I've lost my mind.

But it continued. Baranzir's woman too began unlocking their manacles. Damez got to Rebbaelah and turned the key, not even bother to look her in the eyes, and moved on to the next.

She stared at her raw wrists. Then she tripped over herself, breaking for the stream. Already, some were on hands and knees, putting their face into the trickle of water and guzzling what they could.

It wasn't good water—not this far from the source. Dusty, laden with sediment and grit. It was better than mud, at least. She got on her knees, ignoring the way the sand burned, and cupped her hands in the stream to draw up water for herself. She didn't stop to think about how many times she was drinking; she just knew she had to swallow as much as she could before they were made to march again.

She realized, in the back of her mind, that she was crying, crying because this was the last trickle of natural water she would see for gods knew how long. And all she could think was that she was wasting water, crying like that. She needed to conserve that moisture for the desert.

She reached her hands into the warm, shallow water again, and she touched something. Something solid.

As she brought up another handful of water, she looked at it. A stone. A smooth stone, resting in the river.

She stared at it—then the water rippled. A blur of motion. The splash of something breaking through the stream.

She gasped, her head snapping up.

A man was running, sprinting across the sand. His gangly arms and legs flailing as he went. Every frantic step kicked up puffs of dust.

Something inside her screamed. Hope. She felt hope for him. She wanted him to get away. If he could get away, then that meant—

The bowstring thrummed, the arrow whistled.

The running man cried out, clutching at the bolt sprouting from his lower back. He fell to the ground.

Rebbaelah watched him churn the sand as he writhed in agony. He started yelling, cursing Baranzir and his bowman in the words of the Holy Poets. Every sort of doom and damnation reserved for the wicked, he heaped upon their heads.

"May hands of fire break you over boulders,

"And feet of flame trod you in the press!"

Rebbaelah turned aside. Everyone was watching the man.

Which meant no one was watching her.

She could run. She would be shot too. Or maybe Damez would catch her first and hit her with his rod. Maybe she wouldn't even get to die—she'd just get beaten, punished, and made to walk on.

The stone pulled her attention.

Or what if…?

Her hand closed around the stone.

She looked again. No one was watching. She was alone. All alone, in the midst of a dozen others. Were the gods watching, at least? She doubted it.

Her fingers clenched. She would have to be quick. Strong. Before anyone could stop her.

Her breath shortened. She grit her teeth.

She lifted the stone high, turned her head. With every shred of strength left in her sapped body, she brought it down on her temple.

But a hand closed around her wrist.

All was silent. All was still.

The stream did not run, and the dying man did not cry.

She gasped, looking at one who had not been there before. A man, dressed in the robes of the Mithallkiym tribes. His touch was warm. He kneeled beside her at the riverbank, and he looked at her with the strangest gaze. One eye was blue as brightest sky, the other brown as richest earth.

"Rebbaelah," said the stranger, "you are not to die today."

Whether by her own shock or the authority in his voice, her grip slackened. The stone fell from her grasp and struck the sand.

Motion and sound returned to the world. The screaming man went on screaming. The slaves went on observing, then returned to their drinking.

Rebbaelah gaped at the empty air where, moments before, she had seen...

Who did I see?

All throughout the day, the question tormented her. For years she had begged the gods, she had railed against them, she had returned to begging, and so the cycle had gone.

But today, in the moment she made to end her life, a man had appeared to stop her, to tell her that her death was not yet come. A man dressed in the robes of the nomad tribes, the Mithallkiym. The tribes who worshiped as preeminent among the Four Gods, the one called ha'Mithalleik. The Wandering God. The one who takes souls to the place of rest.

The one who did not hear her prayers when she begged for her father's life.

Her heart hammered in her chest. When she lay down to sleep at the end of the day, she feared to close her eyes, lest he come again in her dreams.

But ha'Mithalleik had appeared to her. He had saved her life. She had seen the eyes of a god. She had felt his touch. She had heard his voice. Twelve years of silence, and now this.

She wasn't sure if she should hate him for it. She couldn't find the words to pray to him. So easy had it been to cry against him when he had been silent—but now? What was she to say now?

So she said nothing. And she resolved never again to raise a hand against herself, lest she look him again in those mismatched eyes.

3

DEVILS' LUCK

A SANDSTORM BARRED their passage north, their passage into Zarush. This angered Baranzir, and the day after the storm, Rebbaelah noticed a bruise on his woman's face. Why he would have struck her for the will of the gods, she did not know. But he was a man who would put others in chains, so perhaps she should not have expected anything else.

But then the storm went on. It whipped the sands into a frenzy, and the winds howled a horrid tune. Rebbaelah covered her ears against it, remembering what was said about desert winds—that they were the chorus of the dead.

The impossible, immortal storm ahead of them, Baranzir made the only choice he could and decided they would go west to Parthava. This lengthened the journey through the desert, and thirst reined. Two slaves dropped dead on the sixth day. Baranzir's anger grew.

Rebbaelah began to fear he would lash out against her. He beat other slaves, but often passed over her, as if he could not see her there.

One day, Baranzir's woman was giving them their allotted ration of water from the skins. "What's your name, girl?" she asked.

It had been the first time anyone asked in…well, in quite some time. "Rebbaelah," she croaked.

The woman did not let her drink just yet. "Amestris." When Rebbaelah stared, she went on. "My name. Amestris. Do you know why he doesn't strike you?"

Rebbaelah looked at the purple mark over Amestris' eye. She shook her head.

"He wants you pretty for the market. Some men will pay very well for a lovely young virgin. You could be a concubine. Even a wife. Lucky you, hm?"

She held out the skin, and Rebbaelah took her permitted two swallows of water.

When she was finished, Amestris waited a moment. "Or maybe you'll go to a brothel. And they'll beat you enough to make up for what you're missing out on now."

She finally left, and Rebbaelah's stomach turned such that she had to fight to keep the precious two swallows of water inside.

EVENTUALLY, they left the desert behind. The sands turned to brush lands, then to rolling green plains. Rebbaelah gaped at the sight. Even in the *maiir*, there was always the awareness of the desert all around. The press of death upon the bounds of the oasis.

But here, for as far as the eye could see, there was greenery. She ran her hands over the grass in the morning, feeling the cool dew. She even ran her tongue over it to collect the moisture. Once they came across a river and could refill the waterskins, Baranzir had them drink again. He never let them off anymore, though. He had lost too much merchandise, and the Parthavan grasslands were the sort of place a slave could actually survive if they got away.

They journeyed along the main roads, the fear of running awry of Talynisti law a distant memory. Rebbaelah felt life returning to her in these days. There was less thirst, though not quite enough food still.

Anytime Amestris got the opportunity, she reminded Rebbaelah of her fate. The greater measure of water was so she would look healthy to the buyers. Rebbaelah took the remarks as best she could. She fought to keep them from ruling her mind. It was difficult, but if she did not master her own thoughts, then hours would wend by, hours dominated by dark musings.

Her dreams, however, afforded little comfort. She could not control those as well as her waking mind. So often she found herself on some brutish man's floor, bruised and battered from his displeasure. She would run out the door and find a dozen more men waiting for her. They tore at her clothes and stuffed her mouth with coins until she burst.

For a time, she avoided sleep, trying to lie awake as long as she dared. During the daytime marches, she'd stumble and earn herself a strike from Damez' rod. Never severe enough to break anything or leave a bruise that lasted beyond a day. She noticed this and thought again of Amestris' words.

She tried taking solace in the greenery, but then she would think of how every step was a step closer to her doom. She started to think again of how she might take her life, but then the eyes of the Wandering God would flash through her mind, and she would bury the thoughts.

One day, they reached a village. It was small, not particularly populated. Damez and the archer kept close watch of the slaves, to discourage both escape and any enterprising locals who might try to carry one off for themselves.

Rebbaelah relished the chance to sit on the grass. She stared downward, trying to appear unremarkable. It occurred to her that Baranzir might sell her soon. So she couldn't help but listen in as the slaver loudly spoke with the village headman. The two of them spoke broken trade Karellan, so there was much repeating and clarification, but that was just as well, as her command of the language was no better.

At first, they negotiated for supplies, but then the conversation turned to Baranzir's plans for the rest of the journey.

"Sandstorm kept us from going north," said Baranzir.

"Devils' luck," spat the headman. "But why come all this way? Could've skirted up the border and gone into Zarush."

"Heard good things about Parthavan horses. Thought I might trade for one."

"Aye, well, the best horses in the world are here, and the best of *those* are with the Hunter tribes. But a word of advice—don't try to deal with them."

"Why not? Never heard of them."

The headman made an uncertain sound, then went on with hesitation plain in his voice. "There're these old families living off the land. They stay away from the roads and cities. We trade with them now and then, but not if we can help it. They don't like the Imperials, but they won't join the Coalition army to fight against them. They go on their own. They, ah, think the gods talk to 'em."

Baranzir scoffed. "Don't care *what* they think if they'll sell me a horse."

"Don't take well to slavers."

"It's legal in Parthava, isn't it?"

"O' course, but they're odd folk. They got their own laws, their own ways of doing things. If you want a good horse, then go up to the capital. Folks come from all around to buy and sell. Best chance you'll have."

"Good slave auction there?"

The headman grunted. "Good enough, I hear. Yu really want a good price? Take them to Lazarra."

Baranzir spat. "Didn't you hear me? I'm getting a horse and going back to Zarush."

"I heard, I heard. But ah, that girl there? She a Tal?"

Rebbaelah's fingers twitched. She kept her head down.

"Aye. You want her?"

"Pff, the wife would never let me hear the end of it. But they don't get many like that in Lazarra. You'll get triple what you'd get here. Mountains more than you could sell her for in Zarush. She catches the eye of some senator or legion commander? You'd be set."

Rebbaelah's fingers closed around a clump of grass.

She knew Lazarra. She knew what they'd done to her people. She knew first hand.

Baranzir hummed. "Triple, eh?" She could feel his eyes on her. "Well, always did want to see Lazarra. The roads good as they say?"

"Best roads in the world. Between you and me, I hope they just take this whole country and be done with it. They've got one half of it already. Sure, our Coalition puts up a fight, but one of these days the Imperials'll send one of their Adepts—and that'll be that. Then they'll finally get Talynis, and then there'll be plenty of Tal girls on the auction block. Not as lucrative."

Baranzir hummed. "May as well extend my trip. Besides, my daughters would like souvenirs."

"Tell you what—I'll give you these supplies half-off if you cut me in on what you get off her. Twenty percent."

"Ten."

"Fifteen, and you're still walking away with a better deal. I'll even let you borrow my horse for the journey—show of good faith."

Baranzir shook hands with the headman. "I'll see you on my return."

When night fell, Rebbaelah curled in on herself. Try as she might, sleep took her eventually. And she dreamed again, this time of Lazarran soldiers. She watched them kill her father, then they carried her off to their city.

She opened her eyes, the stars still overhead, and sobbed. The nightmares were hardly different from the reality she found on waking.

4

WARD OF THE EMPIRE

As they drew nearer to the Ixian Reach, the heartlands of the Lazarran Empire, the roads grew smoother. Paved, even. Legionnaires patrolled frequently, keeping them free of bandits. And so the pace of the caravan hastened. Every day, they passed other travelers who hardly batted an eye at the sight of a train of shuffling captives.

This was the Lazarran Empire. This was the engine that had brought death to her household.

Baranzir made a point of wearing his finest clothes, and he even dressed Amestris in better garments. She seemed to take well to this, and her brightened mood manifested in more frequent taunting.

She would whisper horror stories to Rebbaelah of what legionnaires were like with women. Of how the Lazarrans had invented forms of debauchery unknown to any other culture in the world. Of the special pleasure they took in inflicting these inventions on young slaves. Slavery was part of the core structure of Lazarran society, Amestris said. Rebbaelah would find no sympathy here—she would forever be a slave, and even if she were freed, she would forever be a former slave. Barely human.

And then, somehow, the day came when the fear of Lazarra was no longer just something of night terrors or whispered taunts. The famed city lay on the horizon. The city of her doom.

Baranzir's mood lifted the closer they got to the city, so beatings decreased. Rebbaelah guessed that this was not only a result of his happiness, but also out of the desire to not place 'spoiled goods' up for sale. In a strange way, the absence of stinging pain on her skin became its own sort of torment—a constant reminder that a whole new sort of pain was about to become her reality.

As they approached, they passed yet more legionnaires. This close to the capital, they wore the best-polished armor and rode the finest horses she had yet seen. Not as fine as Baranzir's Parthavan horse though, which caught many eyes as they went. The slaver puffed up under the attention and began styling himself as a 'traveling merchant' to any who deigned to speak with him.

The effect was somewhat ruined by his plainly pedestrian use of trade Karellan. Rebbaelah could practically see the sardonic air the legionnaires suppressed when dealing with Baranzir. Anyone who could speak Lazarran, she guessed, would be better esteemed.

All this added to her own fears. She spoke the same trade dialect as Baranzir—would she be able to communicate in the city? Would her new owner force her to learn the Imperial tongue?

She wondered whether she'd ever speak Talynisti to another soul again.

The morning they were to enter the city, they went to the river. All the slaves were made to bathe themselves. It was the first bath she had taken in weeks. The others' teeth chattered, and they shivered horribly, but Rebbaelah found it life-giving. As the sun rose, it dried her hair and the ragged remains of her dress. But if anything was cold, it was her stomach, as if a frigid river stone had settled in her gut, and with every step it weighed down more and more.

The city Lazarra was a city of seven gates, and they entered through a gate marked with an I overhead. Simple enough—this must have been the First Gate. More legionnaires guarded the way, and she saw the way they looked Baranzir and the rest of the train over—a mixture of curiosity and contempt.

She was beginning to notice a paradox: Lazarrans loved their slaves, but they also saw it as a dirty business. So, as they let Baranzir into the city with directions to the auction, they did so with upturned noses.

Foot traffic packed the streets, and if her hands had not been shackled, Rebbaelah would have plugged her nose against the stench. A hot city, wherever in the world it happened to be, had a horrendous reek all its own.

The noise was equally oppressive. Not only did she catch smatterings of trade Karellan as people of all lands and cultures haggled their wares, she also heard the incomprehensible clipped flowing sounds of Lazarran, and even now and then the fringe of a language that—while not Talynisti—might have been close. Zarushan perhaps, or the strange demotic tongue that was common on the lips of New Mizkhari.

The clothing was similarly varied—but most arresting was the sight of the Lazarran toga. Amestris had told her about this—the toga was the exclusive right of a full Lazarran citizen. It was a mark of pride and status to wear one. More acutely than ever before, she felt aware of her tattered rags.

The urge to try and slip away into these massive crowds snuck into her mind. Surely she would have to be taken off the chain at some point—then, if there was an opening, she could fly away and lose herself in this massive city. How could they find one little girl?

But as the faint hope blossomed inside her, a pair of filthy looking men leered out from an alleyway at her. She froze, petrified by their gaze, which only elicited sickly, gap-toothed smiles from them.

Damez shoved her forward. "Keep walking, busy day," he grumbled. The burly man seemed just as offset by the city as Rebbaelah felt. A part of her wanted to dig in her heels just to spite him more.

But onward she walked. She didn't want Damez watching too closely. Sure, she would have to be wary of strangers who might have it out for her—but she had survived crossing the desert, she had survived years without her father, years *with* her mother.

And still, she had the dreamlike saying echoing at the base of her mind, just beneath conscious thought but always present: '*Rebbaelah, you are not to die today.*'

The auction square was the biggest of any plaza she had yet seen. It rivaled the Artisan's Round in Shugrith for scale, but instead of gems and silks, the wares here were human. All shades of skin, all heights, men and women, young and adult. Only the elderly were lacking amongst the number—although she spied a few. What someone would want with an old slave, she had no idea, but maybe they went for more affordable prices.

Her theorizing ground to an abrupt halt as she saw the auction block.

The scaffold was long as ten men laid head to foot, and it rose a man's height from the ground, so that all gathered could see the slaves. People in the crowd shouted out—all the business was being done in the trade language. The crowd, much like the slaves, was a variegated mix. Men and women, and going by attire, there was every degree of wealth. People who, if she had seen them in Shugrith, Rebbaelah would have pegged as of meager means were present and bidding. The only distinction was that the most finely attired seemed to have someone else calling out their bids for them. Slaves buying slaves? Were some people so rich they didn't even come in person, but merely sent slaves to do their purchasing on their behalf?

It was all so...horrendous. Barbaric, that was the word. This wasn't something people should do to each other—there was a reason the Four Gods had set down in the law of Talynis that one shall not buy or sell their fellow Talynisti. It simply was not something you did—not if you had even the slightest measure of respect or love in your heart.

But here she was, by her mother's hand, about to be hauled atop the block, and she'd stand beside who knew how many others who had been reduced to this fate.

She finally forced herself to look at the people standing on the scaffold. They stood in a line, so that people could get a look at them for some time before they came up for auction. Then the auctioneer would bring them forward and would read off the starting price before make comments on the person: "Well-muscled. Youthful. Said to know six languages, including…"

They're all naked, she realized.

Her heart lurched inside, and her stomach knotted up again. Looking at the crowd, her head started to spin. All of these people—hundreds, maybe thousands—she would have to stand in front of.

Many of the slaves were already without clothes, she realized—indeed, she was in the minority for still having anything on. How far had these people been driven, naked under the hot sun, under the cold night sky? Had they shivered through the rain and wind with no comfort against the elements?

She pulled at her dress, feeling the fabric—the ruined, threadbare, patched mess of fabric—that right now was the most precious thing in the world to her. She didn't have anything—but at least dignity, she had some of that left, didn't she? She still had that after being shoved and pulled and crated and chained and beaten and demeaned—she still had a shred of human dignity, didn't she?

But no, here she was just a good to be inspected, evaluated as an investment like one would inspect a goat at market.

Her stomach roiled, and she feared she'd vomit.

Baranzir was chattering about something, but the words were meaningless to her. Empty sound.

Damez was prodding at her, making her step forward. She was in a line now—she could count how many people were between her and the scaffold.

The manacles were still on her wrists. She was still on the ever-clinking chain.

Six people between her and the scaffold. There was a woman at the steps. She would speak to the person selling, look the slave up and down, have them stripped of their clothes—if they still had any—and then send them onto the scaffold. Then she passed a narrow slate block to a man (probably a slave himself, Rebbaelah guessed) who would then deliver the appropriate slate to the auctioneer when the time came for the given slave to be bid upon.

Five left until her turn. The first of Baranzir's slaves was inspected, his thin loincloth torn away, and he was walked up the steps, tugging the rest of them along with the chain. Baranzir told the woman how much he wanted to start the bidding at. She made a face at what he said, but wrote on the slate and passed it to the attendant slave.

Four left. The world was spinning. She strained against the manacles, knowing it was fruitless. Even if she could free herself, there were far too many people. She would be caught. She would be put on the block and—

A rough, calloused hand clamped on her shoulder. She gasped, coming to an abrupt stop halfway through her step.

She spun to look at who had touched her and found herself looking into the hard eyes of a man in uniform. A legionnaire? But unlike most legionnaires she had seen, this man wore a red cloak around his shoulders, with golden trim at the edges.

A memory stirred, something her father had told her in his last days...

The man said something she didn't understand, then pressed something cold against her forehead.

Rebbaelah swallowed, going still as a stone.

Something changed in the atmosphere. All of a sudden, it was like a space had opened up around her—like everyone had taken just one step away.

The solider with the red cloak moved the object along her skull. The cold metal against her forehead felt...odd. Almost like it was alive.

The man's eyebrows raised. A strange light came into his eyes.

Suddenly, Baranzir was there, chattering in his typical way. "Hey! You can bid with the re—"

The slaver went pale. His eyes, wide as bowls, fixed on the man's red-swathed shoulders. His lips opened and closed like a fish pulled from water. "M-my apologies, sir. Lord. I di-I didn't realize who—"

"This girl," said the soldier, speaking with all the confidence of a man who expected no resistance, "is now a ward of the Lazarran Empire. Remove her shackles."

What?

"Yes!" squawked Baranzir. "Of course! As—ah—as for payment, I think a fair remuneration would be—"

The man scowled. "You misunderstand me, slaver. She is *now* a ward of the Empire, manumitted by law and entrusted to the care of the Adept Corps."

Rebbaelah realized what he meant a half-second before Baranzir. As he recovered a bit of his spine, she could only half-listen, drowning in bewilderment.

"Hold on, I brought this girl here at great expense—and clearly she is worth that, given your interest. I think it only fair that—"

But as he went on, he seemed to realize no one was coming to his defense. Even Damez had taken a few steps away, looking suddenly like he wanted to make himself as small as possible despite his stature.

"The Empire," drawled the man, "will reward your labors with the right to continue doing business within her borders. Or go on obstructing the Corps and see what happens, slaver."

Baranzir looked ready to go on another diatribe, when Amestris appeared at his side, clutching at his arm and bowing toward the soldier. "Please forgive him, sir! He's simply weary from the travels and can be quite a fool when he hasn't had his proper rest." She dipped her head low again and again as she spoke, like a worshipper making obeisance in a temple.

Her fingernails pressed into his forearm in sharp depressions, and Baranzir shook her off. His arm bore sharp marks where her nails had dug into the skin—so tightly some of them were even bleeding. "Fool woman," he spat. "I'm not about to be conned out of—"

"The woman," sighed the soldier, "has twice the brain you do. I'd suggest you listen to her."

As he spoke, Amestris had already sprung forward again, and using the keys (which Rebbaelah could only guess she had lifted from Baranzir) unlocked the manacles. As she did, she gave Rebbaelah a severe look. Her lips pursed as though she meant to say something, but once the shackles were off, she stepped away.

The soldier nodded. "There we are. Callis! Maren! Get this one to the Sanctum."

He passed Rebbaelah to a pair of legionnaires, one of whom readily looped his hand around her thin upper arm. "Aye, Adept," said one, a man with a nasty scar along his jaw and a head of graying hair. He then looked down at Rebbaelah with an appraising eye. "Can you walk, girl?"

Rebbaelah stared, then nodded slowly.

"Good, come on. And no running, would you? My knees have been giving me hell this week."

The legionnaire tugged her along, not roughly, but also not in any way that could be described as gentle. As he and his partner brought her through the crowd, people readily made way. Even the auctioneer, Rebbaelah realized, had been distracted from his clamoring and shouting by the incident.

She threw a look over her shoulder and caught sight of Baranzir gawping after her, red in the face. Amestris was at his side, speaking hastily at his ear, pawing at his shoulder and gesticulating madly.

And all the slaves, too, were watching her. Some with vacant looks. Some with envy. Hate. Hope.

Then the legionnaires pulled her around a corner, and the auction block disappeared from sight. For a while longer, she could still hear the auctioneer's warbling voice echoing off the stones of the street and the buildings lining the way.

5

STRANGE BEYOND BELIEF

Rebbaelah marveled at the sight before her.

The Sanctum was an enclosed compound whose walls ringed a wide area, the stones piled high and cut to precision. The gates stood many times her height, set into a magnificent archway, and at either side stood a number of legionnaires on duty. Callis and Maren, the legionnaires who had brought her here, said something in Lazarran to these guards.

Instantly, they were looking at Rebbaelah with curious, even wary, eyes. A smaller door set into the gate opened, and she was ushered through. As soon as they were inside, she stretched her neck to look around, trying to count just how many buildings were inside.

She saw people marching to and fro in armor, others in uniform. She saw young people, even youths her age. Some of these noticed her and began nudging one another and whispering, pointing at Rebbaelah as she was brought along.

"Plenty of time to get to know them later," said Callis. "Now you meet your master."

Rebbaelah's stomach turned, her feet dragged along the stones. *Master.*

So she was a slave after all. She was going to be a slave to—that's right, the Adept Corps. She knew the word *Adept*. It was spoken in hushed whispers in Talynis.

That was what her father had told her, as he shuddered against the aches of his fever. He had seen one of the Lazarran Adepts when he had fought against the invasion three years ago—a single warrior who, in mere minutes, had killed dozens of good Talynisti men with impunity.

The devils of the Empire. Sorcerers and witches who used malicious powers mortals were not meant to wield.

She would be a slave to one of those monsters.

As they took her through the compound, she observed and did her best to memorize paths and doors—which ones were more closely guarded, which ones were locked. Getting out through the gates would be the biggest issue, but there would have to be some other way, maybe a sewer tunnel...

But the sheer number of turns, hallways, and passages soon became a jumble in her mind, and her nutrition-racked body struggled to process so much information. Her mind was slower than normal. Her need to escape struggled against the need for food and water—she hadn't had either since early this morning, and the slightly more generous rations that Baranzir had given them weren't enough.

The legionnaires stopped at a plain door. Callis, the only one who spoke to her, opened it and waved her forward, releasing her arm.

Cautiously, she stepped in. There were two chairs in the room, and a small table to the side between them. On the table were a pair of cups and a pitcher.

"Help yourself," grunted the legionnaire. "He should be here soon." And with a nod toward the far wall, added, "Door's locked by the way."

And with that, the door shut, and Rebbaelah was alone.

The girl from Talynis sagged against the wall.

Think. Plan.

She was alone for the first time in months—this was an opportunity.

She wasn't about to try the door at her back—the two legion-naires were doubtless outside. The other door, the one he had said was locked, she moved toward, padding as silently as she could.

The thought that she was being watched crept into her mind, that there were holes in the wall or the ceiling. Possible, but irrelevant. Besides, everything the legionnaire had said made it clear they expected she might try to escape, and if she was going to be made a slave anyway, what point was there in not testing the bounds of her cage?

So she put her hand on the door handle, and—

It turned on its own.

Rebbaelah jumped back, pulling her hand close to her chest.

The door opened, and a man stood in the frame.

"Hmph." He cast a dry look behind her. "Didn't even touch the water."

Rebbaelah scrambled backwards, tripping over herself and falling to the ground.

The Adept sighed. "Here." He reached into a satchel at his hip and retrieved something wrapped in a linen. With precise motions, he unfolded the fabric and held out something she hadn't seen in...

"What," he snorted, "never seen bread?"

Lashing out like a viper, she snatched the loaf from his hand, tearing into it and ripping off as big of chunks as she could manage. It was fresh, soft—not like those crumbling, burnt morsels Baranzir had kicked to them. She barely chewed before swallowing, and she could feel the food hit her shriveled stomach.

"Easy—you'll get sick scarfing it down like that. Have some water."

He shut the door behind him and moved to the little table.

Rebbaelah watched him go, still devouring the bread as fast as she could.

His back was turned.

And he hadn't locked the door.

She sprang to her feet, reached for the handle and—

His hand covered hers.

A morsel of half-chewed bread lodged in her throat, and she started to choke. The Adept pounded her on the back until she spat it out. She sank to her hands and knees, staring at the wet glob she'd coughed up.

A part of her told her to pick it up and eat it—it was too precious to waste. She hated that she thought like that now.

"Right," he sighed, getting down on one knee. "Normally I wait until we've had a bit to eat and drink, but you're a determined one, eh kid?"

Mustering up her most hostile expression, she tried to glower.

He cracked a smile. "Mm. You *can* understand me, right? Do they not speak Karellan where you're from?"

"I understand," she snapped.

"Ah! She does speak! So what's your name?"

"You're a killer."

He leaned back, a new aspect coming into his expression. "I've killed, yes. Does that bother you?"

"The Empire killed my father."

The Adept clicked his tongue. "I see. Well *I* didn't. I know that doesn't matter to you. In your position I would hate me too—I *did,* in fact, because I was in your position a long time ago. We all were."

"You're going to kill me too."

"Are you listening, kid?"

"I won't be your slave. So you'll have to kill me."

Another grunt. "Well, at least sit down and have some water before I have to kill you."

He stood and made his way back to the chairs. She noted he took the seat facing away from her. If this were anyone but an Adept, she would have thought that stupid. But after seeing how fast he had moved to stop her from opening the door...

The message was clear. Nothing she could do could overwhelm or outmaneuver him.

"I've got more bread," he said eventually. "A little bottle of oil too. Can't have bread without oil, can you?"

Rebbaelah stared at the back of his head for a moment. He sat like that for a bit, then retrieved another loaf of bread—this one bigger than the first. And sure enough, he brought out a little stoppered bottle. He pulled the cork with his teeth and spat it to the side. She watched as he tore off the edge and drizzled some oil over it before popping it in his mouth.

Slowly, she walked to the chair opposite him.

"Are you going to sit?" he asked with a full mouth. "You can stand if you like, but you look like you've walked a long way."

She lowered herself into the chair, doing her best not to show the relief she felt.

Without prompting, the Adept tore another piece off the loaf and handed it to her. She took it, then the bottle he offered.

"Pour as much as you like, but too much makes it soggy and ruins the flavor."

She frowned. "I know how to eat bread."

"And where are you from that they know how to eat bread?"

"Everyone knows how to eat bread."

The Adept smirked. "I suppose. I hear some places don't have bread though. Far-off places."

Rebbaelah furrowed her brow as she considered that. *What would you eat if there were no bread? Just fruits and vegetables? Meat? Fish?* Bread was reliable, consistent.

"Well," continued the Adept. "I'm Alyat. I'm from the Northlands. You know where those are?"

Rebbaelah shrugged. "Not south." The bread was good. The oil was fine as well—smoother and purer than any she'd ever tasted.

"Aye, and quite a ways from it. Across the Frozen Sea."

She looked up from her meal, frowning. "The what?"

"Frozen Sea, some call it the Sea of Salt and Ice. Lots of icebergs."

Rebbaelah blinked. *Icebergs?*

Alyat scratched at his beard—a wiry blond thing. "You're from out east. Your father was killed during an Imperial campaign. Talynis." He didn't state it with the slightest bit of doubt.

Rebbaelah lowered her eyes, focusing on her bread again. "So?"

"Talynis is a ways away. You were brought here from the slave market. Not a lot of Talynisti end up as slaves in Lazarra. You must have quite the story."

She swallowed, then tore off another piece of bread.

Alyat made a grumbling sound in the back of his throat. "How *I* got here is—I was on a longship. Maybe, oh, thirteen years old. We were going to raid along the Hyrgallian coastline. But a storm swept us off course. Our ship capsized, and only all the devils' luck saw me wash up ashore without drowning."

Rebbaelah's eyes were still low, but she had stopped eating the bread.

"Turns out, we'd ended up all the way down in Gallia. This was before Praetor Marcus turned Gallia into an Imperial Province. And I was alone, I didn't speak the language—none of them—and it was winter. I tried to live off the land, but it was an unfamiliar land, a strange territory. And before long, I was found out. Some Gallians trussed me up, recognizing me as a Northlander, and they intended to kill me. Got the sword all sharpened and everything. The night before it was to happen, they tied me to a tree. It was so cold I wondered if I'd die of the winds before they could get to me in the morning."

Alyat stopped to take a sip of water. Then he took another. Carefully, he set his cup on the table, then tore a piece of bread and popped it in his mouth.

"And?" blurted Rebbaelah.

"Hm?"

She bit her tongue. "What happened next?" she muttered.

"Oh, so you were listening. Well, believe it or not, a pretty girl in the village took a liking to me. She cut me loose, sent me on my way with a knife in my hand and a woman's shawl around my shoulders. Never even got her name; we couldn't understand a word of one another's speech."

"Then how do you know she liked you?"

Alyat shrugged. "Makes me feel better about myself to tell it that way."

She snorted, then quickly forced the grin off her face.

Alyat didn't comment on her expression, and just went on with the story. "My luck held. I knew the stars, like any boy on a longship had to, and I headed south. All I cared about was getting warm. I rooted for vegetables, I caught what little game I could—hares mostly, but they were thin things in that clime. I even stole a horse."

Rebbaelah frowned. "That's wrong."

"If you had the chance, while you were being hauled here across the world, to escape the slaver who had hold of you, but you had to steal a horse, would you do it?"

She swallowed. Then nodded.

"Me too. And I thought I would die, so I took the horse. That doesn't mean it was right—I probably did harm to whoever I took the horse from. Maybe they really needed that horse. But I was scared of death in a foreign land, so I put myself first. I didn't even know what I intended to do with myself. Every day I got further and further from my homeland. My chances of getting back were nonexistent. But big things like that don't matter when you bed down at night, shivering, and you close your eyes only to see life and death swinging behind your eyelids."

She thought back to her nights in the slave caravan. She thought of the man who had tried to run in the desert and been shot. She thought of Amestris' terrible words and the terrible future she had painted of what life in Lazarra would be like for Rebbaelah.

"I kept stealing. Spring was long in coming that year. I was hungry all the time. I tried not to take too much, but it was stealing."

"I've been hungry and didn't steal."

"Good for you. You're better than I was."

"I wouldn't say that," she mumbled. "We had people to help us."

"That's better still. But you didn't have anyone to help you when you were put in chains and brought here."

Rebbaelah shook her head.

"I know the Empire killed your father. I know you probably hate everything about this place. You probably hate me. I hated the man who put me through this whole routine, too. His name was Gamollo, and he was a right bastard every day of his life. And just like you, I thought he meant my death. Because I had made my way all the way down to the Ixian Reach, and I had stolen from a Lazarran military patrol while they were sleeping. The lad on guard duty had been snoozing. Someone else must've heard me though and woken up. You know what they did to the guard who had been sleeping? Killed him right there. That's what the Lazarran Legions do to people who fall asleep on guard duty. It's high treason. And if that's what they would do to one of their own, then I was certain whatever they had in mind for me was far worse. And it probably was, knowing what I know now. But the strangest thing happened. There was a man with the patrols. He had a red mantle, like this one I'm wearing, and a funny thing around his neck."

Here Alyat pulled on a chain, tugging a pendant out from beneath his tunic. It looked the same as the thing the Adept in the auction square had pressed to Rebbaelah's head.

"And he did with this the same as was done to you earlier today. I couldn't understand a word of what he said to his fellows, but for whatever reason, they didn't kill me. They hauled me all the way back here to this city, and then to this building, and in this same room I sat where you're sitting now. Took them hours to find a translator, but once they did, Gamollo explained what he was, and what I was."

Alyat held up his hand, and then, softly, a coruscating stream of *light* went up from his palm. The light splashed across the ceiling, bright as the light of the sun. "I am an Adept of the *Ars Lumens*, the Art of Light."

Rebbaelah shook her head. Her breathing was coming fast now. "No."

Alyat tilted his hand so the light painted the wall, illuminating a map that had been in shadow. "You see that? That's the world, girl. I'm from that strip of land along the top—cartographer couldn't even fit the whole thing because he didn't know what it looks like. That purple shape? That's the Ixian Reach, and that star is Lazarra, where we are now."

Rebbaelah hugged her knees to her chest. Tears were threatening to spill over her cheeks.

"Go east, across the Ixian countryside and through Parthava, and *right* before that mountain range at the far edge of the map—that's where you come from. Talynis."

Rebbaelah wiped at her eyes. *It's small. Too small. It can't be that small!*

But there was the whole world she had crossed—and her aching feet told the testimony of just how far it was.

"You came so far, and you've ended up here, girl."

She shook her head. "You're going to kill me."

"You're lying to yourself."

"I won't—I *won't*! You killed my father! It's your fault I'm here! If he hadn't—" she sobbed. "If he—"

She buried her face in her hands. She couldn't stop the tears now, couldn't stop the cries racking her hunger-thinned body.

"It's not fair," she hissed, gritting her teeth.

"No," said Alyat. "It's not fair. You're right about that. It's strange beyond belief that you'd end up here instead of dying along the way, or getting sold off any of a hundred other places you might have been taken. But that's how it goes. Somehow, we find ourselves here. And we find out who we are."

"Shut up!"

"You're going to be an Adept, girl."

"I don't want to! Kill me first."

She sat like that, crying and groaning, hiccuping and sobbing. Eventually, she steadied, and she peered at Alyat with her stinging, waterlogged eyes.

"You can say no. But I won't kill you—you haven't committed any crime that I know of, and as harsh a land as Lazarra is, it holds its laws in high regard. Instead, you'd be returned to the slave market. And there are some folks who take a particular interest in prospective Initiates to the Adept Corps. They think there's something special about them. Which is true. Is that what you want?"

Amestris' harrowing warnings of rich men with strange tastes lurked in the back of her mind.

"So let me tell you," said Alyat, "what you'll get if you cooperate.

You get a crack at freedom. Being an Adept means security. Power. Respect. Admiration. *Authority.* Those are very important things, more so in Lazarra than anywhere else. You have the chance to become a Lazarran citizen—something most folks would give an arm for. You'll become the sort of person no one in the world dares try to step on or shove out of their way. You'll never want for food or clothing or anything else a person could desire. People will all but *worship* you. And it will be the hardest thing you've ever gone through. Seven years of training, and at every turn, the chance to fail and wash out. You'll be stretched in body and mind further than ever. You'll probably even wish you took the choice to go back to the slave market. You'll try convincing yourself that it wouldn't have been so bad. You might even try to run away—some always do, and you have the look."

Alyat leaned back. His eyes had taken on a ferocious glint. "The Empire ruined your life. Now the Empire wants to give you a life beyond imagining. You can spit in the Empire's eye. I might even respect you for it. Or you can be smart and take this chance. You can become an Imperial Adept. You have *magic* in you, kid, something humans have dreamt of and chased after since time immemorial. Divine power, some say. So what do you want? Do you want to get a life beyond measure from the Empire? Do you want the Empire to wash your feet and polish your boots? Or do you want to turn away and go back to the mud?"

Rebbaelah pursed her lips. She felt hollow. She felt angry. Every inch of her quivered with fiery rage. She wanted to strike him. She wanted to break out. She wanted to run.

A part of her cautioned reason, warned that it would be better to take the offer now and then come up with a way to escape later. Another part of her relished the idea of taking riches from the Empire that had hurt her family so badly.

But in her fury, none of it amounted to anything more than a whisper. "No," she said. "No! I won't."

Alyat sighed. "All right. I lied when I said I'd respect the choice. You're a fool, girl. A principled fool, but a fool."

"Take me back to the market. I'd rather be naked on the block than wear any clothes the Empire gives me. I'd rather starve than eat another bite of this bread, or drink another drop of this water."

The Adept got to his feet. He strode to the door he'd come through, opened it. Two people she hadn't seen yet were waiting outside. Youthful, but not quite adults yet. They had red mantles around their shoulders, but without the golden trim of Alyat's.

The older Adept spoke to them in the Lazarran tongue. They listened, glanced at Rebbaelah, and then dipped their heads to Alyat.

Rebbaelah was already standing. One of the youths, a girl, moved to put a hand on her shoulder, but she shook it off. This was rewarded with a firm grip on her arm. Rebbaelah tried to stomp on the girl's foot, but she easily pulled her leg away.

The two youths grabbed hold of Rebbaelah, their strength easily surpassing hers. Fighting against them was like trying to fight nature itself—they were Adepts, like Alyat, and even though they were only a few years older than Rebbaelah, she had no chance of overcoming them. They hefted her off the ground, leaving her legs kicking furiously at the air.

"Let me go! I'll leave, let me leave on my feet!"

A sympathetic flicker crossed Alyat's face. "You'll leave—but not yet."

"You lied to me!"

"No, I said you can leave, and you will. But first you'll stay here."

"I want to leave now."

"Until you're returned to the slave market, you are still a ward of the Empire. You'll be tended to for a brief while, and then if you still want to leave, you can."

Rebbaelah spat at Alyat's feet. "You tricked me."

"No, I didn't. Now go. I'll see you again in a few days."

Rebbaelah kicked and fought the whole way, earning grunts and what she assumed were curses from the two young Adepts hauling her. They brought her up a flight of stairs and, with great difficulty, tossed her into a room and hastily shut the door. The *click* of the lock echoed in the space with grim finality.

Rebbaelah tried the handle, but it wouldn't budge. She ran to the window, but there were bars across it, too narrow to squeeze through, even as thin as she was.

Like a caged animal, she paced to and fro, checking every corner of the room. She looked under the bed, behind the chest, behind the tapestry decorating a wall—not a single method of escape presented itself.

So, feeling months upon months of exhaustion, she dropped to sit on the floor. Even this was wearisome though, so she flopped onto her back, then turned on her side and curled in on herself.

A long, shuddering breath passed her lips.

The words from that day by the stream came back to her. *'Rebbaelah, you are not to die today.'*

"Well, I wish I was. Then. Now. I wish it was all over." She whispered to the empty room, and heard nothing back. A bird's cheerful song came to her through the window.

She felt the urge to cry again, thinking of how beautiful the birdsong was and how the singer could fly wherever it pleased on the four winds. But the tears didn't come anymore. The sorrow compressed into an ashen lump and settled deep in her chest, and hollow layers of grief wrapped themselves around the sorrow, forming a shell.

She lay on the floor, building her shell, and she did not cry.

6

INITIATES

MEALS CAME to her room three times a day. The number itself gobsmacked her—at most she had eaten twice a day in Shugrith. Then once a day in the slave caravan—if she was fed at all—and meagerly at that. Not that her meals in Shugrith had been much more than meager.

At first she refused to eat. She contemplated starving herself, just to show Alyat how determined she was to keep her word—not a stitch of fabric, not a drop of water, not a morsel of food from the Empire would she enjoy. If they wanted her to eat their food, they could force it down her throat.

As it turned out, they didn't have to. If she hadn't starved for months before, she might have endured, but the need for sustenance had ruled her mind for so long. By the second morning, her will crumbled, and she sipped at the thin porridge they prepared in the mornings. She felt it trace its way from mouth to throat to stomach—and when the gnawing in her gut finally eased, she felt something inside her crack.

The meals came with bread and oil, as she had eaten with Alyat, but they also brought a thin sort of wine. Bitter, and hardly stronger than the water, but it helped her strung out stomach work through the food.

Along with the bread came vegetables—all fresh—and for dinner she even got a cut of meat. Some days she didn't even know what sort of meat she was eating, but always the savoriness of it thrilled her palate.

The bed was amazingly soft, the covers not scratchy in the least. She also found that the chest lying against one wall was filled with long tunics that fell to her knees.

She thought back to what she had said to Alyat—that she'd rather be naked as a slave than wear clothes from the Empire. Well, she'd already broken that vow by eating the food and drinking the water.

On her third day, Alyat appeared at the door with an offer—not to return to the auction, though.

"How would you like to use the baths?"

Rebbaelah recoiled. Washing did sound wonderful, but she'd heard about foreigners' bathhouses—they sounded like filthy things, filled to the brim with people.

As if he read her thoughts, Alyat said, "You'll have the bath to yourself—the Sanctum maintains a number of facilities for our use."

"The Sanctum," she echoed, the word feeling rough in her mouth.

"The compound where we are now. The headquarters of the Adept Corps."

"You tricked me before."

"I didn't. Besides, wouldn't you rather clean yourself before being put on sale?"

"I bathed the morning I went to the auction."

"Probably in a freezing river. There's a heated pool here."

Heated?

"I'll...take a look."

Alyat smirked.

"I know what you're trying to do," she grumbled.

The Adept shrugged. "I'm sure. Go with Marali here, she'll show you the way."

Alyat stepped aside and a woman who looked to be in her forties stepped forward. She wasn't dressed in a uniform and did not wear the Adept's mantle. She smoothed her apron before bowing lightly toward Rebbaelah. "If you would follow me, lady."

Lady?

She stepped out from her room, eyeing Alyat suspiciously.

The Adept turned away, heading down the hallway. He called over his shoulder as he went, "If you try to escape, do leave Marali out of it. She just wants to help."

Rebbaelah frowned. Marali didn't seem to react to the remark, simply making her way in the other direction with even, unhurried steps.

Rebbaelah followed, hurrying to catch up. Alyat's words sounded in her mind. As they descended the stairway and exited the building, she scanned the courtyard. The grand gate was there, and though she couldn't see any legionnaires on duty, she guessed a few were stationed in the small structure beside the gates—likely a guardhouse.

Here and there, men and women with the red mantle around their shoulders were walking—some in haste with their eyes low on bundles of papers in their hands, while others strolled leisurely, lost in thought.

If she tried to make a break for the gate, she'd be caught. Either by one of the Adepts or by the legionnaires likely lurking inside the guardhouse. Or who knew, maybe even more Adepts manned the interior guardhouse. So she kept following Marali.

The woman led her down a set of stone steps, lined by wide-boughed trees casting cool shade. Once down the steps—and there were quite a few of them—Marali headed for a single story building, far longer than it was tall. There was a columned portico at the entrance, and the walls were decorated with mosaics depicting the strangest of scenes: it was a lake, and there were naked women riding creatures that seemed to be half-fish, half-horse; men (also naked) flew atop clouds, breathing winds that whipped the lake's surface into waves; and through the water all manner of strange creatures made their way—things that looked like armored bugs with axes for hands, snakes that wound through the water as if it were sand.

"What...is that?" she asked.

Marali glanced back, then followed her gaze. "Water spirits. The bathhouse is dedicated to them. This side shows the ocean spirits, and the other side river spirits."

"Ocean. A lake of saltwater." She wrinkled her nose. "Dead water."

Marali chuckled. "Where are you from?"

"Talynis," she said, standing straighter.

"Well yes, you can't drink it, but it's lovely to swim in. Especially in the summer. It's quite a popular thing for the Initiates on their free days."

"Free days? Are they prisoners the rest of the time?"

Marali chuckled. "If Adepts are prisoners, what does that make the rest of us? The Orphans ensure Initiates don't leave when they are not permitted, but I'd hardly call this place a jail."

"Orphans?" Reiva's voice dropped.

Marali's eyes widened slightly. "No, not as in... The Second Legion is called the Orphaned Legion. Every two legions are paired, with one praetor over both. The First Legion disappeared a long time ago, along with their praetor. So, legionnaires of the Second are called Orphans."

Reiva nodded. "I see." She cared little for the history lesson, but at least it took her mind away from thoughts of her family.

They stepped through the portico, and instantly Rebbaelah felt the humidity of the interior air. She heard voices, which instantly set her on edge. Marali noticed, because she waved her on further. "Those doors go to the public ones—Adept Alyat arranged for you to have use of one of the smaller rooms."

Still on alert, Rebbaelah followed Marali through a small antechamber, where there were folded linens and drink pitchers, and then into the baths themselves.

The room was small, with two pools. The nearer one was larger, and its surface curled with steam; a set of steps went down into it, so you could gradually immerse yourself. The further one was smaller, and it looked as though you had to drop into it in one motion.

"Hot and cold," explained Marali. "Would you like some wine?"

Rebbaelah shook her head. "How hot is it?"

"Very."

Rebbaelah bit her lower lip. "Are you...a slave? I know what you said, but..."

Marali shook her head. "I'm not anymore, but some people here are."

"*Anymore*?"

"My father got into bad debt, and so he sold us all into slavery until we could pay it off. I ended up working here in the Sanctum. A few years in, they paid off my debt fully, and now I work and live here."

"And that's...common?"

Marali pursed her lips. "Not always. Many people die enslaved."

"It's illegal to enslave someone in Talynis."

Marali's eyebrows shot up. "Really? But how do you handle debt? What about criminals?"

"People work, but...they aren't *owned*. Criminals are punished."

"With execution?"

"It depends." Rebbaelah twisted her features. "It's just...not right."

Marali shrugged. "It's interesting that your people can get by with your ways, but the rest of the world isn't like that. It just...wouldn't work."

"Why not though?"

Marali sighed. "You'll see. But come on, you're here to experience a Lazarran bathhouse, aren't you? I'll go pour a drink for you."

Rebbaelah hugged herself as Marali departed. It didn't make sense. She had seen for herself the auction block—she had been about to stand on it herself. Had Marali been spared that? Just how many channels for buying and selling slaves were there?

She shucked off her tunic and dipped a foot into the pool. It *was* hot, but not unbearably so. If anything, it was comforting. She made her way down the steps, letting out a long sigh when the water came up to her chin.

Sleeping in an actual bed had been nice, but she still had a whole host of aches in her muscles and bones. Wasn't that what old people were supposed to feel like?

Marali returned with a goblet. "It's just water, but let me know if you want wine."

"Thank you," she muttered, taking a sip. She stood there for a moment, staring into the cup. "How often do you do this?"

"I work the bathhouse most days, but sometimes—"

"I mean *this*." She gestured at herself. "They're trying to get me to stay. They want to convince me that Lazarra is a good place." She scoffed. "As if a place where I was about to be a slave could be any good."

Marali hummed. "I do attend to ones like you, now and then. But I'm not trying to convince you of anything for the sake of the Adepts."

"They would have told you to say that," she muttered. "Even setting you free from your debt—they could have done that just to make you grateful so you would *think* you're doing this freely."

She shrugged. "Believe what you like. I understand how it could be different for you, coming from a place with such different laws. But to me, growing up here, this is life."

"That doesn't make it right."

"Maybe not. But you don't have to think it is."

Rebbaelah frowned at her reflection. "What do you mean?"

Marali sighed, getting on her knees beside the pool. "I've seen what happens, sometimes, to the children who choose to go back to the auction. It's not common, but it happens. Sometimes they end up doing the worst sort of work—working in the mines, working in brothels."

Rebbaelah's stomach turned. "It's a big city—how could you see them if it barely happens?"

"Because they come back."

Something in her voice made Rebbaelah look up, look into the woman's eyes.

Grief. Pity.

"They don't come right away," she continued. "Usually it's a few months later. Maybe even a year. I can barely recognize them sometimes. I'll be tending the garden outside the wall and they'll stumble over, clutching at my feet. They'll beg me to remember them, and I do, eventually. They want to change their mind. They want to join the Adepts after all."

She looked askance, swallowed. "But by then...it's almost always too late. The Adepts' training is long and hard. And the law that permits the Adept Corps to manumit a slave for initiation only holds for first discovery. Once they have given up their right to the child, it is the new owner's right to charge as much as they wish—and they know how desperate the Adept Corps is for new recruits."

"But if they're desperate, then—!"

"They used to buy them back anyway," she sighed. "They have the funds for it. But almost always, those ones—what do they call it? —*wash out*. They fail. If they're lucky, they'll end up getting sent to join the legions, but some of them are just too broken by that point. I don't know much about how their magic works—that's all secret and nothing I'd care to know even if someone offered to teach me—but something goes wrong with those poor children. They can't do it right. They end up hurting themselves, or other people. There was one boy, they say his heart burst inside his chest the first time he tried to do magic."

Rebbaelah clutched at her own chest, dropping the goblet into the waters of the bath.

Marali drew her lips into a thin line. "So that's why I try to make young things like you see that there's something good for you here. I know what you think about the Empire. Maybe you're even right about it. The gods will judge that. But..."

She shrugged, shaking her head. "Well, you must be getting hot in there. Wouldn't want you passing out. I'll get a towel for you."

Rebbaelah hugged herself. If she hadn't been in a pool, she'd have crouched down into a ball, like her first night in the room.

Her fingernails were digging into her arms. Despite what Marali had said, the pool hardly felt hot. If anything, it felt tepid. The mournful lump in her chest burrowed deeper, and more layers crystallized around it.

After she dried off and returned to the room, she sat on her bed. She ignored lunch when it came, then dinner. She stared out the window, then down at the floor, at the walls.

She took in the tapestry adorning one of the walls—she had looked at it for hours by now, but it always held some new detail to uncover.

It was a scene of victory. Most of the setting was cast in darkness, represented by black and violet thread, but then at the heart there was a golden burst of radiance, like the sun's light breaking through the clouds to shine upon one spot. In the darkness were mounds of defeated warriors, dressed in all sorts of ways and bearing all sorts of weapons. To Rebbaelah's continual shock, most of them wore the Lazarran toga—but a dirtied, tattered representation of it.

In contrast, the people standing in the light wore spotless white togas, with seamless fringes in luxuriant dyes. They were elevated, standing atop an outcropping of rock that rose from the earth like a spear thrust heavenward.

In the dead center was a handsome man wearing a piece of armor that looked more like art than actual protective gear—it outlined his musculature in impressive detail, and it bore subtle reliefs of yet more figures, images within an image. The fringe of his toga was the richest purple she had ever seen. Atop the man's head was a laurel crown, and in his upraised hand was a spear unlike any she had ever seen, all gold and platinum, having a look of vibrant energy such that it almost seemed alive in its own right.

Imperator Primus floated over his head in gilt threading.

Around him stood a number of similarly beautiful warriors, men and women, who held no weapons. One held a roiling sphere of water between his hands. Another seemed to be cloaked in rushing winds. Another held her hands high, and the more Rebbaelah looked, the more certain she became that *she* was the one raising the pillar of rock upon which they all stood. All these had red fringes on their togas.

She stared at the tapestry for a while, her eyes lingering on the red fringes, on the displays of arcane power. She heard laughter through the window, and when she went to it, she saw a cluster of youths wearing red mantles going out through the little door set into the gate. She recognized the two who had taken her up to this room.

They didn't have any chaperones or supervisors that she could see—they were just...*going.*

Maybe they're going to the ocean, like Marali said.

Rebbaelah sat on the floor after that, hugging her knees. The sun went down, but it was a full moon that night, so she was not plunged totally into darkness. She watched the silver disc arc its way through the star-strewn sky.

The stars always followed the same courses, night to night, year to year. They were bound to their paths. Yet they were divine. The Four Gods had set the stars in their ways, and the stars held to them. How wonderful to be a star—to know the way you were meant to go, to understand always the right thing to do.

'*Rebbaelah, you are not to die today.*'

She did not sleep that night. She just sat on the floor, watching the moon and the stars.

She thought about her brother. Did he know what had happened to her? Had their mother lied? What if she had told him something terrible—that a wild animal had devoured her, or that she had run away, leaving him behind?

How long until she sold him too?

Again, Rebbaelah found herself unable to cry, even though it seemed she must. Marali's words echoed in her mind. '*There's something good for you here.*'

'*Rebbaelah, you are not to die today.*'

The sky lightened. The sun burst over the horizon.

Breakfast came, announced by the *click* of a key in the lock. As always, it was delivered by one of the young Adepts in training—Initiates, Marali had called them. He opened the door, glanced at Rebbaelah, then set the tray with the food and drink on the floor.

Just before he shut the door, she raised her head.

"Where is Alyat?"

The Initiate stopped. He looked over his shoulder at her.

"Where is Adept Alyat? I need to speak to him."

Slowly, the Initiate nodded. He didn't lock the door when he went. He must have known she wasn't going anywhere.

7

SEVENTH COHORT

The ceremony was a quick and simple affair. Rebbaelah was made to kneel before a statue of the First Emperor—the same man she had seen depicted in the tapestry—and swear her loyalty to the Imperial Authority, to all the Emperors and Empresses of Lazarra.

The oath was simple. To give her life in service to the Empire, to be a blade in the hand of her lord, and to carry the Imperial Dominion forward. The statue was painted to look like a real person, but Rebbaelah thought it only looked eerier than if it had been plain marble.

Alyat witnessed her declaration, and when she had said the words, bade her rise and presented her with a precisely folded mantle. It lacked the gold fringe of a full Adept—it would take seven years for her to earn the gold. But anyone who saw the red would know she belonged to the Adept Corps and would give her the respect due one of her stature.

Hearing those words seemed like hearing a fairy tale. The respect due her? When had she last received anything like that? It almost seemed childish to imagine such a thing existed. Days ago, she had been a slave, the lowest of the low. Now all she had done was speak a string of words (clumsily recited in Lazarran tongue with Alyat's guidance) and don a swathe of fabric, and she jumped leagues. She was *human* again.

All she had needed to do was turn her back on the Four Gods of Talynis.

Well, they turned away from me a long time ago.

Those mismatched eyes of blue and brown seemed to peer from the recesses of her memory as she spoke the oath, but she shoved the memory away. He had saved her from herself, declared her doom was not yet come—and this was where that had led her. What else was she to do? If anything, the god had pushed her on. Rather than let her die a Talynisti, he had sent her to live as a Lazarran.

Fine then.

The final blow, as it were, to her old identity was when Alyat touched her shoulder after she had donned the mantle.

"Rebbaelah," he said slowly. Like all Adepts, he was not Lazarran by birth. He still carried the Northlander burr in his speech, and so he spoke her name carefully, working the sounds out as best he could to how she had told spoken it to him.

But now he said, "It would be wise to choose a new name for yourself. Not required, but it will ease things."

She swallowed, feeling as though she stood before a yawning chasm. "I don't know many Lazarran names."

"Doesn't have to be Lazarran. Just something that sounds closer, not as..."

"Not as Talynisti."

"Aye. What about Rebba?"

She knit her brow. "No."

"Rava?"

She shook her head again. Then, something clicked together. "Reiva?"

Alyat sucked on his teeth. "Reiva. Sure, sounds good enough to my ears. I'll have that marked in your record. Initiate Reiva."

She rolled the name around in her mouth, feeling it move like a breath.

Reiva.

"I like it," she said suddenly, more to herself than to Alyat.

The Adept snorted. "Good, you're stuck with it. Now get to your lodging."

She was about to move to leave, but Alyat raised an expectant eyebrow. There was something she was forgetting...

Ah, right.

Awkward and unfamiliar with the motion, she closed her fist and set it over her heart. "*Ave Imperator,*" she said carefully.

Alyat nodded. "*Ave Imperator,* Initiate. Dismissed."

Finally released, she departed from the shrine to the First Emperor. The spot was located smack in the central courtyard of the Sanctum, the beating heart of the place. The girl christened Reiva headed toward the southeastern corner of the compound. She had been told her quarters were tucked away in the area, that she couldn't miss them.

She had also been told that she was expected, and any tardiness would be noticed if she dallied.

Still, it was odd to her that she was being sent there with no accompaniment. What if she got lost?

They're testing me already, she realized. It seemed so simple—follow these directions and get to where you need to be—but she felt sure that was what was going on. Already she was under evaluation. '*Can you be the sort of soldier we expect? Are you going to wash out?*'

That put an extra kick in her step as she hustled toward her destination. The Sanctum was expansive but not massive, and before too long she heard what sounded like young people's voices. A surge of pride burgeoned in her chest, and she stood tall as she opened the door.

A wall of noise struck her—shouting, cheering, laughing, yelling. She came to an abrupt stop at the threshold, taking in the scene before her.

A boy with dark skin was pinning a smaller boy with blond hair, holding his arm back in a way that had to have been painful. The blond boy struggled against the other's grip before pounding the floorboards.

A cheer went up from the assembled crowd—all people who looked to be in roughly the same age range as Reiva—the oldest might have been fourteen, which would have been about two years older than her.

For a moment, she got lost trying to work out if her birthday had passed during her travels with the caravan, and so she missed the question the first time.

"Hey! You got wax in your ears?"

Reiva blinked, suddenly aware that the whole room was staring at her.

A pale boy with red hair (which was jarring enough on its own) had stepped forward, and he was snapping his fingers at her.

People were whispering, glancing at her with barely disguised curiosity and suspicion.

"I can hear," she said. "My name is—"

"Didn't ask your name," barked the boy. "You're late."

Reiva balked. "I came right after the—"

"Did you *run*?"

"No. Nobody told me I had to—"

"All Initiates in their first year of training must run to their destinations, *without exception.*"

Reiva frowned. Her eyes swept across the room, searching for any sign that this was a joke.

All she saw were dead serious expressions, even contemptuous ones.

Weakly, she tried to say again: "Nobody told me—"

"Well, I'm telling you now. Now, on the ground, fifty pushups."

"Excuse me?"

The boy's eyebrows shot up. By his face, he looked youthful, but he was a good deal taller than her, taller than most of the others, actually. So despite his face, she guessed he must have been on the older side. "I *said* you do fifty pushups."

"I don't even know your name."

"You get names after pushups."

"But why—"

"Give it a rest, Phetan," groaned a male voice. The whole room's attention swung toward the speaker—the dark-skinned boy who had won the wrestling match. "She's not biting."

The mood in the place seemed to deflate.

The red-haired boy sighed. "Come on, Tolm, she was gonna crack."

The other boy, Tolm, snorted. "Right." He wiped his forearm against the glistening sweat beading on his brow. "Better luck next time." With that, he slipped by Reiva and out the door, briefly glancing down at her as he went.

Phetan glowered after him.

A girl with dark ringlets of hair sauntered forward from the corner of the room. "Hi," she said, waving to Reiva. "Sorry, it's a running joke. Every time someone new shows up, we try to get them to do something like that. Pushups, run around the perimeter—you get the idea."

Reiva narrowed her eyes. "Uh-huh."

The girl smirked. "Really, it's nothing personal. I'm Domi. Welcome to Seventh Cohort."

"Reb—Reiva. Thank you."

Domi nodded, as if approving of the name. Based on what Alyat had said, probably everyone here had changed their name once they'd come to the Sanctum. "You're probably the last to join us. Next week they're going to start putting new Initiates into First Cohort. Word of advice, though," she whispered, "if *anyone* else tells you to do something—push ups, running laps—you do it. Everyone in this place who isn't at our level is above us, and that means they can order us around however they please. And then someday we'll get to do the same!"

She said that last part quite excitedly.

Phetan scoffed. "Yeah, if you don't wash out before then."

Domi made a strangled sound. "If anyone's washing out, it'll be you." She leaned over exaggeratedly to Reiva before saying in a stage whisper, "Fifteen minutes in the sun and he burns red as a robin."

Phetan puffed his chest out. "Discomfort builds fortitude. Once we get our focuses, I'll be outpacing the lot of you by miles."

Domi shrugged. "Yeah, we'll see. Until then, just keep on slathering yourself with fish oil."

"It's not—!"

But Domi was already snickering, dodging away from Phetan as though he were about to whirl out with a blow.

Reiva watched the exchange with a growing sense of unease.

There was so much she was out of the loop on. Everyone here knew each other, they knew how things worked around here—she had been told almost nothing. Just that she should follow the others in her quarters and get the hang of it.

As Phetan stomped after Domi, the blond boy who had been pinned by Tolm came over to Reiva. "Hi," he said, smiling easily. "You said your name is Reiva?"

"Yes." She fought the urge to take a half-step back.

As if he could read her nervousness, he laughed. "It's all right, we were all new once. I'm Caulo. I got here a few months ago. You already speak Karellan—that's good. You speak any Lazarran?"

She shook her head.

Caulo clicked his tongue. "Well, you'll learn quick. We're supposed to only speak it here, technically, but if anyone hears they won't mind since we've got a new face."

"I heard from Alyat that I'll need to be fluent soon." She hated that her voice betrayed her worry. She needed to look strong here.

Caulo scratched at his sweat-dampened hair. "More or less. One year until you're tested, but if you pay attention in your lessons and get used to speaking it daily, you'll be ready way before then."

Reiva nodded. "Um, thank you. I'll try."

Caulo laughed—he seemed to do that a lot. "Yeah, you'd better. You have to try if you want to get anywhere here."

A girl appeared at his side. "Don't talk like that on her first night here!" The girl pouted, her bright blue eyes filling with reproach. Then she turned to Reiva and her features instantly warmed. "I'm Mylla."

"Reiva."

"Sorry, lots of names, huh?"

Caulo nudged Mylla with his elbow. "You tell me not to overwhelm her, but then you introduce yourself."

Mylla swept her jet black hair back from her face. "What's that supposed to mean?"

"Have you ever *met* yourself?"

Mylla turned her nose up. "I'm sure I don't know what you're implying."

"You know what, I'm sure you don't either."

"Hey!"

Reiva smiled weakly. She tried cataloguing the faces and names she'd learned so far. Mercifully, there were a few people still standing off for now, either content to wait until later to introduce themselves or just not interested.

"What was the name of the boy who left? He argued with...I think Phetan. Toll?"

"Tolm," said Mylla. "He's really something."

Caulo rubbed at his shoulder and grimaced. "Yeah, you could say that."

Reiva glanced at the spot on the floor where they'd been wrestling. "Why were you two...?"

"Oh. Well, someone asked Tolm if it was true that he was going to get his focus soon. I said there's no way Tolm could manage it—and I said this with the most benign intentions I'll have you know—but people thought I was calling him out. One thing led to another, and either we had to try for a fall or show ourselves cowards. So we tried, and I fell."

Reiva nodded, getting the gist of what he meant. "The focus is the necklace."

Mylla's eyes lit up. "The *necklace*? It's a key to everything you've ever wanted. That mantle around your shoulders is a symbol, but the focus is what makes that symbol meaningful. It's how Adepts pull power through themselves and shape the world!"

"How does it work?"

Mylla faltered here. "Well...we don't know, exactly."

Caulo jumped in. "Adept training is mostly physical at the start—exercises and martial drills. They don't bother explaining all the magical parts when there's a chance we might not even get to try for the next stage yet."

"And Tolm," Reiva ventured, "is getting close to that next stage?"

Mylla nodded eagerly. "I think he is. He's always been at the top of the physical examinations, and I know for a fact a lot of the full Adepts have their eyes on him."

She had a few ideas as to why that might be, but she asked anyway.

"Just because we're a long way from serving in the field," Mylla said, "that doesn't mean what we're doing won't have ramifications for those days. Lots of high-ranking officers in the legions keep their eyes on promising Initiates. Adepts can do wonders in war, and there's always a struggle for the best ones."

Reiva had suspected that was more or less what she was going to say.

Mylla tilted her head. "You got a funny look just now."

"Hm?" Reiva felt like she'd just been hit with cold water. "What do you mean 'funny'?"

Caulo rubbed his chin, a mischievous smile growing on his face. "Like you just heard good news." He nudged Mylla. "She's gonna fight for the top spot, I guarantee it."

The girl frowned. "Well we *all* are."

Caulo shrugged. "Yeah, but not everyone goes for it in the same way." Another shrug. "Ah well. Come on, Reiva, we can show you where you're gonna sleep. And I know it's all exciting, but do sleep. You're gonna need it."

Reiva followed, surreptitiously wiping her sweaty palms on her tunic as she did. She kept her eyes on Caulo and Mylla as they led the way, studiously avoiding the glances of anyone else who might want to fill her head with more names, more advice, more curiosities and questions.

She noted, though, that no one had asked where she'd come

from. No questions about her accent, her features—no guesses as to what they betrayed about her origins.

Being a collection of children from all around the world, the Initiates were a variegated bunch. She had expected they would be interested in hearing where she was from and telling her the same about themselves.

Maybe it all had to do with that oath to serve Lazarra. And she supposed that made sense. Whoever they had been before, now they were Adept Initiates in training to serve Lazarra. That was their identity. Maybe there were even rules about asking each other questions or talking about their past lives... She would need to ask about that, subtly.

There was some more chatter around—much of it in Lazarran, so she couldn't comprehend it anyway—but the force of the day was hitting her several times over. She hadn't slept the night before, and after the whole process of listening to Alyat explain what would be expected of her and going through the oath-swearing ceremony, she was more than ready to sleep. It didn't matter in the slightest that she had to leave beyond the wonderful bed she had enjoyed for a plain cot in a shared dormitory (Mylla said they would eventually get real beds once they rose to the next stage of their training). As soon as her head was down, she was drifting away.

An Adept Initiate. Yesterday Rebbaelah the slave, today Reiva the Adept Initiate.

It seemed she had hardly shut her eyes before she was violently shaken awake, someone yelling like a god of thunder.

"Up up up! Gonna be late for morning exercises!"

Reiva blinked, her eyes and mind foggy with bleary sleepiness.

Then the blur of motion around her resolved. Phetan was screaming at her, tying his sandals. Everyone in the room was either on their way out or long gone.

Reiva scrambled off her cot, fumbling to tie her hair back. Where were those sandals Alyat had given her...

Phetan huffed, grabbing them from right under her nose and grabbing her ankles to shove them on. "Didn't you hear the horn, new blood? Come on—one person's late and we all get it!" He expertly tied her sandals and sent her out the door with a hearty shove.

Arms pumping, all semblance of sleep shocked away by the cold morning air, Reiva fell into the back of the Initiates' pack. Phetan passed her in a blur, moving to take up a position near the head of the group.

Reiva's lungs burned, unused to this sort of explosive exertion. Her body could handle long, drawn out drudgery, but this sort of instant burst of activity was beyond her. Already her side was cramping, and the new footwear was chafing at her ankles. She began to fall behind.

Then someone grabbed hold of her arm and tugged her forward. Reiva gaped, realizing Mylla had dropped back from the main group.

The black-haired girl didn't say anything, just pulled Reiva along, her breath puffing in the pre-dawn atmosphere like plumes of steam. Caulo too had fallen back from the main group. "Come on," he huffed. "First run's always the worst."

Reiva felt tears blistering at her eyes. When was the last time someone had done something like this for her?

Sucking in another stinging breath, clutching at her pain-lanced side, she pushed on, tackling the uphill run one step at a time.

Drenched in sweat and wincing, she managed with Mylla and Caulo's encouragement to avoid falling too far behind. She hated that she had kept them back, but she nodded her gratitude to them as they came to a stop.

The Initiates were organizing themselves into lines, and Reiva found herself standing at the very end of the last line. The other lines seemed to be older Initiates—other Cohorts, Reiva guessed, though she didn't see all seven. There were at least twice as many people here than had slept in the dormitory last night. The birds hadn't yet begun their morning choirs, so the only sound was a mass of young lungs gasping for air. Reiva glanced down the line, and she was just barely able to make out Tolm standing all the way at the other end of her line. He didn't even seem winded. She didn't remember seeing him on the run, come to think of it...

Her thoughts were interrupted by a gruff bellow, a single word rumbling through the air with enough force to reverberate in her bones.

She had no idea what the word meant, but then she saw the unified ripple of motion rolling through the others. Half a second behind the rest, Reiva got her fist over her heart in a salute. She turned her head to see who had spoken, but Mylla hissed from the corner of her mouth, "*Eyes forward.* Straighten your back."

She did her best to comply, feeling a painful twinge between her shoulder blades as she fought to hold her posture.

At the edges of her awareness, she realized someone—probably the man who had called for the salute—was walking down the line. As he drew nearer, Reiva felt acutely aware of the sweat trickling down her back, the cool breeze against her face.

Finally, the man stood in front of her. He had a square chin, nicked by a half-dozen scars, one of which reached up his cheek to stop just below his left eye.

He barked something at her.

Reiva's heart somersaulted.

The man scowled.

Caulo piped up, yelling louder than Reiva had thought he was capable. He spoke a brief string of Lazarran.

The man glanced at Caulo with a sour expression, then turned his gaze on Reiva.

"Name and position!" he snapped in Karellan.

"Reb-Reiv-Reiva!"

"*What's your name,* Initiate?"

"Reiva! Sir," she added meekly.

"Wrong. What's your rank?"

Her stomach dropped. How could her *name* be wrong? What was her rank?

"Initiate, sir!"

"Wrong. Twenty pushups, the lot of you."

Before she could question if this was yet another joke, a few muttered groans went up from the line. Everyone was dropping to the ground. Reiva followed their lead.

As she struggled to lift herself up, cursing her twig-like arms the whole way, the man bellowed something over the group in Lazarran. A moment later, he barked another word.

Caulo huffed, coming to the top of a pushup. "If one soldier is unprepared—*gasp*—the whole company suffers." He went down again, up. "You suffer together for your failures—*gasp*—and you learn your lesson."

Reiva's arms trembled. She could barely process the meaning of what Caulo was saying—all she knew was that she didn't have the strength to finish the set. From the corner of her eye, she could already see people standing up. She had barely done half the required number.

Her face burned with shame. They had all been through this before, hadn't they? This wasn't abnormal?

Even if so, it couldn't have been as bad as this. By her thirteenth, everyone else was already through their full twenty. She fought with all her might to lift herself, but her body remained in the dirt. She groaned, gasped, did everything she could to muster up another ounce of strength, but her muscles failed.

Someone further down the line shouted something. The instructor replied, setting his foot on Reiva's shoulder. She took that as a sign to stop.

Feet pounded the grass. All of a sudden, another Initiate dropped to the ground right next to her, a boy whose name she didn't know. He hastily worked through another twenty pushups, then popped to his feet.

Reiva glanced up at the instructor, who nodded crisply. The boy who had done the extra pushups ran back to his spot in the line without a word.

"Someone," drawled the instructor, "teach her what name and rank is."

Domi stepped forward. "Initiate Domi, Seventh Cohort. First year, *probatia!*"

The instructor turned to Reiva. "Go."

"Initiate Reiva, Seventh Cohort. First year, *probatia!*"

"Faster next time, and get on your feet, Initiate!"

The instructor switched back to Lazarran, barking another set of orders. The line broke into another run, moving single file with Tolm at the head.

As the instructor moved off out of earshot, Mylla whispered to her. "We should've told you. Our fault."

"What did that boy do?" Reiva whispered back, suppressing a groan at the thought of running again.

"If one person can't do an exercise, someone else has to do it for them. It's called a reprieve, and you have to request permission. Don't worry, we've all been there. Luo did it for you this time, someone else will do it next."

Reiva felt herself wilt. Great—so she was the dead weight they'd all have to carry until she could get up to speed. Her legs and hips screamed in protest as she started into the run, following Mylla. Her constitution was frail as could be after months of meager nutrition and dull trudging. More than once, black spots danced in front of her, and she had to lean on the others before unconsciousness seized her.

All the while, the instructor kept pace alongside the line, moving back and forth, bellowing orders. When she raised her head, she could see the other cohorts ahead of them, each with an instructor. They were moving the cohorts at staggered rates and assigning different exercises.

Now and then, their instructor would call for another set of pushups, or sometimes sit-ups, or for them to crawl the next fifty yards on hands and knees. Every time Caulo or Mylla had to explain what the orders were, and for everything besides the crawl, someone had to give Reiva a reprieve. Sometimes she knew the person's name, most times she didn't. She never even got the chance to say thank you, and almost always the person didn't even spare her a glance. She was just an obstacle, a task to complete. They did the work and moved off.

After what felt like hours, the instructor gave another command, and everyone dropped to the ground, heaving sighs of relief.

"Ten minute rest," breathed Caulo, "then the obstacle course. Get a drink from the well over there. Not too much or you'll puke."

Reiva nodded her understanding, not sparing any breath to speak.

The ten minutes disappeared like mist under the rising sun's face. She hadn't even gotten up to drink from the well—she had just sat there, covered in mud and itching from crawling through grass. When the order to move again came, she got onto shaky feet, took a shallow breath, and joined the line again.

Everything ached. Everything inside her was screaming for her to stop. It was only the first day—how much more of this could she take? Might as well just quit now instead of wasting more time and effort and suffering on this.

But then she looked toward the front of the pack, at the way Tolm and Domi and Phetan pushed through the tasks with grim determination. She looked at how Mylla and Caulo huffed and puffed their way through with more difficulty than the leaders, but still gave a showing that seemed borderline miraculous to Reiva.

She grit her teeth.

I'm not getting left behind. I'm not going to be the weakest anymore.

She watched keenly as Tolm burst forward with lightning speed, first onto the obstacle course. He clambered over logs, crawled between stakes, vaulted fences, climbed walls.

She made a decision, standing at the back of the line. The new blood. The first year *probatia*. The Adept Initiate.

She was going to make it. She was going to prove to this place, the Adept Corps—to the whole damn Empire—that she was stronger. Stronger than the other people in her cohort. Stronger than *anyone*.

She would not let the Empire break her. She was going to become unbreakable.

When her turn to run the course came, she stumbled over the logs. She lost her footing and nearly twisted her ankle. She dropped face-first into the mud as she scrambled over the fencing. She lost her grip once on the wall climb, and her arms failed her halfway up the second time. She needed a reprieve to finish.

But she burned every mistake she'd made into her mind. She stoked her will with a singular fire—the raging flames of anger.

She was going to climb to the top. However long it took, she would climb to the top.

8

POTENTIAL

HER BODY RAGGED, Reiva trudged with the other Initiates to the mess. Thankfully, she still could cling to Mylla's side. Caulo had drifted off to traipse with Phetan and a blonde girl whose name Reiva didn't know, so she was left with Mylla—not that she minded that. It would be good to have some time just with another girl. Neither of them said much of anything on the way, though. They huffed, shoulders hunched and eyes downcast the whole way, not sparing a breath for anything save recovery.

The trip to the mess hall, however, was not a direct one. First, the Initiates had to go to the river and dunk themselves until they were sufficiently de-mucked. As *probatii*, they had not yet earned the right to use the actual bathhouse for this. This involved a great deal of wringing out clothes and hair, and the water was frigid, even though the sun had risen well into the sky.

Reiva sucked in a sharp breath as she hauled herself onto the riverbank. "Good enough?" she muttered to Mylla through clenched teeth.

The other girl, her lips tinged blue, nodded—the motion accentuated by her shivers.

Just moments ago, thought Reiva, *we were dripping sweat. Now we're half-frozen.*

And this was only the midpoint of their day.

Reiva swallowed, her throat and lungs still burning. Her determined self-declaration during the obstacle course suddenly felt like a flame burned low, almost reduced to ashes. They still couldn't go to eat, though, because they needed to wear their mantles at meals. And as they were required to wash off the dirt and mud at the lowest point of the river, by the drainage grate (lest their muck filter anywhere important) they would had to trudge nearly the entire uphill length of the Sanctum to get to their food.

Now she was beginning to appreciate why she had been given other sets of clothing—the Corps didn't want grubby Initiates dripping water and reeking in the mess hall any more than could be helped. She hastily shucked off her damp tunic and pulled on the dry one stored in a trunk at the foot of her cot.

Heat crept into her cheeks as she glanced at the curtain dividing the boy's half of the room from theirs. She nudged Mylla, keeping her eyes low out of self-consciousness. "Do they ever...?"

Mylla blinked, then realization dawned in her eyes. "Oh, no. Someone always keeps an eye out." She nodded toward the entrance, where Domi was leaning against the wall and keenly observing the divider. When she noticed Reiva, she threw an easy wave, an amicable smile playing on her lips.

"The nice part," said Mylla, "is that we get separate dormitories once we make *acolyta*."

Reiva agreed, that would be nice. But then she asked how long that would take and Mylla explained most broke through in their second year.

At least a whole year then—and then six more until training was done. Another wave of exhaustion shook Reiva to her bones.

Seven years. She would have to endure seven more years of training—waking up early, straining her body to the limits, and who even knew how things would change once they began practicing their magic...

Magic. She would have to do magic. She already had the potential deep in her soul—that was the only reason she was here at all. What would she do? Shake the earth? Stir the seas?

She shut her eyes against a sudden spell of nausea.

Don't think about that right now. Think of today. Think of food.

In response, her stomach made known its desperate plea for sustenance. Mylla cracked a weary smile. "Sorry to say, but we're always last in line."

She had assumed that would be the case, and she was no stranger to waiting for meals—things had been plenty hard in Shugrith after her father's death. That, plus the even sparser rations she'd received in the slave caravan, meant her stomach capacity was already minuscule. The full meals they had given her during her stay in the upper room with the window had been like buffets, and she'd almost eaten herself sick two days in a row by trying to clean her plate.

But despite all that, she still suppressed a groan. This morning was the hardest she'd pushed her body in months—probably in her whole life—and she could tell just by looking at the other Initiates that she was well behind them in nutrition. Food was going to be just as much a part of succeeding as exercise and will.

After suffering through the final stretch of the trek to the mess hall, they stood outside, waiting as the line shuffled forward. Now and then, higher ranking Initiates (as evidenced by their wearing focuses or, in the case of the most advanced, having silver fringes on their mantles) would walk past, not even sparing a glance as they took up their rightful places further in the line.

If any *probatii* grumbled or groused on this point, they did so quietly. After all, someday they would enjoy the privileges of rank and status. If they made it that far. Reiva couldn't help but notice how much fewer were the numbers of Initiates with silver-fringed mantles. Though she couldn't differentiate between the other cohorts precisely, it was plain to see the numbers of Seventh Cohort surpassed even the combined sums of several others.

Her ragged throat knotted; her empty stomach turned. She almost wanted to ask how many Initiates made it all the way through, but she was too hungry and tired to weather what she was certain would be a frightening and wearying answer.

When she and Mylla finally got their turn, they each received a loaf of bread and a bowl of stew—both long cold, though Reiva hardly cared, and by the wolfish eagerness with which Mylla tore into hers, it seemed neither did she.

They hadn't sat at a table though—all the *probatii* had to take their food outside and eat on the ground. There were only so many seats inside, and they were a privilege that had to be earned.

It also added another social dynamic to things, Reiva realized. Whereas with the tables, you had to sit somewhere, had to sit *with* people, out here on the grass, no one was forced to do such a thing. You only ate with someone if you chose to, and already Reiva felt her stomach knotting out of fear. What if someone sent you away, or got up and left when you arrived?

She cast a glance toward Mylla, who was devouring another chunk of stew-soaked bread. Thank the gods—if they cared—for this girl.

Mylla happened to look up, then gave a kind, full-cheeked smile. "Thorry," she muttered around her food, "wa' hun'ry."

Reiva smiled back, almost involuntarily, then took another bite of her own meal. She had eased enough that she managed to swallow another bite without her stomach revolting.

They didn't speak for several more bites, wholly focused on getting down the sustenance. Reiva had to stop now and then to let her stomach rest, though. She still hadn't acclimated to regular portions.

"Oi, Mylla. Mind if I sit?"

The two girls looked up at the speaker—a boy with gangly limbs and a perpetual half-smile.

"Luo!" chirped Mylla. "Yeah come on."

Luo sat down, his own meal half-gone by now. Had he left someone else to come here then? "Gruesome morning, huh?"

Mylla groaned. "Terrible."

Reiva's cheeks flushed. "I'm sorry."

The two of them turned to her, brows knit. "What was that?" asked Luo.

"I said sorry. It was my fault you... Well, you helped me. You had to work more."

Luo blinked slowly, and it seemed something was working behind his eyes, thoughts tumbling around. His lips moved silently. At last, comprehension dawned on his features. "Oh! You're the new girl!"

Reiva sat there, immobile, fingers tightly clutching the last of her loaf. "Y-yes?"

Luo nodded, his half-smile expanding. "Right, I gave you that reprieve. Don't worry about it, we all do it for each other. Someday you can return the favor."

Mylla nudged him with her knee. "Her name is Reiva."

"Reiba."

"*Va.*"

"Rei-*va.*"

"There you are." Mylla patted Luo on the head, prompting him to duck down and scratch at the back of his neck.

"Sorry, I *ohshit*—"

Hot stew spilled onto his leg as he tipped his dish too far to one side.

Mylla snorted, covering her mouth as the boy hopped to his feet, desperately batting and wiping at his thigh.

Reiva had to bite her lip to smother a laugh.

"Yep," said Mylla, "that's Luo."

He muttered a few more curses as he sank back to the ground. Casting a dejected look at the recently beef-flavored grass, he clicked his tongue. "Ah well. It happens."

Reiva offered her bowl. "You can finish mine—I can't eat all this."

Luo's eyebrows went up. "Are you sure?"

With a nod, she explained how her appetite hadn't come back yet. Luo let out a low whistle. "Auction-find, eh? That's hard."

Reiva's throat closed a bit. "How else do they find us?"

Luo opened his mouth, only for a feminine voice to say, "Province surveys, mostly."

Domi dropped to the grass to sit beside Reiva—quite nearby, in fact—without stopping to ask permission. How long had she been listening?

"All the Imperial provinces get regular scoutings of the population, testing for potential. You have the knack, they haul you straight here and give your family and village a stipend. Quite generous, really."

Reiva processed that. "So, are most of you...?"

"Province-born," Domi confirmed. "Auction-finds are second most common though. Then there're the outliers."

Reiva recalled Alyat's story of how he had gotten picked up by the Empire.

"Either way," Domi went on, twirling her finger in a circle, "look around. Dozens of us here today—and maybe three or four will remain by the end."

Reiva's stomach seized up again.

Luo stiffened. Mylla's face darkened. "Domi, don't talk like that."

"What happens," muttered Reiva, "to the rest?"

Domi's expression was somber as she spoke. "If you make it to at least your second year, decent chance you end up in the legions or some other sort of Imperial service. Empire wouldn't want to totally waste what they've put into us, eh?"

"And if we don't make it to that?" Frightful memories of the auction block swarmed her. Unconsciously, she clutched at her tunic, suffering again the fear it would be torn from her, leaving her exposed like merchandise to be inspected.

Mylla had turned somewhat pale. Luo was looking askance.

Domi shrugged. "Depends how you wash out. I've heard some people go crazy, and then you're locked up in some dark cell the rest of your days."

"That's just a rumor," snapped Mylla.

"Well, what would *you* do if an Initiate lost her mind? A psychotic Adept on the loose is bad news for the rest of us."

Luo cleared his throat. "Excuse me, I'm gonna go wash off the last of this food before afternoon lessons. Nice meeting you, Reiva."

Reiva gave him a perfunctory nod. "Thank you again for earlier."

"Not a problem."

Mylla's lips pressed into a tight line. "I know it's easy for you to talk about this sort of stuff, Domi, but we're not all as comfortable."

The girl whipped her head around to Mylla, sending dark curls flying. "I'm not comfortable talking about this. I just want Reiva to understand the stakes."

"You know what I meant. And I'm sure she understands them perfectly."

Domi sighed. "All right, I'm sorry then."

Mylla pouted, turning aside.

Reiva balled her fists again, clutching at her tunic. "Thank you for telling me," she murmured to Domi. "I appreciate it. I know you weren't trying to scare me."

Domi blinked, then her lips split into a smile.

Reiva felt uneasy. "Did I do something wrong?"

Domi drew her eyebrows down and stuck out her chin. "Thank you for telling me," she grumbled in what Reiva guessed was supposed to be an impression of her, then slapped her on the arm. "So stoic."

"What's that?"

"It's when you never smile."

Reiva huffed. "I *do* smile."

Domi snickered. "Well, I'd like to see that someday."

"Just five minutes ago I—"

"Sure, sure, I believe you." She patted Reiva on the shoulder. "Maybe someday you'll even tell a joke. Anyway, we need to get to lessons—you don't want to be late on your first day."

Mylla was already standing. "I need to stop by the dormitory," she said in a flat tone. "Just go with Domi, Reiva."

Reiva's hands clenched again. Mylla was still upset—what could she do? She wasn't good at this sort of thing...

But the girl was already walking away to clean her dish in the water trough set out for the purpose.

Domi pulled Reiva to her feet. "I'll apologize more to her later."

She scratched at her eyebrow. "Sorry, that must have been awkward for you, especially on your first real day."

Reiva shrugged. She wasn't about to complain to Domi about how she behaved, but she also wasn't sure enough of the social web going on that she would dismiss Mylla's frustration.

So, she settled for asking a question. "Why did Mylla say you're comfortable?"

"Ah." Domi led them to the cleaning station. "When we take our bowls in, look at the wall with all the placards mounted up."

Reiva did so. She hadn't noticed them earlier, but now she saw seven boards hung up on the near wall. The writing on them was in Lazarran script, which she couldn't decipher, and to make things worse the boards were filled with wax into which the letters had been incised with a stylus—so it could be erased and rewritten, Reiva assumed—which made them even harder to read.

But she could tell that the nearest board had the smallest amount of writing, and the far seventh had the most. She made an educated guess. "Are those the cohorts?"

Domi nodded. "That they are—with our rankings."

Reiva swallowed. "Rankings."

"Come on, we can take a quick look and not be late for lessons." She grabbed Reiva's hand and tugged her to the farthest board. "Can you read Lazarran script? Well, right here at the bottom, that's your name."

She blinked, staring at the odd shapes that apparently symbolized her. "At the bottom."

Domi actually patted her on the back, and it felt sincere. "That's okay, really. Everyone's at the bottom on their first day."

"So where's your name?" she asked, though she already had a decent suspicion based on what she'd seen at the exercises that morning.

Domi stabbed her finger toward the top. "Looks like I'm fifth this week. Tolm's still at number one."

"And Mylla?"

Domi pointed to a name slightly below the middle of the list.

She nodded slowly. "I see."

That warmth that had been building in her during the meal, the laughter that had bubbled against her lips—all of a sudden it felt ashen and bitter. This was all a competition. She had known that, of course, but to actually *see* it written out here for all to see...

It did something to her. She cast a glance around the room. Most of the other Initiates were gone by now, but of those still here, Reiva wondered exactly what their rankings were. That boy there who carried himself easily—was he sitting at the top, without the slightest of worries about whether he'd still be here by the end? That girl with dark rings under her eyes, was she holding on to the bottom?

A month from now, where would Reiva be? A year? Would she even still be here? Would she prove herself skilled enough to make it to the legions? And what then—would she die in a couple weeks in some front line clash, her body mangled and trodden underfoot in the manic press of battle?

Domi tugged at Reiva's arm. "Come on, lessons are another opportunity to rise."

Reiva swallowed, feeling her fists clench again.

Rise. I can do that.

"Thank you for showing me that," she said.

Domi snorted, bumping Reiva with her shoulder. "Still so stiff. Ease up a bit. I saw how hard you pushed yourself this morning—we all did. You're not going to wash out anytime soon."

The shape of the auction block burned in the back of her mind.

"No, I won't."

Domi's eyebrows rose.

Reiva blinked. "Hm?"

Domi snorted again, shaking her head. "Sorry you just—you got a fiery look in you all of a sudden. It's how you looked when you ran the obstacle course." She nodded, almost in an approving manner. "That's a good look to have. You'll be striking terror into the hearts of your enemies in no time."

INNER FLAME

9

THE GREAT SECRET

THE FIRST DAY melted into the first week, and then the first month of training. The schedule became second nature to Reiva. In the morning, always at a slightly different time, one of the more advanced Initiates would blow a horn in front of the dormitory. The house would have to be out in under a minute and at their muster point within five. If rain turned the hill to mud, there was no accommodation. "War makes no exceptions," they were told.

And neither did their instructors. While Reiva's strength gradually grew—thanks to the hearty meals they were fed, her ribs disappeared beneath a layer of toned muscle—the difficulty of the exercise accelerated. As soon as she managed to overcome a hurdle that had frustrated her for weeks, the standards were elevated.

Even so, she grew to love the physical regimens in the morning. The challenge never diminished, and that made her proud. She could cope better with the rigors thrust upon her. She was getting stronger day by day. She found herself standing up straighter, keeping her eyes up. She had grown taller, she realized—something that had completely escaped her notice through months of walking hunched over with downcast eyes. By the time she finished growing, she'd probably be among the tallest of all Talynisti women, though that was only slightly above average by Lazarran standards.

After the physical regimens, the Initiates quickly bathed and ate a meal, then attended their lessons. For first years like Reiva, this largely consisted of learning the Lazarran language and history.

The language was a tough nut to crack. She was no stranger to learning a new language—just about everyone in Shugrith spoke at least two, Talynisti and either Karellan or Zarushan. What was difficult was the *formality* of it. Declensions, verb tenses, moods. It was enough to drive her mad. And it was made only worse by the fact she was learning in her second language, which was itself a trade dialect and not Karellan proper.

Still, with the help of Mylla and Caulo (who insisted upon only speaking Lazarran for her benefit), she started to pick things up. She had to accept that she would never excel in language study, though.

History was easier to learn—she'd always had a mind for stories and the meaning they imparted—but the worse struggle. Entirely because she rejected most of the instructor's lessons on principle.

"But it doesn't make *sense*," she vented to Mylla after one particularly taxing lesson. "She says the Empire was founded by the First Emperor after the High God Arkhon taught him the secret of creating the arcane focus, which enabled him to found the Adept Corps and bring Lazarra out of the Dark Days."

Mylla nodded, already looking disinterested at what had become a somewhat regular routine for the two of them. "But..." she drawled.

"*But*, if that's true, then why did we—why did Talynis defeat the Lazarran invasion just a few years ago. If Arkhon really is the strongest god, then how come he couldn't defeat the Talynisti Four?"

Mylla rubbed her eyes, leaning against the tree she had been napping against before Reiva had stormed over. "Just write down what you're told, Reiva. What's it matter? Eventually Lazarra will conquer Talynis, even if it takes a few tries."

Reiva groaned. "But you see how it doesn't make sense, right?"

"I'm not a theologian."

"But the whole story of the Empire hinges on that! Who ever heard of a 'High God' before this? What if—"

"Or what if you're just going to keep getting yourself—and the rest of us, eventually—in trouble?"

She bit her tongue. "Doesn't the truth matter?"

Mylla shut her eyes. "Of course truth matters. But you can't eat truth. Or wear it. Or have it hold you when you're cold at night. If this is what the Corps wants us to know, then there's a good reason for it. I'm not going to question them. I *get* your point, Reiva, but what do you gain with this fight? You get assigned extra laps, weighted push ups. Didn't Luo have to give you another reprieve the other day?"

"First one in weeks," she grumbled.

"Still. If you keep making yourself a target like this, it's going to follow you. Don't you remember what Caulo and I told you on your first night here? People watch Initiates long before we get commissioned. We're going to have field exercises, serve alongside the legions as part of our training. You need to have a good reputation. I really don't care about who the Lazarran gods are. I'll do the sacrifices they say we need to, I'll participate in the rituals when they say we need to, and then I'll go back to my bed and it won't have made a difference."

Reiva popped to her feet and started pacing back and forth. "No, I've *lived* that life. I lived like that with my mother, then when I was enslaved and brought here. It *kills* you, Mylla. When your heart and your actions are misaligned, *it kills you.*"

"You know what else kills you? Me if you don't let me catch this nap before my session. And even if you get away from me, you'll still have to deal with the whole damn Empire who thinks what you're saying makes no sense."

"Then they should give me an explanation that makes more sense."

Mylla threw her hands up. "Maybe the commander of the legion attacking Talynis didn't say his prayers often enough, or he made offense by giving an inadequate sacrifice. That sounds like something a god would do, right? Let the army lose so they learn to behave? Nothing to do with whose gods are stronger. Besides," she muttered, squirming in her spot, "I like the system here. Arkhon on top, and all the other gods fit in below."

"That's humiliating."

"No," she snapped, her eyes opening with an intense glare. "It isn't. All I have left of my village in Gallia is a little song we used to chant every winter to our goddess. No one else in the world knows that goddess—we called her Lhivera—but even though I'm hundreds of miles away in Lazarra, I can still sing that song, because Gallia is part of the Empire, and my goddess is part of the pantheon. She might be a small part, but she's part of it. Someday the gods of Talynis will be too. Don't you *want* that?"

Reiva let her response die in her throat.

Do I?

She had a sudden vision of Shugrith burning under an Imperial banner. She thought of what her dad had paid to stop something like that from coming to be.

"I need to go to my session," grumbled Mylla.

As she dusted the grass off, Reiva folded her arms over her stomach. Mylla turned to leave.

She got two steps away before Reiva called out to her. "I didn't mean to say... I was trying to... I'm sorry, Mylla."

The black-haired girl pursed her lips. "It's fine, Reiva. I just don't want you to get in trouble over this. Every day, I see the gap widening between Tolm and Domi and Phetan—and the rest of us. You're getting stronger much faster than I am—anyone can see that. And if something happened where you had to leave...I just don't want that. Some of the older Initiates told me that as the years go on, the cohort splits into the elites and the average. Elites make it through. The rest of us just hang on as long as we can."

"But you're—!"

"You've seen the rankings in the mess hall, Reiva. Right now I'm just a little behind the curve, but that's going to get worse over time. Two paths can set out at just the *slightest* different angles, but as you walk them, that becomes miles and miles of separation. Trust me, we all see how the instructors push you. Yeah, you got here last of us all, so you're still making your way up the rankings—but they know you could be one of the elites. *That's* why they want you to drop this arguing about the history lessons. And that's why I do too. I...I need you to be here."

Mylla dashed her hand across her face. Reiva looked aside, pretending not to notice the tears welling up in the other girl's eyes.

"I'm going to be late," she muttered, turning her back to Reiva. "I'll see you at dinner."

"See you," murmured Reiva, watching her hustle across the grass.

As Mylla went, Reiva felt that sorrowful seed in her chest grow.

What am I supposed to do?

It wasn't long before her own session. As often as possible, Initiates met with their mentoring Adept. Since their mentors still served the Empire in many other capacities than just training the next generation of the Corps, there could be lengthy stretches of time during which an Initiate couldn't have a session.

And even though Alyat did much of his work in Lazarra, he frequently cancelled sessions without telling Reiva; he just didn't show up. If he was feeling particularly generous, he'd leave a note.

Her feelings toward her mentor were complicated. Over time, he had shown much more of his natural demeanor. He was brusque, often biting, and absolutely unconcerned with stepping on toes. That was a plus for Reiva. She liked this face of him much more than the diplomatic host he had presented himself as when they first met (apparently diplomacy was one of his many functions in the Empire).

What she didn't like was the nonsensical stuff he put her through in the name of 'training.'

"Deep breath in," he growled, not even hiding his own frustration at this point.

They had been going for well over half an hour by now, and her breathwork still wasn't up to his standards.

She inhaled deeply through her nostrils. Her legs were folded as she sat straight-backed on the floor of Alyat's office.

"Visualize," he said.

She pictured the breath curling through her lungs, into her veins, rushing throughout her body.

"Exhale."

She let it out through her nostrils, totally emptying her lungs.

"You're still fighting it."

Reiva opened her eyes. "It's ridiculous."

"It's essential if you ever want to make *acolyta*."

Reiva frowned. *Acolyta* was the second stage of an Initiate's training. That was when she would get her focus and started practicing her arcane Art—which was supposed to manifest in the process of earning the focus.

But for some reason, Alyat insisted she practice *breathing*.

"Isn't there some other method I could try?"

"If there is, I don't know it, so I couldn't help you with it."

"I hear other mentors give their apprentices different exercises."

Alyat sighed, running his hands over his beard. "Look, you want to carve wood? You want to take leisurely walks? You have free time. You even have a free day now and then. But breathwork is superior, and it's what we all learned with. Everything else is a waste of time."

"I can't *see* it, though! I can't touch it. I need something like that."

"That's what the visualization is for. Unless you want to admit you have no imagination," he said flatly.

Reiva opened her mouth, then shut it. She looked away, scowling at the wall of Alyat's office. It was sparsely decorated. He really didn't do much to make it welcoming. Books, scrolls, and sheaves of parchment occupied most of the floor space. Alyat was one of those Adepts who served the Empire more with the pen than the sword.

"Tell me what your problem is," said Alyat, "and maybe I can fix it."

Reiva rubbed her face. "It feels like the days just get worse as they go on. The high point is the physical regimens. Then I have the lessons—don't get me started on those—and then *this*."

Alyat snorted, his expression totally flat. "Kid, if you talk like that to your instructors, I can tell you why it's so painful."

"I want to do the best I can! But this place is just..."

"Not built for you," he offered. "We *all* think that. Some people, it takes a few years to hit that point, but eventually it happens to everyone. Part of your training is learning to overcome that. You think every single man and woman in the legions is exactly the same person? A human cast from a mold? No—but they are forged into squadrons, into companies, into legions. And if you can't hack that, then you wash out. Get it, kid?"

Reiva dropped her eyes to the floor. "I get it. But if I need to be a soldier, then why am I learning to *breathe*? I was born breathing. And I don't understand why you say I'm doing it wrong. In the physicals I'm getting stronger. I can speak Lazarran a hundred times better than when I started. But *breathing*?"

When she glanced up, Alyat was smirking at her.

"What?"

"Why do you think you're getting so strong?"

"Because I'm training every day and eating a mountain of food."

"Yes, but wrong. That could make anyone strong—but not *as strong* as you, this fast. Come on, somebody must have told you by now that you're smashing expectations."

She remembered what Mylla had said earlier. "Well..."

"Here's why kid." He took a knife from off his belt and cut a small gash in the pad of his thumb. A drop of bright blood welled from the cut.

He wiped away the droplet, and the cut was already gone.

Reiva threw her hands up. "You can do magic, I know. Everyone here knows how Adepts can heal."

"But you don't know *how*, so shut up and listen."

Her eyes widened. This sort of information usually wasn't given to *probatia* until they were ready to try for a focus, certainly not to any first years.

She shut up readily.

"All around us is energy. A substance that pervades all reality.

Aether, we call it. Aether is the great secret, even though it's hardly a secret. Philosophers, mystics, prophets—countless people throughout the ages have sensed it. All people know it, to some extent. When a shrewd merchant gets the sense that he's being cheated in a deal, purely on intuition, that's the sleeping part of his mind recognizing a shift in the aether around his trade partner. Aether responds to emotion, to life, to intent. A man about to murder moves aether. So does a woman in love.

"And so do Adepts. More than anyone else, we understand the flow of aether—we feel it as easily as we feel the water on our skin and smell flowers in the spring. With aether, we heal. With aether, we work our Arts."

His palm glowed with light.

"When you discover your Art, you'll draw aether through your body—with the aid of a focus—and change the world. That is magic —the power to change the world by working aether."

Reiva swallowed. The room seemed to tilt.

Alyat continued. "The reason you're getting strong faster than you should be able to? These ridiculous breathing exercises are training you to attune to the flow of aether. Sure, there are other ways of doing it. Some people walk a particular way. Others carve wood. And all those methods have their advantages, but learning breathwork is the most valuable thing an Adept can do. You learn to enrich your body and mind through control of breath, then learning to do the same with aether is a natural progression."

Her head was truly spinning now. "But, the physical regimens..."

"Just as aether healed the cut on my thumb, so it helps you build your muscles, hone your reflexes. You can't consciously control aether yet, but the conscious part is only one tenth of what matters. True skill with aether is found in the unconscious mind, in the same place that produces dreams and intuitions. Once you have that— which is what these breathing exercises are teaching you—you'll take to the deliberate manipulation of aether like a fish to water."

Reiva's jaw shut with a click. "That...ah..."

Alyat snorted. "Yeah, it's a lot to take in."

"Is it just the physical exercises?"

"No—aether attunement will help you with mental work as well, but most people have a natural inclination. Yours, from everything I hear, is to the physical. Before the Adept Corps was founded on the revelation of aether and how to control it, many people understood parts of this, at least in small ways. The great heroes of ancient legends? The ones who lifted boulders and wrestled with bulls? They were like you. The philosophers who upended centuries of accepted wisdom with one carefully formulated question? Same principle, only skewed toward the mental faculties.

"Sensitivity to aether is the small nudge that separates normal men from exceptional men. People call it talent, or inspiration, or luck—but this is what it is, at its root. It's the slightest edge that, over years of practice and labor, adds up to mountains of difference. Men have said such people are chosen by the gods—and maybe that's true—but they didn't understand the mechanism. In the Adept Corps, we've unlocked the secret. And if the Empire comes to rule the world someday, it will be on the back of that one secret."

Reiva suddenly felt something slide inside her and *click* into place, like a puzzle piece just out of alignment shifted into position. She seemed connected to a grand purpose and project that extended far beyond her own body.

Alyat must have noticed the change in her, because he nodded. "I think that's enough for today. Don't go around sharing this."

Reiva nodded furiously.

"Good. So next time you come in here, the second I hear a complaint, you're getting tossed out on your ass—understand?"

"Understand."

10

BELONGING

Amid all the drudgery and frustrations of training, there was one precious bright spot that could always be relied upon for a true spot of *fun*, and that was hand-to-hand combat.

While a legionnaire, and by extension an Adept, was more likely than not to have a weapon when facing foes, it was an essential pillar of an Adept's martial education that she know how to handle herself with nothing but her own hands and feet. And though Reiva had never experienced a formal education in this manner of battle before she came to the Sanctum, she took to it readily, building upon many impromptu (or not-so-impromptu) instances of having fought other children in Shugrith for the sake of her little brother.

The memory of his scraped and bleeding face sent horrible pangs of guilt and longing through her, so she smothered it with a fanatical focus on the task at hand—beating her opponent.

The chill in the air had not yet abated, as the sun still hung low in the sky. Hand-to-hand combat training was one of the regimens the Initiates rotated through as part of their early morning disciplines, switching out with the obstacles course and whatever other sequence of exercise the instructors saw fit to inflict upon them.

Despite the cold, though, Reiva did not shiver. Her breath puffed great clouds of steam, but her body streamed with sweat and a flush lingered in her features from the warm-ups. Though the exercises were just as grueling as they had always been, they no longer reduced her to a near-vomiting, shuddering mess.

So it was with no small eagerness that she sized up her opponent—a pretty blonde girl with a petite nose. Her name was Ela, and Reiva had watched her fight plenty of the others. She already had a sense of how their fight would go once it began.

And the beginning would be soon. Reiva and Ela, along with a gaggle of others, stood in a circle watching the final moments of a match between red-haired Phetan and a dark-eyed boy named Sciro. Both of them had sturdy builds, both held places of pride on the cohort rankings, though Phetan was often the higher.

Reiva observed as Sciro tried to put the other boy into a headlock, only for Phetan to deftly break the move and retaliate with a vicious elbow to the gut, followed by a leg sweep. The wind rushed out of Sciro as he hit the ground, and Phetan pounced on him before he could recover, planting one knee on the boy's chest and putting both hands around his neck.

"My win," huffed Phetan, features screwed up in equal parts aggression and exertion.

Sciro slapped the grass, acknowledging that Phetan had him beat.

The two got to their feet, nodding to each other. Sciro's eyes held a sort of quiet anger, and Reiva had to suppress a shudder at the way he glared at Phetan. The latter hardly seemed to notice or mind though, as he puffed out his chest in victory. Turning to the half-dozen Initiates assembled around, he spread his hands. "Well?"

Reiva wasted no time. "Sciro's footwork was weak, leaving him open to strikes he should have dodged or shrugged off. Phetan left no chances for Sciro to recover, always pressing to keep him from taking control of the match."

As she spoke, one of the instructors walked by, nodding in approval at Reiva's explanation. Her heart lifted, and her shoulders squared. She was still pushing her way up through the rankings, and that would go toward pulling her higher.

Some other Initiates offered their interpretations of why the bout had proceeded the way it did, and then it was Reiva and Ela's turn. Today, they would be going to a single fall, so she would only have one shot to take Ela down before another pair rotated in.

As she stepped up, Reiva ran her eyes up and down the other girl. Ela was taller. She was also older, almost by a year, and it showed in her stature. Each cohort's members were relatively close in age, but today Reiva had the ill luck to be up against someone at the extreme end of that range. On top of all that, Ela's name was a common sight at the tops of the rankings—she was usually the second highest ranked girl after Domi.

Though Reiva had strengthened thanks to the regular nutrition and exercise, she was acutely aware of how uphill this battle would be.

So when the start was called, she wasted no time in pressing her attack.

She lashed out with a quick punch, then flowed into a grapple. Ela's eyes widened at the ferocity of Reiva's opener. She ducked the punch and disengaged from the grab, but she was on the back foot already.

Reiva didn't intend to let her recover from that. She focused on overwhelming Ela, forcing a chink in her armor. When it came to raw technique and precision, the girl had her beat any day. If the match came down to ability or raw strength, Ela would win. So Reiva had to rely on tenacity and momentum. She had to rely on stamina.

The good thing about stamina was, it could be bolstered through sheer force of will and focus. And if Reiva had anything—willpower and focus she had in abundance. Every morning, she pushed her body to the limit. And while Alyat's sessions still hadn't produced any breakthroughs regarding magic, they had honed her concentration to a razor's edge.

Ela lashed out with a precise sequence of jabs. Reiva didn't have the speed to evade them, so she hunkered down and took the blows, gritting her teeth. Every hit rattled her to the bone, and she could already feel bruises welting on her skin. But pain was no stranger. She could endure it.

She couldn't let the tide turn, though. Ducking her head, she darted forward, slamming her shoulder into Ela's midsection and sending her reeling. Reiva chased, throwing feint punches and kicks that she pulled at the last minute.

Ela's eyes whirled as she tried to meet the phantom strikes. Reiva felt a surge of satisfaction in the back of her mind. This was Ela's key weakness. She had a cold, analytical mind, but when too much stimuli came at her, she had to process *all* of it. She didn't know how to ignore things.

And when a mind is stretched a dozen different directions, it cannot hope to attend to the true strike when it does come.

Reiva jabbed at Ela's eyes, and in the half-moment when the girl blinked on reflex, she threw herself forward in a full tackle. They went down in a tumble, and in moments Reiva had Ela pinned. "My win," she huffed, sweat soaking her brow and back.

Ela grunted in acknowledgment, letting her muscles go slack.

Reiva's chest burst with pride. Never before had a fight gone this well for her. Almost to a beat, it had proceeded as she'd predicted and strategized. And Ela was near the *top*. As Reiva offered her a hand, the girl brushed mussed-up blonde hair from her eyes.

"That was good," she said simply. Though well-masked, hurt pride lurked behind her eyes.

Reiva nodded her thanks. "You too. You get distracted easily; if you could hone in more intently on what matters most, instead of trying to account for every little thing, you'd probably beat me."

Ela seemed to accept this. "Thank you. You could stand to work on signaling your moves less obviously."

Reiva received the critique with another nod. She had long ago stopped feeling such comments as personal—she craved them now. Morning regimens were her best chance at climbing the rankings, so she took every drop of feedback she could get.

As the others who had been watching offered their comments on how the fight went, Reiva glanced at Phetan. He was the highest ranked person in this group. She was curious what he would have to say—but it was a curiosity that would go unsatisfied, as he didn't say a word.

Reiva pursed her lips as she stepped out of the center, joining the spectators again.

Not one word? She felt a blistering spark of anger kindle in her heart and spread through her. What was it—did he just think he was too good to bother? Was it because there had not been instructors in earshot at the moment, and so he didn't care?

She shot him another look—which she imagined was a full-on glare, though she didn't bother trying to rearrange her features. He wasn't paying the slightest attention to her, though. Ela had gone to stand next to him and the two of them were cracking jokes, judging by the furtive smirks and smothered laughter. At least Ela had the decency to pay some attention to the next match—Phetan's eyes were firmly fixed to her chest.

A flush crept into Reiva's face. She turned aside, realizing that she hadn't been paying any attention to the match either. A few seconds later, she found herself casting another furtive glance at them. Sure enough, Phetan stole another ogle.

Reiva shook her head, trying and failing to dislodge the embarrassment she felt. She also felt a sudden urge to tug at the hem of her tunic in a vain attempt to pull it lower over her legs.

The rush of victory had faded now, and all she felt was discomfort.

I don't belong here. Her lower lip was quivering. She couldn't hold her attention to the fight anymore, so she let her eyes roam around to the other matches, the other spectators.

They all looked so comfortable. Caulo and Luo were tumbling in another spot, vying for dominance against one another. Some of their spectators had even taken to cheering, so pitched was the struggle.

Domi stood with her hands on her hips, watching a match with keen attention. Her tunic left much of her thighs bare, and she didn't seem to mind—she certainly wasn't pathetically tugging at the hem.

That was how Lazarrans dressed, wasn't it? Why should she have cared?

Mylla was just coming out of a fight of her own—she had been up against Tolm, by ill fate, and the outcome had gone as expected. Her eyes were downcast, but she nodded graciously to the victor. Tolm seemed to be offering her pointers on some sort of hold. Mylla watched his demonstration eagerly, then offered her thanks.

An ugly sort of jealousy surged through Reiva. She hadn't had the chance to fight Tolm. How helpful would that advice be? Why did Mylla get to—

The blue-eyed girl noticed she was watching. Her eyebrows knit in concern, and she mouthed the words, 'Are you okay?'

A wave of shame slammed into Reiva, wiping out the envy. Her insides roiled as she forced a smile and a small nod.

Mylla returned the smile, though her eyes still plainly bore the mark of worry.

Reiva hugged herself across the stomach. When the match she was meant to be watching ended, she didn't have any feedback to offer. She just stood there, quiet. Naturally, an instructor floated nearby, and she was sure her silence would be noted. Fine then— what did it matter, really? After all, she had just been playing at belonging here. She didn't really deserve to climb the rankings. What did she think would happen—she could win a few fights, run an obstacle course, and she would be worthy of something? She would *belong*, finally?

She would never belong—not like the others so clearly did. It was all she could do to hold back tears as morning regimens came to a close and they were sent to dunk themselves in the river.

Moving quickly as she could without looking like she was bolting, she made her way to the water, hopping in without a second thought. When her head was under, she screamed. Then, quick as she could, she hopped out and started for the dormitory, dripping frigid water. She didn't even stop to wring out her hair.

She struck her toe against a stray rock, though, earning a hissed curse. The pain faded to the back of her mind in an instant, though, as she realized how her clothes were sticking to her body. Another flush burned her face as she tried to peel the tunic away from clinging to her skin. She started tugging at the hem of her tunic again.

Then she only cursed again, this time at herself. Ela hadn't minded the way Phetan looked at her—and she had obviously noticed. Why was Reiva so concerned about whether people could see what her body looked like? She was entering womanhood; wasn't that what happened at this point in life?

Bile rose in the back of her throat as the thought of Phetan leering at her chest flickered through her mind.

No. No no no! Gods, no.

She folded her arms across her chest as she reached to the dormitory—she was the first back today, and she was glad for it as she shucked off her wet clothes and pulled on a dry set as quickly as she could.

She spun on her heel, intent on making it to the mess hall before—

Mylla nearly bowled her over as she half-ran out the door.

"Reiva!" she yelped. "What happened? I've been trying to catch up."

Reiva came up short. "Huh?"

Mylla blinked. "You were almost *running*. I would have called after you but I thought you wouldn't want that."

That was true—it would only have made her more self-conscious. What was she supposed to say, though?

She settled for muttering something about her tunic.

Mylla furrowed her brow. "Your tunic?" Her eyes flitted down. "Oh, yeah it's a little short huh? *Ha!* You're finally getting taller."

Reiva stared. "Um, yeah. I guess so."

"Have you ever requisitioned from the Quartermaster's staff? Let's hurry over to lunch. If we have enough time after, I can show you how."

Blindsided, Reiva felt the prickle of tears yet again. "Th-thank you. That sounds good."

"Just let me change really fast."

"Mhmm."

She leaned against the outside as Mylla went in, avoiding looking at anyone else as they arrived. Blessedly, no one bothered her.

True to her word, Mylla was quick to return. She swept damp, dark hair out of her eyes as they hustled for the mess hall. "Was that really all that bothered you?"

Reiva swallowed, tasting sour. It seemed there was too much to even articulate. Where to begin? She was worried about her rank. She was worried about fitting in like a Lazarran. She was worried about growing up. Worried about how people perceived her. Worried about whether she would ever manage to have a breakthrough with Alyat's stupid breathing exercises.

She shook her head slightly. "I just..."

Mylla's attention was rapt on her, that now-familiar crease between her eyebrows, the slight frown on her lips.

Reiva scoffed at herself. "It's nothing." She managed a smile. "Really. Just getting lost in my head. Thank you."

Mylla returned the smile. "Okay, if you say so. And if you need to be alone, you can tell me. But I'm always willing to listen."

It sounded, on the surface, like any sort of common pleasantry. The sort of thing said in courtesy and then forgotten by both parties. But somehow, Reiva detected a note of...almost desperation. A desire from Mylla that Reiva would let her in.

Reiva's stomach knotted again. Was that kind of her? Was it foolish? Weren't they in competition here? How could Mylla so readily offer of herself for Reiva's sake? People just didn't *do* that. They played tricks. They used and betrayed you when it was convenient. They sold you for a clinking bag of silver.

"Thank you, Mylla. But really, I'm okay." Her teeth almost groaned as they ground them together through another smile. "I'm okay."

11

AN ADEPT IN GLORY

One day, after physical regimens, the Initiates were sent to hastily bathe and change into formal dress. As Reiva had never done this before, Domi assisted her.

"And then you knot *this*, and done. And your mantle should have the tail hanging off your left shoulder."

As they stepped out from the dormitory, Reiva fidgeted at the stiffness of the uniform. It was the finest piece of clothing she'd ever worn. She could have lived off its value for *months* in Talynis.

"All this for a parade?" she asked.

Domi pursed her lips, fussing over her own uniform. "Not just any parade—a *triumphal* parade. We've won a war."

Luo snorted. "With how many wars we've got going on, it doesn't seem like quite a rare occurrence."

Domi stuck her tongue out. "It's not every day you get an unconditional surrender from an enemy. The Empire has expanded yet again. And since *we* are the future face of the conquest, we have to be there. All Initiates will be—and our mentors will be watching. So just stand straight, look official, and give praise when everyone else does."

Reiva wiped her palms against the uniform. "Who was conquered?"

"Parthava. Now come on, we can't be late."

Parthava. She'd come through there. That was the nation where Baranzir had cut a deal for a horse with a Parthavan man—a deal that had hinged on her being sold in Lazarra.

She had a vague recollection of the slaver speaking with that man about the struggle between the Lazarran military and the Parthavan Coalition. He had said that as soon as the Empire sent an Adept, the fight would be over.

"Will there be an Adept in the parade?" Reiva asked.

Domi glanced over her shoulder. "Hm? Probably. I don't know who though."

She would have to ask Alyat then.

The Initiates assembled at the gate of the Sanctum according to rank and cohort. At the fore, just behind the commissioned Adepts, were the highest ranking Initiates. These had silver fringes on their mantles and were called *subordinati*. There were few of them—not only due to attrition but also because *subordinati* served on field missions, proving their capabilities in genuine combat. After them came the *acolyti*, who had earned their arcane focuses. Lastly were the *probatii*, among whom Reiva stood.

Looking at the older Initiates, it seemed almost impossible to Reiva that she would be like them in just a few years.

If I make it...

She bit her tongue. No thinking like that—she had to hold fast to the determination that she would find victory here. She would prove herself.

With every passing day, however, it got a little harder to believe. She was doing well in the physical regimens, and she had even started cooperating with the lessons from their teachers, but Alyat's tutoring was still about as pleasant and productive as pulling teeth.

What if she never got past this wall? What if she washed out before she even finished her first year of training?

Such thoughts swirled around her mind as the company marched forward. It was still morning, but already the streets were filling with spectators. A triumphal parade was a holiday for all the city, and Lazarrans were never remiss with chances to celebrate their military.

The assembled throng presented no difficulty to the Adept Corps, however. People parted for them with deference, some even bowing their heads to the ground. There was a strange sort of mystique some people held about the Corps. Reiva could understand it—before she joined, she had only known of the Adepts as whispered horrors of war.

But it was certainly disquieting to be on the receiving end of such obeisance.

The parade route stretched from the First Gate at the eastern side of the city and wound all the way along the central promenade to the palace, where the Emperor himself would receive the victorious legion.

The representatives of the Adept Corps divided. The most senior Adepts sitting on the Circle of Peers and the *subordinati* Initiates headed toward the palace, where they would attend to the final honors and celebration of the parade. The rest, Reiva included, headed toward the First Gate, where they would welcome the victorious as they entered. Alyat was among the Adepts responsible for overseeing the Initiates going to the First Gate, so Reiva tried to get his attention by tugging at his sleeve.

"Eh?" He growled, looming over her. He was not, Reiva noticed, looking particularly celebratory.

"Is there an Adept with the legion coming in?"

Alyat's face changed, so much so that Reiva blinked in surprise. She had not known Alyat long, but she'd never known him to have an expression of such...trepidation?

"Aye. Adept Sharasthi. *Ars Tenebrae.*" He gave her an expectant look.

"Shadow," Reiva translated.

Alyat nodded, satisfied that she was keeping up with her Lazarran. "If you haven't heard much about her yet, then you will."

Reiva frowned. "About Adept Sharasthi?"

Strange name, too...

Or rather, not that strange a name. For Reiva, it rolled off the tongue easily, sounding almost Talynisti. But it certainly sounded like a name Lazarrans would struggle with.

"She's done a great thing for the Empire," said Alyat. And that was all he had on the subject, turning his face forward.

When they reached their place, Orphans had already cordoned it off to prepare for their arrival. The Initiates were placed at the fore, so that they would be closer to the parade, while the commissioned Adepts like Alyat stood behind them. Actually, Alyat was directly behind Reiva—much to her chagrin. She'd have to hold perfect posture the whole time.

The air was dense with noise—countless voices chattering back and forth about the news. Reiva only caught snatches, but from what she could garner, the victory over Parthava had been sudden and unexpected. Apparently, even the most optimistic projections for the campaign had not predicted such a sweeping success in so little time.

Reiva found herself wondering about that as she waited. They had been forced to assemble well in advance of the procession, and now there was nothing to do. They had been forbidden from chit-chat, told it was imperative they project decorum. The eyes of senators, aristocrats, and military veterans would be on them, wondering what the future of the Adept Corps looked like.

At least, until word came that the parade was approaching the city—then all eyes turned toward the Gate.

Even before the first legionnaire was through, the cheers were beginning—cheers of "*Ave Imperator!*" and "Glory to the victors!" And then, the aquilifer stepped into sight, and the crowd went well and truly mad.

Every legion had its aquilifer, its standard bearer. This legionnaire carried the great gilded Eagle—the *Aquila*—that symbolized the spirit of the legion. The aquilifer held aloft the Eagle, and below it was a vertical banner emblazoned VII. The Seventh Legion. And beneath that were words that, to Reiva's best guess, translated to something like "By Vigilance and Preparation." The legion's motto.

As the sun glinted off the golden *Aquila*, the crowd's roar hammered Reiva's eardrums. She actually gawked upward—a moment ago, the sky had been overcast, but now the sun shone through the clouds, as if to signify divine favor.

But the crowd's cheering and shouting only grew louder as the spoils of war rolled through. Legionnaires walked alongside carts laden with loot. There were flags, banners, furs, all manner of fine clothing. Pulling these carts were some of the most majestic horses Reiva had ever seen—Parthavan, of course—and many of these steeds had armor of their own, which glittered and jingled as they walked.

As the din of the people grew ever louder, Reiva clapped her hands over her ears, only for Alyat to flick her fingers. She scowled—glad he could not see the expression—and put her hands down.

Her mind whirled with curiosities about how the legion had overcome the Parthavans—perhaps the strongest cavalry army in the world—with their infantry legionnaires. How had they won these leather belts with gilding, these beautiful works of glazed earthenware? How had they pilfered from the Parthavans' temples these innumerable religious idols? The enemy had been stripped bare, and Reiva would have been agog to hear anything substantial yet remained in the Parthavan homeland.

She knew from her lectures that much would remain, of course—after all, Parthava would now be under the rule of the Empire, surrendered to the Emperor and High Arkhon. But even though she knew that, it was hard to believe as yet another cart full of masterfully carved totems came trundling along the street.

Smiling legionnaires laughed to one another as they drank in the praise. People threw laurel wreaths at them from the rooftops, which they caught and placed atop their heads.

Reiva couldn't help but smile herself. She understood that glee—she had felt a hint of that at the end of her first day of training. The knowledge that she had survived what came before—that she had a future now. And these men and women had not only survived war—they had *won* it.

Suddenly, another scream pounded her eardrums, and only the

threat of another reprimand from Alyat kept her from covering her ears.

If the horses pulling the carts had been magnificent, they were like common mules compared to *this* specimen. Its chest was broad, its chestnut coat perfect in the golden light. Atop it sat a middle-aged man dressed in formal legionnaire kit, every bit of metal on his body polished to a gleam. As he rode, he kept one arm raised in a perpetual acknowledgment of the laud heaped upon him. This was the legate, the military commander of the Seventh Legion. She had never seen a legate this close before—but her eyes only flicked over him before a glint of gold caught her eye.

The Initiates' lessons had taught them, at great pains, the various honors one could win in the Empire. It was expected that they, as Adepts, would win several in their commissioned service. The rarest of all honors was the personal dispensation from the Emperor to wear Imperial Purple—perhaps one in a hundred Adepts had ever earned the distinction, and it was even more precious among the common ranks of the military, reserved only for the greatest of generals.

Of a different sort was the second highest honor: the golden laurel. This glory came not from the Emperor, but from the legion. When the time of victory came and the triumphal parade marched through the capital city, the legion selected the soul who, in the eyes of the soldiers, had contributed the greatest work to the campaign.

More often than not, the legion elected to bestow the golden laurel upon the legate, an acknowledgment of the leadership that had taken them through the crush of battle and death, but this needed not always be the case. Sometimes it was given to a lesser officer who had led some daring, suicidal charge that turned the tide of battle. That sort of honor changed a legionnaire's life and career like nothing else.

But today, the golden leaves of the laurel crown sat atop a head of raven hair, coiffed in curls that flowed starkly over the crimson red of an Adept's mantle. Framed by the dark ringlets, the gold and the red, the Adept's face was severe, befitting someone who was more than

human, someone who almost seemed as though she had no awareness of the pomp surrounding her.

Reiva heard Alyat's voice call for the salute, and she numbly put
her fist to her heart.

Why do I feel like this? she marveled to herself.

Time seemed to unfold slowly as Sharasthi's horse cantered down
the promenade. Alyat had said Sharasthi did something great—but
to have earned the golden laurel? Reiva realized her heart was
pounding. There were gasps and murmurs among the other Initiates
as they took in the sight, and then it clicked for Reiva. Then she
understood why the sight had stirred her so.

That could be me.

And not only because this woman was an Adept, but because of
what she saw in her features. Her name, Sharasthi, had been the first
sign, and now Reiva only saw more—the ruddy brown complexion,
the strong nose and thick hair. This woman, like her, came from the
eastern realms. Was she Mizkhari? Zarushan?

Her eyes—hard eyes, dark as granite—glided over Reiva, and she
thought she'd almost fall to her knees and bow her head to the
ground.

This was an Adept in glory.

This was what she could achieve.

Her heart did not stop pounding—not when Sharasthi disappeared around the bend, not when the parade was long over and the
Initiates returned to the Sanctum, and not when she lay down to
sleep. Long into the night, Reiva stared up at the ceiling, her mind
spinning with fantasies of herself coming through the First Gate, gold
in her hair and the mantle around her shoulders.

The next day, when she fell on the obstacle course, she thought of
Adept Sharasthi's entry, and she stood up. She did the same when her
tongue caught on a complicated line of Lazarran poetry. And again
when Alyat chided her for lacking focus in her breathwork.

"Adept Sharasthi," she muttered, "seems incredible."

Alyat drew his lips into a thin line. "She is," he said eventually.
"She almost died, you know."

Reiva's eyes widened.

Her mentor sighed, pinching the bridge of his nose. "She got cut off from the main company. Stranded behind the Parthavans' lines. Everyone else with her got picked off by their cavalry archers. It was impossible to escape—but she had the shadows on her side. She hid, and she fought like a ghoul from the darkness. What she did with her Art was insane in the extreme."

Reiva realized she was leaning forward, her breathing shallow.

Alyat grunted. "She got into the command camp of the Coalition army. Reports differ, but she killed as many as three of their most important generals single-handedly. The surrender came in two days later. That's why she got the gold."

He peered into Reiva's eyes. "You want it? You want to climb the ladder we call an Empire? Here's a rung: *breathe.*"

And she breathed.

12

DEALS, EXCHANGES, MATTERS OF CONVENIENCE

REIVA PASSED the first year Lazarran competency exam with minimal difficulty. She knew she hadn't done so with any particular distinction, but she had proven herself as capable as she had to be. She wouldn't be writing any political treatises or philosophical discourses, but she was fluent in all the ways required of her.

As a second year Initiate though, she faced a more pressing challenge. She needed to break through to *acolyta*, which required she manifest her Art. Second year was the most common point in an Adept's training for that to occur. Now and then someone hung on until their third year, but if they didn't manifest quite early in their third, they washed out.

There were rumors of Adepts who'd manifested in their first year of training, but no one could verify whether someone like that had ever happened—not recently, at least. Even Tolm had taken until two months into his second year to manifest his Art of Water, the *Ars Aquae*. Phetan had taken three for his Art of Life.

Mylla and Domi had already manifested their Arts. As had Luo, Ela—and every single other Initiate remaining in Seventh Cohort. Reiva was the only person who had not reached stage two, which meant she was, once again, at the bottom of the rankings. About a fifth of their cohort had already washed out. And Reiva was behind the curve, which put her in dire straits of becoming one of those failures and losing her dream of glory.

To add insult to injury, it wouldn't have even been particularly bad if her sessions with Alyat held any promise, but no, they only diminished her hopes further.

She continued to excel in the physical regimens, and she had started parroting back what the lecturers drilled into her. Since moving on from history, they had begun lessons in military strategy and campaign logistics. While not particularly thrilling, she enjoyed working through the puzzle of how best to prepare an army for war, and how to keep it sustained in the theatre of combat, far from home for many months.

But she'd never get to stand in a battle line or to coordinate a supply train if she never manifested her Art.

At the end of one of their increasingly frustrating sessions, Alyat wiped his hand over his face. His palm barely muffled a groan.

"I'm doing everything you say," protested Reiva.

"No, you're not. Your breathwork is impeccable, I'll grant that. And your concentration, solid as the marble of the Palatine Throne. But you're not opening yourself to the aether. You're closed off."

Despite how many times they'd gone down this road, she couldn't stop herself from lashing out again. "I'm *trying*! Let's just go to the Trial Chamber and—"

"Trying isn't good enough. If you went to the Trial Chamber now, you'd just embarrass yourself. In another cohort, your physical performance might be enough to keep you in the game until your third year, but your group has too many high performers to justify keeping someone around who hasn't manifested her Art yet."

She bit down hard on her lower lip. She knew it was true. Tolm was the darling of the group—supposedly there were already legates who had their eye on him. He continued to be elusive, barely interacting with the other Initiates beyond what was required of him. Other elites like Domi and Phetan could tell they were pulling ahead of the others, and they relished it. The better they displayed their competence, the more confident they felt, and the more confident they felt, the more they seemed to breeze through the regimens and disciplines required of them. Every time someone gained a focus, they moved into another dormitory to stay with other *acolyta*. Reiva was alone, surrounded by the faces of First Cohort *probatii*.

Alyat scratched at his beard, the way he always did when he something was bothering him. "Have you tried the stillness meditation?"

"Yes," she sighed. "And I can't find it."

"The stillness."

"There's nothing *still* about anything in my life. I wake up and run, and fight, and then I scarf down enough food to last me through my lessons, and in every spare moment all I can think about is how I'm falling behind."

"That sort of worry is exactly why you need to find the stillness."

"You say that like I'm going to be walking along one day and then find a nice brick of inner calm by the wayside."

The Adept made one of his distinct groans—almost a growl, really. "Do you think in the heat of battle, a legionnaire has the chance to stop, ask for everyone to hold off a moment while he finds his bearings? Is that what *you're* planning to do when you're in the field some day? You think all the archers who've been told to target the person with the red scarf are just going to relax their draws? All the cavalry are going to go off and graze their horses for a spell? Because as far as I can tell, that's what you think you're going to get. Your life now is *gentle as rain* compared to what it will be."

"Well then, I might as well quit now, because *I can't do it!*"

"You *can*, and damn the gods if I'm going to let you walk out now. I wasn't padding your ego when I said you have one of the best intuitive grasps of aether attunement I've ever seen in someone your age."

"Fat good it's doing me now."

"The only person in your way right now is *you*, kid. So sort yourself out before something else gets in your way—something too big to overcome without a focus around your neck."

"I thought your job was to help me."

"Don't start with that, kid. I told you—if you talk to me about what's going on inside your head, I might be able to."

"I don't—"

"You don't trust me. You don't trust anyone—we've noticed. Yeah, not just me—*we*. You've got allies, sure. Initiate Mylla. You train with Luo and Caulo now and then. But you don't have *friends*. At the end of the day you mope back to your dormitory to wipe the noses of the new blood. You can't keep expecting to breeze through training with alliances, kid. Alliances are deals, exchanges, matters of convenience. You need more than that. "

Reiva grit her teeth, feeling heat rise to her face. "I'm competing with them."

"You *were* competing with them. Now you're at the back of the pack again, barely clinging to their heels. They helped you when you first got here, didn't they? Tell me, what did that benefit them?"

Reiva blinked, turning aside. "They...I don't know. We always help the new kids. We know what it's like to be in their shoes. It's courtesy. That's not friendship."

"It *could* be. Hell, it could be family."

Reiva opened her mouth, but Alyat cut her off with a wave and a gruff, "We're done today. If you won't talk to me about what's going on, go talk to someone else. Or talk to yourself for a while. Spend your extra time puzzling thing out—maybe something I said will finally lodge inside your skull."

She deflated, staring at the flooring.

"Get some air, kid. No one ever had a spiritual breakthrough sitting in an office."

Without a word, feeling bitterness well up inside her like a black fountain, she picked herself up and left. As she exited, she could feel the waves of frustration rolling off Alyat, and they only intensified her own anger. Anger at Alyat, anger at herself.

Supposedly that sort of heightened emotional awareness was part of touching the flow of aether. Alyat said it was a good sign that she felt things so intensely. But it too had only become a constant reminder of how badly she'd been hamstrung. It was like she'd been hitched to a cart of granite slabs and told to haul it up a mountain. Her feet churned the mud, her shoulders and back ached with the strain, her hands burned as she clutched the ropes—and all she managed to do was hold her place and fight the inexorable downward pull.

She felt tears pricking at her eyes, wiped them away surreptitiously with the edge of her mantle. She couldn't be seen crying. Whatever of her reputation she had, she had to hold on to it. Let people see her as strong, determined. Let them think she was completely unbothered by her problems, completely confident that she would manifest her Art when she was ready.

She was so focused on looking composed, she didn't look ahead—a mistake that made itself painfully clear when she walked into a stone wall.

She grunted, backing up.

The wall grunted as well.

Reiva felt her face heat up again. "Tolm!"

The other Initiate raised an eyebrow. "That's me."

"I—sorry. I should've moved to the side. I was...thinking."

"Thinking."

"Um, yes. Sorry."

"You already said that."

"I...right. I did."

Tolm cast a glance behind her. "Coming from a session?"

She nodded, careful to project ease in her posture. Shoulders straight, chin high.

"It went well?"

"Yeah, it did."

He cracked a smile. "Really?"

Her face heated further. "*Yes*, really. I'm sure your sessions are going well."

He shrugged. "I suppose."

Gods, what kind of person talks like this?

...someone kicking my ass by every measure.

"Well," said Tolm, "I'll get on my way."

He—somewhat exaggeratedly—stepped around her, then started off down the pathway. He looked to be heading toward the mess hall. Grabbing an early dinner, maybe.

Before she could stop herself, she blurted out, "I don't have my focus yet."

Tolm stopped, turned at the hips so he could look back at her. "I can see that. You're also wearing sandals. The sky is cloudy today. Any other observations?"

She chewed the inside of her cheek. "You...you broke through to *acolytus* so fast, and I'm falling behind, and—" She stopped, feeling panic well up in her chest. One more word and she might break.

No tears. No screams. Strength. Composure.

If Tolm saw her fraying, he didn't register any change of emotion. He also didn't turn around fully, still standing in that half-turn that said he was only partially committed to the conversation.

But he wasn't leaving either.

She took a breath. "How did you do it?"

"You're asking me for help?"

On instinct, she wanted to deny, to come up with any other plausible reason for her question. But there was none—it would only be humiliating to pretend otherwise.

"Yes. I need help. My mentor says I need friends. Not that I'm asking you to be my friend!"

Tolm cracked another smile. "Thank the gods."

She resisted the urge to smack her own face. "What I mean is—"

"I get it. Look, I only broke through so fast because I hung around a lot of *acolyti* from Sixth Cohort. I'd offer to carry stuff for them, to run their clothes to get mended—and they gave me pointers in exchange."

Alyat would call that an alliance.

"But what *really* helped me," he continued, "was the stuff that wasn't related to training. The ways you mold yourself to be like those around you." He shrugged. "Don't know what that's worth as far as advice goes, but your mentor's right. But also, yeah, maybe don't go around telling people you want to be their friend so you can break through faster. Not the best foundation for a relationship."

Reiva blinked. "Right," she said eventually.

"And one more thing—find what drives you. Find the thing you would do anything for, and put your whole mind to just that. And that's how you get through the days. Make sense?"

"Yes, thank you...*thank you.*"

"You said that already."

She scoffed. "*You* said that already."

He actually let out half a chuckle. "So I did. Good luck, Reiva."

"Thank you, Tolm. Wait, you know my—?"

"I keep track of everyone I think could be competition. Don't prove me wrong."

He got another ten paces away before she remembered to close her mouth.

"Competition..." she whispered to herself.

REIVA OPENED the door to the dormitory. Not her dormitory—the dormitory for *acolyti* girls.

Sitting against the wall, Domi popped her head up from a book, her tresses flying every which way with the motion. "Reiva! You're...here."

She tried her best for an easy smile. "And you're wearing a tunic. Any other observations?"

Domi grinned. "Sorry, I was just surprised. You haven't come over...ever since I moved here, I don't think. How are the kids in First Cohort treating you?"

"They're fine—there's enough of them who get the gist of things now that I don't need to explain when a new one comes in. But forget that. I was—ah—was thinking of going to the bathhouse and was wondering if anyone wanted to come. I...miss the rest of you from Seventh."

Did I say that right?

She panicked, worried she'd somehow bungled the words she'd been rehearsing for the last thirty minutes.

Domi perked up. "Sure! If you want to wait a bit, I think Ela and Mylla will be back soon. They'll probably want to come."

"Yeah, that sounds good."

She stood by the door, hiding her white-knuckle fists behind her back.

"Uh, would you like to sit?"

"Oh. Yeah, sure."

She slid down the wall.

Domi snorted. "I meant by me, but suit yourself."

"*Oh.* That would make sense."

She hopped to her feet and scampered across the floor to sit beside the other girl.

"What are you reading?" she ventured.

"Tactylus' *Annals of Early Conquest*. My mentor gave it to me as a gift once I earned my focus." She snorted. "Homework as a gift—typical, right?"

Reiva laughed. "Classic Adepts. That's about the First Emperor, right?"

"At the start—but that's just the first section. Tactylus goes from the end of the Dark Days all the way to Empress Viviana."

"Fifth on the Palatine Throne," Reiva recalled.

Domi snorted, setting the book aside. "Yes, but this isn't class, Reiva. How have you been? I heard you got two falls out of three against Sciro. He was steaming about it in the mess hall the other day."

"Why?"

"Because a *probatia* three inches shorter than him beat him in a match." She said it so plainly.

Reiva shrugged. "It's his footwork. I couldn't stand a chance against him if he kept his center of weight low. He's stronger than me, but he's sloppy with his grapples."

Domi hummed. "His footwork was always shoddy, but he used to be better, if you ask me. I think he got careless once he earned his focus. When he's against other *acolyti*, he can channel aether to fortify himself. He's one of the better channelers around, so it makes up for his weaker technique."

Reiva frowned. "Why would he do *that*? If you have a focus *and* good technique, then you'd be even stronger."

Domi leaned her head close to whisper in Reiva's ear. "And that's why Phetan's scared shitless of when you finally get yours."

Reiva felt herself blushing. "Come on, I'm the only one in our cohort who hasn't broken through. That's why I'm not sleeping in here with you all."

"Yeah, but it'll happen. And then you'll knock Phetan off his high horse, and I'll sweep to the fore amidst all the carnage."

Reiva let out a quick laugh. "And what's your plan for unseating Tolm?"

"Tolm..." Domi trailed off. Reiva caught something at work behind the girl's eyes. A flicker of something—sorrow?—across her ebullient features. "Tolm, I will handle when I get to him."

Domi reasserted her easygoing smile, but Reiva felt the urge to ask why she'd hesitated. Did she know something about him?

Before she could work up the courage to ask, though, the door opened and Mylla and Ela strutted in. At first, Mylla broke into a wide smile. "Reiva! What brings you?" But then her smile faltered, and a pang shot through Reiva's stomach. "You haven't come by in so long."

Before she could get a word out, though, Domi threw her arm around her. "This one came to suggest a trip to the baths. Are you ladies interested?"

Ela sighed with relief. "That sounds perfect. Let me grab a change of clothes and we can head down." Reiva didn't know Ela much outside of martial bouts—but from that, she knew her to be a hard hitter. At least, so testified a few still-healing bruises. It would be interesting to get to know her in an environment where people weren't throwing punches at each other.

Domi bounced to her feet, hauling Reiva up with her as she went. "Well, hurry up, Ela—we've only got forty-five minutes or so before they close the thermal pool, and I've got at least thirty minutes of wear in my lower back. Did you bring a bathing tunic, Reiva? You can borrow my spare."

Ela snorted. "No, for taking so long to visit us, Reiva must be punished—I say she goes naked."

Mylla slapped the blonde girl on the shoulder. "Uh-huh, like that one time you stole those bottles of wine and—"

"Shh!"

Domi rolled her eyes, herding everyone out the door. "Stop wasting time and corrupting the youth."

Ela's eyes flashed. "Oh, this from *you*, Domi?"

"I only corrupt the youth on free days—it's called having ethical standards."

Reiva couldn't help but smile as the girls traded jabs and jokes all the way down the hill.

She didn't know any of the attendants on staff this late—which disappointed her, as she hadn't seen Marali in some time. But her sorrows were quickly forgotten in the soothing heat. And for a while, the conversation stayed light-hearted—but before long, the topic turned to Reiva's latent Art.

Domi let out a long sigh. "I'm telling you, she'll be *Thalassan*, like me, and together we shall master the sea! We've got the same *mmph*."

Ela arched an eyebrow. "*Mmph*. What is *mmph?*"

"You know, *mmph*. Like *grrm* but more refined."

"Somehow, that makes even less sense."

"Figures—you wouldn't know, lacking *mmph* yourself."

"Well, *I* think Reiva will manifest *Theron*."

"And how do you figure that?"

"She has the tenacity of a wild beast, so she'll have the Art that lets her control them."

"Tenacity," echoed Domi. "That's a synonym for *grrm* isn't it?"

Reiva let herself sink a bit, feeling the hot waters cover her throat and chin.

Domi and Ela kept going back and forth. Around their necks, the chains of their arcane focuses glittered. Reiva suddenly felt acutely aware, once again, of how she was the only one lacking a focus.

Mylla sidled up beside Reiva. "Hey," she said softly. "Are you okay?"

Reiva nodded, sending gentle ripples across the surface of the pool. "I just need to figure out what's blocking me."

Mylla hummed. "What do you mean?"

"My mentor says I'm too closed off, and it's preventing me from opening myself fully to the flow of aether."

"I see."

"Do...do you think I'm closed off?"

Mylla pursed her lips. Reiva saw pain flickering behind the other girl's eyes. Her eyes flitted briefly toward Domi and Ela. Her lips trembled with words half-formed and abandoned. "Sometimes," she said eventually. "You're very forward with your opinions. And you never shy from giving your thoughts on a fight. But aside from that— even though I've known you over a year at this point...I don't know, it's hard to say much."

Reiva grunted her agreement, letting herself sink further. "So what do I do?"

Mylla shrugged. "Just try talking."

"About what?"

Mylla's gaze fell. "You were able to talk to Domi, weren't you?"

Reiva searched the girl's expression. "Mylla, you know I value you, right? You know I care about you?"

She smiled faintly. "Yeah, of course I know that. Sorry, let's not...I once told you about Lhivera, the goddess we sang to in my village, remember? Tell me about where you're from. Talynis is a desert, right?"

Reiva twisted her lips. "Mostly yes, but we don't live on the sands. Only the Mithallkiym tribes do that; and they just wander around their whole lives. Everyone else lives in what are called *maiir*. Oasis cities."

Mylla's eyes widened. "How big an oasis?"

"Well, the source of the water is deep beneath the ground, and the water flows through the *maiir* from that source. Sometimes it emerges as rivers or collects as a lake. There's a legend that says all the water in Talynis flows from one source—the Origin Spring."

"Really?"

"It's just a legend. It doesn't make sense if you ask me—why wouldn't the whole desert be full of plants and life if water were running all the way to every *maiir* from a single massive source?"

"Still, that sounds fascinating. I'd love to see it someday." She grinned. "What's the name of your *maiir*, then? Maybe someday I'll get to go and I can bring you back something."

"Shugrith," she answered automatically. She pushed away the grief that came with uttering the word after so long.

If Mylla ever makes it to Shugrith, that will mean the capital has fallen...

Reiva bit down on her tongue as fear roiled her insides. The horrible image of her little brother picking up a sword too big for him and running to join the defense.

Don't think about that. That's a world away.

"Hey!" barked Domi. "No moping allowed!"

A wave of water bowled over Reiva and Mylla. The two of them came to the surface, sputtering and coughing.

Mylla snarled. "No magic! That's unfair."

Ela chirped up, "I agree." And she tackled Domi around her midsection, taking her beneath the surface.

The water roiled, then a spout of water burst up from the pool, carrying Ela to the surface.

Domi burst up, whipping her hair out of her face. "Fine, three on one. That's even, right?"

Reiva swallowed, seeing currents—currents in a pool—shift around Domi as she summoned her *Ars Thalassan*.

Mylla pushed her hair back. "Why does the Art of Sea work in freshwater, anyway?"

"You could also translate it as *Lake*, but that doesn't have *mmph*. Now come at me, girls—show me a good time."

Ela sniffed. "Reiva goes for her left. Mylla and I take the middle."

Mylla nodded.

Reiva felt a smile splitting her lips. Fights—she knew fights. "No. I'll take the middle, you two go for the sides."

Ela glanced over, shrugged. "Fine by me."

Mylla cracked her knuckles. "On three?"

Domi yawned. "Before I fall asleep, please."

"One," murmured Ela.

"Three!" snapped Reiva, throwing herself head-first into the fray.

REIVA BANGED her knee against the slick tiles as she tackled Domi down. Domi shrieked, twisting her arm against Reiva's grip. She writhed like a fish, fighting to tug herself back toward the pool, where her powers would return.

"Help!" cried Reiva.

Mylla piled onto her legs, and Ela grabbed her other arm, planting a knee between Domi's shoulders. Somehow—after a dozen half-drownings and sputtering recoveries—they'd wrestled her out of the pool onto the tiles.

Domi groaned. "Gentle, girls, please. I bruise easily."

"Yield," huffed Reiva.

"I yield, I yield, now get your foot off my back—I told you I'm stiff there."

They all disengaged, flopping onto their backs.

"So much for a relaxing night at the bathhouse," scoffed Mylla.

"What are you talking about?" Domi sighed. "I feel more at ease than ever."

"Round two then?" asked Ela.

"Not *that* at ease."

Reiva laughed, wiping water from her eyes. She took a second to look around.

"Uhh..."

Domi perked up. "Hm? What's—*oh*."

The thermal pool had lost about three-quarters of its depth. The rest of the water was sloshed all around the room. The walls bore splash marks as high as fifteen feet off the ground. The tiling all over was wet, and the *frigidarium* seemed to have gained a foot or two of water.

Domi scratched behind her ear. "Good thing there's a drain, eh?"

"Yes," drawled a stranger's voice. "Good thing."

The girls yelped, unconsciously forming into a line like they did for morning exercises.

A bathhouse attendant Reiva had never seen before—a grim-faced woman with most of her hair gone to gray—stood with her arms crossed. "I'll be informing your mentors of this, Initiates. I look forward to your assistance in refilling the pool."

The girls deflated. Ela bowed her head. "Our apologies."

"Apologies don't haul water. Now, on your way before you break curfew. I'll see you tomorrow."

They hastily changed into dry clothes and started trudging back to the dormitory. Everyone heaped accusations on Domi, who repeatedly asserted she had only been acting in self defense.

"You started it!" Reiva protested.

"Okay, but you fought back—so I had to defend myself."

Ela nudged Domi with her shoulder. "Proper philosopher you are."

"Well I am the best read here."

Mylla wrung water out of her hair as they walked. "Any chance they'll let Domi use her Art to refill the pool?"

Reiva groaned. "I wish. Oh, here's me."

"Hm?" Mylla stopped. "Oh, right, you're in the *probatii* dormitory. I forgot."

Domi stretched. "She's only here for a little longer, anyway. Soon you'll be putting up with Ela's snobbery all night long."

Ela slapped Domi's shoulder, but smirked.

Reiva waved goodbye to them. When she lay her head down, she was smiling to herself.

13

FINEST BREAD

THE NEXT AFTERNOON, after her lessons, Reiva spent hours hauling buckets of water from the designated well. There was a well just behind the bathhouse, but they were forbidden from using this one, told it was having issues—whatever that meant. The girls didn't even bother asking why they could not get water from the river, having gotten the hint by now. So, they had to make a trek about five minutes each way. The bathhouse was downhill from the well, which would have been a mercy if it hadn't rained during the night. Reiva took more than one spill on the way down, losing the water and coating herself in mud.

The other three grumbled about how they were missing sessions with their mentors for this—Mylla and Ela blaming Domi more than once for their woes, though eventually they just lapsed into silent labor. So as Reiva filled another two buckets at the well and set off for the bathhouse yet again, her thoughts turned to Alyat. When she had gone to his office to tell her she was being disciplined and had to miss the session, she had only found a note nailed to his office door (there were countless such nail marks pocking the wood).

'Called to LI, back morrow. R, work on it.'

Translation: 'Called to Legion Intelligence, back tomorrow. Reiva, work on your problems.'

Well, now she had ample time to reflect amidst the drudgery, and her mind kept circling back to the same thing.

She had a choice to make.

Specifically, she had a choice to make about Alyat.

She appreciated him. That was honest truth. But she didn't *like* him. She was even grateful now and then for what he did on her behalf. And they had some good days. But despite the brief glimmers of success in their relationship, he still represented the Empire. He had brought her into the Corps. He had pressed her with the choice.

In the seasons where he was off on missions or service and she hardly saw him, things were fine. She even missed his dour mood and sardonic mien. But when he was back and they had to do sessions, all she could think of was how he—he above all the other Adepts and instructors—was responsible for what she was becoming. And what she was becoming was an Imperial Adept.

It was easy in the day to day to forget that, strange as it was. The physical regimens and martial practice, the classroom lessons—they were just daily life now. She had acclimated. But day by day, moment by moment, they were making her into a killer who would serve the Empire's goals.

He had said she needed friends, not allies. Well, all right, she could do that. There was even a sort of grim camaraderie in being punished with the others for what they'd done. But he also said she needed to open up to *him* if she wanted to find success with the aether.

So she needed to decide what to do, and she needed to do it soon. Alyat was due to set off on a diplomatic mission next week. Then two months would go by before she had another chance at trying for her focus. The fact that he was gone today was an ill omen in that regard. Wars, political disputes, these things didn't always happen according to a timetable—what if he had to leave early?

After the laborious work of refilling the thermal bath was complete, the four of them learned they were barred from the baths for a month as punishment. They could only access the washrooms—antechambers before the baths proper—where they could cleanse themselves of dirt and muck. They readily took to these, heaping water over themselves to get rid of the muck before trudging back in sopping wet clothes.

"We're getting looks," sighed Mylla.

"Yeah," said Domi, "but at least they're not smirking like while we were hauling buckets. You all going to the mess? Sun's almost down—don't want to miss dinner after all that."

The others concurred, agreeing to quickly change into dry clothes and meet at the mess hall. Again, Reiva had to diverge from the others. Since her dormitory was the farthest away, by the time she got to the mess, the others had already gotten their meals and sat down. Another small reminder of how she was still beneath them.

Dinner was tasteless, though the others said it was rather good. They spoke little aside from that, hunching over their meals with barely masked fatigue. Afterwards, Reiva had to walk back alone. The sun had fallen, so curfew was quick approaching. That was fine—all she wanted right now was sleep.

But once she lay down on her cot, her mind flooded with thoughts of what to do in tomorrow's session. She dropped into sleep amidst a dizzying fog of anxious imaginings.

REIVA KNOCKED on Alyat's door. Instead of his usual gruff 'Get in,' he opened the door.

"Come on," he said, offering no further explanation before blowing past her and heading down the stairs.

She frowned after him, suppressing a sigh before giving chase.

"Alyat," she said, coming even with him. "I've been thinking about what you said, and—"

"None of that right now."

"I—what?"

"We're doing something different today."

Reiva gaped. "But you're leaving in a week."

The Adept snorted. "Thank you for reminding me—a dodderer such as myself could never remember such important details."

"I mean I don't have much time."

"I know. And I said we're doing something else today."

Reiva realized he was taking her to the gates, which meant they were going into the city. *That* set her curiosity aglow. She had been outside the Sanctum only twice since her training started—once for the triumphal parade where she'd seen Adept Sharasthi, and again to walk in a procession celebrating the founding of the city.

They didn't need to worry about crowds—as soon as people saw the red mantles, they made way, some even adding bows and respectful murmurs, salutes to the Emperor's authority. Alyat gave no response to these, simply keeping his eyes ahead. Reiva did her best to mimic him, but her curiosity often got the better of her and she found herself locking eyes with many of the pedestrians scrambling to the side.

A little over a year ago, these people would've seen me as nothing more than livestock. Now they trip over themselves to show respect. To avoid my ire.

Well, more likely they feared Alyat than a little girl at his heel.

She remarked as much to him, quietly. "They're scared of you."

"You too," he grumbled.

At first she thought he implied she feared him as well, and she took umbrage—but then she took another look at the people clearing the road.

Alyat was right—they were looking at her with fear. Furrowed brows, wide eyes, tight lips.

"Why?" she whispered back.

"Hardly anything is more precious to the Corps than an Initiate," said Alyat. "If anyone raised a hand against one of you, they'd receive more than the full force of the law in their punishment. Now quit your gawking, you look like a tourist."

Reiva snorted, but did her best to fix her eyes forward. She couldn't help that, as a *probatia*, she'd hardly gotten to leave the Sanctum—of course she was gawking.

Even keeping her eyes ahead though, her other senses experienced waves of stimulation. The smells of the city took her back to that first day she'd come through the gates, shackled by Baranzir. What was he doing now, she wondered. What explanation had he given to the Parthavan who lent him the horse in exchange for a cut of profit from her sale? Was he still beating Amestris, or had she maybe gotten away from him?

A sudden horror gripped her stomach as she wondered whether she might encounter one of the others on these streets—the ones from Baranzir's caravan who had gone to the auction when she had escaped. What did *they* think of her? Were they glad one of them had gotten away? Spiteful that fate had chosen her? Did they think of her? Were they even all still alive?

Her mood subdued by such ponderances, she lost any urge to analyze her surroundings. She slipped into a fugue, only giving the barest attention as Alyat led the way through the streets of Lazarra.

"Here," he announced with little fanfare.

Reiva snapped out of her reverie, taking a moment to look around.

They were on a narrow road lined with shops—mostly foodstuffs, from what she saw. A grocer here, a butcher there.

Alyat waved his hand toward one of the shops. He looked almost...expectant.

Then the aroma of baking bread struck her, and her stomach loudly reminded her she had eaten a sparse lunch. The smell was coming from the building Alyat had indicated—waves of heat rolling off it confirmed it to be a bakery. And not just any bakery, but—

Reiva's stomach seized up, all hunger dissipating from her consciousness.

The sign over the door bore the angular script of the Talynisti language. Reiva gaped at the lettering, her mind swimming as her tongue and teeth quietly shaped the syllables.

Alyat gave a grunt—one that sounded positive, as far as his

various mutterings went—and nodded toward it. "You have coin? Never mind, here."

Alyat tossed her a denarius. "Be inside the gates before curfew. Session as normal tomorrow."

As he took a step to leave, Reiva blurted out, "Wait, what am I supposed—"

"To do?" A shrug. "Whatever you want, kid. Go inside, go to the docks, go to a vineyard—your call."

Before she could say anything more, he strode off the way they had come.

She stood in the street, clutching the coin in a white-knuckled fist. The metal seemed to burn a circle into her skin as she held it, her hand trembling.

She couldn't say how long she stood there, weighing what she ought to do—but she never ended up making the choice. A man with a thick beard stepped outside, dusting floury hands on an apron.

"Hm?" He furrowed his brow, noticing Reiva standing there. His eyes fixed pointedly on the red mantle around her shoulders. "Can I help you?" he said in carefully constructed Lazarran.

Reiva swallowed, her throat dry. "H-hello. You're a baker."

His eyebrows drew even closer together. "That I am." His gaze flitted to her awkwardly raised fist. "Would you like to take a look? Finest bread in the city."

Before she could reason against herself, she nodded—perhaps a bit too ferociously—and stepped closer.

The baker waved her toward the door. "Normally my wife works the front while I handle the bread, but she's been ill. Go on, before the batch cools."

She slipped inside, watching her feet, fearing she might tread upon—well, she didn't know what she feared. It was like stepping into another world, and she had no idea what could lie in her path, so she stepped carefully.

The smell indoors was even better—warm, welcoming, the scents and flavors of years that seemed long lost.

The baker lumbered over to his oven, sparing a glance at the loaves currently baking. He made an appreciative sound, then picked up a basket resting on a table.

"These came out in the last hour. Still warm. Barley, for the most part. These ones have olives in them. And these—"

Reiva cut in, her mouth watering. "Are those *qnashoth?*"

The baker blinked. "They are." He suddenly seemed to see her in a new light. "*Talnishte debar?*"

You speak Talynisti?

She nodded, not trusting herself to say as much. More and more, her thoughts were all Lazarran.

The baker made another sound—this one more contemplative, more surprised.

Reiva offered him the coin. "Please. One *qnasha.*"

The baker selected a loaf and handed it to her. He waved the coin away.

Reiva frowned. "But—"

"Where are you from?" he asked in their mother tongue.

She came up short. "Shugrith," she said eventually.

"You're wearing red," he observed. "Strange thing to see."

Slowly, she formed words in a language she hadn't spoken to another soul in over a year. "I was sold and ended up here."

The baker glowered. "*Sold?*"

Reiva nodded. She offered the coin again. "Please, sir."

But after what he'd heard, he only seemed more insistent that she take the loaf—and he handed her a second. "Save it for later."

"I was given this to pay you."

"Save it for later," he said with a conspiratorial wink. "And like I said, my wife handles the front. I don't know anything about the money. Come back when she's here."

Reiva's heart jumped into her throat. "I will." She swallowed, nodded. "I will."

"What's your name?"

"Reiva." A pause. "Rebbaelah beyt'Avadh."

The baker hummed. "A good name. Strong. *Avadh.* Never knew an Avadh. We're from Dav-maiir."

The capital of Talynis. "I never saw it. Is the Temple truly—"

"*Twice* as magnificent as they say." He seemed to puff up with pride. "Someday I'll go back. All of us should, I think."

Reiva wilted. "That sounds...it would be nice."

The baker seemed to realize he'd hit upon something. He glanced at the red again. How much he knew about the Adepts and their laws, she had no idea, but he quickly changed the topic.

"Levin's my name. Ah, but you saw on the sign, I'm sure."

She had seen, but she'd been so startled by the letters she hadn't even really read them—just marveled at their shape, their presence.

She remembered then how Alyat had left her here, telling her to spend her time as she wished.

And she knew what she wanted—what she *needed*.

"Excuse me, sir, but I must go. I...I will come back. Maybe not soon, but I will."

Levin seemed disappointed, but he nodded sympathetically. "A woman with responsibilities, I see. You promise?"

"I promise."

"Good—the Four don't look lightly on a promise between our people."

Our people—when had she last thought of herself as a Talynisti?

"I'll come back," she said, and after one final (failed) attempt to give the baker the coin, she tucked the loaves under her arm and dashed through the streets, heading straight for the Sanctum.

14

———

ARS VULCANA

THE LEGIONNAIRES at the gates seemed surprised to see her— probably Alyat had told them to expect her back later—but they let her in without any questions.

When she'd first gotten here, the run to the Sanctum would have left her gasping for air, but by now she had strengthened to such degree that she was hardly winded. When she found Alyat in his office, she only had to take half a breath before she said, "Thank you. I need to tell you something."

The Adept looked up from his papers, wrinkling his brow. "I said you—"

"I know what you said, but I need to say this now." She took another breath, a steadying breath, then blurted out the words that had been rattling around inside her for over a year.

"I hate you."

Alyat barely twitched. "Is this meant to be a revelation? Shall I call an archivist to mark the date and reckon the moment?"

Reiva wiped her hands over her face. She was sweating. Her skin was hot. Actually, everything felt hot. Her insides, her spirit, every fiber of being she could recognize as herself seemed to vibrate and smolder.

Alyat set aside his work, leaned back in his chair. "I brought you in. I'm the means by which you came to serve the Empire. I still hold that I never tricked you or coerced you, but it wasn't certainly wasn't an even choice—of course you'd resent me for it."

Reiva shook her head. "But why the baker?"

Alyat sighed. "I know what it's like to lose your language. I don't have much besides my *r*'s and *t*'s. I thought it might help you open up —to yourself and to others—if you could experience a taste of what you lost."

"Levin asked me to come back."

Alyat answered, "What you do on free days is not the business of the Corps—so long as you are not found to violate our statutes."

A diplomatic way of saying, *'Keep it under the table.'*

Reiva tried to swallow, but her throat seized up.

She shut the door to the office. Words started spilling out. "My father joined the defense of Talynis against the Empire. He was wounded in battle—in the very last battle of the war—and developed an infection. I had to take care of him for a week, feeling his skin burn at my touch, seeing the life ebb out of him."

She grabbed at the red mantle around her shoulders. It seemed to constrict like a snake, choking her.

"And here you are."

She clutched at the mantle, not tearing it away but still fighting against it, trapped between competing urges. "He's dead." The words came out in a hiss. "Dead because of you."

Alyat held her eyes. There was a force behind his gaze. An impelling power, urging her to go on.

"Dead..." Her voice failed. She sank to the floor. "Dead because— because of—dead because of me."

Her hands were tangled in the red.

Alyat stood up from his desk. Carefully, precisely, he produced a key, which he inserted into a drawer and turned.

Reiva's heart and stomach switched places. "Not now," she murmured. Hadn't he been listening to her?

But Alyat shook his head. "You're ready now."

"That's impossi—"

"Which one of us is the Adept?" He held the focus aloft, letting it catch the light.

Reiva wiped at the tears on her cheeks—when had those trickled down? "I can't go to the Trial Chamber like this."

"Just take it."

Her hands were still wrapped up.

"Take your hands out of the mantle, and take hold of your focus, Reiva."

She stood, shivering, frightened—frightened of a dozen things, none of which she could name for the way they all blended together into one indescribable, many-faced horror.

Alyat didn't move to help her—he only held the focus out for her.

Slowly, she extracted her hands and cupped them. Alyat dropped the focus into her palms. The metal was cool to the touch, but somehow the artifact seemed to radiate a tingling sensation. Whether that was just in her head or a true property of the item, she'd never asked.

"Now, *breathe.*"

Reiva closed her eyes. She took a long breath in, felt it rejuvenating her body from head to toe, and exhaled. She breathed in again, repeating the process with rhythm like that of the tide. The breath moved through her, and she felt her awareness of herself expanding—every stitch of clothing scratching her skin, the sweat beading on her brow, the metal focus warming in her grip.

"Look inside," said Alyat, "and tell me what you see."

She pictured what 'inside' might be, seizing upon the first image suggested by her imagination. It was an image she had seen many times before—seen in the curious way the spirit intuits the shape and essence of those things which have no true appearance.

"There's a boulder. Gray. Rugged. Not one solid piece of rock, but many layers that have grown atop one another. It's a living thing."

"Go into it."

"It's solid."

"*Go.*"

She swallowed, pushing her mind vision deeper. "It's hot. Every layer is hotter than the one above it. They're shaking—they're in a rage. Like a nest of wasps going to war. There are so many of them—wasps that live in the rock, wasps born from the rock. I can feel them in my heart, spinning in a storm of wings and stingers. They have faces—horrible faces."

"Focus on the swarm, and go further."

"They'll sting me."

"The only way to rid yourself of them is to go further."

What if she didn't get rid of them, though? What if she chose to go on like this, harboring them deep inside the stone shell, where their whirling rage was muffled and muted?

"I'm going," she whispered.

"Keep the rhythm of your breath. Don't let the wasps overtake you—you do not obey them. *Breathe!*"

She sucked in another breath, and the swarm buzzed louder, angrier. She could feel them crawling inside her heart, nipping with their mandibles. She took another breath, and they began to jab their stingers into her. A myriad of knives and needles stabbing and tearing.

"It hurts."

"What is *it*?"

"The wasps, how they bite and sting."

"What are the wasps, Reiva?"

She breathed. "Hatred. Sorrow. Pain. A hundred things I can't name."

"Name them. One by one. Look at their faces. Name the wasps."

Another breath, another burning, aching wave inside her chest.

"The Empire."

"Another."

"The Adept Corps."

"Yes, another."

"You."

"Good, go deeper."

"I see Tolm. The impossible task I'll never succeed."

"Deeper."

"My mother. My own mother who sold me as a slave."

"And even further."

The room felt too hot to breathe, but she forced the air through her lungs. Sweat was pooling beneath her arms, running down her neck.

"The gods. The Four Gods. They did nothing for me. He let my father die, and then he made me live."

Reiva's voice died in her throat. She saw more—and what she saw made her want to run away. She began to retreat, and the shredding ache in her heart subsided just a smidge—a tantalizing promise: *'Give up, turn back, and the pain stops.'*

Alyat's voice sounded like a bell, goading her on. "Reiva, you do not serve the fear and the pain."

She pushed forward, the agony redoubling far beyond what it had been. "Father left us. Left *me*."

Alyat shouted something, but she didn't hear it—all her awareness, all her mind turned toward a coal-black gnarl at the center, the center she had at last reached, the center of the rocky shell that had long been growing.

"I see myself. I'm turning my back on my brother, leaving him to languish in the crucible I escaped. He's starving. He's alone. He needs me—but I'm a world away. I see myself, alone."

As soon as the words left her lips, something changed—the blackened whorl cracked, and the crack ran on, breaking through all the layers over it.

And she felt something kindle in the ashen heart—a spark of fire. A Flame.

"Fire!" she gasped. "There's fire!"

"Then let the fire devour the swarm."

She hardly had to think—the action was as fundamental as flexing a muscle. The Flame roared, washing over her in a blaze and whirling in an incendiary tempest.

"Open your eyes, Reiva."

She marveled at the Flame, at how its storm consumed all the wasps and stone.

"Reiva!"

The Flame was beautiful, all-encompassing, a power she had never thought possible, resting within her.

"*Breathe!*"

She gasped, opening her eyes.

She could still feel it, the Flame. She could feel it burgeoning inside her chest, expanding every moment in a blistering, sweltering rage.

"It's burning, it's burning!"

"Stretch out your hand," barked Alyat, "and put it there."

She obeyed, uncurling her fingers, and with the barest impulse of will—

Fwoom!

All the power roiling inside her raced down her arm, and appeared as a ball of crackling, hungry fire.

Reiva's jaw dropped. A half-choked scream sounded from her throat, and the fire grew larger. She yelped, but Alyat was smiling madly.

"Good! Now control it. Rein in your emotion. Refine the power flowing through you."

She shook her head, staring in terror at what she had done.

"You've lost the breath—return to it."

She did, and at first: nothing. Then, gradually, as the rhythm returned, she felt the power still, and the fire shrank.

"Now quench it."

She tried to will it away in the same manner as she had summoned it—but it only grew larger.

"I can't," she whimpered. "Should I drop the focus?"

"No! You need to control the aether; your focus regulates the flow. If you drop your focus now, the power will kill you in seconds."

The fire crackled louder, expanded.

"Not helping, Alyat!"

"*Concentrate.* You are more than your anger. You are more than your fear. Focus on your breath, on your being. Steady yourself, and you will steady the fire."

Reiva felt a deep fatigue encroaching—weariness of the soul after channeling so much power. She needed to get ahold of the aether, of the fire.

She thought of the Flame that had burst alive inside her. She thought of how it had devoured stabbing swarm and solid stone. She thought of all the things—all the people, the faces—she had pushed through to reach that sore, buried center.

And she went through them all again. She experienced her fear of being left behind. She felt her hatred of the Empire, she felt her gratitude. Her mother's callous gaze. Her father's faltering heartbeat.

Again and again, she moved through them, and when the pain of it began to subside, when she knew every shred and fiber of it, she set them all aside.

The Flame in her inner being quelled.

And the fire snuffed out of existence.

Reiva felt her legs tremble and nearly give way—and then she jumped for joy.

She'd done it.

She had manifested the *Ars Vulcana*. The Art of Fire. The Art of Flame.

15

OPPOSITE ESSENCES

After Reiva moved into the *acolyta* dormitory, it was like everything in the Sanctum shifted. Not just topographically—though being closer to everything important (besides the bathhouse) was certainly a plus. No, the biggest shift was in her relationships with the other Initiates.

In the mess hall the first night after Reiva moved in, Domi immediately declared a celebration was in order—ignoring any opinions Reiva had about whether this was needed or justified—and she set to work preparing just what the celebration would be. From the mischievous quirk of her smile and the sly wink she gave before disappearing from the dormitory, Reiva got the sense it was not about to be strictly legal by the Corps' regulations for Initiates.

Before she had long to worry about that though, a great deal of other congratulations swarmed her. There were familiar faces—Mylla, of course, as well as Luo and Caulo. Phetan didn't congratulate her, but she caught him giving her a different sort of look than he had before. A wary look, like one might appraise a wild animal on a hunt. There was a glint of respect in that look. Also an edge of murder.

Tolm said nothing to her, only glancing at the focus around her neck as he passed her by. She almost got up from her seat to go after him and thank him for his advice, but as soon as he'd appeared, he vanished, moving forward with that singular purpose that suffused his every action.

She felt a familiar hollowness in her stomach. She quickly worked through it, dismissing it from her concern, as she had finally managed during the climactic aether meditation in Alyat's office. Tolm's face had adorned one of the wasps humming in her heart-shell. He presented a threat. An obstacle.

She tried to ask subtly about who Tolm spent time with nowadays, remembering how he'd said he broke through quickly because he had befriended older Initiates who'd given him pointers. Ela pursed her lips and shrugged. "None of us—I've heard he's around the Silvers a lot. They're off on war games and field missions plenty though, so oftentimes he works in solitude in the Trial Chamber."

So Tolm was still looking ahead. 'Silvers' was the common way of referring to the *subordinati*, those Initiates who had reached the third and final stage of their training, when they went on field missions under Adept supervision. They had a silver fringe on their mantles— the sign they were only one step away from reaching full stature as a commissioned Adept.

Reiva stowed that away for future reference. If Tolm was working in the Trial Chamber, where Arts could be used freely, then he was concentrating his efforts on strengthening his aether tolerance. She would do the same. Alyat had told her not to worry about the next steps yet, that she should take a day or two to let her soul rest from the exertion of manifesting her Art for the first time, but she couldn't help the thrill fluttering in her gut. She was catching up. She had a chance. And now that she'd started making progress again, she wasn't about to fall into another slump—no matter how hard she'd need to sweat and strain and push herself.

Even if she'd wanted to take time off worrying about her Art, though, the others wouldn't have allowed it. Once they got out of her that she'd manifested the *Ars Vulcana*, she could hardly have a moment's peace. The Art of Flame was one of the most precious and coveted in the arsenal of the Adepts. Powerful, rare—it was no wonder people were treating her differently than they had before. It wasn't just that she'd finally escaped probationary training and earned her focus—it was that now everyone had a hint that Reiva's ambition might actually hold up. Sure, they'd all seen how she trained, but any soldier could do that. Sometimes excellent Initiates washed out because they couldn't swing it in the arcane aspect of their vocation, but they went on to become distinguished warriors in the legions.

Now though, people could see that Reiva had a real shot at making it through training. And even if they hadn't looked down on her before, now they certainly treated her with more reverence. She noticed the acute attention Ela gave to her words, the way she inclined her head toward Reiva when she spoke. Caulo nodded along more readily when she made a comment about a practice bout in morning regimens.

In the back of her mind, Alyat's words about needing friends, not just allies, echoed. That was true, she acknowledged. But not a person in the Sanctum wouldn't give Reiva more weight as a person because of what she'd accomplished. Did friends do that? It was a cynical possibility—and maybe it was so. She hoped not. She hoped that was something allies did. Competitors. She hoped friendship could stay separate from that sort of evaluation. She wasn't sure if she placed much weight on that hope, though.

After dinner, she walked back to the dormitory—the *acolyta* dormitory—with Ela and Caulo. She was exhausted, both residually from her trial and from all the conversation and attention she'd received at dinner, so she didn't mind that the two of them weren't particularly talkative. Maybe they had sensed her fatigue and were giving her—

"*Now!*"

No sooner had Reiva heard Domi's cry than she found herself lifted up by a mass of arms, cheering Initiates swooping from the shadows to join the effort. She shrieked, instinctively thrashing as she left the ground, but her captors only laughed and whooped.

She caught a glimpse of Domi's mirthful face. "To the river!" she shouted.

Before she'd even gotten the words out though, the host of Initiates was already on the move, moving with a familiarity that told Reiva this had either been rehearsed or done as a sort of tradition. If it was, she'd never heard of it—but maybe that was the point.

She was also laughing, she realized, her cheeks hurting from the unconscious smile splitting her features. Her heart threatened to burst, so great was the joy pulsing through her.

The river wasn't far, and the Initiates had hurried. So hurriedly had they gone, in fact, that Reiva hadn't even thought to wonder what their plan was.

"Hey, hey—*ahh!*"

With a collective heave, they threw her into the frigid waters. She broke the surface, sputtering and coughing. The crowd roared even louder, whistling and clapping and pumping their fists. Some of them even cheered her name.

Hauling herself onto shore with what she hoped was at least a measure of grace and dignity, Reiva gave a shivering bow. "Wow, thank you," she drawled. "I feel so c-c-congratulated."

Domi had positioned herself at the fore of the crowd, and she eagerly stepped forward with a waterskin. "Here, this'll warm you."

Reiva frowned. Had she heated water? That seemed like it would be disgusting to—

Again, she found herself sputtering. The crowd burst with glee as she gave the skin a disturbed look.

"What kind of wine is this?"

Domi stabbed a finger in the air. "Brandy, not wine. Now drink and be merry—it wasn't cheap to get that!"

Reiva shook her head, though she couldn't help the silly grin reasserting itself on her face. She braced herself and took another swallow, this time managing to get it down with only a minor amount of grimacing.

It *did* feel warm—it burned a trail from her lips to her stomach.

After making an appreciative sound, she took a longer drink; based on the reaction this elicited from the crowd, they approved.

She gave a clumsy bow. "I thank you again—but could I please have a blanket or something?"

Mylla—smiling widely—stepped forward with just such a thing, but someone suddenly blocked her way. It was Luo, the boy who had taken Reiva's pushups on her first day of training.

"Hang on," he said, nodding to Reiva with an expectant look. "Let's see it."

Reiva cocked her head in confusion. But soon everyone was adding their voices to Luo's suggestion.

Domi clapped Reiva on the back. "Come on, show us what you can do! *Oh*, better take that first." She snatched the brandy from Reiva's hands, surreptitiously taking a sip as she backed away.

Then it clicked for her.

She swallowed, suddenly feeling small beneath the weight of all those eager, curious eyes. The heat of the alcohol in her stomach pushed against the chill of the water on her skin and the cool night-time breeze, creating a paradoxical sensation—one not unlike the sensation of existing in the physical world while touching the immaterial flow of aether. Opposite essences united in her person.

She touched the focus at her neck—not out of any necessity for working her magic, only out of a desire to ground herself, to remind herself that this was *real*, she truly had come this far—and cupped her hands before her.

A small, wisping orb of fire kindled into being. Steam curled off her hands. Logic told her that should have hurt—or at least felt uncomfortable—but it barely tickled.

A chorus of gasps went up from the crowd. People pushed closer, and a small spike of nervousness shot through Reiva, sparking the fire even bigger.

Domi—her eyes full of waxing light—looked on the ball of flame with awe. "Incredible," she breathed.

This from the girl who can summon waves with a thought.

But she understood. Even though they were all capable of

amazing feats of magic and power, they were still human. Had the prophets of Talynis ever ceased to marvel when they heard the Four Gods speak in thunder, or when messengers of heaven descended from the stars with swords of lightning and shields of onyx? It was human to be awed, even by one's own acts.

Reiva stoked the fire hotter, holding it close to herself without fear, trusting it to warm her without burning.

Before long, the fatigue in her spirit struck again, and she was forced to extinguish the fire—breathing a sigh of relief that it hadn't taken as much effort as the first time.

She got her final cheer of the night, and Mylla wrapped the blanket around her. Reiva nodded her gratitude, giving a tired smile.

Domi whistled, cutting short any lingering acclaims. "All right people, curfew was five minutes ago, and I'm not doing any more disciplinary work this month. If you're caught, this was Ela's idea. Break!"

Quick as they'd appeared to pick Reiva up, the Initiates vanished into the nighttime gloom, hustling to their various dormitories. Domi, to her credit, didn't leave. But she did grab hold of Reiva by the arm, leaving Mylla to grab the other, and together they towed Reiva along. "Come on! The guards give us a little leeway when someone breaks through but they can't ignore us forever!"

Laughing and half-stumbling, they made their way back under the moon's light.

As soon as Reiva's head hit the pillow—and she did have a pillow now, as well as an actual bed instead of a cot—she was out, plunging into the dark waters of dreamless sleep.

With Reiva's ascent to *acolyta*, a special day had come upon Seventh Cohort. They were all initiated in the working of aether and had manifested their Arts.

That meant they were finally eligible to learn the Adept Corps' secrets.

There would be things kept from them, of course—no one expected to learn *everything* there was to know about magic and the Empire's arcane history within their first year as *acolyti,* but there was an unmistakable thrill buzzing through the air as they filed into a lecture hall. Some, Reiva saw, had arrived early, taking a spot at the front of the room—Tolm was there, as was Luo. She cursed herself for not thinking to do the same. The instructors would notice that, she was certain.

That was another thing—their instructor today would be an Adept. In physical regimens, that was not always guaranteed; there wasn't really anything an Adept could teach that a legion drill sergeant could not. Most of Seventh Cohort's morning disciplines had been run by a *triarii* veteran—the most revered class of legionnaire infantry.

But now, that would change. Now they would begin learning how to become more than elite soldiers—they would become *divine* soldiers.

And that began today.

"Reiva!" Mylla called, waving her over. Reiva smiled in relief, glad to have a friend. She knew everyone by now, but she would rather sit beside someone she trusted—she had heard rumors that there was something...intimidating, about this lecture. What that meant, she had no clue—and when she asked Mylla, neither did the other girl.

As it turned out, they were not long in waiting.

"*Ave Imperator!*" called a strong voice.

In unison, the cohort jumped to their feet, snapping off salutes and returning the cry.

"At ease," said the Adept.

The Initiates sat down on their benches again, facing the front of the auditorium.

The Adept was not one Reiva was familiar with—he had brown hair and a rather easygoing demeanor that seemed at odds with the booming harshness of his voice. He looked out over the assembled Initiates before nodding. "All on time—very good. Better than I can say for my cohort back in the day."

When he allowed a lopsided smile to break onto his features, Reiva and the others let themselves laugh. As best she could tell, it was a running joke with commissioned Adepts to see how uncomfortable they could make the Initiates. Telling jokes and then acting dead serious about it was one of Alyat's favorite ways to do it.

"I am Adept Jan," began the lecturer. "*Ars Theron*. Any other beast-masters here?"

Reiva saw Luo's hand go up, as well as two other Initiates she did not know as well.

"Excellent. And you don't even have any feathers in your hair or mice in your pockets—doubly excellent. I serve in the Imperial Post, dispatching messenger hawks across the provinces and beyond. But today, I have been assigned the *delightful* task of teaching you about relics."

Jan paused a moment, surveying the Initiates.

A buzz of excitement filled Reiva's stomach. She had heard whispers of relics, but she didn't really know anything about them. And Adept Jan seemed one of the most affable Adepts she'd yet encountered—she was feeling high hopes for today.

"Judging by your expressions, some of you already know what a relic is. You, tell me something."

He had pointed at Phetan. The redheaded boy stood, back perfectly straight as he answered. "Initiate Phetan, Seventh Co—"

"Yes yes, that's all right. Go on."

"A relic," Phetan said without missing a beat, "is a magic item that lets anyone use an Art. They take many forms and most are ancient. "

Murmurs went through the Initiates at this, increasing in volume when Jan nodded approvingly. "Almost exactly right. Can anyone correct that?"

Domi raised her hand and stood when indicated. "Adepts cannot use relics as it interferes with their Arts."

"And what do you mean by *interfere*?"

"That's...how my mentor explained it."

Jan cracked another smile. "That's fine. Leaving me to do the heavy lifting—I see how it is. Very good, sit. The intricacies of *why* relics interfere with the Arts are complicated and, if I were to be honest, not of interest to nine out of ten Adepts. *Maybe* one person in this room will go on to graduate and serve in the Imperial Reliquary. For most of you, it just matters that you know not to try it yourself."

Jan paused, taking another look over the room. As he lectured, he had been glancing toward the door frequently, as if expecting something. Eventually, he honed in on Reiva. "You, are you bored yet?"

Reiva's heart leaped into her throat. She practically jumped to her feet as she tried to formulate a response. "No! Not at all!"

"Well, I am. Enough about relics for now. What's your Art?"

Reiva blinked. "*Vulcana.*"

"Fire! Excellent. Do you know why Fire is such a rare Art?"

Reiva shook her head, a blush creeping onto her face.

"Does anyone? Good—that's the correct answer. We don't actually know why three of you manifested *Theron*, a handful of you have *Ventas*, and maybe one or two are *Thalassan*. But tell me," he said, turning his attention back on Reiva, "do you come from any of the following: Zarush, Mizkhar, Talynis—"

"Talynis," she called out, then chided herself for how loudly she'd said it. You didn't want to sound *too* excited about your birth nation.

"Talynis—rare bird. Now, why was I able to guess that? I could have started out with Gallia and Aspagne, yes? What do you think?"

Reiva swallowed. "There must be a connection between birth location and what Art someone manifests."

"Quite so. But it is not everything. There is one other living Adept of Flame at the moment, and he hails from Aspagne—opposite side of the world from those other countries I listed. An Art can appear anywhere, but there are certain probabilities involved. *Fraja*, the Art of Frost, appears most commonly in Hyrgallia and the Northlands—not hard to imagine why, given how cold those places are. *Thalassan* almost always appears in coastal lands.

"Now," he went on, "the strange bit is, even when we account for recruitment proportions, some Arts are just plain rarer. In other words, if the Corps took in a hundred recruits from Talynis, very few of them would manifest Fire. We would have more than we do currently, since our recruitment from the eastern lands is so weak, but most of them would have *Terra*."

Jan took another significant pause, looking at the door. He waited long enough that eventually Reiva (who had sat down by now) and a few others started looking back as well.

Jan sighed. "All right, onward we go. Lost Arts! Has anyone heard of these? How about you?"

He had chosen Tolm, who, of course, had an answer. "Several of the arcane Arts recorded in our histories no longer manifest. It seems like something changed about a hundred years ago, but a precise date or cause is unknown."

"Can you name any?"

Tolm actually hesitated. "*Divina*?" he said eventually.

"Good. Your mentor wasn't supposed to tell you that yet though, so bad. Trick question." He flashed Tolm a grin before waving him back down. "Yes, there are some Arts that we don't see anymore. Even though we call them Lost Arts, though, theoretically they could appear again. About thirty years ago, for instance, we got a *Fortuna* Adept, first one in ages. She never lost at gambling and almost got driven out of the city for it. The Senate actually passed a law because of her. We don't have a clue why some Arts vanished like that. Arkhon only knows, and he only knows whether Arts we have today will someday vanish. Or, for that matter, whether new Arts will someday—oh thank the gods."

Jan ran a hand through his hair, looking to the back of the room. "Finally we can be done with the gabbing and get to the good part."

Reiva perked up, turning her head.

She almost wished she hadn't.

So that's what people meant by 'intimidating.'

Stepping through the door was a man with a shaved head, dressed entirely in black—save the bright red of his Adept's mantle. Even the mantle, though, had a fringe of sable. He held a wooden case in his right hand, which was shackled to his wrist by a manacle.

Her stomach turned, instinctive fear boiling up. As the man's cold eyes swept over the room, she had to fight the sudden urge to run and hide.

Someone—it sounded like Phetan—muttered something under his breath. "Carnifex." Others shuddered, a great many of them pale.

Tolm was watching with intense focus, but even he looked nervous.

The Carnifex walked to the fore of the room, and Adept Jan slid to the side. "May I present to you all," Jan began, "Carnifex Seyun."

Seyun did not react to the introduction, merely kneeling to the ground to set down the vessel chained to his wrist. He then reached into his tunic, retrieving a heavy key.

"Relics," said Jan, "are of the most controlled artifacts in the Empire's possession. No one below the authority of a legate can requisition one for use, and such requests are granted only in cases of extreme need. One of the Empire's great generals once said that it would be better to lose a war than have a relic fall into the hands of an enemy."

He paused dramatically. "Today, you will all touch one. Follow my instructions very carefully, and we should all be fine. Seyun?"

The Carnifex had unlocked both the manacle around his wrist and the case itself—he had used separate keys for the two locks. He opened the case, retrieving a sword much longer than a standard legion gladius. The blade was single-edged, with a curve that had an almost organic, elegant shape. The flat of the metal was etched with swirling lines, and Reiva thought she could detect an almost blue-green tint from the iron—if indeed it *was* iron.

When Seyun spoke, his voice was grave and flat—as though he not only took no pleasure in being here, but more than that, as though he actively resented the task.

It's not just that, thought Reiva, observing the manner with which he presented the sword to Jan. *He actually doesn't trust Jan. An Adept!*

She thought through what she had seen—the man had an Adept's mantle, but she knew nothing about black fringes. Did that mean a Carnifex was a special kind of Adept?

And then the word itself—it was easy enough to translate, being a rather common word: *butcher*.

"What's a Carnifex?" she whispered to Mylla.

The other girl blanched, shooting a glance at the black-clad man. She leaned in so close that her lips brushed Reiva's ear, and even then, when she spoke, Reiva could hardly make out her words. "They hunt rogue Adepts. *Ars Sanguis.*"

Reiva had never heard of that Art, but like the man's title, it was simple enough to make out. Art of Blood.

She suppressed another shudder, wondering at just what sorts of things an Adept with that sort of magic could do. And how dangerous and single-minded they had to be for this one to look upon Adept Jan —a commissioned warrior of the Corps lecturing in the Sanctum itself—with plain suspicion.

Jan took hold of the relic and experimentally gave it an easy swing. "Light as a feather," he observed. "This is a windsword, a relic of the *Ars Ventas*. Now, all of you will line up in the usual order. And as I said—follow my directions. You will use your aetheric sense— your mentors should have instructed you in the basics—to probe the nature of this item. So you *Ventas* Initiates will need to be particularly cautious, since the relic's power will be familiar to you, but you still must not draw it forth."

The usual order meant they lined up by ranking. This put Reiva at the back. That was fine, in this case. She did not relish having to stand under the Carnifex's gaze.

On the other hand, having to wait so long only gave her more time to dread the moment.

One by one, the Initiates took their turns holding the relic. Some make sounds of surprise or awe, others simply seemed to hurry through the process as quickly as they could manage.

About halfway through the line, Adept Jan said, "An excellent question has been asked. If someone were to try to use two relics at once, they would experience the same sort of interference effect that an Adept would."

Reiva puzzled over that. She also wondered just how many relics the Empire held. With such powerful weapons, surely the legions would want to use them to bring down their enemies?

She also thought about the Carnifex. She would have to ask Alyat about them, and why he had never mentioned them. Was he scared of them too?

Adept Jan seemed at ease enough, but…

It might just be my imagination, but he seems tense.

There was just a bit too much of a gap between him and Seyun. A bit of tension in his smile.

Mylla had said Carnifexes hunt down rogue Adepts. But was that all? Who did this Seyun answer to? The Emperor alone? And how many others were there like him?

She racked her mind trying to think of whether she had heard of any Initiates from Seventh Cohort manifesting the Art of Blood. Was it rare like her Art of Flame? Rarer?

Suddenly, she found herself alone at the front of the room, under the twin gazes of two Adepts who could not have been more different in her eyes.

Jan hummed. "Last with *Vulcana*. You're the most recent manifestation, then?"

Shame warmed her face. "Yes, sir," she said through gritted teeth.

Everyone else had only gotten directions. He didn't have to remind the room that she had taken the longest—they all knew already.

Her inner Flame stoked, a rush of anger coursing through her.

Well, she wasn't going to stay in last for long—just like she'd climbed the ranks when it was all physical discipline, so she would do the same now that magic was on the table.

She cast a brief glance over the room. People were either disinterested or watching with a critical eye. The Flame burned hotter. All these had been pale and trembling not a moment ago—fine. *She* was not going to be known as fearful.

"Carnifex Seyun," she said, before her better judgment could stop her. "May I ask a question?"

Seyun blinked slowly. His expression betrayed absolutely nothing—neither surprise nor curiosity. "Ask."

Reiva's Flame shivered, but she pressed on. She could sense the tension in the room, the weight of so many eyes. "What is it that makes a rogue Adept?"

The Carnifex made a sound in the back of his throat. His eyes changed, though Reiva could not say for certain what they communicated. Predatory intent? Approval? A mixture of both?

"To go rogue," he said, speaking very slowly, very deliberately, "is to betray the faith of the Emperor. To act against the interests of the Empire. It is the sin of many an Adept who falls in love with his own power. It is pride. Vanity."

He leaned forward, bending almost double to go eye to eye with Reiva. "Initiate Reiva, *Ars Vulcana*. Seventh Cohort, second year, *acolyta*. Your mentor is Adept Alyat, *Ars Lumens*. His office is in the first wing, second floor, three doors from the stairs, and it has one window. Alyat received his commission fourteen years ago; his rank was second. He serves the Emperor by seeking out enemies within. He seeks those who do things in the dark that would harm the integrity of Lazarra and the strength of Imperial rule. He exposes them. It is like what I do—only I hunt my prey among the strongest, among those who have received the most from the hand of our Emperor, and those whose betrayal is most heinous. Does that make sense, Initiate Reiva?"

Reiva regretted ever having opened her mouth. She felt light-headed. Her guts were in a knot. Her knees, she prayed, were not shaking. She nodded, then, fighting against the dryness of her tongue, tried to form words. "I understand, sir."

"Carnifex," he said.

"I understand, Carnifex."

"Hand me the relic, Adept."

Reiva was dimly aware of Jan giving the windsword to Seyun. The Carnifex presented the sword to her. "Take hold of this, minding the edge. It's sharper than anything you've held before, I assure you."

She hated how her hands shook as she accepted the relic from him. For a moment, their fingers touched, and his skin was startlingly hot. Was that an effect of his Art of Blood, or was she just that cold from fright?

"Now, similar to how you can sense aether around you, turn your aetheric sense to the relic itself. Run your fingers along it and seek out its nature. But do not indulge its pull—or else things will get difficult."

She swallowed. She had barely paid attention to any of that—she could still feel the phantom touch of his too-warm fingers.

Thinking back to Alyat's training, she took a breath. Then another. How long had she been standing up here? Five minutes? Ten? Were they all staring at her?

For a moment, she thought she'd pass out.

Breathe!

She shut out the world. Her vision became only the metal in her hands and the power it contained. Reaching out with her aetheric sense, she searched the object.

It seemed to glow in her perception—not visually, but still in a way perceptible to her. She inspected it, running her fingers along the etchings in the blade. They seemed to vibrate to her touch, and from within the metal came an unmistakable sense of tempestuous motion. Rushing winds, swirling in the cold iron, eager to be let out— almost *begging* to be released, to flow through Reiva and out into the world.

She wanted to experience that freedom. Wanted to let the winds loose and turn this room upside down.

Stop!

She pushed the relic back toward the Carnifex.

Seyun observed, one eyebrow rising slowly. After what seemed an eternity, he said, "Potent. Well done, Initiate."

He took the relic back, kneeling to return it to the case and lock it away.

Jan's hand touched her shoulder. "You may sit, Initiate." She couldn't read the intent behind his words, as if he were striving to sound as neutral as possible.

Reiva's feet seemed to glide as she drifted back to her seat—as if someone else were controlling her body. She didn't make eye contact with anyone, just headed straight back to where she had sat earlier and slipped onto the bench.

As she sat at the edge, Mylla pulled away—ever so slightly, but unmistakably so. A dagger went into Reiva's heart. She looked at the Gallian girl, but Mylla's eyes were fixed straight ahead.

"Well," Jan said, "you all performed admirably. You'll be practicing your aetheric sense more throughout your training, but from what I've seen here today, I'm confident you all meet our standards for new *acolyti*."

Carnifex Seyun was already walking out, and Jan did not spare a word of farewell for him. When he had left, it was as if the whole room eased.

Jan said something more, but Reiva did not hear it. Her eyes were downcast, looking at the gap between her and Mylla. Her insides were cold.

After they were dismissed, Reiva made her way to Alyat's office. If anyone spared her an extra glance or tried to catch her eye, she missed it. She kept her chin high, her gaze forward, and her jaw tight.

16

THE NINE-KNUCKLE HOUSE

REIVA HAD BEEN EXPECTING their final session before Alyat departed on his mission to be focused on further training her magical abilities. Instead, he quickly stood and bid her follow him, much as he had when taking her to the bakery.

Reiva hurried after him, still full of swirling emotions from the lecture.

"Alyat," she said once they were clear of the gates, "what do you think of Carnifexes?"

To his credit, her mentor didn't so much as break stride as he spat out a curse. "Steer clear. They're a necessary evil—and they're zealous to a fault. Never give one cause to look at you for more than a moment. If you've got the misfortune of working with one, comply absolutely. And don't speak of them this close to the Sanctum. They know more than they should."

She felt a knot in her throat. "I see."

"Relic lecture?"

"Yeah. I uh...asked him a question."

Alyat swore again, more elaborately. "No wonder you're rattled." They walked on a while longer before he spoke again. "Best-case scenario, they'll admire your courage and your ranking will get a kick. Worst case...let's just hope for the best."

"What do you—?!"

"You won't die, don't worry. It's just never a good idea to get the attention of the sable-fringed. Now enough of that—you need to look confident for this."

"How do I look?"

He spared her a glance. "Just try to ease up on the teeth grinding."

THE PLACE he led her to was at the border of the markets and the worse-off area of the city. It wasn't a slum—those were outside the walls, as the city ensured that all areas within the walls were at least *decently* impressive—but there was a certain roughness to the place. The streets were more narrow, the air denser with sour odor.

Alyat stopped in front of a wide building, all wood and nails. It looked like a tavern, if Reiva had to guess. She didn't smell any food, but there was a buzz coming from inside—as if the walls barely constrained a raucous chorus.

"This is the one place outside the Sanctum you're allowed to take off your mantle."

Reiva frowned. "What is it?"

"The Nine-knuckle House." He opened the door.

Right away, the force of dozens of shouting voices struck. Reiva actually took a step back, amazed at how thoroughly the sound had been muffled.

"Either get in," drawled Alyat, "or go home. I'm not holding the door like a manservant."

Reiva hustled inside, pulling her mantle off as she crossed the threshold. It felt strange not to have it around her shoulders—and Alyat looked even stranger without the familiar red.

"Come on—and don't stare at anyone."

Easier said than done. Reiva had hardly seen a crowd like this since coming to Lazarra. She was almost always kept inside the

Sanctum, which had all the military discipline and stiffness of the legions.

This though—this place had *life*.

At the center of the room was a bar; not set against a wall but circular, with stools all around filled with all manner of folks. Some were tall, others short—but all had the same gruffness, the same barely constrained aggression. They yelled at one another, they laughed, they even threw one or two punches—though these quickly drew the ire of the bartender, whose voice sounded over the din with clarion force.

"Keep it in the ring," he bellowed, "or I cut you off!"

The warning was instantly heeded.

Along the near, right, and far walls of the establishment were tables filled with the same sort of people as the bar—though Reiva noted there were more elderly folks at the tables. Gray hair and missing teeth, though, did nothing to allay their fervor. They argued and jested just like the younger ones, and they did so with just as much—if not more—alcohol in front of them.

To the left, the room stretched out. There was a stairway, on either side of which were stands, like in an amphitheater. Reiva couldn't see what the stairs led to, but the roar of the audience was so deafening she could hardly hear herself think.

She glanced at Alyat, and she saw something that truly mystified —he looked *pleasant.*

"Jalis!" he called. "How long do I have to stand here?"

The bartender honed in on Alyat's voice—and a moment later, a wide grin split his features. "Ice! *Haha!* Get the hell over here, I'm already pouring a round."

Reiva padded after Alyat, doing her best to avoid people's elbows as her mentor cut effortlessly through the room.

Alyat leaned on the bar, and he actually *tossed his mantle across.* Jalis caught it effortlessly and stowed it out of sight. At a nod from Alyat, Reiva handed hers across.

"New protégé, eh?" Jalis looked her up and down as he handed Alyat a mug. "Bit short, this one."

Reiva's Flame crackled.

Jalis laughed. "She's already learned your glare though." He stuck his hand out.

Reiva took it, squeezing harder than she needed to. "Reiva."

"What—are you putting magic into that grip?"

She quickly let go, embarrassment replacing anger.

Jalis shook his hand exaggeratedly. "Didn't break anything, at least. Where'd you find this feral badger?"

Alyat shrugged. "Same as the last."

Jalis clicked his tongue. "How it goes, eh? And where're you from, Reiva?"

She hesitated. "Talynis."

"You don't say? I knew a girl from Talynis once...she didn't like me either."

Alyat snorted. "Good intuition on all counts."

Jalis looked wounded. "Now is that how you introduce a friend to your—?"

Another uproarious clamor from the audience swallowed the last of his words. Once it subsided, Jalis made a sour face. "That's another loss for me. Polnoff's pulled ahead in the betting as of late."

Alyat gave him a flat look. "Isn't Polnoff always ahead in the betting?"

"I had him last winter."

"Right. Well, you know the drill." He took a long pull from his mug of ale. "Mm, good swill."

"Only the best. So tell me, *Reiva*—you know how to fight?"

She shot a look at Alyat. "I'm an Initiate."

Jalis waved his hand through the air. "Aye, but there's fighting, and then there's *fighting*. Which can you do?"

"I can fight."

"How do you do with crowds?"

"If Alyat brought me here," she said, "then I can do whatever it is you do here." She turned to the audience. "It's a fighting ring? I'm learning from the best in the Empire."

Alyat tapped his mug against the bar. "You're learning how the legions fight. But there's more to it. You practice against people who've learned the same holds and techniques. On the battlefield, you won't have that luxury. What's more, in the Nine-knuckle House, you won't have the luxury of fighting with aether. You'll have to keep your fundamentals strong. You want to truly be the best? You'll come here and learn in the ring. It will humble you. Refine you. And it will give you an edge."

An edge. She could use one of those.

Jalis leaned across the bar. "Now, there's not many fighters your age, fewer still who are girls, but we'll find something that works."

"I can fight boys my size."

Jalis rolled his eyes. "Teenaged boys won't come back even if they did know it was an Adept-in-training who kicked their asses. Not rational actors, if you catch my drift."

Aether exposure granted not only greater strength and speed in the moment—it also conferred, over time, such benefits naturally. As a result of drawing aether into their bodies, Adepts were just plain stronger and faster than normal humans.

"Eventually," Jalis said, "more people will take you on. But we've got to build you up first. There's an art to it. Once folks in the House accept you as one of their own—then you can fight anyone. Take Ice here—he showed some fifteen years ago a grumpy sourpuss no one wanted to be around, and now he's a grumpy sourpuss people can tolerate! That's the spirit of the Nine-knuckle."

"Why 'Ice'?" she finally asked.

Alyat pushed away his now-empty mug. "Everyone gets a name once they became a full member. To become a full member, you have to fight and beat another one. Most folks here are just in it for the fun. Only about a fifth of the faces you see here have actually fought their way to membership in the House. The only thing that matters here is what you can earn with your hands. That man with the bald spot in the corner? He's a senator. The one he's talking to? Dock-worker. Under this roof, they're equals."

Now she was getting it. That's why they had taken their mantles off—being an Adept didn't matter in this place.

She felt a grin splitting her face. "So how do I start?"

IT HAD BEEN REMARKABLY easy to find a match. Polnoff, Jalis' business partner and the man who ran the ring, kept a mental ledger of everyone looking to hop into the ring. Alyat had hardly gotten past introducing Reiva to him than he had already thought of a competitor.

She was going to be up against a girl named Iula, who was two inches taller and two years older. Reiva guessed that with her enhanced constitution, it would be about fair.

But she had better training—even though she could see Alyat's point about learning different ways of fighting. She was almost certainly going to win.

It hurt to hand her focus over to Alyat so soon after she'd earned it, but Alyat was insistent that she do so. Once she had more experience, she would be able to fight with it. At her level, though, she was liable to draw in aether on reflex to heal herself or to channel it to boost her strength.

Worse than giving up her focus though, was how she was supposed to dress.

"Do we *have* to?" she asked.

Iula and she had stepped into one of the rooms adjoining the ring where fighters could prepare. Ordinarily they would take separate rings, but Iula had agreed to help Reiva learn the ropes.

She was also smirking at her. "Haven't you ever seen athletic games? Been to a gymnasium?"

"I've haven't even been in Lazarra for two years. We didn't do this sort of thing in Talynis."

"Oh, Talynis. It all makes sense now."

Reiva felt heat creeping into her cheeks. "What's wrong with Talynis?"

"Just a tendency to be...weird about things. Like this." Iula gestured at herself. She was dressed in a bandeau and loincloth, which she insisted was standard attire for an athletic competition in Lazarra.

Reiva insisted it was ridiculous. "In the Sanctum, we fight dressed normally or like we're going into battle. It's about practicality and preparation."

"And here it's about not giving your opponent something loose to grab hold of. Now change, or I'll use your cloak to tie your hands together when we're in the ring."

Reiva pressed her lips together. Iula raised an eyebrow.

"Fine," she muttered. "But if those people out there say anything weird—"

"They'll get their teeth kicked in. The House is a place for fighting —we don't let anything buck the sanctity of that."

It felt strange to hear fighting referred to as sacred, but she could respect the notion.

"Now, here's how you wrap your fists. Not required, but trust me when I say you don't want bruised knuckles for the next week. Also, it's considered rude if your opponent doesn't agree."

Reiva followed along easily enough. She was struck again by the strangeness of fighting just with arms and legs for the sake of it. Their hand-to-hand training in the Sanctum was more for augmenting their ability to fight with weaponry and their magic. Here though, it was everything.

As she followed Iula into the ring, she started feeling less confident.

"Into the ring," shouted Polnoff, "our next two competitors! Neither has earned membership in this House yet, and one is a familiar face. These fighters seek your approval!"

The crowd stomped their feet and sent up a cheer.

Reiva scanned the ring. There was a ring of torches set up atop the wall, illuminating the fight. Beyond that was the audience. Alyat would be somewhere, watching and evaluating. Her performance might even reflect in her cohort ranking, if she did well enough.

Iula didn't look like she was about to let Reiva manage that sort of performance easily, though. She was rolling her head side to side, tapping her fists together, bouncing up and down—there was a thrill to her. A mirror eagerness grew in Reiva.

With everything that had happened recently, she'd almost forgotten there was actually something *fun* in combat.

Polnoff waved the two of them over to him. "Standard rules, you two." He shot a look at Reiva. "That means no lethal holds or strikes, easy on the head and neck. And no funny business from you."

Reiva frowned. "I fight fair."

"Good—and just as important as that, give 'em a show, eh?" He sent them to opposite sides of the ring.

Reiva steadied herself with deep breaths. One of the worst things in a fight was to lose yourself to lightheadedness, getting too swept up in the action to breathe. Men had passed out on the battlefield from such things.

Well, if Reiva passed out today, it would be from a strike. And she didn't intend to allow even that.

Polnoff was shouting some to rile up the crowd—to great effect—but Reiva had fixed her attention entirely to her adversary. Iula had slightly more reach, but she was also probably cocky, expecting an easy win against the newcomer, eager to trounce an Adept Initiate.

Well, she was about to find out just what the Sanctum instilled—and why it was a grueling enough program to spit out almost every soul that attempted it.

"Fight!" bellowed Polnoff.

Reiva took the initiative. She burst forward, leading with a clean jab.

Iula blocked, but Reiva was already following with another series of strikes. Each blow was textbook, perfectly to form.

If only they had been landing. Half the time, Iula dodged out of the way before Reiva's strike even landed. She was reading Reiva's motion and slipping away, and no matter how well Reiva threw a punch, it didn't count for anything if it didn't land.

Reiva grit her teeth.

Time to pour on the pressure.

In a fight, all else held equal, the victor was the one who stayed on the offense. Reiva stepped forward, driving her opponent on the defensive.

In a frustrating twist, Iula kept her footing and used her retreating movement to duck even further away from Reiva's fists.

And then she turned the tables.

Quick as lightning, Iula jumped forward, catching Reiva's arm at full extension and putting her into a lock. Reiva was helpless as her opponent swept her feet out and threw her across the sand.

She went tumbling, only managing to pop back to her feet and keep her balance by good fortune.

And now she was angry.

Iula was faster—she could recognize that. But Reiva would have staked her life that she was stronger. If she could hit hard enough, then it didn't matter how much Iula could dodge—she only needed to land the one hit.

So she rushed into an even more brutal series of attacks. She threw haymakers, stepped inside Iula's reach, poured on so many attacks and with such vicious intent that Iula couldn't possibly account for them all.

And indeed Iula couldn't—she started taking hits, she had to put up more blocks and plant her feet, lest she been knocked off them. But she also started fighting back. She threw rabbit punches and quick hooks, then danced out of reach. Reiva pursued, throwing a wild jab, only for Iula to bat it aside and return with a knee to the gut.

The blow knocked the wind from her, doubling her over. She almost dropped to the sand then and there, only keeping her footing thanks to countless morning regimens. Discipline overcame human frailty, and she stood up straight, readying her hands for the next exchange.

Iula cracked a smile. Reiva snarled.

Her opponent took the initiative now, throwing crosses, sweeping kicks, and all around moving just too fast for Reiva to keep up with. The hits weren't overwhelming, but they chipped away at her resolve. Every blow was another stinging pain tugging at her mental awareness, and each one made her more likely to miss the next.

She was forced onto defense, hopping backward and trying to shield herself.

But then Iula slipped, leaving her side too open.

Reiva seized on the opportunity, lashing forward with abandon.

This was her chance—the one hit she needed to get in to turn the tide.

And then Iula twisted, turning what would have been a solid gut shot into a glancing blow.

Reiva hardly had time to realize what had happened before Iula's fist clocked her between the eyes. She went sprawling, feeling the sand bite into her back.

In an instant, Polnoff's voice was next to her, counting down.

She had eight seconds left. Seven.

She took a breath, forced her eyes open.

Five.

Her limbs strained. She ordered her body to move, but it was resisting her. Or rather, perhaps it just didn't have anything left.

Three seconds.

Reiva sighed, and with what little energy she could muster, put up her hand in surrender.

Alyat had said the Nine-knuckle House would teach her humility. Well, at least she already had enough humility to admit when she was beaten.

The crowd roared as Polnoff called the fight, raising Iula's hand high.

Reiva caught a few more breaths before hauling herself to her feet and padding back to the prep room, eyes downcast.

She may have had enough humility to admit defeat, but she also had more than enough pride to feel the shame of the loss.

"Hey," said Iula, catching up to her as she pulled her clothes back on. "That was a good fight—you did a lot better than I did my first time."

Reiva muttered her thanks.

"Oh come on, have you never lost before?"

"No, I have, just...I thought I would do better than that at least."

Iula shrugged. "Like I said, it was a good fight. You have good basics, but you let the emotions get to your head. As soon as you got frustrated, your form went to pieces. At that point, I could control you pretty easily."

Reiva nodded along. This was good feedback—she would think over it again later, considering how she could do better. For now though, she just wanted to be out.

"Thank you," she said eventually. "You're an excellent fighter."

Iula shrugged. "Thanks. I hope to see you come back."

Reiva nodded. "I will." She wasn't particularly excited about the prospect, but she knew she would. She had to. Not because Alyat said so either—she had to *win*.

Iula left first, getting another round of applause and cheers from the crowd. Reiva followed shortly after, and to her surprise, she did get a fair amount of acclaim. Maybe they appreciated when a new fighter tried their hand.

When she made her way back to Jalis' bar, she found the barkeep waiting with a mug of ale for her. "Usually it's winners who get a free drink, but for your first fight I can make an exception."

Reiva grimaced. "I...don't like ale."

Jalis looked stricken. "Seems we've even more work to do with you. Ah, there's the man."

Alyat reappeared beside Reiva. "You know what you did wrong?"

She nodded, repeating the feedback Iula had given her.

"Good," Alyat said. "And don't forget to control your footwork."

Jalis nodded sagely. "And try not to blush so bright when you come out—it's a prey response. Like painting a target."

Reiva snorted. "I'll work on that."

The barkeep cackled. "While you do, don't get too hung up on the losses. I could see some talent while you were in the ring—and we've got a saying here: 'No one sees talent like Jalis.'"

Alyat, with a completely sincere expression, said, "I have heard that. Always from you, but I've heard it."

Jalis spread his hands. "I'll be ahead of Polnoff before you know it. And I think this girl might be part of my winning strategy."

Reiva stood up straighter at that. "Well, I'll be back soon as I can."

Alyat nodded. "Good. And this is a good place to make your way without anyone from the Corps—including me—hovering over you. Even if someone does come, the mantles stay away."

She remembered what he had said earlier: what people had here, they earned with their hands. She flexed her fingers, feeling the stiffness and the shock still receding.

Yes, she could enjoy it here.

PART III

ELITE

17

ANYTHING FOR THIS

ALMOST TWO YEARS to the day after she manifested the Art of Fire, Reiva was sitting, legs crossed, on the floor of the Trial Chamber. Despite the name, the Trial Chamber was really an assortment of rooms, all of them prepared in various ways for the training of the arcane Arts. Reiva hadn't gone for anything special today though—she was in the center of the first room, well away from anything flammable, her eyebrows knit in concentration.

Her hands were folded in her lap, a ball of fire floating a few inches above her palms. As she breathed, it swelled, shrank, and swelled again, responding to the impulse of her will. In the time since she first manifested, her ability to control the fire had so developed that she could hardly believe it. But she still had a long way to go.

By necessity, *acolyti* devoted a great deal of time to training aether tolerance. When an Initiate first began to work their Art, their soul could only handle a meager amount of aether flowing through it. Overextending oneself could lead to aether sickness—a condition that was uncomfortable at first, but soon progressed to more dangerous stages, including insanity and eventually death. With time however, and effort, the soul acclimated and grew stronger, in much the same way muscles did as they labored. Instead of food to fuel the growth, though, the soul required sleep and mental exercises.

It would have been challenging enough if she had only labored in the Sanctum, but much of her free time went to the Nine-knuckle House—and to great effect. She was without question the best hand-to-hand fighter in Seventh Cohort. It was the one area where she could truly say without question that she had established her superiority—she even beat Tolm two times out of three. All her fighting and training had paid off about six months ago when she made full member in the House—besting Iula (who had become a member long ago) in the ring.

As a reward, Jalis had christened her 'Red.' At first she had told herself it was because of her mantle, but the barkeep had been quite explicit that it was a reference to how she blushed bright red the first few times she'd stepped into the arena. "Don't forget where you came from," he had admonished her, before sliding her an on-the-house mug of ale so potent she had needed to burn its effects off with aether channeling.

All told, as an *acolyta*, Reiva's schedule had become even more packed. While the required exercises and lessons remained at the same level of frequency, she was expected to build aether tolerance on her own time. This meant shorter lunches and dinners. She had to sleep early so she could get enough rest before starting her day—which now began long before sunrise. The predawn hours were some of the only available segments of time for solid, uninterrupted aether work.

So when she heard the door to the Trial Chamber open, Reiva frowned. Time dragged on at a snail's pace when performing tolerance exercises like this one. That meant someone else had come in early—which wasn't particularly common.

She blinked as Luo stepped into sight.

"Reiva," he said, eyes widening. "How long have you been here?"

She shrugged, letting her fire lapse and puff out of being. "Since fifth hour, same as always."

"Today's a free day."

She shrugged again. She'd stopped feeling bashful about this a long time ago. Other people thought it was crazy what she was putting herself through, but Reiva had higher ambitions. In the time since she had become an *acolyta*, she had soared through the rankings of the cohort.

Last month, she'd finally broken into the top ten. Last week, she'd made it to the top five when Sciro, the former holder of fifth place, had washed out. Rumor had it he'd suffered a seizure while practicing his Art of Mind, losing control of himself and screaming about things that didn't exist—spirits following people around, dragging chains everywhere they went.

His departure—tragic as it was—from the Sanctum was Reiva's gain, but she only felt the distance from the top more acutely.

Tolm and Domi had earned their silver fringes last month. They were *subordinati*. Phetan was desperate to claw his way back to second place, having been eclipsed by Domi. He was being evaluated for *subordinatus* this very moment. As a wielder of the Art of Life, the *Ars Viva*, he would have to demonstrate his ability to perform *Viva* surgery—an intense and challenging form of medical work that combined the best surgical methods with the Art of Life's preternatural capacity to heal the body. It made normal aether healing look downright primitive—and Phetan was confident he would prove himself competent.

Well, Reiva wasn't one to let herself slip. Next week, Alyat was taking her to clear out a bandit camp. If she performed well, he would clear her for field work—and she'd be a *subordinata*.

That was why she couldn't afford to slack now. She *needed* to stay at the top of her game, she needed to—

The door opened, and both Reiva and Luo turned. Mylla came inside, and right away, Reiva's heart ached.

The Gallian girl was downcast. Her eyes were ringed by dark circles, and her lips tugged down at the corners. She made it four steps in before she realized Reiva and Luo were there.

"*Oh*, excuse me." She quickly put on a smile, but Reiva could see the strain in her cheeks, the way her eyes didn't match her mouth. "Extra training for you two?"

Luo scoffed. "On my mentor's orders. Reiva just does this on her own, apparently."

Mylla's smile strained a bit more. "Well, that's Reiva."

Luo didn't seem to notice the tension in her, or if he did, he didn't pay it much mind. Luo wasn't an elite, strictly speaking, but he was in a comfortable position. He probably didn't worry about washing out. Reiva could understand that—she didn't have those worries anymore either.

That sort of thing created divisions among the Initiates. Even among people who had been friends since the early days.

Reiva got to her feet. "Actually," she offered, "I was about to be done for today. I'm going into the city. Do you want to come, Mylla?"

Luo scoffed. "Fine, fine, I see how it is. Leave the man behind."

Reiva shot him a deadpan look. "I was about to invite you, but now I'm questioning the wisdom of that."

He perked up instantly. "Buy you a pastry and I'm forgiven?"

Reiva shrugged. "You don't have to buy me anything, but sure, pastries sound good." She had been planning to visit Levin anyway, so at least she'd be visiting a baker. She couldn't risk any of the other Initiates finding out about a connection to a Talynisti family in Lazarra. That sort of thing could fall under 'courting sedition,' depending on how strictly one interpreted the Adept Corps' statutes.

Mylla was shaking her head though. "I'm all right, thank you. I do need to train today."

Reiva frowned. "Mylla, you look exhausted. Did your mentor approve this? It can't be healthy."

"Who cares what my *mentor* says?" she snapped, her face briefly flickering into a contortion of pain. As soon as it had appeared though, it was gone. "Sorry," she whispered. "Slept poorly. You two get going, please. Don't let me hold you back."

Even if he wasn't the most socially conscious, Luo wasn't so dense as to miss what had just happened. He glanced over at Reiva. "I know a good place near Third Gate. Bit of a walk so we should go before all the good stuff's gone."

Reiva gave one more look at Mylla. "Are you sure you don't want to—"

"I'm fine, Reiva. I don't need anyone's pity."

"I'm not pitying you. I just—"

"You know, I still remember the days where you were fighting to keep up at the back."

Reiva blinked. Where was this going?

Wherever it was, Luo had no interest in seeing it through. He scratched the back of his head, muttered something about waiting by the gate, and slipped out.

Which left Reiva facing Mylla, whose face had gone cold and stiff as stone.

"Mylla, I—"

"Just listen, Reiva. You always have something to say now, so listen to me for once."

Her gut knotted like she'd just taken a hit. "I *always* listen. We've talked since day one."

Mylla's eyes shone. "Have you even noticed how long it's been since we ate together in the mess?"

Reiva felt the sudden urge to wrap her arms around herself. She held still. "You know where I sit."

"That's not an answer, and we both know why you're putting this on me."

"If it's because Phetan is there, you know I would force him to—"

"I don't give a damn about Phetan! I give a damn about the fact that I shouldn't have to use you like a shield if I want to eat with you. I shouldn't have to worry about that sort of confrontation happening at all."

Reiva opened her mouth, but Mylla waved her hand through the air. "No, don't even try. Like I said, I remember the days when you were in the back, Reiva. I remember how you gave everything you had to climb the rankings. I remember how badly you wanted it. I admired you for that, and I *cheered* you. But now I get it—when you said you'd give anything for this, you really meant it."

Reiva clenched her fists at her side. Her Flame was roiling, itching to be unleashed. "What are you saying?"

"I'm saying you're throwing me away. Now that you're an elite, you've taken to hobnobbing it up just like the rest of them."

"Alyat says—"

"I don't care if he advised it or ordered it or whatever. I know *why* it happens. I know you need to have those alliances built for when you're in service. You're all the most likely to make it through, so you might as well consolidate now. *But you could at least eat with me once a week!* Is that too much? Is it like training, Reiva? You need to get every last drop in so you can have a chance of taking on Tolm someday for the top spot?"

Tears stung Reiva's eyes. A scream had been building in her throat with every word Mylla spoke—and then it broke free. "I came from *nothing*! You're province-born. You got picked up by a survey, and your village got a stipend for sending you here. *I came here in chains*. I didn't join the Adept Corps because I wanted to be important or powerful—I joined the Adept Corps because it was the only thing saving me from a living death! So yes, I'm not going to take a chance. I'm going to become the best one here, because anything less than that is risking too much. You don't understand how far down it's possible to fall."

Mylla's lips twisted into a sardonic smile. "Oh, I don't? It's just you —you're the only one who understands suffering. Fine. Go enjoy some cakes. I need to train, because I don't have the luxury of considering anything less than first a failure. I'm hanging on to the bottom by my fingernails and you know it."

Reiva's throat closed up. She dashed her hands across her eyes and stomped past Mylla, slamming the door as she went.

'I'm hanging on to the bottom by my fingernails and you know it.'

She did. As more and more Initiates had washed out, Mylla's once respectable position at the middle of the pack had become the lowest. They'd lost half their cohort.

But why had she taken it out on Reiva? Didn't she understand? Sourness built at the back of Reiva's throat.

Do I *still understand?*

When she got to the gate, she waved Luo off. "Sorry, change of plans. I need to be alone."

Ignoring his dismayed protests, she made her way to Levin's.

REIVA'S DAYS OFF—ONCE an awkward stretch of time where she didn't know what to do besides wander the grounds of the Sanctum aimlessly—had become a treasured escape from the drudgery and culture of the Adept Corps. She *did* train on her days off (albeit less intensely, letting her body and soul take the extra time they needed to recover properly), but she always made sure to visit Levin and Artha.

Even before she set foot inside the bakery, Reiva could tell the baker's wife was not having a good day. The first day she'd met Levin, he had told her of his wife's ailing health. She had a persistent cough —on the best days it was only a nuisance, but those days were more and more precious. She'd often double over for minutes at a time, hacking her lungs out. Sometimes blood came up with the phlegm.

Any doctors they visited were baffled. After several months of pressing, Reiva had convinced them to let her try to channel aether to heal Artha, but it had only given her a temporary respite. Aether could only do so much.

Reiva slipped inside the hot, delicious-smelling shop. Artha was standing near the door, coughing into a kerchief. When she saw Reiva, she smiled weakly, her pale skin creasing with well-worn laugh lines, her eyes twinkling.

"There's my *akhyana*." Reiva smiled sadly. She always insisted on calling Reiva 'niece.' She and Levin had no children of their own, and what family they did have they had left behind in Talynis when they moved to Lazarra years ago. Artha's cough had been lighter then. Now she probably could not have made the journey.

"How are you?" she asked, pulling off her Adept's mantle to stow it in her satchel. She didn't like wearing the thing while she was in their presence—it felt too divisive. For a few precious moments every few weeks, she could pretend to be Talynisti again.

Artha shrugged. "The same. Not wor—" A fit seized her, and she spent the better part of a minute hacking into her kerchief. She smiled faintly. "Not worse," she finished belatedly.

Levin quickly appeared from the back, mopping his brow of sweat and coming to put his arms around his wife. She leaned into him, letting him take her weight.

Reiva's lips drew into a thin line. Artha always teased her for the way her brow furrowed when she looked concerned. She probably looked like that now. Taking a step froward, she stretched forth her hand.

Artha nodded gratefully, and Reiva laid her hand on the woman's arm. Gently, she channeled a measure of aether to her.

Artha shivered. At first, she and Levin had been hesitant about letting Reiva do this, unsure about whether it was right to benefit from Imperial magic. Once Reiva had finally broken through, though, Artha had become quite receptive.

She recovered a bit of color to her cheeks, and her breathing evened out, becoming less laborious. For the rest of the day, she would have fewer coughing fits, and the pain in her chest would abate. Within the next day or two, unfortunately, things would return to how they were.

Reiva's aether channeling could only heal the internal damage created by the coughing, as well as reduce any inflammation. Artha kissed Reiva on the cheek. "Thank you, dear. The Four blessed us with you, may they bless you in kind." Levin nodded solemnly, his face contorted with the pain known to every man who could not succor his beloved's suffering.

She always said that, and Reiva still felt an uncomfortable twinge in her chest at those words. It wasn't the Four Gods of Talynis doing anything, after all. It was by the power of a Lazarran focus and arcane Art. And even if the Four had somehow sent Reiva, why couldn't they have healed Artha herself?

Why couldn't they have healed her father all those years ago?

The memory of a frail desert stream brushed the edges of her consciousness, and she shoved it away.

The Adept Corps was always researching the power of aether healing, and the Initiates were drilled constantly—painfully—in its application. This entailed inflicting wounds on one another to heal—both oneself and one's partner. Anyone who delivered an injury lighter or heavier than mandated by the exercise was punished severely—often with yet another injury to heal.

Levin and Artha had been aghast when Reiva first explained the method, so she didn't bring it up anymore. She didn't bring up anything about her training, for that matter, unless they asked. And when they did, she clung to the banal things, the things one would expect of any soldier in training. So she would tell them of which weapons she was training with, which she was best at (the sword) and worst at (the bow). She would talk about her cohort members and about her place in the rankings.

They were kind enough to avoid pressing Reiva on her relationship with the Four Gods. They knew, of course, that she was required to swear fealty to Arkhon and the Lazarran pantheon, like all Lazarran soldiers. When she didn't join in saying the prayer before dinner, they didn't complain, and they never asked whether she'd like to join them in attending the local Talynisti meeting house.

Also, they never pressed about her family. They knew her father had died in the Lazarran invasion, but they didn't know it was her mother who'd sold her, and they didn't know that she hardly ever thought of her brother anymore. She couldn't—for her own sake. Another piece of her past, thrown into the abyss.

Reiva wondered if the two of them had ever mentioned her existence to any other Talynisti in Lazarra. One part of her hoped they had, another, more sensible, part hoped they had not. The fewer people who knew of their relationship, the better. It meant her connection to Talynis was a frail thing, but at least it existed. At least she had this.

Then in the course of conversation, as the time drew near for

Reiva to return to the Sanctum, Levin, his brow furrowed and his arms crossed, muttered, "We may leave the city soon."

And Reiva's world spun for a moment.

"*Leave*?" she echoed. "You mean...?"

Levin nodded, and Artha laid her hands—her thin hands—on his arm. The baker went on, "The air's not good here. If we can get out into the countryside, maybe..."

Reiva understood the reasoning, but the words still cut like a blade to the heart. "And you would just...be gone."

"Depends," grumbled Levin. "Most Talynisti this far west stay in the big cities. We might not have a prayer house to visit if we moved. We'd have to come back for the seasonal feasts."

Artha's lips formed a mournful smile. "But yes, for the most part, we would be gone."

Reiva's gut turned. "What about my healing?" she blurted out. "It helps—we can all see that! I can't do that if you're far away. If you stay, I-I'll come more often. I'll find an excuse, I'll have my mentor write something up for me, and I'll come here in the mornings, or late, and—"

"Dear," murmured Artha.

"And maybe if I keep giving you channeling more often then—"

"*Dear*."

Reiva's voice died in her throat.

"It's okay," whispered Artha. "You've said yourself it can't heal longstanding illnesses. I don't think getting away from the city will do much either, but..."

"It will make things... easier," muttered Levin.

Reiva had been trained to assess people. To examine an enemy and decipher the weakness in his stance, the gaps in his defense. Or to evaluate a speaker and discern his overconfidences and anxieties.

But even without that instruction, even if she were still a little girl who'd never gone more than ten miles from the place she was born, she would have recognized the pain haunting the baker. A different sort of pain than afflicted Artha. Levin only bore his suffering as well as he did for his wife's sake. And he held up under it like a creaking wagon under a pile of raw-hewn granite.

Reiva stifled the sob building in her chest.

She had had this, and it had been lovely.

And now it would be gone.

"When are you going?" she managed eventually.

The man rubbed at his forehead. "It's not certain yet, but...next month. There's someone at the prayer house who's looking to buy the bakery from me. He won't knead a *qnasha* quite as well, mind you, but he'll do. This city won't lack for good bread just yet."

Artha looked at her husband with such pride, Reiva almost couldn't comprehend it.

You're dying! She wanted to scream, to grab her by the shoulders and shake her. What did it matter whether the bakery was still here? Whether there was good bread? What amount of bread or money or *anything* wouldn't she have traded to undo her father's death?

But instead, she put on her soldier's face—the inspection face, the one that held like a mountain against lashing rain no matter how the instructor yelled or berated for the slightest scuff on a uniform—and she said, "I'll come before then. I'll be sure of it."

Levin said he would be sure to have some of her favorites ready for her. Artha gave her a kiss on the cheek and prayed a small blessing over her.

And Reiva was out in the night, walking the streets of a city that went on as it always had. Her mind spun with memories of Shugrith and mourning songs, wailing tunes that went on all the day and night. That sort of thing never happened in Lazarra. Maybe if the Emperor died.

Death was so different in Lazarra. They burned bodies instead of burying them. They set coins atop the eyes—a toll for the ferryman of the dead. There were seven rivers in the underworld, so they said, and if the toll was incomplete then the spirit would be stranded, waiting who knew how long until the ferryman finally had pity on them. What was time to a ghost? Did centuries pass in seconds, or did every second last a century?

The Lazarrans took such things seriously. Every house had a shrine to the families' ancestors—they were like meager gods, blessing descendants who remembered them well and cursing those who were derelict.

And that, in a very real sense, was the entirety of the Empire. Every man was a son, every woman a daughter. The Emperor was the great priest, the first father, tracing his lineage all the way back to the Founders, the man and woman who had birthed the first Lazarrans. From that one family lost to the mists of the past to today's sprawling city and far-reaching Empire.

That was the place Reiva had found herself in.

It was grand. She could plainly admit that. The roads were wide, the buildings tall. The sight of a legion in parade dress could not help but stir the heart with awe. The rich Imperial banners flying from the impregnable walls, the glittering gold of the Legion Eagle. It was majestic.

And without Artha and Levin, it would be hollow. What would she have? Only a number by her name? A reputation with the Corps? Would she give a life in service only to die on the battlefield or retire and consort with the same ilk that had ordered the campaign on Talynis?

She came to a stop in the road. Her stomach was turning. She clutched at her gut, fingers digging into the skin. She willed the revulsion to still. She sucked in one breath, then another.

"This is all you have," she hissed. "Don't throw yourself off the cliff to chase a coin."

Yes, life would be hollow. It would be missing so much.

But what was she to do? She'd come this far. She'd survived this much. Either she could sit and sob, or she could keep moving forward.

Forward. There was always something ahead. Always something to strive for.

She saw the number beside her name. *Five.*

She would keep climbing. Ela. Phetan. Domi. Tolm. Four people. She could overcome four people. She *would* overcome four people.

She would move forward until there was no one else in front. Until she had something no one could take from her.

By will and strength, she'd hone herself into the greatest Adept there was. Then what could be taken from her? Nothing that mattered.

When she made it back to the Sanctum, there was a commotion going on outside the infirmary. Someone had likely been hurt—training exercise, perhaps.

She took a step toward it, but stopped. Two Initiates were running a litter, which bore a girl. A girl about her age, with familiar locks of straight black hair.

Reiva broke into a sprint.

"*Move*," she snapped, shoving her way through the crowd and following the litter-carriers. People tried to hold her back, telling her to let the *Viva* Initiates do their job. She ignored them, pressing forward.

At the door, someone tried to bar her entry—she shoved them aside with a burst of aether empowerment.

"Mylla!" she cried, finally catching up just as they brought the litter into a healing chamber.

The Initiates looked up in annoyance as Reiva barged in. "Hey!" barked one of them, a silver-fringed mantle around her shoulders. "You can't be—"

Reiva ignored her, going straight to Mylla's side. They'd lain her on a cot, with a pillow beneath her head.

Mylla's head lolled toward Reiva, and a jolt of fear went down her spine.

The girl's eyes were wide open, darting to and fro in a manic, senseless pattern. Her lips opened and closed like a fish plucked from water.

For but a moment, she seemed to focus on Reiva, and a strangled, incoherent sound came from her throat.

"Mylla," Reiva pleaded. "Mylla, what happened?" She turned to the Initiates who had carried Mylla in.

The *Viva* Initiate with the silver fringe made a distasteful expression, but sighed and began explaining. "Aether sickness. Your friend over-extended her soul. Someone found her a few minutes ago and came for us—thought it was a seizure."

Reiva swore. "Will she...?"

The Initiate looked away. "We'll see. But you really need to go, before—"

"Aether sickness?" called a masculine voice from the door.

The *Viva* Initiates snapped to attention. A full Adept had just stepped in—a man with curled locks of black hair and handsome features.

"Adept Gylos," announced the girl who had spoken to Reiva. "This *acolyta* was found minutes ago in the Trial Chamber. Symptoms suggest acute aether sickness."

Adept Gylos' grimaced. "And you?" He nodded to Reiva. "You found her, or you were with her when it happened?"

A hand of guilt seized Reiva's heart. "No, Adept."

Gylos grunted, motioning for her to step away from Mylla. "So you don't know anything to help."

Reiva slid back. "I'm her friend. She's *Ars Ventas*."

Gylos took Mylla's head in his hands, inspecting the motion of her eyes. "Doesn't matter which Art she holds. You didn't notice she was overtraining?"

The hand of guilt gripped tighter. "I asked about it this morning, and she said she was being careful."

"Well, she should have had someone supervising her. You recognized the danger. Next time, don't leave her alone."

A nascent gleam of hope lifted Reiva's spirits. "She'll recover then?"

Gylos gave her a grim look. "Perhaps. We'll know in the morning. Now go—we need to examine her."

Reiva swallowed, staring at Mylla's features. The Gallian girl kept repeating those strange motions, looking around at everything indiscriminately.

The *Viva* Initiates ushered her out of the room. Then they shut the door.

Reiva stood there for another minute before finally turning to leave.

No one was outside the infirmary anymore. The excitement was over, so they'd likely gone to the mess hall to tell what happened.

Finding she didn't have the stomach for dinner, Reiva made her way back to the dormitory. Domi said she had a Sixth Cohort friend in the infirmary. She'd see what information she could get.

At lunch the next day, Domi told her Mylla's condition had not improved. After the meal, Reiva had tried to go visit her, but was told she couldn't receive visitors, as it could worsen her mental strain.

Still, Reiva returned the next day. And the next day, and the day after that. Every time, they turned her away, until one week after Mylla's admittance to the infirmary, Reiva received the news that she had been discharged.

Not only discharged from the infirmary though—discharged from the Adept Corps. She had pushed herself too far—beyond the point of recovery. If she ever tried to wield aether again, it would almost certainly kill her.

She had washed out.

Reiva felt a pang in her chest. She thought back to the last conversation they'd shared. The shouting. She remembered the first one, years ago. The laughter. She'd never get another of those. When she asked Alyat, he refused to investigate where they had taken Mylla. Or if he knew, he refused to tell her.

"These things happen," he said. "Someday it'll be a friend bleeding out in your arms. You don't always get closure. Learn to live with it now. Learn to sleep with it—we've got an early start tomorrow."

She felt a prickle behind her eyes, then blinked it away.

She could weep elsewhere, alone. There was work to be done: she had a sword to sharpen, armor to polish.

She had sworn to serve, no matter what.

18

THE WORK OF A WARRIOR

MERE HOURS after receiving the news about Mylla—with a few scant shreds of fitful sleep under her belt—Reiva donned her armor and buckled on her sword.

For the past couple of years of their training, the Initiates had trained in full kit—hand-me-down sets of armor they looked after and tended to as though their own. Every morning of training, they were inspected to ensure they had shined their armor, hammered out any dents, and mended any tears or rends. Though they might have aides in a real campaign as full Adepts, that was no guarantee that they *always* would. As such, they needed to know how to care for their own gear and to be comfortable moving in it as though it were a second skin.

This gray morning, however, Reiva felt a different sort of gravity as she fastened her breastplate and tugged on her greaves. Today she was going on a real mission. The weapons wouldn't be dull practice blades. There wouldn't be rules about striking for the head and throat. People would be wounded, maimed, and killed.

When she showed up to Alyat's office, he took one look at her and smirked. "Nerves?"

She nodded, not trusting herself to speak. Her mentor was

dressed in his own armor, and he even had a sword buckled to his belt.

"Keep clutching your helmet like that and your fingers will cramp before you even get a chance to draw your sword."

"Right." She made a mental effort to ease her grip.

Alyat snorted, picking up a shield leaned against the wall. "Like I said, we won't be in the front lines. Come on, we've got some legionnaires to burden."

The sun had not yet risen by the time they got to the Third Gate of Lazarra. On the dewy grass outside, standing in the fog, was a detachment from the Second Legion. Reiva counted forty Orphans milling around—about half a company. Most of them were on their feet, packs sitting on the ground.

A man with a captain's insignia noticed their approach and strode over to meet them. He seemed unperturbed by the chill. "Adept Alyat," he said, snapping off a salute. "*Ave Imperator.* Captain Darin."

Alyat returned the greeting. "Well met, Captain. My apprentice, Reiva."

The captain gave her a stern nod, glancing at her mantle, with its conspicuous lack of silver. "First outing for you?"

"Yes, sir," she said, inwardly cringing at how loudly she'd spoken.

If the captain thought it amusing though, he gave no sign of it. The man's face was hard and impassive as chiseled stone. "The troops are ready when you are."

"Then lead the way," said Alyat.

The captain grunted and called an order for the legionnaires to muster. This was repeated by who Reiva presumed were the man's sergeants. In moments, they were all in ranks and ready to march. Reiva followed Alyat to the rear of the file. Eventually, she knew, they'd walk at the middle and even the front, but for now Reiva's role was simply to observe and absorb the energy of legionnaires on the move.

She'd practiced marching in the Sanctum of course, but they were all Initiates. Right away, she caught the difference in attitude. Whereas she and her cohort had marched with an eye toward receiving marks on their evaluations, these men and women marched with real intent. There was grim certainty to it.

That made sense. Sanctum marching exercises weren't much more than loops around the training fields. This was out in the open. Of course, this close to the capital city there was little chance of anything happening. Violence was a ways away. But it was ahead of them, and every step was a willful approach, a bringing near of pain and death.

And it was a lengthy approach. Even with her aether-toughened constitution, Reiva began to feel a burn between her shoulders from her pack. Her neck ached from the weight of the helmet. And still they went on.

A legionnaire had to march twenty miles a day in full kit—at minimum—to be considered fit for service. She had the advantage of aether, but these men and women only had their bodies and their discipline.

When a rest was called, they'd wordlessly move off the road, drop their packs. Reiva had been about to sit on the ground when she realized none of the legionnaires were doing so—they were kneeling. She did the same. Alyat gave her an approving nod. As she took a sip from her waterskin, she guessed at the reason. Sitting down might let the body ease too much, and then the muscles would have to warm up again on the march. Kneeling did not permit that.

Before she knew it, they were on their feet again, on the march.

Hours ticked by like that. The only substantial rest they took was during the hottest part of the day. Legionnaires nibbled on salted meat from their packs then, washing it down with a few swallows from their waterskins. Nothing much, though. The risk of a cramped stomach on the march wasn't worthwhile. They'd eat a full meal for dinner—everything until then was just about the most efficient way to get from one location to the next with the minimum necessary discomfort.

Reiva had never found marching exercises exciting, but she had underestimated just how boring a full day of the stuff could be. For the first hour or two, she'd fixated on every hill they crossed, every copse of trees they passed. For one, it had been years since she'd been this far from the city. Two, she was hyper vigilant for any threats.

Alyat watched all this with a wry look. "You know," he drawled, "we're not getting anywhere near there until tomorrow evening."

Heat rose to her face. "I know."

Eventually, the novelty of it wore off though, and she found herself drifting off into spirals of thought. Initiates went on field missions as they became available—a combination of chance and the schedules of their mentors—so there was little consistency in who had gone on one. Tolm had, of that Reiva was sure. Word was he had performed—as was to be expected—excellently. Phetan had done well.

Domi's success had been assured. Her Art was particularly well suited to working with the marine legionnaires, so she had been one of the first Initiates to go on a field mission. She'd spoken breathlessly about the beauty of the sea, the sheer scale of it. She had not been quite as excited about her work—pushing the ships to sail faster, essentially. "We didn't even run into any pirates," she had pouted. "I didn't get to bathe for two weeks either."

Reiva's mission wouldn't be lasting that long—it was planned for about a week, perhaps a week and a half. The specifics would depend on how things shook out with the bandits.

Besides guarding the city of Lazarra, the Second Legion oversaw the protection of the Ixian Reach—the land making up the heart of the Empire. This was territory that had been Lazarra's since the days of the Republic. It was a point of pride for the Empire that the rule of law was well-maintained in her heartland, as well as a matter of practicality. One could hardly conquer other lands when one's own was out of order.

But humans were humans, and now and then something slipped through the cracks. The particular thing that had slipped through the cracks this time was a roving band of bandits called the Sons of Stoborro. They had taken up residence in a less-patrolled part of the reach roughly forty miles from Lazarra. It was hilly terrain that jutted up against long stretches of forest from which the bandits would emerge, then fade back into.

Towns in the area had petitioned for aid, and now aid was coming. Step by step, they were coming.

Dinner was a simple affair—meat stew. It seemed that whatever was on hand had been tossed in—which meant some salted beef and a couple of chickens that had been caught in the afternoon. Legionnaires carried their own wooden dish and a pewter spoon. When the cook gave the word, everyone lined up according to rank and received a helping from the pot.

Alyat was at the fore, naturally, while Reiva was at the very back. She didn't mind particularly, but her stomach did loudly make its wishes known as she waited—much to her chagrin.

Despite her skepticism, the stew was flavorful. Alyat said that a company's cook was as essential—if not more so—as its captain, and Reiva concurred.

They slept in the open air that night, Reiva using her folded up mantle as a pillow. She did not feel the cold—it had been almost impossible for her since at least a year ago.

After another day of marching, they rendezvoused with the advance deployment—a select group of Legion Scouts encamped with a small number of legionnaires. Alyat brought Reiva to the officers' meeting.

The Scouts' faces were smeared with dirt, their clothes dyed a mixture of browns and greens. Dressed in camouflage, they would have spent the last few nights surveying the forests and seeking out the Sons of Stoborro.

The captain greeted the Scouts curtly, then asked for their report on the bandits.

One of the Scouts stepped forward. "We've found the core of their operations," she said. "They keep patrols, but they're sloppy and irregular. Stoborro himself holds court in a camp about three miles northeast of where we are now. The camp has elevation and good tree cover, and of an estimated forty bandits total, about thirty live in the camp. If it weren't for the noise they make, you could walk within ten yards of them and not know they were there."

"Only ten or so of the bandits are out on patrol, then?" asked the captain.

"Aye, sir. One of my men caught some chatter that they're planning a large raid on the town two miles north of here."

The captain grunted. "We have the element of surprise for now. What are the odds we can keep it?"

The other Scout officer at the meeting, a man, spoke up. "The way I see it, Captain, we have two options. If we wait for them to move out so we could strike them while they're strung out on the move, it would be down to luck. The bandits patrols are lazy and disorganized, which makes it impossible to predict. If one stumbles over us, we'd have to take the gamble on no one noticing he's missing."

Alyat stroked his beard. "Not risk worth taking."

The male Scout concurred. "Our team agrees that a sudden strike in the early morning would be preferable. The bandits spend much of the night carousing, so the ideal opportunity would be sometime between fourth and sixth hour."

"What's the layout?" asked the captain.

The female Scout began sketching in the mud with a stick. "This circle is the camp. This line"—she said, tracing a winding trail toward the northwest—"is their usual route when they go out raiding. Stoborro himself sleeps in the center, surrounded by his most trusted lieutenants. There are hostages in this area as well—mostly women the bandits have taken from the neighboring villages. The lion's share of the plunder is with Stoborro, who deals it out as he sees fit. Most of the bandits sleep in tents and crude shelters radiating out from the chief. The tree cover is thicker on the western side, which is also where most of their lookouts are positioned. Approach from the south is almost impossible given the recent rains—a sheer cliff of mud."

Alyat scowled. "Meaning we'll have to circle around the encampment to get at them from the back."

"Correct. My Scouts have picked out two routes—one looping in front and over to the north, the other under and up to the east."

"Then we'll split into two forces," said the captain, "and move in during the night. Stay out of sight and go quietly. Then, at the signal, swoop in and crush them before they know what hit them. You run into anyone on the way, kill them. One hour after daybreak, I want this finished."

THE COMPANY soon learned the plan, and the officers divided their troops into the appropriate detachments. Reiva and Alyat were with the unit that would attack from the east. It wasn't lost on Reiva that this was the group less likely to encounter trouble on the way, given that they didn't need to cross the bandit's regular route. She said as much to her mentor, who acknowledged the point.

"If it were just me, I'd be on the riskier route. When you're a full Adept, you'd damn well better put yourself there. That's what you're here for."

Reiva clenched her jaw. "So why put us on the eastern force? I know how to fight, and you're here."

"Because mistakes happen. Plans fall apart. It would be a disservice to the legionnaires on the northern detachment—who are already in more danger—that they also work with the added responsibility of protecting an Initiate. Every single legionnaire in this company, every Scout on that team, would die for you without question. Adepts are the most valuable asset in the Empire's war chest.

"You say you know how to fight? In a ring, sure. On a practice field. But this is war. There will be casualties—gods send mostly on the enemies' side. You're still in training. You haven't seen the ugliness of it yourself, understand? Eventually, aye, you'll go where the fighting is worst, where death lies heaviest on the battlefield, and you'll lead the charge—but only once you've become the sort of person who *can* lead that charge. What if you lose concentration and can't maintain your magic in the melee? What if you overtax yourself and come down with aether sickness? People *will* die to keep you alive. So you'd better be damn certain that you're someone worth dying for. You owe it to the legionnaires who will follow you, and who will fall in front of you when it comes to that. Not if, *when*. Understand?"

Reiva ducked her head. "I understand."

"Good. Now get your kit in order—we're marching in ten."

The company left their packs and supplies with the small legionnaire force that had been part of the advance deployment. All Reiva took was her sword, shield, what she was wearing, her waterskin, and two pieces of salted meat.

She and Alyat left their mantles behind in the camp. Stealth missions were one of the few rare instances where it was acceptable for an Adept to do such a thing.

The weather turned sour right away. First the rain drizzled, then it poured. The forest floor turned to mud, sucking at Reiva's boots. Her feet went numb from the chill, and she was shivering beneath her cloak. Visibility was so poor, she could only see Alyat's back in front of her and the vague outline of the legionnaire in front of him. At the front of the file was one of the Scout officers—the man, the woman having gone with the northern force. Another Scout, Reiva knew, was further on, ensuring they didn't trudge headlong into an ambush.

The march—if it could truly be called a march—was miserable. Even though Reiva's magic helped keep her warm against the sopping cold, before long she felt a headache building behind her eyes. For as long and hard as she'd trained, she still was nowhere near Alyat in terms of aether tolerance. She forced herself to endure the full force of the cold like anyone else, preserving her stamina for the fight itself.

Though the bandit camp lay just three miles from where they had set out, the elongated route they took to avoid detection and get into place added considerable distance. The elements slowed their pace even further, stretching the trek into what seemed hours. Reiva doubted whether they'd even make it to the camp in time to execute the assault as planned.

It was while muddling through such thoughts that she saw the body.

The corpse lay to the side, staring off with vacant eyes. The man's whole expression summed up to a look that might have been about to transform into full blown shock, if only death hadn't come upon him so quickly.

The sheeting rain had soaked him to the bone, which gave an odd cleanliness to the precise slice in his throat. The blood washed away too quickly, and his roughspun clothes were too dark to tell where it had flowed.

He must have been a bandit on patrol, caught unawares by the vanguard Scout.

All this she saw in an instant.

She lost her sense of self, her foot slid out from under her. A half-scream escaped her lips, and then a strong set of hands grabbed her.

The legionnaire who'd caught her helped her regain her footing. "Adept?" he said, his voice muffled by the downpour.

"I'm all right," she said, not bothering to correct him on her rank. "Thank you."

He nodded, waving her on. She was grateful for the rain then, obscuring her features and cooling the embarrassment flushing through her face.

It's just a body, she reprimanded herself. *You'll see plenty more before this is said and done.*

Alyat must have heard her because he glanced back. Seeing her to be fine, though, he moved on.

Reiva found herself wondering how many men Alyat had killed. From what she knew of his work with the Corps, he didn't spend that much time in combat. His Art wasn't as easily applicable to war as hers—though he assured her it was a useful one. He mostly worked with Legion Intelligence or Imperial diplomats.

He hadn't lost a step at the sight of the corpse though. Someday she'd be like that—not having a second thought at the sight of a man with his throat slashed.

Some people baked bread, some carved stone. Some killed.

This was the work Reiva had to learn. She squared her shoulders and set her feet confidently as she followed Alyat into the gloom. Years of training had brought her to this. She knew how to swing a sword and heft a shield. She knew where to strike and how to kill.

She was going to seize honor and glory—today was a necessary step on that journey.

ALYAT RAISED HIS HAND, crouching. Reiva followed his lead, knowing that the file would come to a silent stop. The rain had let up—not entirely, but enough that it would be possible for the bandits to overhear them if they made too much noise. Because if they had come to a stop, that meant they were at the camp.

Alyat crept forward. Reiva followed. All her fatigue evaporated from her, adrenaline coursing through her veins, sending tremors through her limbs. She fell into her well-practiced rhythm of breath, seeking the stillness of mind needed to keep one's head.

They moved uphill. Thanks to the rain, the earth was muddy and loose, forcing them to haul themselves by roots and branches. Every slight clatter of armor buckles, every slap of the scabbard on her thigh made her heart twist. Any second now, they would be found out —she was certain of it. Or the squelch of mud would give them away. Or someone would slip and go crashing through the brush.

Alyat put his hand for stillness again. Reiva was halfway from one root to the next when she froze. She waited like that for what seemed minutes. Her muscles burned, so she shunted a measure of aether to strengthen them.

What were they waiting for?

And then she heard the voices. Gruff and harsh.

Slowly, Reiva lifted her head.

Two bandits were walking along, just twenty feet above. They were moving perpendicular to them—but if one moved his head just an inch toward them, just stole a glance...

Then, like phantoms, two Scouts melted out from the trees and brush, looking less like humans than spirits of the forest. In unison, they clamped their hands over the bandits' mouths and cut their throats.

The bandits thrashed against the Scouts' grasps, but the Scouts did not relent. Their grips held like iron vises as they lowered the bandits' stilling forms to the ground.

So quickly, death had come to them. Reiva swallowed, acutely aware of how her own throat was exposed.

One of the Scouts melted back into the trees, the other made a signal. The file moved on.

When near the top, they formed into ranks. It wasn't as neat as the legion preferred and drilled—but the terrain simply wouldn't allow it. That was fine—the legions prided themselves on adaptability. They'd fight as they were required, and they would fight to the end.

The Scout who had been bringing up the rear slipped by Reiva, moving to join his compatriot and Alyat at the fore. They conferred briefly in hushed tones. Alyat motioned for Reiva to join them. She crept closer, still terrified of making too loud a sound.

The rain had nearly ceased.

Reiva got to them just as the Scout who had left returned. Her face was hard-set as she murmured, "The north-attacking force is in position. The captain will give the signal when he knows we are ready."

Alyat cast a glance over the arrayed ranks. Reiva took the sight in: about twenty legionnaires, dripping wet, miserable, chilled to the bone.

"Tell him we're ready," grumbled Alyat.

The Scout nodded, slipping away.

A few seconds later, Reiva heard what sounded like a birdcall. It was still too early for birdsong—but hopefully no one in the camp would notice.

Alyat waved them on, and Reiva kept pace with him. She still hadn't drawn her sword—Alyat had been emphatic that marching through these conditions with a naked blade was an easy way to gut yourself by mistake.

As they crested the hill, Reiva caught sight of the camp. It was just as the scouts had described. She easily picked out the central tent where Stoborro must have slept with his bounty—its peak rose higher than all the others.

Alyat pushed down on her head, nearly planting her face into the mud.

She grunted, but nodded, keeping her face low. She took a handful of mud and smeared it over her face and helmet. The sun wasn't up yet, so there was no risk of rays glinting off her armor, but every bit of camouflage helped.

One by one, legionnaires crawled into place beside them, behind them.

Reiva narrowed her eyes, trying to glimpse the Scouts. Was one in those bushes? And another up in the trees?

She turned toward the north, trying to spy any signs of their comrades. Nothing. If she hadn't had the word of the Scouts, she would have sworn she and the legionnaires were alone with the bandits.

And then, the waiting. Bugs and slugs crawled onto her arms, brought up by the rains. The cold of the mud was disgusting, but she thought back to all those wretched morning exercises when she had first made it to the Sanctum. Compared to that, this was easy—she was just lying in wait.

And she waited, and she waited.

And then, another birdcall.

They got up from the earth. Slowly, swords came clear from sheaths. Shields were hefted. Prayers murmured.

Alyat's voice was at her ear in a hot whisper. "Keep to the line. Shield high. When I say *down*, you put your head down fast as lightning. Don't overuse your fire—aether sickness in combat has undone many Adepts. Understood?"

She nodded. "Understood."

Alyat grunted, rolling his neck side to side. "And be sure to yell—gets the blood up."

One second ticked by.

Another.

A horn blasted from the north.

The legionnaires yelled—and Reiva yelled with them, the sound torn from her in a rush of instinctual fervor.

And then they were running.

Bandits were stumbling from their camps, half-dressed or totally nude, bleary eyed and scrambling for weapons.

Arrows zipped from out of nowhere, skewering throats and sprouting from chests.

By the time Reiva and the legionnaires reached the tents, the camp was already in the grip of panic and terror.

Reiva's world narrowed to the cone in front of her. A legionnaire covered her left, Alyat her right. All that mattered was the space right ahead.

A bandit with a club stumbled forward, only for Alyat's sword to dart forward like a snake and drop him, his battle cry dying in his throat.

They easily swept through the outer reach of tents. By the time they got further in though, they hit stiffer resistance. The greater number of the bandits had massed together in the center of the camp, surrounding their leader—and perhaps more significantly, their treasure.

"Man up, boys!" bellowed a voice equal parts annoyed and enraged. "Double share to anyone who brings me a buckethead's sword!"

That must have been Stoborro, and the promise energized his men.

Eagerness and the promise of reward were little match for legion drilling and equipment, though.

Even less of a match for Adept magic.

Alyat jumped forward, slightly ahead of the line, sword hand outstretched.

A miniature sun burst to life in his hand. The bandits' faces crinkled into agonized squints. Some of them even covered their faces. They were like a scene illuminated by a bolt of lightning.

And the front line was just seconds away from slamming into them.

Reiva's breathing turned shallow—she forced herself to deepen it.

Five yards, four.

Her grip tightened on her sword—so tight her fingers went numb.

She saw her mark. A man with a hatchet that looked more suited to chopping wood than people. Alyat's blast of light had left him peering around in confusion, clutching his weapon to his chest in bewilderment.

In fear, even.

For a moment, she felt a snag of sympathy in her stomach. He wouldn't even see it coming.

She hesitated, her sword arm pulled back, ready to stab. The legionnaires around her pushed forward without slowing a beat, milling through their enemies and trodding them underfoot.

The bandit finally saw her, baring his teeth in a snarl and raising his hatchet.

A groan slipped from between her clenched teeth, and she stabbed for his gut.

The blade sank in, its well-kept edge parting flesh easily. The man looked down at it in shock, his lips curling back.

But he was still standing. He roared, lifting the hatchet high overhead, about to split her helmet and soul as far as he dared.

Alyat's sword flashed through his neck, removing his head in a crimson spray.

She spat, trying to clear the coppery tang of blood from her mouth, when she realized another bandit was stepping forward—and he looked perfectly able to see her. He swung a club in a double-handed grip.

Reiva yelled, hefting her shield high. She channeled a rush of aether to her arm and shoulder, and her body took the force of the blow as easily as it had taken the drizzling rain. She followed through with a stab to the gut, then another to the chest. The bandit shrieked, stumbling backward into his fellow.

Reiva stabbed again, this time striking him square in the face. He went down after that.

She could still taste blood. Instead of letting herself think about it, she threw herself forward again. She had to keep pace with the line. She had to maintain the shield wall.

Every moment flowed into the next in a frantic medley of images and sensations. She felt her sword biting into bone. Her boots churning mud and blood and viscera underfoot. The wails of the wounded and dying became a choral counterpoint to the metallic clash of weapons and armor.

As the bandits dispersed, so did the legionnaires. The ranks no longer served their purpose, so the battle turned into a melee. By now, though, the number of bandits had dwindled such that it was often two legionnaires to every one of theirs. Reiva stuck to Alyat's side. Her mentor blinded another one with a burst of light, and she followed through with the kill strike.

A few tried to run—these dropped with arrows in the back.

Reiva stepped aside as a bandit swung an ax for her head, sending a jet of fire into his face before stabbing him through the throat. As he went down, she cast her eyes around, taking a deep breath. Her head ached with the light pressure of minor aether sickness.

Thankfully, the battle was almost over. The legionnaires were closing in on the central tent, where Stoborro—

A flash of movement in the corner of her eye.

Reiva whirled on it, raising her shield against any surprise attack.

At the edge of the forest, right where the trees grew thick, she had seen a man, thickly built with a fine leopard skin around his shoulders, running. And he'd had a girl hardly older than Reiva in his clutches.

Stoborro.

"Alyat!" she called, whipping her head around.

Her mentor was in the midst of disemboweling a bandit while simultaneously blinding another. Amidst the din and chaos, he didn't seem to hear her.

Reiva grit her teeth, turning back to where she had seen the bandit leader vanish into the woods.

She started running.

Reiva tore through the forest, sword clutched in a white-knuckled grip. She threw her shield aside. She didn't even stop to check if anyone was following her, pumping her legs full of aether so that she'd outstrip the pace any normal human could achieve.

Just when she was beginning to fear she had missed the bandit leader and blown right past them—she caught sight of them.

Stoborro was trying to hush her, but then he caught sight of Reiva and put a knife to the girl's throat. "Not one more step or I kill 'er!"

She stopped, cursing the uneven ground below her as it almost made her trip.

Stoborro bared an ugly grin. "A *girl* legionnaire? Hah! That's all they can muster up for me?"

"We brought enough for you to turn tail and run."

The bandit's mouth turned down in a frown. A trickle of blood ran down the girl's neck. "Say that again. See what happens."

Reiva bit her tongue.

"Now here's what's going to happen, *lass*. I'm going to walk out of this forest. If I hear even one twig snap behind me, the little lady gets it. Same if I hear even one whistling arrow or one twanging bowstring —I'll slit 'er throat so fast she'll die before I can be hit. Now nod if you understand me."

Reiva nodded slowly. Her mind was racing, her heart pounding.

"Drop your sword."

She did.

Think! Think!

Stoborro took a step away, tugging his hostage with him. "Move!" he snarled. The girl whimpered, screwing her eyes shut.

Reiva clenched her fists. She couldn't throw fire and hit only Stoborro—she didn't have that sort of finesse. She couldn't run for help or they'd lose track of him. And if they *did* find him, then he'd follow through on his threat to kill the girl.

Another step, then another.

"Wait!" Reiva called.

Stoborro glared, knife pressing into the girl's flesh.

"Take me instead. She's an innocent."

Stoborro looked at her like she'd gone mad. Reiva reached for her breastplate buckle and unfastened it, letting it drop to the ground. She drew the knife on her hip and tossed it to the side.

She put her hands up. "Take me instead. You can ransom me, and you'll get more than for some village girl."

The bandit leader's eyes glinted. She had his attention.

His eyes moved over her slowly, head to toe.

Slowly, Stoborro nodded, his lip splitting into another wide grin. "Step away from the sword, come 'ere slowly."

She did, taking care to keep as great a distance from her weapons as was possible.

"Let her go, and you can take me."

"I'm calling the shots here!"

From the distance, the sound of shouting voices carried through the trees. The legionnaires were drawing near.

Stoborro swore. He tossed the village girl roughly to the side, then sprang forward to grab Reiva by her hair.

Reiva let him grab her hair—but she clamped one hand over the wrist of his knife-hand. Immediately, he snarled and tried to slash her —but he hadn't been expecting for the flesh on his arm to start *burning*.

Reiva poured as much power as she could into setting her hand ablaze. Stoborro shrieked, dropping the knife on instinct. Reiva punched him in the nose with her other fist, adding a hearty dose of aether enhancement to the strike. The resulting *crunch* was eminently satisfying.

Pouring on more aether empowerment to her muscles, she put the bandit down on his face, pinning his arms to his back.

"Try to get loose and I burn more than just your arm."

Stoborro groaned and wailed. "Where's the mantle? It's the law! Adepts *have to* wear mantles!"

Reiva was actually impressed—a bandit leader was quoting Lazarran law to her.

"We do," drawled Alyat, stepping down the hill at an almost leisurely pace. "But we don't like to get them dirty. Pick a cleaner hiding spot next time."

He nodded to Reiva, and she felt pride blossom in her heart.

A FEW HOURS LATER, the bandit camp was clear of all stragglers and hostages. The wounded were tended to—Alyat and Reiva providing assistance with their aether channeling—and the bandits' holdings were catalogued and appropriated.

After they made camp that night, well away from the forest and with the surviving bandits under heavy guard, Alyat and Reiva sat by a cook fire.

"So," he began, "what went wrong?"

Reiva swallowed. She had hoped they would start with the successes.

"I hesitated."

"How many times?"

"Just the first time. I struck him but...I couldn't kill him."

"What changed?"

She looked down at her hands. They were clean now, but she still thought she could feel blood underneath her fingernails. "You did it so effortlessly. And I realized that if I couldn't do that, then I'd end up the dead one."

"Good lesson. You didn't kill Stoborro, though."

Reiva nodded. "I didn't. I don't know why."

"Did you want to kill him?"

"Yes," she answered, surprised at how easy it was to say.

"Why?" Alyat's voice stayed the same flat pitch.

"He was going to take that girl away. And when I played my trick on him…he gave me this look that turned my stomach."

"So why not finish him off? You had all authority to do so as part of this mission—he's going to be executed tomorrow morning. You had the right of self defense as an Adept Initiate. What stopped you?"

She drew her lips into a thin line. "It's not…an easy thing. When I was in the melee in the camp, that was one thing. It's not personal, in that moment. Everything is just weapons and faces and body parts. But when it's one-on-one like that…I know that doesn't make sense but…" She spread her hands. "That's what happened."

Alyat nodded slowly. He sat like that for so long, Reiva wondered if he expected her to say more. But then he said, "No, it is understandable. Perfectly understandable. Listen kid, I've taken plenty of Initiates on field missions—taken plenty before you and I'll take plenty after. There's two sorts of extremes I'm wary of. On the one hand"—he held out his right fist—"you see the ones who can't do it at all. They lose their breakfast, they piss themselves, and you practically have to haul them out of the battle to keep them alive. Then they quiver for the next week. They stare at their blade, and they can't believe they've harmed another person. A lot of folks wash out, then and there.

"On the other hand, you see the ones who take to it too readily. They even enjoy it. They see it as a game, sometimes. And those ones, I'll tell you right now, can make it *very* far in the Adept Corps. Sure, there's a few like me who raise questions about the wisdom of that, but we're all killers, in the end."

Reiva digested that. "And I'm not either of those."

"No. You're in the middle, like most people. *But*, you have an inclination. You tilt more to this"—he raised his left hand—"and you'll have to be wary of that your whole life. You might not feel it right now, but I saw you. When you manage to silence the hesitation and doubt, you're a warrior through and through. You'll do well like that. But always remember, the work of a warrior is just that—*work*. You can take pleasure in a job well done, such as it is, but never let yourself forget the severity of what we're involved in. We're death-dealers, kid. And you don't want to wake up one day and realize you're more comfortable around corpses than the living."

Reiva's stomach turned. "Yes, sir," she said quietly. "That...I don't want to become that."

Alyat nodded. "Good. That Flame of yours will push you to it, push you to get angry. Use it as a tool, but don't let it control you."

"I understand."

"Good." He scratched at his beard. "Now, your homework. I know your days off are important to you, but if you want to come out on top —like you say you want—then you'll have to invest extra time."

"I already train on my days off."

"Yeah, but I've got something else for you—so shut up and listen. I want you to go to the gladiator matches. Get a feel for the fights. Get used to seeing violence. It'll help keep you from freezing up in a fight. You should also practice analyzing combat—professional combat, not the piddling stuff with holds barred and tap outs you get up to in the fighting ring. Now, under what circumstances should you *stop* going to the gladiator fights?"

Reiva felt that uncomfortable turning in her stomach again. "Bloodlust."

"Right. Look for that middle way and stay on it. Understand?"

"Yes."

"All right. Think you can fall asleep?"

"I think so."

"Good, because I don't sing lullabies."

Reiva snorted. "Of course not."

Alyat cracked a smile. "All in all, good work, kid. High marks. You've earned your silver."

Reiva sat up straighter. She couldn't have asked for anything more.

19

———

JUST CAUTIOUS

By the time Reiva returned from her first field mission, Levin and Artha were gone. She took her first free day available to go visit them, only to find the bakery run by another man whose face she didn't know. He was Talynisti—so Levin had sold the place to one of their own, after all—and he had no idea who Reiva was. So they had kept her a secret. She was grateful for it, even as it hurt.

She bought a loaf of bread that day, picked at it on the walk back to the Sanctum, before ultimately giving the more than half that remained to a beggar. Her stomach was hollow, and it just wasn't the same bread as what Levin had baked.

Now and then, as the weeks and months rolled past in the slow, breakneck pace that is time's nature, she would suddenly miss the taste of Levin's bread, the crunch of the crust, the warmth of it on her tongue and in her stomach. And she would wonder if Artha was still alive. She would wonder if the climate was treating her better, or if she lay in the ground now. And she would try to convince herself that they were well and healthy, and they were still thinking of her. It was a better fantasy than the alternative.

She would also think, in those moments, of Mylla, wondering

where she had been sent. Back to her village in Gallia? Had her symptoms retreated, leaving her more or less like any other person? Or had the sickness refused to abate, leaving her mind forever scarred? Of all things, she refused to countenance the dreadful rumor she had heard on her first day of training—that all that Mylla would know the rest of her days was a dark cell, sequestered from the world.

Again, Reiva chose to believe in the easier possibility—if only so she could go about her days without chains of guilt hanging off her.

Without the bakery to occupy her free time, she visited the arena as Alyat had suggested. Unlike the Nine-knuckle House, fights in the arena happened with weapons. They had an obscene number of spectators, and there was enough blood to soak a field. Gladiators died—not often, since the training and equipping of a gladiator was often a significant investment, and it made no good economic sense to create a professional fighter only to throw him away in a single match—but they did die. The crowd loved those in particular.

For Reiva, it was all an exercise in observation. She would study the fighters as they stepped into the sandy pit, observe how they carried themselves and confronted one another. She examined their stance, their grips. These men—and they were mostly men, though female gladiator matches were a well-attended novelty when put on —were largely convicts or slaves. Even though they were not likely to die, there would be consequences for failure. Beatings from their owners, cut rations. Success, on the other hand, was well-rewarded— good food, prostitutes, even a shortening of their tenure as a gladiator if they performed exceptionally well.

The stakes were not too unlike those faced by a legionnaire in the field—few things could matter more to a gladiator than what transpired in the arena, whether the day ended in victory or defeat.

So Reiva watched, and she grew numb to the blood and gore. She began to look forward to the matches, looking up the names of who would be contending. She even developed a few favorites and began jockeying to get her free day when they would be in the pit. Once or twice, she placed bets—not unsuccessfully, though the thrill of winning meant more to her than the money. The Corps paid for her necessities, and she didn't spend coin on much else besides a ticket to the arena and food while she was out.

Her fights at the Nine-Knuckle House were affected as well. She didn't realize it at first, but one day Polnoff pulled her aside after a match, nodded to her face and muttered, "Good show, Red—but next time, maybe not look like you're enjoying it so much. People are getting scared of going up against you."

It was a somewhat off-putting revelation, but not an unwelcome one.

She never froze again during a field mission. Not when men clutched at spilled intestines and begged for mercy, not when their flesh crackled and sent up acrid fumes under the blistering force of her fire.

The Flame within her was pleased, and she was pleased in turn.

In her fifth year as an Adept, she climbed to number four in the rankings, surpassing Ela. Only Domi and Phetan, who continued dancing back and forth between second and third, stood between her and Tolm.

As the frequency of field missions increased and the final year of their training drew near, the elite Initiates spent more and more of their time together. At first, Reiva felt guilty about this. She remembered how Mylla had called her out for spending no time with those who had once been her friends.

The problem was, hardly anyone else was going to be left. Socializing and building alliances and relationships with the lower ranked Initiates was an almost pointless endeavor—you hardly knew who would even still be around by the end of the month, let alone the year or the overall training period.

That said, it wasn't *only* the elites who spent time together. There were others, not quite as high in the rankings, but who were expected to maintain their position throughout the course and likely endure into full commissioning. Caulo, for example, was still hanging around. After speaking to him on and off throughout her time in the

Sanctum, Reiva once again found him eating at the same table as her. If he thought it odd that Mylla was no longer present, their old trio long-since broken, he never mentioned it, and neither did she.

Years had passed, and they had all changed.

Phetan was less obnoxious than he had been. He still burned with envy for Tolm and took every opportunity to display his own skill, but he had learned to be cautions and precise. He didn't go out of his way to make a fool of himself when he knew Tolm would outclass him.

Ela was beneath Reiva in the rankings, but she hardly showed any difference in her attitude toward Reiva. That surprised Reiva, since Ela was an incredibly proud girl. Reiva had once said as much to Domi when they were alone in the baths, and the other girl had shrugged. "It's because she's resigned to it, Reiva. Hell, I'm resigned to it. I wouldn't be surprised if you passed me up next week, or next year, though I doubt it'll take that long. Hardly anyone has the same drive as you and Tolm. Sure, I keep Phetan on his toes, but not with the same tenacity you have. I swear, sometimes you get this look in your eyes and it's like you're fighting for your life—even while you're in the safest place in the world."

Maybe the safest from a military perspective, Reiva thought, but not from a status perspective. In fact, almost anywhere else in Lazarra would be safer. She could go out on the streets with her red mantle and receive deference and obsequiousness like she was a goddess enfleshed—the Sanctum was the only place, save the Emperor's presence—where Reiva was acutely aware of just how precarious her position was.

It baffled her beyond words how casually Domi could talk about the rankings.

"So, you're all right with where you are?" she asked eventually.

The sea-worker shrugged. "Third place? Could be worse. Fourth, once you pass me? Still good in my book. I'm the only *Ars Thalassan* wielder in Seventh Cohort—as long as I don't screw up royally, I have a sure spot in the Corps. They could always use more of us on the sea patrols. Pirates have been uppity lately. I hear marine legionnaires are getting more bold in requisitioning supplies, arms, even Adepts when we can be spared. So yeah, I'm all right with where I am. Graduate, get my commission, spend my years kicking around the sea. What's not to like?"

Domi leaned her head back, closing her eyes and taking a deep breath. "The smell of salt water, the sounds of a dozen different port towns. We'll have shore leave, I'm sure—lots of fun to have in towns where you'll never be seen again. At least, not for a while," she added with a laugh.

Reiva marveled. How different Domi's way of looking at things was. It almost made her question why she was taking things so seriously...

But then her old instincts reasserted themselves.

That's the sort of thinking that will lead to a slip. You can't afford to count on a commission with the marines. You need to distinguish yourself for field service. You need to be too good to ignore. You need to be the best.

Domi laughed again, and Reiva realized she had cracked one eye open. "You're making the face again."

"What?"

The other girl shook her head. "Never mind. Say, you've got a free day coming up?"

"I do," Reiva said hesitantly. She guarded her free days zealously. If Domi was about to suggest something silly like—

"And you like the arena, right? Gladiators and all that?"

Reiva blinked. "I go when I can."

"How about we go as a group? It's not often so many of us are home at once. I think Ela's coming back from a field mission this afternoon. We can ask the table at dinner."

Reiva perked up. "All of us go see the games? That sounds...nice."

Domi sighed. "Yes, it does sound nice. I swear, you're hopeless."

"Hopeless?" asked Reiva, smirking. "How so?"

"Because anyone else would have thought to invite the rest of us months ago. What—are you scared our perception of you will change once we see you drooling over some blood sport?"

Reiva scoffed. "No, and I don't *drool*. I just enjoy the fights."

"Mhmm. But those gladiators must be quite the physical specimens, no?"

"Of course—their whole lives center on training for the games. You can see their strength and discipline in every movement."

Domi sighed again. "I mean, they're handsome? Like you might want to spend a night with one after his victory?"

Reiva's mouth shut with a *click.*

The others talked like this—a lot, actually. Ever since their third or fourth year, this sort of thing had become a common enough point of conversation—at first just between the girls, but eventually someone (probably Domi, Reiva imagined) had shattered a barrier and the whole group was speaking freely of their romantic aspirations.

And Reiva just...had never had that. It was like she was missing something the others had—she never had that ache to hold someone else, the heart-shuddering desire to wrap herself around a man.

And she normally was able to just avoid the subject.

"I...no, I don't feel like that."

Domi frowned. "Never? I know you come from Talynis, but you've been in Lazarra for five years now, Reiva. You can open up about this." Her lips curled into a sly smile. "I promise I won't tell. A woman's oath."

"I really have no interest in that sort of thing."

Domi shrugged. "If you say so."

WHEN THE DAY CAME, five of them set out from the Sanctum: Reiva, Domi, Phetan, Caulo, and Ela. As per regulations, they wore their red mantles—all of them with silver fringes. Reiva had hardly been in public with such a number of other Initiates—aside from public functions such as triumphal parades in the aftermath of a conquest —and so she was acutely aware of how much attention they drew as they made their way to the arena.

When they reached the arena, the throng of people in front

rapidly parted. The others stepped forward like this was second nature, and after a moment, Reiva realized it had become familiar to her as well. She had become accustomed to the special treatment an Adept received. She just felt awkward now that it was a group of them—now that she had more opportunity to observe how people reacted to an Initiate. She didn't have eyes in the back of her head, so when she was by herself she didn't catch it as much—but now she could see it plainly. The deference—the fear, even—that common citizens displayed toward them.

And why shouldn't they display such reverence? Adepts were more than human. They were the chosen ones, the Emperor's finest machine of war, the great engine of Imperial conquest. So what if they got to skip the line at the arena, and so what if they were led to the best seats—among senators and retired legion commanders—without hesitation? They were going to put their lives on the line so that all these people could continue living behind the shelter of the Lazarran walls and borders, so they could spend their day watching men beat and hack one another for entertainment.

Yes, Reiva had earned this for all she had put in—and she leaned in eagerly when the horn sounded and the warriors stepped into the pit.

The day's events began with a simple duel—two relatively well known gladiators duking it out with shields and swords. From what Reiva gathered, there was some sort of perceived slight from one to the other. They did that sort of thing now and then, try to tell a story, to create some dramatic tension around the fight. None of that truly mattered—all Reiva needed was the fight itself.

Domi, however, was rapidly caught up in it. She leaned forward as one gladiator bellowed to the other about how he had insulted the man's sister. Or...cousin? Reiva wasn't paying close enough attention. But as the men drew close, weapons raised, Domi put her hands on her knees, took a breath, and muttered, "Now that's something."

"You really care about all that?" Reiva whispered back. "It's all made up, I'm sure."

Domi frowned. "So? It's dramatic—it adds stakes to it. Otherwise it's just two men beating the tar out of each other."

Reiva shrugged. "Good enough for me."

Domi sniffed. "Well, some of us have more complex interests."

"Is that what you call it?"

Caulo, who was sitting on the other side of Domi, batted her on the arm. "Would you two shut up so we can just—"

The crowd erupted in cheers as one gladiator got a strike on the other. A shallow cut across the upper arm. It likely did little more than sting—a real blow from a sword like that could have taken the arm off entirely if they weren't pulling their strikes—but the sight of blood had whet the crowd's appetite.

Sure enough, the fight only built in fervor. Insults were hurled back and forth, appeals were made to the gods and to Lazarran virtue, and before long, Reiva couldn't help but acknowledge it did add something to the fight.

One swung his sword, the other ducked and retaliated with a shield bash, sending the first sprawling across the sands, tracking red as he went. Before the downed man could rise, the standing gladiator rushed upon him with sword held high and planted his knee on the other's chest.

"Yield!" he gasped, lungs heaving. "Or I claim my rightful satisfaction in spilt blood!"

The downed gladiator coughed, spitting a glob of reddened saliva into the dust.

The whole arena was in fits, half yelling for death, the other half yelling for them to both get up and continue the fight.

Then the man on his back raised his hand, signaling his surrender.

The victorious gladiator sprung to his feet, his opponent forgotten, and saluted the audience all around with sword held high. He basked in the adulation and the cheers—Reiva and her friends adding their voices to the acclaim—before bowing to the Imperial banner and taking his leave. The defeated gladiator had been carried out of the pit long ago by then.

"Okay," Reiva said, "I see your point about the drama."

Domi had a look of satisfaction. "*But?*"

"But that fight was probably staged anyway. The winner started to duck well before the loser even began that wild swing."

"*Well* before?" protested Caulo. "He ducked it like anyone else would have."

Phetan leaned over. "No, Reiva's right. That wasn't a real fight. Entertaining, but staged."

Reiva nodded. "See, Phetan gets it."

Caulo scowled. "Then why did we pay good money to get in here?"

Domi patted him on the knee. "Hush, bloodthirsty one. There will be real fights later, right Reiva?"

"Right. It looks like next there's going to be a melee. Those are almost always real."

A great throng of gladiators began filing into the pit. Almost entirely, they were poorly equipped. Some had little more than a loincloth and a sword Reiva wouldn't have trusted to pare her nails.

There were only three warriors out of thirty, from what Reiva could see, that seemed to have proper armor and weaponry.

"Well, this doesn't look fair," mused Domi.

"Criminals?" asked Ela.

"Most likely," said Phetan. "Sentenced to the games as punishment—they live if they can make it through the day. Those three, on the other hand, are professionals."

"However," Reiva put in, "they're going to fight to the death just like the rest of them. A melee is a common way for a rising gladiator to make a name for himself."

Caulo scratched his chin. "And what happens if all the condemned decide to join forces and rush the professionals? Does that never happen?"

There was a moment of silence.

Reiva fidgeted. "It does occur... In that case, the arena might let out the beasts. Starving lions. Or if there are too many to risk the lions on them, then they'll call for the Orphans to put the insurrection down. It's a slave rebellion, effectively."

The words sounded strange as she said them. It was almost analytical how she had described it. It was something that happened to someone else—someone completely unlike her.

And well, in a very real sense, it was someone completely unlike her. She was an Adept Initiate, she was someone the common folk deferred to and even feared. No longer was she someone to tread upon.

From the bottom of the world, she had climbed. She had climbed so far, but now, thinking about those people in the arena, thinking how five years ago she had been a hair's breadth from finding herself in the same position they now found themselves in...it only reminded her how far she might fall again.

"Here we go!"

Phetan's eager outburst snapped Reiva from her musing as the thirty bodies in the pit clashed in the melee. The free for all had begun.

THE MELEE, predictably, ended with the victory of one of the professional fighters. Reiva didn't know his name, but she assumed she would see more of him. He had bought himself recognition with blood and death, and people would look forward to the chance to see him work his craft in the future.

Throughout the day, there were more such events. Another melee. Some beast-games (mostly ending in the demise of the condemned, but one lucky fellow actually managed to slay the lions set upon him, and he walked free into the streets).

There was even a gladiatorial duel between two female fighters—much to Phetan and Caulo's delight.

Ela frowned. "That's not armor—those are costumes."

"So?" retorted Phetan. "Why can't we get something staged like the first fight?"

"Because those men didn't have their tits flopping around."

"Oh, don't tell me you didn't check out their thighs. Those men were sculpted like statues of the Founder himself."

Domi nodded like this was self-evident.

Reiva shook her head.

Once the show was over, the day ended with a true duel to the death. This was an expensive proposition, and the betting was high.

Reiva leaned forward. Sure enough, the tension in these fighters was evident. It was a testament to their discipline that they looked as calm as they did, but she could read the nerves.

She knew both their names. Both men had a strong reputation in the arena, but one was favored, Gianno the Ironborn. As they were introduced and raised their arms to the audience, the arena seemed split over who received more acclaim—the expected victor or the underdog.

"Who's your money on?" asked Domi.

Caulo answered readily. "The champion."

Ela shrugged. "I couldn't say."

Phetan concurred Gianno would take the day. "He has more experience—and look, you can see he's more relaxed. He's confident, assured. That's a man who knows victory well."

Domi hummed. "And you Reiva?"

"I put a bet on Brascho. The underdog."

Phetan whistled. "The one who's shaking like a leaf?"

"I've seen him fight before." And that was all the explanation she was willing to give before the duel began.

Right from the outset, the substance of this fight was different from the one that had opened the day. There were no flashy maneuvers, no boasts of prowess and divine favor.

These men were fighting for their lives.

The roars of the crowd were so deafening that Reiva could hardly hear the clang of sword and shield.

They danced to and fro along the sand, simultaneously aggressive and cautious all at once. In a battle, especially a one-on-one sword duel, victory most often went to the one who pressed the advantage. Truly was it said that Fortune favored the bold.

But skill and discipline were just as crucial. A single slip, the slightest misjudgment of the opponent's line of attack, or just one falsely believed feint, and that could be the end.

The shield, in such fights, was more important than the sword itself. Two men with only swords would end their fight within the minute—if that. But with shields, the opportunity to survive, to defend, to attack—it multiplied, and so it multiplied the length of the struggle.

But a fight to the death was taxing, and these men—consummate athletes that they were—still lacked the aether reinforcement that an Adept possessed. So as they began to flag and tire, Reiva guessed that a mere two, perhaps three minutes had passed. That was impressive —had either of them been any lesser a fighter, it would have been over a *long* time ago.

But now the tide was turning, and it seemed in favor of Gianno, the champion. His arms were strong, his footwork sure. He moved forward like a bull, unhindered. The cheers built as he pressed on, shield high and sword at the ready. Soon his blade would leap forth like a viper, skewering Brascho and leaving him dead—or if he had a theatrical flair, maimed. Then he would leave the choice to the audience—spare him, or put him to death?

And, as always, the audience would favor blood. What else had they paid for, after all?

Reiva leaned forward, realizing she had been biting her lip. Her hands were sweating. Not at the thought of losing money—at the thought of Brascho, her chosen warrior, suffering defeat. She had seen him in the arena before—she had been *sure* he would pull out a win. She had a sort of affection for him, a belief, like a mother has belief in her own son's capacity to achieve great things.

It was an odd way to think about a man well older than her, but it was what came to mind.

So when she saw the turn coming, she jumped to her feet,

grasping the railing and leaning over. She had a vague awareness of others doing the same—of a raucous cheer louder than thunder.

Brascho made a desperate play—as was his only opportunity, as was the only way for a man sure of death to have any chance at snatching victory. He reversed course, turning from retreat and throwing himself right for his opponent.

The champion Gianno reacted like any consummate fighter in this position—he held forth his gladius to skewer the fool, to let his own inertia carry him onto the blade.

And Brascho threw himself down, tumbling just beneath the blade's pass. Even as Reiva saw it with her own eyes, it seemed impossible, seemed that everything before her suggested he ought to have ended up stuck like a pig.

But Fortune favored the bold.

Brascho slashed out with his sword as he went, slicing open a gash in the champion's calf.

A deep gasp echoed from thousands of throats as Gianno buckled, his leg failing, his knee striking the sand.

Brascho came up to his feet, and Reiva saw that his desperate gambit had been costly—a sheet of blood was spouting from his neck. And it was no shallow wound. Only the fact that he was still standing suggested that the crucial vein had been missed, and that the gods' luck indeed had been with him.

For a moment, he stood there, transfixed, as though his own survival was a miracle he could not believe.

The champion turned himself about to face his opponent, still kneeling. The audience was rabid now—he was not yielding. He could not stand, and still he intended to fight to the death.

The two warriors stared each other down.

Reiva's fingers clamped so tightly to the railing they went numb.

Domi was at her side, cheering and whistling. "Finish it!" Reiva had no idea who she was speaking to—and truth be told, she had no idea who could better manage it.

She had placed her bet on Brascho because she had seen his raw fervor, like a feral beast cornered. He didn't have the cool confidence of a more experienced fighter—but he had the terrible drive to live, to survive against the odds. He won his fights in the final moments, at times like these.

But now, looking at Gianno, she saw the same emotion. Perhaps it had been there in his early days in the arena, but victory after victory had left him cold. He had been immortal, untouchable.

Now his wound, his spilled blood, had woken that same primal strength that characterized his opponent.

They were two beasts cornered, staring doom in the eyes.

And in a flash, they sprang into action.

Brascho ran forward, shield ready, sword high. He had the advantage, by all accounts. His steps were longer than earlier—a sign of confidence.

Reiva clenched her jaw.

Too much confidence.

Brascho brought his sword back, ready to lop his opponent's head clean from his shoulders.

The champion tensed, like a lion about to pounce—and then did just that.

At the critical moment—the only instant such a move could have worked—he exploded into motion, hurling himself from the ground with a burst of strength from his legs, both whole and maimed, and with his shield up to block his opponent's sword, he slammed into Brascho.

They went rolling. Reiva's ears rang, her stomach turned, her throat went raw.

In the dust-up, the fighters' bodies became a whirling mass of limbs and blades. The shields lay in the sand off to the side, the swords' effectiveness hampered by close quarters. For a moment, Reiva almost thought the two of them might kill each other, so devoted were they to their quest.

Then the champion threw off his opponent, and the younger man went rolling. He left dark red tracks in the sand as he went, and the grit sheeted off him in rivulets as he stumbled to his feet. A dozen wounds scored his flesh, at least half of them possibly fatal, if the blade had gone deep enough to strike arteries or puncture organs.

The champion, still maimed, pushed himself once again to his kneeling position. He too bore a great many cuts and gashes. He coughed, and a spray of blood jetted from the grille of his helmet.

The battle, miraculously, was not over.

Or so it seemed.

Brascho rose to his feet. He took a step forward, then another.

And then the sword slipped from his grasp, dropping to the sand.

A great intake of breath sounded throughout the arena.

Then his knees struck the sand, then his face. He lay still, his wounds faintly spurting blood, his heartbeat so weak by now it was all but assured to cease.

Gianno the Ironborn stayed kneeling, still grasping his blade.

Then, slowly, he raised his sword, arm trembling. He had to support his sword arm with his other.

The whole of the arena went mad, and if anyone had not been on their feet, now they jumped high, the rabid spirit of the moment possessing them.

After a few moments, the champion's arm drooped, the blade biting into the sand—but he did not let up on his grasp.

From the side tunnels, a coterie of men rushed to the victor, picked him up between them. One was a physician, who quickly began fussing over the champion's wounds. It wouldn't do to have the victor succumb to death after such a spectacular conclusion, after all.

As they carried him out, Gianno raised a victorious hand once again, his fingers stained red by blood that might have been his own or his defeated foe's.

Domi wiped an arm across her glistening forehead. "Damnation. Think he'll make it?"

Reiva shrugged. "They'll do their best—might even take him to a *Viva* Adept. He'll be able to afford it with his winnings from today."

Caulo whistled. "Well, if he ever wants to fight again, he'll *need* *Viva* surgery. No ordinary doctor could repair a maim like that to the calf muscle."

Ela shrugged. "I'd retire at that point anyway. Could you imagine going down in history with a finish like that? People here will tell the story of this fight for years."

"I will," chuckled Phetan. "What an end, eh? So—how much lighter is your purse, Reiva?"

Reiva twisted her lips. "Let's not talk about that."

Everyone laughed at that, earning a rueful grin from Reiva. "Well," she said, "even if I lost the money, at least I got a hell of a fight, right? I feel like I've spent a day on the battlefield after all this."

Domi pouted. "Come on, you can't be ready to go back *now*. Let's go get dinner—I haven't eaten outside the Sanctum in nearly a week."

Caulo arched an eyebrow. "Excuse me? How much of a stipend are you getting that you can afford to make a complaint like that?"

Domi had the decency to blush—which was a rare sight on her features. "I have ways of—"

Phetan cackled. "You're swindling some poor soul, aren't you?"

"Not swindling, just giving them my company."

"Them?" Ela scoffed. "How do you find the time to string so many men along? There are only so many free days."

Domi twirled a lock of hair around her finger. "I *may* have an arrangement with one of the gate guards."

"One of your many suitors?" Caulo drawled.

"*Many* is an exaggeration. You should try it—there are lots of people, men *and* women, who will pay for dinner to be seen with a future Adept."

Reiva smiled faintly. It baffled her how Domi could so easily move through Lazarran society the way she did. Also, wouldn't there be an expectation for...more than just dinner?

"Well, none of *us* are going to pay for you," Phetan said, "so either go back to the Sanctum or cough up yourself."

Domi put on an expression of mock outrage. "Of course I'll pay for myself. Where should we go?"

Reiva was content to take a passive role as they maneuvered their way out of the arena (an easy feat given how readily people made way for them) and negotiated the restaurant of choice for the night.

As they went, she cast one final glance toward the pit, noting the clumps of dark red sand where the blood had dried. Brascho's body had been taken away at some point during their conversation.

The memory of his collapse haunted her mind.

Yes, she was more disturbed by his loss than she let on—but not because she had incorrectly placed her wager.

In some sense—in a deeper way than she would ever admit to the others—she had seen herself as that fighter, and she had made some implicit bargain that if he could win, then she too could come out on top in her struggle to place first among the Initiates.

She shook her head, dispelling such thoughts.

It's not as if it's an omen, she told herself. *So he lost. I won't. He made mistakes. He grew complacent. I won't. I'll fight every day like death is at my heels, and I won't rest until I'm as secure as High Arkhon in his throne above the gods.*

THE RESTAURANT they decided on turned out to be rather affordable —not least because the owner practically tripped over himself to offer them an extensive discount on all his wares, even the wine, which he selected for them from his private holdings.

"An excellent Karellan vintage," he demurred. "May I?"

Domi was all too happy to let him pour for her, and she lifted the cup to her lips with all the poise one might expect of a senator at a public function. She even paused dramatically. "Exquisite, sir."

The restaurateur practically burst with pride, moving on to empty the bottle in filling the other four cups at the table. Reiva noted that none of them got quite as much as Domi had.

Phetan scowled. "How do you do that?"

Domi shrugged. "How do you swing a sword? How do you channel aether? Everything is skill, action, discipline. I know how to move, and I know how others move."

Ela rested her chin on her palm. "And how did you learn to move so well while the rest of us were slaving away in our martial disciplines? Is this common in Aspagne?"

The slightest flinch crossed Domi's features, but it was instantly wiped away by her typical easygoing expression. "Oh, I'm a special case. And I'll never tell my secrets."

Reiva quickly asked, before anyone could press Domi further, "What's Aspagne like?"

The other girl's shoulders eased, and Reiva was glad to have provided her some relief from whatever she had feared. "It's lovely. A shame I'll never be able to go back, but that's how it is, eh? The orange groves are amazing—such an aroma when they ripen. There's a perfume made there—you have to spend bushels' worth of rinds to get enough oil for even one bottle, but I've never smelled anything so delightful. Once I've got my full salary as an Adept, I'll buy one."

Phetan looked mystified. "And what, wear perfume into battle?"

Ela slapped his arm. "No, you brute. There's more to life—maybe she just wants to wear it for herself. Or, you know, maybe for one of these suitors she has."

Domi smiled in a way that was almost feline. "Who can say?"

Phetan shrugged. "Women."

Ela shot him a lethal look. "What—you wouldn't like it if I wore perfume?"

His responsive look was dry as stone. "I'm focused on other things in those circumstances."

Ela's face turned red.

Reiva's eyes shifted from one to the other. Caulo noticed and snorted. "You didn't know?"

Reiva felt heat rising to her own face. "Look, I've been busy."

Ela turned aside, unsuccessfully hiding her flush. Phetan chuckled, looping an arm around her shoulders and pulling her in. She half-smiled, burying her face into his arm.

"Get a room," sighed Caulo. "I'm eating here."

Phetan sighed. "I'm sorry for polluting your innocent eyes."

"Damn straight—I'm pure as a vestal."

"Vestals don't say 'damn,'" retorted Ela.

"Oh come on—religious figures of all people have the right to say 'damn.'"

"Not how you're saying it."

"Why would the gods care, anyway? You want to tell me Vulcaen doesn't say *shit* when he drops his almighty forge hammer on his toes?"

"I don't think a blacksmith god *would* drop his hammer," Domi offered, swirling her cup. "But who knows? Even the gods get drunk, don't they?"

"I for one could use some more wine," sighed Phetan. "Another round?"

Reiva put her hands up. "I'm all right. I might head back actually, but you all stay as long as you like."

Ela's lips curled into a smirk. "Scared of breaking curfew?"

Reiva's fingers curled. "Not *scared*. Just cautious."

"Phetan and Domi are both here—they'd get demerited too. You won't fall behind."

Caulo stuck a finger in the air. "It's Tolm she's worried about. These two will slip behind her any day now."

Domi shrugged, but Phetan's eyes hardened. "Easy for you to say, Caulo. You're already behind. Some of us take these things a bit more seriously."

Caulo put up his hands in a surrender. "Fine, fine. All I'm saying is, if Reiva wants to go, she can."

Reiva clenched her jaw. "And if I want to stay, I'll stay. I *can* have fun."

"Yeah," said Domi, "lay off the woman. I once saw her *whistling*. Not even as part of an exam, just for the hell of it!"

Another round of laughs circled the table.

Reiva felt the anger of her Flame building.

"Oh really?" asked Ela, a sudden mischievous light creeping into her eyes. "You can have fun, Reiva? Just like anyone else?"

"I can—just like anyone else."

In the corner of her eye, Reiva saw Domi's smile falter a bit. "Ela, what are you—"

The blonde girl leaned in, dropping her voice to a whisper. "The Belletranes. Tonight. Let's go."

Caulo choked on his meal. "*What* did you just say?"

Reiva's throat knotted.

Ela's smile widened. "You heard me. We're all old enough to get in—and I hear they treat Adepts for free on their first visit. Let's all go. I've been with Phetan; and you *must* have been Domi."

The girl's face was inscrutable as granite. "If I have, it's not your business. Come on, Ela, this is ridiculous."

"Oh, so you're just talk after all? I see. Big words until it's time to put up."

Reiva's fingernails dug into her palms.

Domi crossed her arms, leaning back in her chair. "I don't need to prove anything."

"Fine—go home then. But Reiva's the one who said she can have fun like anyone else."

"Maybe Reiva doesn't want to have fun the same way you—"

"I can speak for *myself*, Domi."

The other girl frowned. "Of course you can, I just—"

"Let's go." The words were out before she could think better of it.

Caulo cleared his throat. "Uh, really, I think Ela was just joking."

"No I wasn't," she snapped. "And Reiva knows it. She's a big girl—she can rise to a challenge. A Lazarran like any one of us. Not some—what do people say about Talynisti?—*desert prude*."

The Flame was twisting inside her like a wildfire ready to tear through the city.

"I can rise high enough to surpass you, that's for certain."

Phetan's eyes narrowed. "Watch it."

Ela patted his arm. "No no, that's fair. She's above me in the rankings, and she deserves *all* the praise and acclaim for that. She's capable—fearless, I hear. So let's pay up and go."

"Fine." Reiva went digging in her coin purse for her share.

Once they had all paid their bill and stepped out into the street,

Domi put her hand on Reiva's shoulder and whispered, "Reiva, this is silly. Let's go back. We can get to the Sanctum before curfew."

"Domi, stop."

"But you told me you—"

"I said *stop*. I don't need your help. I'm my own person."

She expected Domi to cool, or just back off, but she only looked more worried.

"All right. If you say so."

20

THINGS LIKE THIS

THE NIGHT AIR was chill against Reiva's face. Clouds sat low over the tops of buildings. Ordinarily she would have pulled her mantle up over her mouth and nose, but this late, the Initiates were breaking curfew. They had to stash their telltale red mantles away—choosing to leave them with a friend of Domi's. Exactly who this friend was or how Domi knew her, she didn't explain, but she said she was trustworthy.

Reiva wondered how many others had someone on the outside of the Sanctum they were not 'supposed' to—like how she used to have Levin and Artha.

It wasn't something she had much opportunity to dwell on—the temple of Belletra was not far.

It was also not particularly quiet at this time of night. While most temples—such as the temple of Marbellus across the street—received most of their patronage during the daytime, the temple of Belletra, for obvious reasons, received most visitors when the sun was down. Humans being as they were, however, meant that there was almost no time the temple's services were not in demand, and as such, they operated at all hours.

As the Initiates climbed the steps, perfumed air from within drifted out, tickling Reiva's nose. Even from this distance, its potency was great enough that Reiva felt her head lightening. Her heart beat faster—though whether that resulted from the temple's incense or her own trepidation, she couldn't tell. Perhaps both.

The lot of them were met at the portico by a man dressed in what most people would have considered an outer garment—if it were not the only stitch of clothing on him. It was a richly dyed fabric, and Reiva kept her gaze fixed on his face for fear it would suddenly shift and expose more than she had any interest in seeing.

She bit her tongue at that thought—wasn't that what they were here for?

"Welcome, honored guests," purred the Belletrane priest, bowing his head. "Our goddess delights in your coming, as do we, her servants. You wish to partake in our rites?" His eyes were half-lidded as he spoke, every syllable laced with suggestion.

Ela spoke for them all. "We do." And she pulled the arcane focus out from beneath her tunic. "We've been working so hard, you see."

As soon as the Belletrane saw the focus, his eyes widened. "By the goddess, we receive an honor indeed tonight." He crooked his finger. "Come with me, let's get you all settled. Fine servants of the Empire such as yourselves ought not wait."

As he slipped inside and down a corridor, Ela and Phetan led the way—the former casting a sly glance over her shoulder. "Well? Come on, everyone. Let's have some *fun*."

She looked directly at Reiva as she said it, which only deepened Reiva's frown.

Caulo shifted uneasily. "Uh, are we going to be...all together?"

Domi shrugged. "I don't know—why not ask Ela, since you all seem bent on letting her rule the evening."

Reiva clenched her jaw. "Hang on, why can't we—"

"You can do what you like, Reiva, but don't act like you aren't shaking in your sandals right now."

Her cheeks flushed. "Are you saying I'm scared?" she hissed it under her breath so as not to be overheard, earning her a dry look from Domi.

"I'm saying this *isn't you.*"

Caulo's eyes darted from one to the other. "Uh, girls, I—"

"Shut up, Caulo," snapped Domi. "Go have some *fun*. Or were you hoping to go for a tumble with the two of us?"

His face went red as a tomato. "I didn't, I don't, I—"

"*Go.*"

He obeyed.

Domi huffed, running her hands through her hair. She actually looked *angry*, which wasn't an emotion Reiva was used to seeing on her.

Reiva's insides turned. "Do you think Caulo really...?"

Domi threw her hands up. "I don't know, and I don't care."

"But he's—"

"He's a man, Reiva. You can't think like we're all still little *probatii*. You really think he *wouldn't* like to get a look at you? Maybe brush his hand somewhere in the midst of the confusion?"

Reiva clutched her stomach. She felt herself going lightheaded. "When you say *confusion*, what do you—"

"Anything someone can dream up, there's a room for it in this place. How far in would you go? Until you proved yourself more daring than Ela? Until you couldn't even remember your name?"

By now, they had begun to earn themselves some looks. A female Belletrane drifted over, cautiously laying hands on their shoulders. "My darlings, is everything well? Wine to soothe your souls? There's a private room just over here, if I may."

Domi's voice was flat. "Wine sounds nice."

Reiva followed silently. The Belletrane poured them each a rather generous cup. No sooner had Domi taken a sip than she waved off the priestess. "Leave us."

The woman, who had been in the act of untying her raiment, froze, then quickly recovered and slipped out.

Domi took a long draught of wine, then shook her head.

Reiva awkwardly held her cup in both hands. Her cheeks were still hot.

Domi gave her a look. Then laughed. "I'm not trying to pull anything on you, Reiva."

Reiva looked aside. "It's not that I—"

"Reiva, *look at me*. Just the other day, you told me how you don't see people that way. Or was I wrong?"

Reiva bit her tongue.

"I'm going to be as direct as possible—have you ever in your life wanted to take someone to bed?"

"No." The word broke out like a horse set free from its stable. "Never."

"So *why the hell* are you here?"

"Because I want to be like the rest of you!" she said, tears suddenly stinging her eyes. Her lips trembled. "Don't look at me."

Domi sighed, "Come here."

Reiva dropped her cup, wine sloshing across the tiles as Domi pulled her into a hug.

"That was perfectly good wine," murmured the other girl.

"I feel your sympathy," sniffed Reiva. "Truly I do."

For a moment, they stood like that, in silence. But it wasn't long though before the various sounds of the temple of Belletra drifted through the walls.

The two of them snickered, covering their mouths to stifle laughter.

Domi glanced toward the door. "Can we go?"

Reiva nodded. "Please. And, Domi, I should've listened to you earlier."

She shrugged. "It's all right. I've seen how you get sometimes. We're all still training, learning to master our Arts. Sometimes you get worked up and I don't think there's a force in the world that can turn you off your path." She smirked. "Except the sea, of course."

Reiva snorted. "I guess so. But...why did you come all the way here then? Why not just go back?"

"I wanted to keep an eye on you. But then when I saw how dreadful you looked at the portico I just...I couldn't take it."

"But *why*? I mean you're...you know."

In an instant, she had composed her face into a perfect mask of innocence. "I'm what?"

Reiva felt herself blushing again. "You know, you're—" she waved her hand awkwardly. "Not like me. You...go to dinners, with people."

Domi snorted. "Diplomatic way of putting it." She hugged herself, rubbing her arms like she had gone cold. "Tell you what—let's leave and I'll tell you a secret. Something only you can know."

Reiva's eyebrows shot up. "Ah, all right. Let's go."

"And let's hurry—before another cleric starts stripping for us."

"What about the others?"

"They know the way back."

Without a moment's hesitation, Domi blazed the trail out. As they went, a number of Belletranes bowed to them, murmuring words of blessing and invitations to return with all haste.

Once they were back into the clear air of the night, Reiva felt her head clearing. "Is there something in that incense they use?"

Domi sighed. "Probably. Meant to lower inhibitions. People get nervous."

"Even in Lazarra?"

Domi arched an eyebrow. "Lazarrans are humans too."

Reiva couldn't deny that. "So..."

Domi nodded. She took a shallow breath, and Reiva noticed *she* was nervous. "Want to go back to the temple?" she joked.

"*Ha ha*. Yes, that's exactly what I need." She swallowed. "Sorry, I haven't told anyone about this."

"That's all right." Reiva felt a warmth building in her heart—the same sort of warmth she'd felt when she first truly connected with the other girls, or when she and Alyat had begun to finally cooperate and understand one another.

"We're friends, Domi. Aren't we?"

Domi's posture suddenly stiffened. Something changed behind her eyes. "We are. And friends tell each other things." Another shaky breath. "Even things like this." She cast a quick glance around. They were alone on this street.

"The woman we left our mantles with," Domi whispered, "is not a friend."

Reiva's muscles tensed. Who were they then? An enemy? An assassin?

Domi put her hand on Reiva's arm. "Relax. She's not dangerous. Well, she is, but not to us." Her voice dropped even lower. "I am...a somewhat distant relative of the current king of Aspagne."

Reiva almost tripped. "*What?*"

"Shh!" She threw another glance over her shoulder.

"How distant?" Reiva hissed.

"Enough that no one knows who I am, but not so distant as for my existence to be unimportant."

Reiva searched the other girl's expression for any hint of a trick or a joke, but everything about Domi's demeanor suggested absolute sincerity. "Okay, I believe you. So your...acquaintance?"

"She keeps an eye on me, makes sure no one has kidnapped me for ransom or anything like that."

"I thought no one knows who you are?"

Domi made an exasperated sound. "It's complicated. That's not the point though—"

"How could that *not* be the point?"

"That's just genealogy. The other part of it—the part that matters to me is this..." She swallowed. "My mother was a courtesan to the king. She wasn't supposed to keep me. Bastards of the royal line in Aspagne are smothered. But my mother had enough favor with the king that she was able to plead for my life, under one condition. Once I was old enough—I think I was five—they sent me to be raised by a religious order, far away from the capital."

Reiva's eyebrows knit together. "What sort of religious order?"

"A virgin goddess," Domi said with a wry smile. "And word spreads fast in a place like that. I was the whore's daughter—and nothing I did could change that. I tried to be the best girl in that house, but they wouldn't even let me handle half the implements. I couldn't even make the beds of the other girls for fear my touch would corrupt their chastity.

"Then one day, the temple was visited by a standard Adept Corps survey. I almost cried tears of joy when I was selected—it was my ticket out of there. But the catch was, the survey still had to transit through the capital—and the king was interested in seeing which fortunate souls his country was providing to the Imperial cause."

"And you were seen in the palace," Reiva guessed.

"I was. I don't think the king would've known, but my mother was still there, and she recognized me, even so many years later. The king must have seen her distress, because sure enough, he realized who I was. And bastard that I am, he's still a father—and bastards have their utilities. All of a sudden, there was a small attachment with the Adept Corps survey. Diplomats supposedly, but really they were just meant to keep an eye on me. I'm sure the Sanctum knows, and turns a blind eye to them whenever they approach me."

The two of them walked in silence for a while longer.

"So," Domi continued eventually. She threw up her hands. "My mother's daughter."

"How do you mean?"

She sighed. "Look, I would be lying if there wasn't a certain measure of...*spite,* to the relationships I seek out. A way of thumbing my nose at those priestesses who made my life a hell. 'Yes, I'm the whore's daughter, what of it?'"

Reiva stopped, grabbing Domi's arm. "No."

"Excuse me? Reiva, I think I know when I'm—"

"Domi, it's your turn to listen now."

The other girl's eyebrows rose, but she put her lips together, curiosity plain on her features.

"I'm not saying that what you do makes sense to me. But I do think...there's a sort of...*liveliness* to you. You know what I mean?"

Domi opened her mouth, looking ready to crack a joke, but then she seemed to think better of it. "All right. But you're lively, Reiva. Anyone who's seen you in combat training can see that."

"Right, but you're..." She pinched her nose. "You have a way of... being...you're..."

"I'm enticing?"

"Sure."

"*Alluring?*"

"Oh shut up."

Domi stuck her tongue out, but spoke no further.

"And that's...fine. I can be Reiva, and you...you can be Domi."

Domi gave a half-smile. "I can quote a half-dozen philosophers who would have rather strong opinions about which of us makes better life choices."

"And I might not agree with all your choices. I could never live—or love—how you do."

"I wouldn't call it love."

"But you're my friend, and there's something beautiful about who you are."

Reiva looked up at Domi, who was blushing furiously.

"Ah," she cleared her throat. "Thank you. People don't talk like that about me."

Reiva shrugged. "Well, that's how I see you."

"Well, my poor heart can only take so much gushing praise. So, how about you hurry back to the Sanctum. There should be an Orphan on duty named Hiran—tell him you're a friend of mine. He won't say anything about letting you in late. I'll collect all our mantles, and I'll meet you back there later."

Reiva nodded. "Thank you, Domi. I'm...grateful you're in my life."

"Me too. Now hustle—before the guard shift changes."

They shared another quick hug before parting ways.

As Reiva walked, the world seemed to open up. The Flame inside her had quieted—and for what seemed the first time in a long while, she was feeling peace. She was even glad, in a strange way, that she had gone on this strange, unusual adventure. Not much of it had gone the way she intended, but all in all—

"Hey there, girlie."

21

A PROPHECY

Reiva tensed, instinct dropping her into the certainty of combat-preparation. She was ready to run, ready to strike—whatever the situation required.

"What's a cute young thing like you doing out so late?"

The man's voice was rough, maybe slurred by alcohol, though she wasn't certain. She honed in on him—he was standing under the awning of a nearby building, cloaked in darkness.

He laughed. "Did I spook you?"

Reiva narrowed her eyes. "You did."

He seemed to find this even funnier. "Aw, shucks. Well, I'm sorry about that. Can I make it up to you?" He waved something in the air, and the sound of sloshing liquid reached her. "No charge."

"I doubt that."

The man clicked his tongue. "Testy testy. You seem fun. Come over here."

"No."

"Ahh, but if you really weren't interested, you'd be leaving already."

"I'm not leaving because I can see your friend lurking at the corner."

The mood changed. It was a subtle change, but Reiva's nerves caught it like the screech of one blade on another.

"Him?" the man drawled. "He's nobody." He took a few steps toward Reiva.

The other man lurched away from his hiding spot, boxing her in. She could run back the way she'd come. That would have been the wise move.

But her Flame was up.

"You're going to get hurt," Reiva said. "I'd suggest you stop now."

The man cackled. "Ohh, you're gonna fight, huh? Go ahead." The glint of iron in the moonlight attested to a drawn knife. "Fight, see what happens. Scream for help, see what happens."

Reiva flexed her fingers. Her anger was building—she could practically feel the fire coalescing around her hands. "You're threatening an Adept Initiate."

A snort. "Not a very clever lie—you don't have the red."

She clenched her fists.

"Come with us."

The other man had gotten into place behind her. From his stance, she guessed he had a knife too.

"No."

The man in front of her made a clumsy grab.

She had an advantage they didn't—they didn't actually want to stab her, not if they could help it.

She had no such compunction.

Reiva clutched his wrist and lit her hand afire.

In the darkness of the night, her fist became a blazing torch, its brightness pricking her eyes.

Right away, the acrid smell of burning flesh assailed her nostrils. An ugly scream hammered her ears.

Quickly, she hit at his side with an aether-enhanced palm strike, feeling a satisfying double-*snap* on impact. The man buckled, his scream turning into a choked wheeze as his side seized in pain against the broken ribs.

She dropped him, letting him fall, and turned to the other.

He was mid-step, as if he had been about to tackle her but froze at the incongruous sight before him.

Reiva set both hands ablaze, illuminating the second man's horrified features.

Whether it was fear or alcohol that possessed him, he wailed and swung wildly with the knife. Reiva danced back a step, letting the blade whistle harmlessly through the air, and threw her hands forward. A jet of fire *rushed* through the space between them, engulfing the man's midsection.

From the moment the first man struck, seven seconds had elapsed.

Reiva let out a slow breath.

Her Flame was still up. Her hands still smoldered with two plumes of fire.

She had trained to fight wars—these had been mere criminals. It was almost disappointing how quickly it had ended. She had half a mind to order them to stand and fight on, or she'd kill them on the spot.

As if in answer to her wishes, the first man groaned and stumbled to his feet. He wasn't moving on Reiva though—the exact opposite. He took a clumsy lurch down the road, moving fast as he was able given his inability to breathe properly.

Reiva almost casually lashed flames at his legs. He yelped, dropping to the stone street and clutched at his singed calves.

The other man was a smoking wreck. His cries of pain were more animal than human, and his chest bore an ugly burn mark, glistening under the flickering light of her fires.

"Hey!"

The word echoed down the otherwise empty street with harsh impetus.

Reiva honed in on the speaker, putting up her hands in case these men had a third after all.

A pair of heavy footsteps raced toward her—and she saw that the two approaching were not criminals at all, but a pair of Orphan legionnaires.

She eased, letting her hands drop to her side, extinguishing the fires.

The Flame was frustrated at that—it wanted more fight.

The Orphans took in the scene at a glance, both of them carrying a torch in one hand, a drawn sword in the other.

"*Ave Imperator*, Adept," said the woman slowly. "You're not wearing your mantle."

Reiva felt her stomach turn a bit. "*Ave Imperator*, ma'am. Adept Initiate Reiva."

From the glint in the Orphan's eyes, she had just had a suspicion confirmed. "And what happened here, Initiate? We heard screams."

The woman's partner scoffed. He was kneeling beside the man with the chest burn. "I think I can piece that one together."

Reiva squared her shoulders, doing her best to look confident, calm. "I was walking back to the Sanctum when these men attacked me. I told them who I was, but they were quite bent on their intentions."

The Orphan woman hummed. "I see." There was an undeniable skepticism in the woman's tone. "Tell me, Initiate Reiva, where is your mantle? It doesn't seem that either of these men tore it away from you."

"I was not wearing it, ma'am." She had almost said, '*I forgot it*,' but that would have been laughable.

"And it's well past dark."

"It is, ma'am."

The Orphan drew her lips into a line. "Well, since you're keeping the streets safe tonight, Initiate Reiva, would you so honor us and help us truss these two up and take them to the jail? I'd like to get your testimony of the incident."

Reiva's stomach dropped further. "I should really get back to the Sanctum."

"You should have been back at the Sanctum a long time ago. Now come on, I assume they taught you to tie a prisoner's hobble?"

~

LAZARRA WAS A LAND OF HIERARCHY. Even though Reiva, as an Adept Initiate, commanded a great deal of respect and honor, even deference, from the common citizenry, within the structure of command—the Emperor at the head beneath divine Arkhon, the barbarian slave at the dregs—she still was subject in authority to the Orphan legionnaires who kept Lazarra secure and obedient to law.

So she had no right or ability to defy the will of the jail warden who demanded she remain at the guardhouse until they could send a runner to the Sanctum. When the man returned, he brought word that she was to be escorted to the Sanctum by Orphans, with a note of thanks and apologies from one Adept Alyat.

Though Alyat did not administer, technically speaking, a court martial, Reiva certainly knew in her gut she had no interest in ever finding herself in front of a *real* trial.

Alyat was seated in his office, at his side standing the Orphan legionnaires who had escorted her back to the Sanctum.

"So," he said slowly, "you stay out past curfew, you shuck off your mantle—both egregious breaches of Initiate code which you are sworn to—and to top it all off you wound and contribute to the arrest of two attempted rapists."

Reiva swallowed. She was standing at attention with such ferocity she feared her knees were about to start shaking, her shoulders to quiver—underlying it all the terror that if she slipped even a mote out of line her mentor's glare would lop off the offending part of her body.

"Yes, sir. All true."

Alyat breathed a heavy sigh through his nostrils. "Well, the last might *in part* ameliorate your offenses, but remind me, Initiate, what is the function of the Adepts as pertains to Lazarran law?"

Reiva knew the words by heart. "Though the Imperial Adept is an agent of the Imperial Throne and Authority, she shall not take it upon herself to unduly use her power to enforce the law. An Adept is no judge, save when it is the will of Empire to furnish her with that noble and necessary vocation."

Alyat grunted. "Now tell me, Initiate"—he kept using that word, so stiffly, so unlike him—"what probable cause does one such as yourself have for attacking two civilians?"

She had been mulling over these words every step of the way back, and she was confident she could even recite them backwards if need be. "Sir, an Adept is the property of the Emperor, a weapon in his hand. My life is not my own, but it exists in servitude to the Empire, Emperor, and Divine Arkhon who selected me for this vocation. When danger was posed to my person, it was a direct threat to an Imperial asset. As such, honor and duty bound me to defend myself as I did."

Alyat actually rolled his eyes. "A long way of saying 'I acted in self defense.' Particularly given that, by your own telling of the story, you did not manifest your Art until *after* the men had attacked you. Perhaps we can obscure that detail when the story begins to spread"—here he gave a significant look toward the Orphans—"but it is never wise to lie, least of all to a populace, Initiate. Eventually, people get wise. And that's when things get very complicated."

"I told them I was an Initiate before they attacked me."

"Mm, and if only there had been some way to prove that before inflicting violence."

Reiva's fingernails pressed into her palms. "The violence was justified, sir."

Alyat waved his hand through the air as if shooing a fly. "You were justified in violence *once they attacked*, but you could have steered a different course of events. No one will give a damn that you burned those bastards—some might say you should have done more. But looking beyond today's events—what could happen five years down the road? Ten? What does it do to the Empire if Adepts are not held to their own laws? Today it's justified, but what if things were more complicated? What if the populace no longer trusted that the laws of Lazarra bind us all?"

"It would undermine the entire Imperial Dominion."

"Correct. And for your own sake, Initiate, it would not bode well to develop a reputation for raising—even dimly—such questions. Particularly as a Fire Adept."

"I understand, sir. I should have used my magic from the start and called for the Orphans."

Alyat nodded crisply. "All of which brings us back to my first question—and I will *keep* coming back to this question, so long as you hide the truth from me—*why* were you out past curfew without your mantle?"

Reiva was glad her hands were folded behind her back, lest Alyat see the glistening sweat covering them.

Just as she had her Flame, so Alyat had what he called his Gleam. And just as Reiva's Flame gave her the drive and anger needed to fight and win, no matter the odds against her, Alyat's Gleam gave him an uncanny sense for the truth—and when the truth was being hidden from him. It made him a formidable asset when he worked alongside Legion Intelligence—he had sussed out and brought about the destruction of numerous cults and political insurrectionists before they could spread and do great harm to the Empire.

It also made him a devil of a person to lie to—even lie by omission.

Reiva's tongue seemed to swell. Her heart and stomach traded places again and again, a sickening, nauseating dance. She hated not to tell the truth—it was an acidic thing, burning her from the inside out.

But what else was going to happen? Was she really going to turn in the others? Couldn't she just take the brunt of the punishment herself and—

Alyat perked up, glancing at the door.

His aetheric senses were far more acute than Reiva's. When she stretched out her awareness, she noticed a rapidly approaching person—someone of her own level of power, roughly.

The person knocked at the door.

Alyat waved for one of the Orphans to open the door, and when he did so, Domi came tripping in, a mantle clutched in her hands. Domi was panting, hair flying free from her braid, her forehead glistening.

She saluted wearily. "Adept Alyat, I was the one who hid Reiva's mantle. I have it here."

Reiva's jaw hung. Alyat reached out, accepting the swathe of fabric from Domi's hands.

"This is yours, Initiate Reiva?"

She nodded numbly.

Alyat made another one of his characteristic grunts. "So why, Initiate Domi, do you have this?"

"The lot of us violated curfew. We stayed out on the town. This was how we meant to stay hidden from the Orphans' eyes."

The legionnaires attending seemed to stiffen. They didn't *glare* at Domi per se—but Reiva was certain they would remember her face.

"Then I have the same question for you as for Reiva. Who was part of your merry little band, and what were you up to?"

Domi seemed to lose some color.

Reiva opened her mouth, about to say it herself, but then Domi beat her to it—

"Phetan, Ela, Caulo. The five of us, sir."

Alyat's eyebrows drew together. The lot of them were some of the highest ranked Initiates in Seventh Cohort. They associated together, so it wouldn't have been a surprise they had been together—but it was still burdensome for him, Reiva guessed, to hear that so many exceptional prospects would receive a mark against them this far in their training.

"I will have that looked into," Alyat said. "The two of you are dismissed and can expect word of your discipline tomorrow."

He tossed the mantle to Reiva. She and Domi saluted.

Wordless, Reiva ducked her head, moving to step outside, when Alyat's voice caught her up. "Reiva—next time, don't give the enemy the opportunity to scream. No quicker way to screw over a stealth mission."

She turned back, throat dry. "Yes, sir."

"And stop calling me 'sir'—this is your punishment, not mine."

Reiva nodded briskly, then slipped out.

Domi was standing outside, waiting, a pained look on her face. "I'm sorry."

Reiva scoffed, shaking her head. "What the hell? What for? How did you even—"

Domi forestalled her with a hand. "When I got back to the gate, Hiran told me two Orphans brought you in. Didn't take long to put things together. I threw the others' mantles on the ground and went running, looking for where you were. Good thing I checked your mentor's right away, hm?"

Reiva rubbed at her forehead. "No, but... Why? I was going to stay quiet! I was going to—"

Domi slapped her.

Reiva's Flame burst into an emotional roar, but at the same moment, shock froze her like the frigid waters of the river at dawn. One hand on her own stinging cheek, the other raised in a fist, she stared at the other girl.

Domi sighed. "Sorry, I just...wanted to do that."

Reiva nodded slowly. "Feel better?"

"Yeah."

"Good."

The two of them looked at each other for another moment before simultaneously bursting into laughter—then covering their mouths and looking around. It was still past curfew, after all. Reiva nodded toward the dormitory, and off they went.

As Reiva wrapped her mantle around her shoulders, she said, "I still don't get why you did that. It doesn't make sense, logically."

Domi shrugged. "Sure it does."

"Explain, O philosopher."

Domi stuck a finger in the air. "If you had seen yourself in that moment, you would have recognized absolute terror. Not terror at being disciplined—we've both been through that before, we'll be lucky if we only go through it once more. You were scared of what would happen if it got out that you squealed."

Reiva frowned, but said nothing.

"Look, we'll all take a hit to our rankings because of tonight. But at least you won't lose face in the sight of the others."

Reiva snorted. "I think I already did."

"What, for leaving the temple?"

"Yeah. And sure, I would have lost more if I had been the one to break the silence about who went out, but I don't know if there's much to salvage."

Domi put her hands up. "All right, well then I should have just left you alone to face the wrath of the Adept of Scowls."

Reiva elbowed the other girl. "He doesn't *always* scowl."

"Well, you must be his favorite, then."

"I'm his apprentice."

"Eh, you never know—my mentor loves Tolm at least twice as much as she loves me."

Reiva scoffed. "Don't they all."

The two of them lapsed into a silence. They came to a stop under the eaves of the dormitory building. Inside, they wouldn't be able to talk anymore—lest they earn the ire of dozens of dozing Initiates with arcane focuses around their necks and the training to use them well.

Domi glanced up. Reiva followed her gaze, noting that the clouds had cleared away, revealing countless stars.

"You want to go a lot higher than I do, Reiva. I'm content where I land. But you're not like that. What did the great philosopher say? 'It is the nature of the elements to move to their proper place, and so it is that fire rises to the heavens'?"

Reiva blinked. "So you *are* a philosopher."

Domi snorted. "I can quote enough to entertain a senator or diplomat. Philosophers themselves are dreadful though. Not enough action or excitement."

"What about that one Karellan—the Dog?"

"Haven't read him. My mentor said he never taught anything worthwhile."

"He was famous for insulting kings and strutting about naked."

"Oh, well..." Domi hummed thoughtfully, taking a long pause. "My sort of man."

The two of them broke into another fit of smothered laughter.

"But I mean it, Reiva. We can all see it. You're not stopping. You're going to keep rising higher—it's what you do." She raised a finger toward the star-strewn sky. "You'll be another candle of fire amidst the gods."

Reiva felt her face heating. "Okay, enough of that—let's just get some sleep so we're not dead tired when we have to carry out our punishment tomorrow."

Domi stretched her arms wide. "And wherever I sail in this world, I will go with the knowledge that every shore I touch will know the name of Adept Reiva, bringer of fire and destruction!" She clapped her hands together. "Consider it a prophecy."

Reiva shook her head, looking away to hide her abashment. "All right, well, I have my own prophecy."

"Oh? Do tell."

"The two of us are going to stay friends, no matter how high *either* of us climbs—or how low either of us falls. I don't care about Ela, Phetan, or Caulo. You're the only one tonight who stopped to consider who I really am. And if who I really am isn't Lazarran to the bone, I would rather have someone by my side who accepts that."

Domi hummed. "A good prophecy," she declared solemnly. "Could use a bit more fire and death though."

Reiva laughed, the tension bleeding out of her shoulders. "I'll work on that."

"It's fine, not everyone can be a natural poet such as myself."

"True enough."

"But Reiva—you know what this means? You're going to have to climb all the way to the top without help from any of them. They're going to see you *and* me as enemies now. Are you sure you want to spend another two years striving against them like that?"

Reiva grabbed Domi's forearm. "Alyat told me once that I need friends, not just allies. What's an ally worth compared to a friend? After tonight, I know you won't turn against me. No matter what I did for or with any of the others, I can't say the same. I wouldn't be able to. Allegiances of convenience, all orchestrated for self-gain. I'd rather have one friend I can count on than a dozen allies who could turn against me in a night."

Domi whistled. "Not exactly poetic, but appropriately dramatic. A future as a playwright, perhaps?"

Reiva's Flame stirred. "I'm serious!"

Domi snickered, patting Reiva's hand. "I know, and it's endearing how seriously you take everything. And I'm grateful for every word. So let's get some sleep. Because tomorrow you need to get back to training. After all—you're not taking number one just because you said some pretty words and made a friend."

Reiva sighed, already picturing the early morning rise that would be demanded of her, and how she wouldn't have a spare minute to herself for the foreseeable future once she received her punishment. "Yeah, let's sleep. Another battle tomorrow."

"Always another battle."

As they slipped inside, easing the door shut, and padded delicately to their beds without a word, Reiva suddenly found herself brought up short. Domi had placed her hand on Reiva's shoulder. She seemed hesitant, in a way that was markedly unlike her.

They stood like that for a moment, before Domi whispered so faintly Reiva could hardly catch the words: "Friends. No matter what, right?"

Reiva nodded in the dark, then realized the gesture was invisible. "No matter what."

Domi squeezed her shoulder. "Good."

Though she lay down, though her body and soul were worn out, sleep evaded her.

She couldn't tell Domi, but she was more distraught than she'd let on. She'd failed to play the game. Even if it was a sick, stupid game to set on Ela's part. She hadn't been able to fit in, and now she was outside the group.

She had Domi. Thank the gods for that. And she'd been honest when she said she'd rather have one true friend than all the rest—but that didn't mean her life hadn't just gotten a lot harder. They'd all get disciplined for tonight—and Phetan in particular wouldn't take that lightly. She was dead certain he'd push twice as hard to keep ahead, just to get back at her and Domi, and of course Ela would assist him in that.

The next two years were about to be more grueling than everything that came before.

PART IV

EMPEROR AND EAGLE

22

DO THE CORPS PROUD

BEFORE SHE WENT DOWN to the docks, Reiva stared at the number beside her name. *Two*.

Tolm had held on to his place with maddening ease. Even seeing the rankings unchanged after so long was enough to stir Reiva's Flame into a rage.

She had passed Domi by the end of their fifth year. Phetan had stood in her way until the end of sixth. But after months and months of labor, training, honing herself to as nigh perfection as she could manage—she still couldn't overtake Tolm. Not throughout sixth year, and not as seventh year slipped through her fingers.

She found herself digging deeper and deeper into the stores of rage afforded by her Art. Her Flame was quite willing to fuel her exploits. Indeed, some days the only thing holding her back from flying into an all out whirlwind of violence seemed to be Alyat's stern gaze and Domi's sardonic tone. The two of them would never let her hear the end of it if she threw a tantrum over something so apparently minor as one place difference in the rankings.

But she knew well the support the two of them had thrown behind her. Alyat stayed up late day after day, instructing her on the finer points of aether manipulation and channeling, introducing her to advanced techniques for maximizing her efficiency and tolerance. Domi—much to her chagrin—joined Reiva in her early morning training routines, pushing her to press her boundaries a little further every time. And sometimes, when she truly was stalled out but too frustrated and proud to realize it, Domi would drag her off the training field or out of the Trial Chamber and force her to relax.

And for all of it, it seemed she could only hang on to her placing by her fingernails. Not second place itself—she knew she was far and away beyond Phetan, who had expanded his lead on Domi after she began slipping in her own regimens for Reiva's sake (something Reiva felt endless guilt over, but which Domi assured her made no difference). No, it was by her fingernails she still held on to the *chance* of ever beating out Tolm.

And now, in the seventh and final year of her training, with one final field mission to go before their commissioning as full Adepts, she was going to be on assignment with the man himself.

It was a balmy spring day. Reiva had never grown accustomed to the reek of the docks—the thick layers of a dozen different stenches of fish, the itchiness of the salt that seemed to settle into her skin after even a few moments.

She had her standard kit, but she couldn't help but wonder how much good it would do her at sea. After all, she wouldn't be digging any trenches or pits on the waves.

Why isn't Domi here?

That was the real question on Reiva's mind—and she had questioned Alyat about as much, earning little more than a belabored shrug from her mentor. "There's the simple truth and the more complicated one. First, they want to test you and Tolm. You and Domi are close allies—it wouldn't say much if you could cooperate."

Reiva had rubbed her forehead. "Why wouldn't Tolm and I? It's not like there's anything *personal* between us."

Alyat simply scoffed. "Well, that's something we'll see, won't we? But that's only the half of it. The darker truth is—they want to know how badly you both want this. It's not unheard of for foul play between Initiates to take place, especially when things are so close."

Reiva tried to take comfort in the notion that she was close to surpassing Tolm—it certainly didn't feel like it.

Standing with her on the docks were two other Initiates, Tolm of course, and Luo—a face she hadn't seen much of in some time, to her great embarrassment. For his part, he didn't seem to take personal offense to Reiva's absence. In his words, he knew how hard she trained, to the point it amazed him she even had time to eat.

He seemed to think she was joking when she said she only ate because Domi reminded her when it was mealtime.

Luo had clung along near the lower tiers of the remaining Initiates; a startling reversal, as Reiva reflected on how he had been the first one to give her a reprieve during physical regimens. In truth, he was likely in danger of washing out—there were nine Initiates left, and he was the eighth. It wasn't often that a cohort would graduate so many in one year.

It was a sobering reality to contemplate—just how many had vanished since Reiva had stood, sputtering and struggling on that muddy field her first day in the Corps. Some of their faces, she remembered, even names. Mylla. She still thought of Mylla with heart-wracking guilt. Another boulder of burden on her shoulders. Another sin that demanded her excellence. If she could only prove in the end that it was all worth it—that all the prices paid along the way truly did take her farther than anyone else...

The arrival of Adept Brefon snapped her out of her reverie.

His hair was the same close-cropped legionnaire style it had been when he plucked her out of the slave auction seven years ago. He looked the three of them over. If he remembered he had been the one to grab Reiva—if he even recognized her now—she didn't catch any hint of it in his gaze as he swept across them, inspecting their posture and stance. "Initiates. On time and in form. Well done. You'll do the Corps proud when you earn your gold."

Reiva's eyes darted to the fringe of gold at the edge of Brefon's mantle. The most obvious sign of a full Adept, in contrast to the silver fringe on hers.

The Adept cleared his throat, casting a baleful glance at the horizon. "Winds up," he said with a sour twist to his lips. "I'll see if the captain's ready to shove off."

Once Brefon was out of earshot, Luo whispered, "So, what's he like?"

At first Reiva thought he was speaking to her, before Tolm shrugged beside her and said in a deep voice, "He holds the *Ars Ventas*. The winds mean much to him."

That was right—Brefon was Tolm's mentor.

She fought a frown. That didn't seem fair. The supervising Adept reported on the performance of the Initiates in the field. If he was going to be weighing Tolm and her against each other...

"Hey."

Reiva blinked, realizing Tolm had spoken again.

He snorted. "Are you going to burn me?"

I would like to.

Reiva forced a smile that hopefully looked sincere. "Just thinking."

Tolm nodded slowly. "Well, enjoy it while it lasts—there's no time to think when you're battling the sea."

Reiva turned a wary eye to the horizon, now seeing the same gray bank that Brefon must have sensed on the winds with his *Ars Ventas*, far away though it was.

Luo shifted a bit uneasily. "We've got maritime training. How bad could it be?"

Tolm actually laughed. "Depends—how big a breakfast did you eat?"

"Pretty sizable."

"Then it will be very bad."

THE STORM, as it turned out, did not materialize. The ship, called the *Valor,* cut through the waves with ease, sails even and strong, oars beating a steady rhythm. Through blind luck or divine favor, the winds died down before they hit any rough seas. The captain of the

Valor, a gray-headed marine legionnaire bedecked with scars, seemed quite pleased about this. "Deep's fortune," he said, almost to himself, kissing a scrimshaw carving hung around his neck.

Every legion had its own character, even a set of stereotypes or jokes associated with their soldiery—but across every legion in the Empire, one thing held true: the marine legionnaires were seen as an odd lot. They were respected—intensely so, even—for their commitment to duty as they served beset by man, beast, and the heavens themselves. But that bevy of challenges often gave rise to dispositions that were viewed as zealous at best, absolutely maniacal at worst.

Tolm didn't seem particularly put off by the captain's mood. As a holder of the Art of Water, he had likely spent much of his training on ships—second only to Domi in that regard among their cohort. Luo, on the other hand, seemed content to give the captain a fair berth as he made his way about the deck. Luo was affable enough, but he seemed drawn to the edges—often looking into the depths below.

He held the *Ars Theron*, the Art of Beasts. It was a somewhat obscure Art, as far as such things went. Much like marine legionnaires, such Adepts often cultivated (intentionally or not) an odd mystique. It was true, many of them simply preferred the company of animals to humans, but many whispered that the nature of beasts somehow wound its way into the minds of *Theron* Adepts.

Reiva tried to remember how Luo used to comport himself. Anyone could change over several years, and Adepts often more so as they grew into their respective Arts and took on the various emotional and temperamental quirks associated with their powers.

But Luo seemed...more different than she would have expected. More reserved, perhaps. Skittish, even.

As she thought about it, she turned her attention inward, looking to her Flame. It had been low ever since they shoved off, but she had attributed that to the listing, sometimes nauseating roll of the vessel over the waves.

Now that her mind was on the task, she saw it everywhere—even in the marines' faces. Perhaps it wasn't as noticeable on them as it was on the less-experienced sea-goers, but Reiva was certain that etched in every visage there was an undercurrent of dread. Subtle sometimes, plain others, but always lurking beneath the surface.

She suddenly grasped the rail, leaning over to peer into the dark waters below. The sun lay behind the clouds, leaving the waves a grim black, impenetrable.

Her fingers fastened on the wood, nails digging into the grain.

"Something amiss?" asked Tolm.

Reiva's stomach clenched. "Just...seasick."

She glanced at him from the corner of her eye. He didn't seem to believe her words.

It was maddening how he seemed to handle himself so much better than her and Luo—another reminder of his incessant over-performance and excellence.

And yet...she could see it in him, too. A pallor in his face. A grim set of the jaw.

He followed her gaze down into the deep. "Afraid of monsters?"

Reiva shook her head. "Children's stories."

Tolm scoffed. "Spend enough time around marines and you'll find they tell very similar tales. But even the wildest maritime yarn doesn't take place this close to shore—and certainly nowhere near where we'll be going."

The mission was simple. A band of pirates had been traced to an island hideaway. Their numbers were not insignificant, but not so great as to present a challenge to a force of marine legionnaires alongside an Adept and three Initiates. They would corner the pirates in their hideaway, keeping them pinned in their cove and fending off any attempts at escape.

Piracy had always been a problem on the waves of the *Mare Magna*, the Great Sea, but since Lazarra's rise to power across the world, one of her greatest accomplishment's was the culling of the sea ravagers—in the same way that she had made safe the roads of the Ixian Reach and was gradually making safe all the world under the auspice of Imperial Dominion.

But always there was the element that persisted against the law and against the Emperor's reign. The work set before Reiva and her compatriots was therefore not uncommon in the grand scope of things—but for Reiva, who had scarcely set foot on deck a ship except for a brief maritime training sequence during her time in the Sanctum, the whole enterprise seemed an ever-widening sphere of foreboding.

For the first day and night, she could not find rest—such that the entire second day at sea slipped past in a groggy, irritable haze, the edge taken away only by a persistent channeling of aether to refresh her restless body and mind. The second night was hardly better, and she lay in her hammock belowdecks, hanging in the air alongside all the snoring, smelling crew—the musky air occasionally punctuated by the foul stench of a stomach turned out by seasickness, the poor bearer of said stomach having been unable to run topside in time and forced to empty himself into a bucket. More than once, Reiva found herself making that run.

And so, laid low by exhaustion and illness, she fell into a deep sleep the third night. As she drifted off, she felt grateful for the onsetting rest, because tomorrow they would to sail to within sight of the pirates' island.

Yet it was on the third night that the storm struck.

23

A DARK ABYSS

Reiva awoke to the hammering of thunder in the heavens. Hardly had she even realized sleep had fled from her did the boat list terribly, like a drunk man reeling through the road. Someone screamed—her, she would later realize—as she tumbled out of the hammock and rolled painfully along the wood.

She stuck out her arms, grabbing for anything that could give a clue to where she was—but then she felt water. All over her body, there was water. The ship was taking in the sea.

All around her, the voices of the crew battered her eardrums as an incessant, senseless menagerie. There were calls for buckets, calls for timber.

Reiva clutched at her neck, and feeling the familiar touch of her focus, stretched out her hand and kindled fire.

It was a stupid action, but she realized it too late.

Her eyes ached as the fire burned away her night vision—and did the same to all the others hustling around belowdecks. Cries of surprise and pain filled the air. Reiva extinguished the fire as a snap reaction—plunging the room into even deeper darkness than had been before.

Then—*CRASH!*

Impact knocked Reiva off her feet, sending her rolling across the boards again—splashing in water high enough to cover her head when she lay on her back.

And the water began to rise like a flood. The hull had been breached.

In seconds, the water level had risen fast enough that, as she stood, it came to her knees.

"Out out out!" came the harsh bellow of the ship's bosun. "Get that fire on, Adept!"

Compelled by the force of the order, she didn't even care that he had mistakenly referred to her as an Adept. She only hoped she lived long enough for the title to become true.

Her torch-like fist lit the way for the crew to stumble and splash toward the steep stairway that led above. Reiva tripped and trudged toward the steps, shouting as she went, "Here! The steps are here!"

Now the fire was a beacon of hope, and the legionnaires flocked to it like moths. She saw fear and determination in their faces, hope and terror on faces old and young. Most were dressed in little more than a tunic or loincloth. They had nothing with them as they fled— the storm had afforded them not a moment to gather weapon or keepsake. Only their lives could they take, and the clothes on their backs.

The icy cold water reached past Reiva's waist. Her breaths were coming more shallow now. She tried not to look at the blackness pooling around her, tried not to think of how much lay beyond the walls.

The ship began to list again, the weight of this chamber tugging the vessel's side lower.

She counted how many crew members were left. She wouldn't go until they were all out. That was what an Adept did, Alyat had impressed upon her again and again. She was there for the legionnaires. She was there to serve.

Finally, when the water had gone so high she was almost swimming, the bosun brought up the rear, grabbing Reiva's shoulder and pulling her up with him. There seemed to be a grim light of approval in his face as he appraised her.

His face came near to her ear as they listed up the unsteady stairway. "When she goes down, get clear! Stay together!"

Somehow, it was only then that the reality of the situation truly impressed itself upon her.

Shipwreck—alone at sea, with no food or fresh water.

Her body settled into the cold efficiency her training had pressed upon her. She had been taught what to do in events such as this.

As she burst into the torrential rain—drops stinging her skin like pelting needles—she stoked her fire. Steam sizzled around her hand, but she kept the light strong.

The captain shouted something, his words lost in the gale and the downpour.

That didn't matter—she had her plan. She was looking for the others—Luo and Tolm and Adept Brefon.

She espied them, as fortune had it. Brefon must have been on watch during the night, for he still had his red mantle around his shoulders and his full dress. Tolm was dressed in naught but his undergarments, while Luo had a tunic on. All looked miserable in their own right.

Reiva more climbed toward them than she walked, given the severe list of the ship. Brefon reached out and grabbed her, hauling her up to the railing with aetheric strength. "The captain's given the call to abandon ship!" he bellowed. "Stay together! Remember your training! Go! I'll find you when the storm clears!"

Reiva stared at the Adept, dumbfounded. Tolm's face was stricken with grief. All around them, men and women were jumping into the dark sea.

Then she opened her aetheric senses, and she realized why Brefon was sending them on without him.

He was a storm of aetheric power in his own right—his *Ars Ventas* roared with all the might of a miniature sun. And Reiva understood, with dumbstruck awe, that the Adept was *shielding* the ship from the brunt of the storm, countering it with his own winds. Had it not been for him, they would have gone under long before.

Her jaw hung, and Brefon actually struck her across the face. "I didn't pull you out of that slave line for you to die here, girl! *Go!*"

Someone's hands closed around Reiva's shoulders—it was Luo—and he pulled her overboard.

For a brief moment, they were flying. And then, the water struck like a dozen whips of ice. Everything was darkness. Darkness and cold and horrible silence.

Kick!

Reiva's head broke the surface, back into the realm of chaos.

The sky split with bursts of lightning and that same dreadful drumming of thunder, casting the ship in a ghoulish light—all torn sails and groaning wood.

Luo tried to tow her away. "Come on!"

"Where's Tolm?" she shouted back.

As if summoned, his head burst from the black waters, closer to the ship.

"Tolm!" she screamed.

But either he did not hear her, or he did not care to—his face was turned toward Adept Brefon, toward his master, standing alone at the highest point of the ship, arms outstretched as gales of power surged around him.

It was like a scene from Lazarran statuary, something that would decorate the center of a great square in the capital. *The Adept Holds Back the Storm.*

And then, in an instant, the scene was shattered by a blinding lance of light falling from heaven at the speed of thought.

The lightning struck Adept Brefon with explosive force, burning Reiva's eyes—and she saw him no longer.

An aggrieved scream tore itself from her lungs, only for bitter seawater to force its way through her mouth. She spit it out, hacking and coughing.

"Tol—!" The water smothered her again, a wave striking her.

Luo's arm was wrapped around her now, and he was towing her away. "Reiva!" he wailed. "Stop fighting me or I'll leave you!"

Clenching her teeth, she turned her back on the ship—almost entirely below the waves by now—and on Tolm, wherever he was. All the while, choking on water and kicking her legs, she saw the terrible image of Brefon illuminated by the smiting fire of heaven.

Don't think about him, she told herself, time and time again as the horrible memory forced its way to the fore of her mind. *Don't think about it. Think about survival.*

Only survival.

As she and Luo swam, empowered by aether, Reiva caught a different sound on the wind—a human sound.

"Did you hear that?" she called. "To the right—I think I heard a marine."

Luo turned according to her words, and together they began to swim. Reiva tried reconstructing a map of the area. The ship—she was fairly certain—was now sunken somewhere to their right. That meant she and Luo were inscribing an arc. Maybe these marines had moved in a similar shape, having leapt from the other side of the ship into the water.

Or maybe they were nowhere near where Reiva thought they were, and the waves had tossed and turned them around too many times to have even the slightest semblance of a coherent frame of reference.

Either way, what mattered was finding others—more people together at sea gave them better odds. They would be easier to spot, less likely to go mad than they would in isolation, and perhaps most importantly, greater numbers of people created a less appealing target for—

A scream split the air.

Reiva poured on even more power. Someone was injured—perhaps a bone had broken in the fall from the ship, or after taking a spill while still aboard. If she could get to the legionnaire in question, she could channel aether and—

Another scream, from a different location. Then another, and another.

And in counterpoint to the wordless cries—which Reiva now realized were not only cries of agony, but of *fear*—she heard another sort of cry, a far more articulate, almost more terrible sort of cry.

"Great Arkhon, save me!"

"Queen of the Sea! Have mercy! Have mer—!"

Reiva lost all forward momentum. Luo similarly stopped. Together, they treaded water for a moment.

She felt her fellow Initiate stiffen beside her—every muscle going tense. She knew that reflex. It was a fear response.

A prey response.

A marine legionnaire popped up over a wave, thrashing and yelling. "My brother!" he yelled. "It took my brother! It took—!"

And his final words vanished in a shocked yell, as he went under, his hands vanishing, clawing desperately at wind and rain that offered no purchase.

"Sharks," Luo whispered through clenched teeth. "I can feel them."

The dark waters surrounding them became a theater of horror. Every rising wave seemed a daggerlike fin, every tossing current was the force of a flicking tail.

Reiva's gut seized up. She almost lost control of her bladder—something that had never happened when facing even the fiercest of human foes.

She pulled herself close to Luo, grabbing his shoulders, forcing him to look at her. "Luo, send them away."

"I've never touched a shark's mind," he pleaded. His eyes screwed shut. "Reiva—oh, they're *ravenous*."

Her mind filled with images of teeth—endless teeth. "They're beasts like any other. Send them away."

"Oh gods above—I can feel one below us. It wants to know what we—"

The thought must have been too horrible, because it dissolved into an empty groan. His head listed to the side, almost like he was passing out.

"Luo, stay with me, Luo! Use your Art."

"It's getting ready. *It's coming.* It's going to—"

"LUO!"

The Initiate made a wretched sound, almost like he had been stabbed.

So close she could have touched it, a massive dark shape burst from the water beside them. Reiva and Luo screamed as the breached shark rose almost entirely of the water, its bright white underbelly stark in contrast to its rugged gray back.

As it fell back below the surface, sending a wave of water over them, Reiva could have sworn she saw a shining black eye, staring at her like a child inspecting a new doll.

She pulled Luo close, looping one arm around his chest so that she could tow him. "Good," she choked out. "Now keep them away."

She began doing the backstroke with one arm, kicking with her legs.

Luo's form stayed rigid. She focused most of her aether on swimming, but now and then she'd spare a trickle to open her aetheric sense. Sure enough, Luo's *Ars Theron* stayed active.

Reiva moved them—much as it terrified her—toward the direction of the screams. If anyone else was still up, she wanted Luo's warding presence to benefit them as well.

When she guessed they might be nearer the other crew members, she began calling out. "Anyone! You're safe with us! We can keep them away!"

She received no answer.

She yelled out again, her throat scraping raw. Surely it had just been that the wind was too strong, the rain too thick...

But still, no one answered.

She tried again, this time earning a mouth of seawater for her efforts.

After the fourth time, she had to focus on breathing again. Breathing and the flow of aether to her limbs.

They went for a while longer, sometimes fighting against the waves, other times fortunate enough to be pushed along by them. More than once, a terribly great wall of water lifted them up and smashed them down, sending them into the pitch blackness. Reiva clung especially tight to Luo in those moments, desperately hoping his concentration had not failed, lest a toothy maw grab hold and never let them surface.

After one such experience, Luo coughed a word. "Left."

"What?" Reiva half-screamed, her head whipping, fearing another monster of the deep was on the approach.

"The sharks don't swim to the left. They see it as...a wall."

Reiva's heart soared. She altered their course. "I'll take us," she huffed, fighting against the twin enemies of fatigue and mounting aether sickness. "Keep at it."

She felt him nod against her, and she threw herself into the work. Now and then, she had to switch arms. But she never let herself stop moving. If she stopped, it would be twice as hard to start again.

Sometimes, Alyat said, the opposition was so great your only option was to keep moving—staying still meant you were knocked on your back, and however hellish it felt to fight a stampede on your feet, it was damn impossible when you were getting trod over.

So she mastered the pleas of her body and soul—the pleas for rest and respite. Occasionally Luo would call out a correction to their course, and Reiva would obey.

It seemed that hours more dragged on, and the storm still did not abate. But eventually, Luo gave the encouraging word that the sharks were farther away now. Though he did not relax his vigil, which Reiva imagined was as taxing as her own work.

At long last, something changed in the water. The motion of it seemed ever so slightly different.

She threw back her arm, and on the downstroke her fingers struck sand.

She almost sobbed, releasing Luo from her grasp.

The two of them got to their feet—they were already close enough to shore that the water was to their waists. Blind hope and relief gave a final burst of energy, and Reiva stumbled onward with Luo at her side.

The dark clouds and torrential rain allowed only a few yards of vision—but it was enough. She could see land.

Her knees broke free from the surf, then her calves, and at long last her feet. Together, they trudged up the beach, going on until the sea felt sufficiently far away—until it was no longer in sight, but was only the distant pounding of waves.

She dropped to her hands and knees and pressed her forehead to the earth. "Wandering God," she gasped.

And then she collapsed, fatigue finally claiming her. She thought she lay like that for an age, but as soon as Luo shook her, she realized it had been hardly a minute.

"*Sleep*," she begged.

"Out of the rain," Luo said, sounding just as weary as she felt.

She groaned, realizing she could not bring herself to lift her own body. It was even worse than her first day of training when she couldn't do another push-up. The pounding in her head warned her against drawing any further on aether.

So she crawled, arm by arm, towing her body through wet sand. Luo similarly made his way onward, though he was at least able to crawl on hands and knees, his body having been spared the exhaustion of swimming.

Blessedly, they did not have to go for long before they reached tree cover. Together they took refuge in a spot partially sheltered from the downpour. As the cold and exhaustion finally settled in, the two of them shivered together, clutching one another in as tight a huddle as they could manage. Reiva never got cold anymore—not in any meaningful degree—but she still shook, aware in every fiber how near to death they had come.

Trembling and drenched, the two of them shuddered until sleep —no longer one to be fended off—claimed Reiva in a sudden sweep, plunging her into dreams of a dark abyss filled with horrible forms.

24

PIRATES

WAKEFULNESS CAME with bleary eyes and full-body aches.

Reiva groaned, stretching out of the cramped, crouched pose she had lowered herself into to escape the chill, death-strewn night. The problem was opposite by now—the sun was in the sky, and it was baking them.

Reiva nudged Luo, who experienced by all appearances a similarly painful awakening.

Reiva surveyed the beach. In the late morning light, it seemed almost idyllic. Their footprints were long gone, but she guessed at the path they had taken from the shoreline. The waves were no longer black and choppy, but a pristine, clear blue. They almost looked *inviting*, were it not for the fact that Reiva currently had no desire to ever swim again in her life.

Luo sighed as he stretched out. He seemed struggling with whether to say something.

Reiva took the initiative. "Think anyone else made it?"

He could only shake his head. "I hope so, but..."

"Yeah."

"I felt a lot of sharks in the water. And their minds..." He shuddered. "So cold. Colder than the water."

Reiva swallowed. She had done the work of towing them through the water, but in some ways, Luo's labor had been worse.

"You were warm though," he added belatedly. "I don't know if I could have slept in that rain otherwise."

Reiva shrugged. "Side effect of the Art. Happens sometimes."

Luo nodded. "*Theron* sometimes creates a general attraction that draws animals to you. Kinda glad I never acquired that."

"Guess the gods really do care sometimes," Reiva drawled.

Luo snorted. "I'll burn an extra offering if they care enough to get us out of this."

The two of them got to their feet, wincing and groaning as they did so. Reiva brushed a great deal of sand off, only to discover that her tunic was encrusted with salt. She glanced at Luo, noting similar white streaks on his—as well as in his eyebrows and hair.

"Do I look as shipwrecked as you do?" she asked.

He glanced at himself, then at her, and snorted. "No, you look worse."

She cracked a half-smile. "Well thank you."

"Any time."

If there was one thing Reiva had learned was essential to the success of the Lazarran legions, it was the ability to make and take jokes at one another's expense even in the most morbid of circumstances.

But the circumstances, eventually, had to be addressed.

"With all that rain last night, we should be able to find some fresh water."

Luo concurred. "And hopefully some food along with it." He was already scanning the trees. "Think that fruit's edible?"

"If it is, you can climb for it yourself."

"Maybe later then."

Going off the lay of the land, they guessed a river might be flowing southwesterly. Survivalist training didn't cover much about deserted islands, but how different could it be, really?

Reiva flexed her fingers as they went, feeling out the wear on her soul. She didn't feel the same headache as she had last night, but she certainly wasn't at full capacity yet. She needed more rest.

"Any animals around?" she asked tentatively.

Luo shrugged. "Some small critters, some birds. We won't starve —but I'd rather not resort to grubs unless we have to."

"What, never ate bugs as a kid?"

"As a *kid*."

"I'll be sure to carve *Killed by Adult Hubris* on your grave marker, then."

"I knew I could count on you."

Their walking was soon rewarded by exactly the sound they were hunting—the trickle of running water.

Luo whooped, running on ahead.

Reiva reached a hand after him. "Luo, wait—"

But then she heard the splash, followed by an eager cheer. "It's good!" he called.

Reiva hurried after him. "We should boil it," she chided.

Luo threw his hands up, sending a splattering of water at her. "If fresh water kills me after all this, I'll compliment the gods' sense of humor when I see them."

He submerged his face halfway, taking hearty gulps.

Reiva wrinkled her nose. "You're swimming in that."

"It's a *river*. Drink. Here, these roots look edible."

Reiva sighed, taking another look around before kneeling down to collect some water—slightly upstream from where Luo was working at tearing up the roots. She *did* want to wash off all this salt and sand, but she'd rather not drink from the same spot she took a bath.

Just as she was lifting the water to her lips, Luo gave another triumphant shout. He took a loud, crunchy bite from the liberated tuber. "See, things are already looking up."

He stretched his hand toward her, offering the rest of the vegetable.

And then something shifted behind him. Reiva only had time to hone in on the movement before a blur of metal spun end-over-end from the brush.

Luo's head whipped forward, the blade of a hatchet buried in his skull.

Heart in her throat, Reiva jumped to her feet, throwing up her hands and throwing a screen of flames at the source of the attack.

Luo was facedown in the water, crimson tendrils leaking from his head, the root still clutched in his hand.

Another hatchet tumbled through Reiva's flames, narrowly missing her.

Then a spear whistled through—and it did not miss.

The head tore along her side. She grit her teeth and forced down a pained groan.

Her head ached again—aether sickness already returning with a vengeance.

With one last look at Luo—at Luo's corpse—she turned and ran.

Despite the pounding pain of aether sickness, she poured aether into her legs, feeling the wound in her side close preternaturally. She ran further into the jungle, knowing that if they caught her in the open terrain of the beach, she was good as dead.

All she knew was the location of the river, the direction of the beach, and the rough direction her enemies lay. Not a lot to go on.

In terms of equipment, she had her focus, a salt-caked tunic, and her underclothes.

Not a lot to fight a battle with. She cursed herself for not grabbing the spear that had pierced her side—that was a novice mistake. Her mind was still weary from the shipwreck and the swim. And the shock of losing Luo.

She shook her head, fighting against the tears that threatened to spill from her eyes as she ran. She ducked branches and leaped over rocks. All the while she heard the crashing of pursuers behind her— pursuers who certainly knew the lay of the land far better than she did.

You give in to fatigue—you die.

Another spear whistled through the air. She threw herself into a roll and felt it *thud* into the soft earth not a foot away. This time, she grabbed hold of it and kept going.

You give in to stupidity—you die.

She came around to the river again—much further downstream. The trees were thicker here. She heard a roaring sound coming from up ahead—rapids, perhaps. That could hide the sound of her movement.

You give in to fear—you die.

She heard shouting from behind—gruff voices, men speaking Karellan. Reiva poured another burst of aether into her legs, leaping up onto a rocky outcropping. The outcropping ended in open air—a fifty foot plunge beneath her. It wasn't rapids that she had heard—it was a waterfall.

So live. You have seven years of training. Live.

She took a breath and jumped, holding the spear overhead and putting her legs together.

Gods be praised—the pool at the base of the walls was deep enough for the plunge.

She opened her eyes, peering into the murky depths around her. The surface was about fifteen feet above—and she knew from when she jumped that visibility didn't reach this low, especially not right where the falls hit.

So she swam against the current, until she was right under the white of the falls, and jammed her spear as deep into the soil as she could manage. She stayed like that for as long as she could bear, until her lungs screamed in agony and every instinct was demanding she surface and take a gasp of precious air.

So she closed her eyes and channeled aether through her body.

Live! she ordered herself.

She ignored the headache from the aether sickness, ignored the aching bones and muscles, ignored the scream in her lungs.

She was an Adept Initiate, and she would not fail in her task.

The aether flowed through her, rejuvenating her fatigue and healing her pains—but more importantly, it acted as a substitute for air.

It was an uncommon technique—one Adepts were only to use in the most dire of circumstances. Air was essential to human survival, and aether could not truly replace it. But it could heal the damage the body incurred by its lack.

Which meant she could stay at the bottom of the river for as long as her soul could bear the strain.

She shut out any sense of time, allowing the muffled roar of the waterfall to overcome her perception. She only cared for the cycling of the aether within. With as much stinginess as she could bear, she measured her draw—a trickle, just enough to keep her from blacking out. Spent air, she let out from her mouth in little bubbles, relying on the momentary sense of relief it gave to help her bear the pain.

Overall, it was agony—everything about her physiology rebelled against this tactic.

But it let her stay underwater, in the one place she was almost sure she wouldn't be found.

And if she was found—then she would join Luo in congratulating the gods on their sense of humor.

'When it's your time, it's your time,' Alyat often said.

Well, if Reiva had any say in it, she'd live to hear him say it again.

She stayed like that until the pounding in her skull became dreadful as a nail hammered through her temple.

She opened her eyes, noting with alarm the black spots decorating her vision.

It would have to be long enough—any longer and she'd progress to a worse degree of aether sickness, and at that point she'd practically be useless.

So she gingerly pulled the spear free and kicked off the bottom, sending herself to the surface.

She let only her eyes and nose out—and she surfaced on the inner side of the falls, beside the rocks. Slowly—even though her lungs desperately wanted mouthful gulps of air—she breathed in through her nostrils. She turned around, scanning what she could see of the trees.

When she was reasonably confident she was alone, she lifted her mouth out and began to breathe again.

She spent a few minutes just breathing, letting her body recover —at least as much as it *could* recover, given what it had been through. She craved a nap more than anything right now—just an hour or so to take the edge off her aether sickness.

Even so, survival took precedence over comfort at the moment. She edged her way to the rocks along the waterside, then again waited for a while. When the time came, she slowly lifted herself, checking over her shoulder and to the sides as she did so. Then, she crept for the trees—even though she was out in the open, she went slowly so as to not draw any attention by a sudden burst of movement.

Spear at the ready, she crept through the jungle. She would need to return to the water later, but right now, the priority was getting away from where she had last been seen. If she could make progress toward a shelter for the night, that would be ideal, but sustenance would be first on the docket.

Once she could no longer hear the waterfall, she knelt down in the dirt. The climate on the island—in the heart of the jungle at least —was humid, and the heavy rains had left the ground thoroughly soaked, in some places to the point of mud. She took handfuls of this and smeared it all over herself. In lighter circumstances she might have smirked at the irony—not an hour ago she had bemoaned how her clothes and skin were caked with dried salt, and as soon as she had gotten clean of that she started bathing herself in dirt.

Once she was sufficiently covered, she did the same to her spear. She had nothing to tie her hair with, so she quickly knotted it at the end and tucked it down the back of her tunic. Not ideal, but better than letting it fly free.

Then she returned to stalking the jungle.

It wasn't long before she came across a path. It wasn't anything close to what would have passed for a road in Lazarra, or any civilized place, but it bore clear signs of foot traffic. Reiva picked a suitable spot nearby and waited, chewing on a leaf to stave off boredom and the pangs of hunger.

It wasn't until the sun was high in the sky that her stake out bore fruit.

A pair of men, both armed and with heavy jackets on despite the heat, strolled down the path. "Aye," said one of them, "captain will be in the tips that we lost the girl—but she was one of them *Adepts.* What were we supposed to do?"

"You scared of a little girl?"

"Oh, she looked old enough if you take my meaning."

The two cackled. Reiva thought back to her encounter with two men in the streets of Lazarra late at night, and she remembered Alyat's words then: '*Next time, don't give the enemy the opportunity to scream.*'

And she would carry that out—but first, she needed information.

So she began to stalk them. It wasn't something she had expected to do, being an Adept of Flame, but it was something the Sanctum had taken care to prepare her for anyway. She had spent time with the best of the Legion Scouts, and they had drilled her thoroughly on the craft of following a target unseen and unheard.

The men were going roughly west on the path. That meant their headquarters likely lay in that direction. By now, Reiva had settled on the assumption that these men—and the man who had killed Luo, if he was not one of these two—were the same pirate band they had been sent to take care of.

"Besides," one pirate said after a bit more walking, "we've gotten, what, a dozen so far? Good enough for a ransom."

"Aye, but Scobo killed the lad earlier. He had one of them necklaces on—captain'll be pissed about that."

"Would the Lazarrans *pay* for one of their Adepts, or would they just send a whole legion after us?"

"Well, you know the captain—*brilliant* with negotiations he is."

"Too right," snickered the other. "Too right."

Reiva continued her pursuit, checking over her shoulder now and then, but mostly focusing on the ground before her—any twigs or animals presented the possibility of alerting her quarry. The real difficulty was the risk of squelching the wet ground with her footsteps. So rather than lift her feet, she just pulled them through the mud. It burned her thighs, and she was reticent to use any aether to add strength and endurance, but it was quieter.

Thankfully, the pirates were loud enough that she could follow at a fair distance and make out every word they said.

"What about the dark-skinned fellow spotted around the northern side?"

Reiva went still.

Tolm.

"Last I heard, he was still loose—killed a couple of ours before he got away though."

"Right bastard."

"Heard they're gonna try to get him in a pincer. Should be trussed up and in the brig afore supper."

"Or dead."

"Aye, or dead."

"Heheh, aye. But I'm sure the captain wants to speak with him personally about what he did."

"Brilliant negotiator, the captain is."

"Too right, too right."

Reiva waited until they were too far for her to hear anything, and then she counted to ten.

As soon as the count was up, she bolted.

25

DESPERATE HOPE

ALYAT HAD ONCE MENTIONED there was a philosophy—or it might have been a religion—that held to the principle of balance in all things. Where one suffered a cruelty of fortune one day, they would find it replaced with an unearned gift the next—and so all life and all the cosmos were thought, eventually, to amount to something approaching fairness.

Reiva had never placed much stock in the theory, but if any force or god was seeking to pay her back for that hellish night in the storm, she was willing to accept, no questions asked.

She ran through the jungle, once again drawing—against her better judgment—on the aether. She was running up a debt, and eventually her soul would force her to pay it off—by rest or by cannibalizing her sanity. The human form simply was not meant to funnel so much power through it in so little a time.

As far as the Initiates went, though, she was one of the best when it came to aether tolerance—maybe even *the* best, Alyat had speculated.

It would have to do.

She followed the pathways when she came upon them, but before long their winding way often diverged from her northward trajectory, and so time and again she had to push her way through the vines and branches and muddy sloughs of the jungle. She wished constantly for a blade—a sword or an axe—that she could wield to blaze a trail, but all she had was the spear. Better than nothing, but not a weapon she had any particular love for.

As she ran, she occasionally opened her aetheric perception.

"Come on," she hissed. "Do something. Give me a sign, something to follow."

She was nowhere near as expert as Alyat when it came to sensing aetheric activity—she could hardly extend her senses to cover the entire Sanctum even in her best moments—which meant peace, quiet, and uninterrupted concentration for perhaps ten minutes. She had none of that now, forcing her to resort to brief pulses of her awareness, and the desperate hope that eventually, one of them would coincide with Tolm using his Art of Water.

Just as she came to within earshot of the northern shore and the surreal calm of the waves, she caught a burst of aetheric power.

Rejuvenated by her good fortune, she tore down the beach, hugging the tree line.

When she found Tolm, he was outnumbered ten to one.

Reiva didn't hesitate, pouring another burst of aether into her legs. The fight was happening in a relatively sheltered cove, with high walls of rock on either side—leaving Tolm truly cornered. He was standing in the waves, a hatchet clutched in one hand—likely taken from one of three dead pirates lying in the surf.

His other hand he held in the air, waving it back and forth in a hypnotic motion. Behind him, several tendrils of sea water rose from the waves, undulating in time with his hand.

This was the key difference between Domi's Art of Sea and Tolm's Art of Water. Domi could manipulate and move great amounts of water at once, but she couldn't use any finesse or precision. Tolm held water like a sword, and he used it to great effect.

Two pirates—either undeterred by their comrades' deaths or determined to avenge them—charged Tolm, one on either side.

Tolm lashed his open hand toward the left attacker, and a tendril of water whipped right for the man's eyes. The pirate must have been expecting the move, because he ducked—only for another whip of water to strike him in the chest, then another in the gut. A final tendril swept around the man's legs, knocking him on his back.

In the same moment, Tolm blocked a cutlass-strike from the right side attacker, using the thick wooden handle of his hatchet. Unceasing in his movement, he flowed into a precise kick against the inside of the pirate's knee. Reiva heard the *crack* even from this distance. Tolm didn't hesitate to press his advantage and open a wide gash in the man's throat.

Before the wounded pirate could even hit the ground, Tolm turned back to the one he had struck and tripped with the water. The hatchet came down straight on the man's chest, splitting it open and spraying Tolm with countless red droplets. It was hardly a noticeable change—the male Initiate was already covered in blood. Reiva hoped it was mostly his enemies.

In just seconds, Tolm had turned the number of bodies at his feet from three to five—but Reiva could see even from this distance that the *Ars Aquae* was exacting a heavy toll. Not only did it take a great degree of energy to maintain so much control at once, Tolm was also splitting his focus, fighting with a weapon at the same time he juggled several strands of aetheric influence.

He was the best the Seventh Cohort had, and he was putting up a worthy fight—but he was going to die.

Or he would have, if Reiva had not reached the pirates just then, catching them totally off guard, so single-minded was their attention on Tolm.

Reiva jabbed the spear through the back of one pirate's neck, pulling it back out with ruthless efficiency. She didn't even slow her run as she moved to a second. This woman had the intuition to realize something was barreling down on her—but it was too late. Reiva thrust the spear through her—in one side of her ribcage and out the other—blowing a spray of blood onto the two pirates on her other side.

By the time they knew what was happening, Reiva had thrown

the skewered she-pirate to the side and raised her hands. Without a single word of communication between them, Tolm dove into a roll, and Reiva unleashed a blazing wave of fire and blistering heat.

The two pirates caught in the blast wailed—one of them dropped right away, while the other had the good sense (or cowardice) to turn and run as soon as Reiva had joined the fray. He dove into the shallow surf, sending up a puff of smoke as he disappeared.

The heightened aetheric draw hit Reiva like a forge hammer, and she saw black spots dancing at the edge of her vision. She withdrew the channeling from her legs, and right away they began to wobble.

Reiva snarled, grinding her teeth together.

Live!

She snatched up a cutlass from the first pirate she had killed, turning on the remaining pirates.

Tolm had not been content to sit on the sidelines and watch, though.

His water whips lashed out in an endless, seemingly unwavering flurry. Though he stood against four pirates, hardly one could even get near him. Salt water struck their eyes, their legs were swept out from underneath them, their weapons knocked aside by arms they could not wound, only shatter for them to reform an instant later.

Reiva jumped into the clash. The cutlass was a longer blade than the gladius she was used to fighting with, but a sword was a sword—and she could count on one hand the number of things she had spent more time and effort on than swordplay these past seven years.

The first pirate wasn't even a challenge; the sudden shift in circumstances shocked him too much to fight properly. Reiva touched blades with him twice before slicing off his hand and following through with an overhead cut—a burst of aether empowered the strike enough to cleave all the way from collarbone to heart, and he dropped to the ground stone dead.

Tolm blinded the second with a jet of water to the eyes, then handily followed up by planting his hatchet between the pirate's eyes.

The third was ready for Reiva, and he had a spear. That gave him better reach—unfortunately for him, it did him no good. One of

Tolm's water whips batted his spear to the side, leaving Reiva a wide opening to close the distance and dispatch him.

The fourth pirate, she and Tolm moved on together. Tolm threw his hatchet at the man, and he made sure to wind-up for the throw clearly. The pirate knocked it aside handily.

And so he was too distracted and slow to respond to Reiva when she executed a precise horizontal cut to his neck, following through with power and elegance that would have made Alyat proud.

The resulting spray of blood from the beheading left the sand a hideous wet crimson.

Reiva took a long breath, letting her eyes sweep over the battle scene.

Less than a minute ago, ten pirates had been standing. Now nine were dead, and the tenth was hiding in the surf, trapped just as he had been cornering Tolm moments before.

She looked at her fellow Initiate. When she had last seen Tolm, he had been dressed in only a loincloth and his focus, drenched in the storm that sunk the *Valor* and killed his mentor.

Now he was painted in red, and he wore what must have been a pirate's leather jerkin. His chest heaved with exertion, and sweat pooled on his skin, mixing with the splatters of blood and trickling down his face, neck, and arms.

Reiva wasn't sure what to do, what to say. So she tapped her fist to her heart.

Tolm nodded and returned the salute.

The two of them turned, wearily, to the last remaining pirate.

"I'm sure you're used to saying this to other people," Reiva began, "but we can do this the easy way or the hard way."

The pirate stumbled backward, clutching a charred patch of his sleeve, the skin beneath which was likely in agony from the burn and salt water. "I'm not like the others! I needed the money, you see? I'll help you! I owe no loyalty to the captain!"

Tolm spat. "You were loyal enough to try and kill me. How much is a pocketful of coin worth to you? How much should I value the loyalty of a man who readily admits he has none?"

Reiva flexed her off-hand, letting a flicker of fire race around her fingers. She did it more for effect—the man was fairly safe with so much water. But the gesture was not lost on him.

"Don't kill me," he whimpered. "Please."

"Show us some good faith by coming out," Reiva called, "before we have to drag you out."

The pirate's lower lip quivered. He looked between Reiva and Tolm frantically, as if one of them would suddenly decide to show him mercy. "If I could just—"

Tolm made a guttural sound and stuck his hand into the water.

The pirate yelped, and a gush of water pushed him closer to shore. He tripped, falling face first in the surf. When he came up, he sputtered, "If I could just—"

Tolm *pulled*, and again the water launched the man forward. By now he had taken the hint and scrambled out of the water on his hands and knees. When he found himself face-to-face with the charred corpse of the fellow who'd taken the full brunt of Reiva's magic, he turned his head to the side, looking like he was about to retch.

"Talk to us or you end up like him," Reiva snarled.

It was a hollow threat, in truth. She would much rather just stick him with the cutlass and be done with it, rather than expend another burst of aether calling forth flames—but he had no way of knowing how worn out she was.

She also realized she was still coated in mud, and with the addition of several hearty gushes of blood, she must have looked more monster than human.

The lone pirate took several shallow breaths. "Th-the others are in our hideaway. On the west side of the island."

"Who are the others?" snapped Tolm. "And how many?"

"The others from your ship!" He pointed eastward. "You wrecked off the coast, a couple miles only. The current brought a few of you here."

"How many?" Tolm reiterated.

"At least a dozen."

"Wounded?" Reiva asked.

"Some. Most surrendered, but a few had bad wounds—shark bites—and didn't make it, or they're good as dead."

"You killed the ones who didn't surrender?"

"No! We were going to ransom them—you can't ransom a dead legionnaire to the Lazarrans. The only one we killed was the lad with the Adept neckla—" The pirate made a choked sound, as if he hadn't realized the words flowing from his mouth.

Tolm's expression turned even grimmer.

Reiva glanced toward the charred pirate. Laying beside him was a hatchet—the weapon that this man had dropped when he ran for the water.

"Were you the one," she asked, voice deathly cold, "who killed Luo? The one who was—*look at me*—the one who was with me at the river? Scobo, is that your name?" she said, recalling what the pirates on the path had mentioned earlier.

The pirate had been shaking terribly, but as soon as she spoke the name, a pitiful groan escaped his lips. She leaned down, going almost nose to nose with him. She caught a miniature reflection of herself in his pupils. Yes, more monster than human indeed.

"It was on Curo's orders," he whined. "You already killed him—that's him right there!" he pointed wildly. Reiva didn't turn her eyes away from him.

"How many more of you are there?" she asked, her voice sounding far calmer in her ears than she felt.

"Another...fifteen or so? Twenty? Numbers aren't my game. A crew just came in from a raid."

Tolm picked up the hatchet laying beside the burned body. "So your whole merry band is on the island?"

"Every one of us—unless the captain sent anyone off, but with the storm last night and the wreck he wouldn't—"

"Describe your hideaway."

The pirate walked them through the layout, the entrances, where they kept the weapons and where they kept the loot, the captain's room.

"And our ship is in port right beside the hideaway—we sail from a cove, like this one but set into the rock. You can hardly see it from the water if you don't know what you're looking for."

"And you only have the one ship?" Tolm asked.

"There's a smaller one, not fit for a full crew. It's a pleasure boat, really—something we brought back from a run. But it can't brave the open seas."

Tolm hummed, moving to stand behind the pirate.

Reiva flexed her fingers around the grip of the cutlass. "What else should we know?"

The pirate babbled, tripping over his words, looking back and forth between Reiva and Tolm, never able to keep both in his sights at once. "There are some other hostages—kidnapped for ransom. Karellans mostly, not Lazarran."

"Karellans are part of the Empire," Reiva said.

"But they're not…"

Something in Reiva's expression made him trail off.

"You're not going to kill me, are you? I *helped* you."

Tolm raised his hatchet. "And for that, I'll make it painless."

The blade struck him at the base of the brain, instantly dashing the light from his eyes. He was dead before his face hit the sand.

Reiva nodded to Tolm. "Thanks."

He gave her a quizzical look.

"He killed Luo right in front of me. I wouldn't have been able to do it as kindly as that."

Tolm shrugged. "Nothing kind about it—I'm too tired for more than one strike."

"Fair enough." She took another look around the beach, scanned the tree line. "I heard some other pirates talking about how this lot was planning to corner you. When these ten don't come back, they'll come looking."

Tolm made a displeased sound. "Where did you wash ashore?"

"Southern coast. It's too close to the hideaway."

He nodded. "We'll go east then. From what I've seen so far, most of the island over there is overgrown jungle—they haven't tamed it yet. We fall back and plan our next move."

"Sounds as good a strategy as any." Reiva sniffed, turning her eye to the female pirate she'd impaled. "But first, let me get some real clothes off this one."

26

———

A FOOLISH TALE FOR SALVATION

AFTER SCAVENGING some clothes and weapons from the dead pirates, Reiva and Tolm headed east. They got off the beach right away so as not to be caught in the open, and they also kept out of sight from any pathways. Freshwater streams, too, they avoided wary of the likelihood the pirates would concentrate their searches around such an essential resource.

Reiva had washed off most of the mud in the surf before donning her new attire, and while she had to admit that slathering herself would have been effective for the sake of staying hidden, she wasn't particularly eager to ruin a new set of clothes so quickly. Setting aside the holes on either side and the bloodstains, of course, which hadn't washed out in the ocean.

The two of them looked the part well enough anyway, with their loose trousers, dark jackets, and cutlasses tucked through their belts. If they came across any of the pirates, they'd likely have the benefit of a few moments of confused identity before their enemies knew what was going on.

Thankfully, they didn't encounter any such foes. The two of them were battling aether sickness—a worse degree than either of them had ever reached under the watchful eyes of mentors and instructors.

Tolm said he had pushed himself almost this far during a field mission once. Reiva couldn't say she had.

After a few hours of trekking, as the sun was on its downward slope toward the horizon, Reiva slumped against a tree. When Tolm asked if it was the sickness, she just shook her head. "Haven't eaten in over a day," she said plainly. "Hardly kept anything down on the ship."

Tolm twisted his lips into a grimace. "All right, wait here. And hand me that spear."

Reiva ordinarily would have never been one to stay behind, but she had to swallow her pride and admit that she just would have slowed him down. As she waited in the shade of the tree, she wondered how those roots Luo had found tasted.

She thought of the moment of his death again—how he must have not even realized it was happening. Was that a good way to die? All at once, not expecting it? Would you blink and find yourself in the afterlife?

A sick feeling gnawed in her gut—and it wasn't the hunger. She tried to remember if Luo was particularly religious. Would he care if his remains were burned on a pyre? Reiva wasn't one for believing in ghosts or hauntings, but what if his spirit held her accountable to what happened? Surely he wouldn't blame her for running—she had had no other option.

She rubbed her forehead, forcing herself to take slow breaths.

Focus on surviving now. Worry about these things after.

Easier said than done, when all she could do at the moment was sit on her backside and hope Tolm didn't run into a troupe of brigands on his way.

As soon as the thought crossed her mind, the man himself reappeared, a still-wriggling fish spit on the end of the spear.

Reiva's eyes widened. "From the rivers?"

He shook his head. "The beach. There are plenty in the shallows."

Reiva kept staring at the creature, mesmerized by its slowing movements. "Still. I never learned to spear a fish in training."

"I did have a life before the Adept Corps."

Reiva perked up at that. "You were a fisherman?" she asked.

"The son of one. The best in our village." He seemed to puff out his chest as he said so. That surprised her. "Nets are better, but..." he gestured to the jungle around them.

"Fair enough," she muttered. "So, are we eating that raw?"

"Do you have it in you to start a fire?"

She nodded slowly, wincing. "I can manage it. Just get me something dry enough."

That proved a more difficult task than anticipated, but before long they had a small cookfire going. Tolm handily gutted the fish and set its meat on makeshift skewers fashioned from sticks.

No sooner had Tolm declared it was ready did Reiva snatch her skewer and pop the whole cut of fish into her mouth. When she finally bit into it, it was the most glorious thing she'd ever tasted. To her surprise, she actually took the time to chew it, savoring every moment before finally swallowing it.

Tolm gaped. "Wasn't it too hot?" Reiva's expression must have been priceless because he actually laughed. "Right, right. Fire." He took a moment to blow on his before picking a piece off with his fingers.

When their meal—such as it was—was finished, they erased all traces of the fire, scattering the ashes and taking the skewers with them before setting out again.

By now, the sun was dipping out of sight, painting the sky in vibrant reds and oranges.

Reiva stopped, her breath catching. She'd never felt well enough to watch it on the ship, always being in some pit of nautical misery.

Tolm noticed, coming to a halt. He observed the sunset. "They say sunsets are greatest in the heart of the sea."

Reiva nodded solemnly. "I can see why." She stared as it sunk down—then, just at the moment when its last sliver vanished over the horizon, a burst of green light flashed across the sky. She actually gasped.

"Yeah, I can see why," she repeated. "Never saw anything like that in Talynis."

Tolm made an appreciative sound. "Sometimes we got that in Mizkhar. I never sailed out very far with my father, but if we were lucky, we saw the green flash. Fishermen down there call it the last signal of the god Atunra before he sails down into the underworld. A promise he'll be back in the morning, when he has defeated the darkness."

Reiva hummed. "Why is it that gods always have to fight their enemies like that time and again—can't anyone have the decency of dying like the rest of us?"

Tolm shrugged. "Maybe if we weren't always dying and being born, they wouldn't have to keep setting the example."

She sighed. "That was rhetorical. I'm not interested in philosophy."

He chuckled. "Good, because I can only steal so many quotes before you start recognizing them."

She cracked a smile.

The moon was waning that night, but still bright enough that they had no need for Reiva to summon her fire as a torch. The skies were blessedly clear as well, with no hint of a storm such as had struck last night.

Eventually, they settled in a cave. The only other inhabitants were a small family of monkeys of a variety neither recognized. The animals didn't seem too happy about the sudden eviction, but Reiva managed to placate them with the offer of some shiny jewelry she had lifted off one of the pirates.

"Told you it could come in handy," she said.

Tolm put his hands up. "I stand corrected."

They spent the better part of two hours constructing a camouflage screen at the mouth of the cave, as well as scattering some twigs about to act as a warning of anyone approaching.

By the time they were both satisfied, sleep was heavy on Reiva's eyes. They still could not afford to rest, though. Using Tolm's hatchet, they cut a makeshift bucket from a log. Then, they retrieved water from the beach, since there wasn't any nearby river or lake.

Though both of them were extremely fatigued and worn, they

had enough in them for one last feat of magic. Tolm lifted the water out of the bucket, holding it in the air in a shimmering, shifting blob. Then Reiva placed her hands beneath the water and summoned fire.

As the fire turned the water to steam, Tolm captured the steam and sent it back into the bucket, turning it back to liquid form.

The process continued, the water heating more and more, and Tolm shifting a greater and greater amount of it back into the bucket. By the end, there was only a small sphere of water floating between Tolm's hands, almost white with the density of salt left within. This water Tolm tossed to the ground, and the two of them drank eagerly from the freshwater they had made.

After Reiva had drunken her fill, she asked, "So you can do that on your own?"

"Much more slowly and with a lot more effort. Boiling it to steam first reduces the load incredibly. Otherwise I'd have to sieve the water out from itself, leaving as much salt behind as possible—it's almost impossible if I'm not fully rested and have an ideal situation for long periods of concentration."

Reiva whistled. A silence stretched out before she finally said what was on her mind. "Why don't they teach us to work together like this at the Sanctum? We had to think of that ourselves—you can't tell me no one with our Arts ever worked that out."

Tolm leaned against the wall of the cave. "Most Adepts work alone in the field once they're commissioned. We're too rare a resource to commit multiples to one conflict."

Reiva rubbed her eyes. "Still, the potential outcomes if we did." An uncomfortable feeling settled into her stomach. "Or they don't want us working together because..." she trailed off, unwilling to finish the thought.

"We would be harder to control," Tolm said.

She sighed. "Right."

Tolm was quiet for a short while. "Most likely. After all, they wouldn't need the Carnifexes if Adepts didn't go rogue now and then."

Reiva shuddered at the mention of the Art of Blood's practitioners. The memory of the one she'd seen years ago still set her on edge. Even her frail aetheric senses had detected the horrible aura of power hanging off of him.

"I'd never go against the Empire if I knew I'd have one of those coming after me."

Tolm shrugged. "But if they didn't exist, what then?"

Reiva stared at him. "What?" she managed eventually.

He spread his hands. "Say there is no Carnifex in all the world. Would you serve the Empire still?"

Reiva pulled herself up straighter. "The Empire...it's given me everything. Why would I ever turn my back on Lazarra? She took me in. I would have been a slave if not for the Adept Corps. I would have been...gods only know where I would be now, what I would be doing —if I were even still alive..."

The memory of the Wandering God grabbing her wrist flashed through her mind. What else might have happened if Adept Brefon had never found her? Would the Wanderer have come for her in the brothel? Would he have rescued her from the mines? Or did he only care that she not take her life on Talynisti soil, leaving her her own in this distant land under a distant sky.

"So what then," she murmured, "you would leave?"

Tolm's eyes turned toward the mouth of the cave. "Do you remember when Viala tried to run away? It was in our third year."

Reiva racked her mind. "I think so. She got her hide tanned for that... A lot of pain and struggle just to wash out a year later."

Tolm nodded slowly. "I gave her the idea."

"*What?*"

His mouth turned into an uneven smile. "Yes, me, the golden boy. I convinced her to try and run away."

Reiva gaped for a moment. "Well why the hell did you do that?"

Tolm sighed. "I wanted to see how they handled it. I really did hope she could get away—I did. But what mattered more to me was whether I could get some sense of how they tried to hunt her down. I wanted to know what I'd be up against if I split."

"I see. And you decided not to."

"Too much risk. And like you said—a Carnifex is just too formidable. I weighed the odds and decided I'd be better off finishing my training. If a good opportunity presented itself, I'd leave. If not—I'd wait until I was a full Adept."

Something clicked in the back of Reiva's mind. "That's what drove you."

"Hm?"

"You told me, that one time we spoke, years ago, before I even earned my focus, that I needed to finding something to drive me—something so irresistible that I'd be willing to do anything for it. Escaping was yours. You found the drive to be the best of us in the hope of getting away."

"That's it." He laughed bitterly. "Sounds far more cynical when you say it out loud."

Reiva rested her head against the cold stone of the cave wall. "I can't believe it. Do you have any idea how long I've hated you? Not personally, I mean, just...the idea of you? You're the one challenge I could never overcome."

Tolm got a strange look on his face. "Well, I won't apologize, but... I can see why that would be frustrating. You know if you had gotten to the Sanctum before me and started your training earlier..."

She nodded. "I've thought of that. A lot, actually. I was the last into Seventh Cohort. I had the farthest to climb."

"Did you resent how things turned out?"

"I did," she said, and suddenly her mouth was moving on its own, words flowing freely. "I killed myself, always thinking that if I just put one more shred of effort in, if I just studied one more technique, figured out one more trick—that somehow it would put me over you. And I could *never* figure out what it was that pushed you to keep ahead of me, despite how hard I worked and how furiously I longed for victory. Freedom. That's what you wanted. That's it."

Tolm snorted. "What do you mean *that's it*?"

"We have *everything*. We'll never want for clothes or food or glory. We'll never have to fear the horrors of scraping out a life at the bottom. We will always be worthy, never abandoned or forgotten.

We're gods among men, only second to the Emperor in our might—and even he cannot do the marvels we can with our Arts. The Empire...for me, it's everything I lost or never had."

Tolm listened, and he seemed to be listening sincerely. "Everything?" he asked eventually.

"What *can't* you get from the Empire?"

"A fishing boat in Mizkhar. A little house by the water, where every evening when I come back from the catch, my Iset is waiting for me, ready to prepare a meal from the fruit of my labor. That's what the Empire can never give me."

Reiva's mouth hung open. "A *woman*?"

Tolm actually laughed.

"You were going to flee across the world from the greatest military power mankind has ever known—for a *girl*."

"She's not just a girl."

"You haven't even seen her since, what, you were eleven? Twelve? She could be married by now."

He shrugged. "She might be."

"And how can you even know when you're that young if you—"

"I *knew*. We knew. And I know if I could see her again, it would be like I never left."

Reiva's jaw snapped shut with a click. Something had changed in Tolm's face as he spoke. He had a...a certainty, an assuredness she had never seen on his face before.

No, that was wrong. She *had* seen it. It was the same look he got when someone really gave him a run in a martial duel, or when he was fighting pirates for his life.

"I admire your ambition, Reiva. But I don't think you'll truly be happy in the Empire, if that's what you're after. You escaped the bottom—but when will you be content? Which mountaintop will finally be high enough?"

"I think you're projecting."

"Maybe I am," he admitted with a small laugh.

They fell into silence for a while. Reiva felt her head listing, but she wasn't ready to sleep yet.

Tomorrow, they would have to prepare for the fight. They wouldn't be able to speak like this again, most likely. They were at the edge of the world, for all intents. What was there to say that could be said nowhere else?

"I'm sorry," she said, "about Brefon."

Tolm stiffened. "I haven't taken the time to think about it yet."

"I saw him. When the lightning struck."

Tolm bowed his head. "He wouldn't leave until every last person had evacuated. He wanted to be sure they had the best chance possible."

"He'll be honored properly when we get back."

Tolm was silent on the point. Then eventually, "He deserves all that and more."

"He's the one who found me. I was about to be sold in the slave market when he passed a focus over my head."

"He told me. He always said he was glad to be the one—that he made sure I had good competition."

She snorted, hiding her grin. "Well, I'm honored to be thought of as such." Another lapse of silence. "After he fell, Luo and I lost sight of you. How did you survive the sharks?"

Tolm's face darkened. "I can't say. Luck, perhaps. I used my Art to propel myself through the water, so perhaps the marines just...were easier targets."

Reiva didn't know what to say to that. Nothing helpful, she could think. "And you came upon the island by luck as well?"

"Something like that. Or maybe neither was by luck."

"What do you mean?"

Tolm took a breath, suddenly looking uncomfortable. "There was...someone. Someone in the storm. When Brefon fell, I tried to get to him. I was sure he had survived, but..." He shook his head. "Well, I was too close to the ship, and its tow pulled me down. I used my Art to break free and get back to the surface, but I'd gotten all turned around. I picked a direction and started swimming with the *Ars Aquae*. But then...a figure appeared. I could see him beckoning me, showing the way. He was pointing the other direction, telling me to turn around. I thought it was a vision, that I was going mad. But then I turned, and sure enough I reached the island, and I forgot all about him in the struggle to find shelter and survive."

Reiva felt cold. "What did he look like?"

"Not dressed like anyone Lazarran. He could have fit in well in Mizkhar. Maybe he was a spirit from my homeland, come to save my life in a moment of death assured."

Reiva turned the possibility over. "Such things can happen."

Tolm turned a curious gaze on her. "And how do you know?"

She swallowed, looking to the entrance of the cave. "Something like that happened to me once. A long time ago. It was in the desert, not the sea—death was inches away. And then he stopped it, and he told me that I was not yet to die."

"What was his voice like? Booming thunder?"

She shook her head. "Like a man's. Firm. Certain. I thought he was...never mind, it's foolish."

Tolm shrugged. "Such stories often sound like it. But we're alive, so who can say? I'll take a foolish tale for salvation."

"I suppose so."

They spoke no more of death and doom. The risk of fire inside a cave being too great, they huddled together to share body heat. Close at their sides were their weapons. Neither could bear to stay awake longer to keep watch, so they placed their trust in the makeshift alarms they had prepared.

When sleep came over Reiva, it enveloped her in a deep, still cocoon.

She dreamed of a man walking among the stars, and just as she was about to glimpse his face, she awoke.

27

FIGHT LIKE DEVILS

THEY DEVOTED the day after they slept in the cave to planning and rest. The two of them had slept, by their estimation, close to fourteen hours apiece. By luck or divine favor, no one had discovered them.

The two of them were starving, so they breakfasted on fish, and Reiva found some of the same variety of roots that Luo had moments before his death. They had a bland flavor.

Reiva felt a weight on her shoulders as she chewed it, thinking how this was the last sensation Luo had known before oblivion took him. He should have had better.

After the necessities of survival were taken care of, and they had done some rounds around the local area to ensure they were indeed as secluded as they had hoped, they began making their plans. They discussed vectors of attack, the possibility of a sneak attack (though the pirates were surely expecting something—unless they were particularly idiotic, in which case this would be a rare turn of luck after everything that happened), and so on.

Reiva stared at the plan of the pirates' hideout they had sketched based on Scobo's description. "And you're saying we can get in *this* way?"

Tolm nodded. "Dead certain."

"You've done this before?"

"Not with someone else, but I'll be able to do it."

Reiva shot him a look. "Drowning after all this would be a sorry end."

Tolm waved it off. "Not a chance."

She sighed. "All right, it's as good a plan as any."

They talked through the hottest part of the day, and then in the cool of the afternoon they relocated. It was never wise, when fleeing an opponent, to stay too long in any one area. If anything, they had already overstayed their welcome in the cave, but their extended rest had replenished their souls well. When the fight came tomorrow, they would be fully capable of fighting with their Arts.

And they intended to fight well.

Night came without incident—the sunset having a particularly blood-red tinge to it, Reiva thought. Something itched at the base of her skull.

"It's been too quiet," she remarked as they dined on yet another meal of fish. "It feels like any moment the trees will turn to blades and spears and come after us."

Tolm took his final bite of fish, washing it down with a drink from another concocted bucket of fresh water. "Well, tomorrow it will all be said and done. So let us sleep well tonight, for hell has few beds."

Reiva searched her memory for the attribution. "King Lanidos?"

Tolm nodded. "On the day before the Battle at the Eastern Springs, against the Zarushan Immortal Emperor."

Reiva leaned back against the tree trunk she had chosen as a rest. "He died, didn't he? Him and ninety percent of all the Myrmidons in Karella."

"They did. But when the Immortal Emperor got to the *Western* Springs, and he saw how many more Karellans had assembled under Lanidos' banner—with the remaining ten percent of the Myrmidons in the front lines, ready to fight to avenge their fallen king—the Zarushan army turned back, knowing they would never win a victory worth the cost."

Reiva hummed. "It's a good story. But—" she waved her hand

through the air. "We're alone on this island. There's no army to be inspired by our sacrifice. The best we can hope for is that whichever marine ship comes here once they realize we're not coming back, they can finish the job."

Tolm clicked his tongue. "Wrong."

"Oh?"

"We can fight like devils and leave not a foe standing. And when some ship comes by—be they marines or merchants or even some other band of merry buccaneers—they'll see what we wrought and remember."

Reiva's lips split into a wide grin. "I'll raise a cheer for that." She held her fist high and called out the legions' mantra: "For Emperor and Eagle."

He nodded, matching her grin. "For Emperor and Eagle."

They arose well before dawn, and without speaking a word, immediately set to their tasks.

Their accumulated weapons were a hatchet, two cutlasses, and two spears. And of course, they had their focuses.

The trek was the part of the initial plan where the most could go wrong—they could run into a patrol, for instance, and an alarm could be raised.

They did run into a patrol, as it turned out, but there was no opportunity for an alarm to go up.

Four pirates walked along one of the jungle pathways, yawning and cursing their luck at having drawn the short sticks, apparently.

Reiva and Tolm crept into position.

Most people were right-handed—as such, they were more vulnerable to attacks on their left side. When two Adept Initiates broke from the tree line, hurling spears and swinging swords, only one of them had the reflexes sufficient to get his right hand across his body and his fingers around the hilt of his cutlass before all four lay dead on the ground.

Reiva let out a long breath, permitting the aether she had chan-neled to dissipate. They had to be sparing with their magic, since they were likely in for a brutal fight.

The upside was that they had cut down the enemies' number before they even made it to the hideout. When you could fight anywhere besides your opponents' home territory, it was an advan-tage you took.

They pilfered more knives and cutlasses. They had to be cautious, lest they go ringing through the jungle, but they would have a use for extra weaponry.

The hideout's exact location they were unsure of, but they could see the rock formation that it likely lay within.

Rather than approach the hideout directly, they made for the northern beach abutting it. This would be the darker side when the sun began rising.

They encountered another pair of pirates on the way—one of them leaning against a tree, the other pissing into the river.

Reiva grimaced. Didn't *they* drink from that river too? Even if it flowed downstream, that was just disgusting to think about.

Reiva set aside most of her weaponry, taking just the cutlass and a knife, and she snuck up on them. At her signal, Tolm dipping his hand into the river. He formed two tendrils of water and smothered the men's faces. Their screams were lost in a muffled garble as Reiva slashed them to ribbons.

They tossed the bodies in a thicket of bushes—it wasn't perfect, but with a little luck, no one would notice them until it was too late.

The beach was deserted, save a group of hermit crabs who seemed to have woken early to trade shells. Reiva stared at them for a moment.

Somehow, nature always found a way to express her absolute lack of interest in the affairs of humans.

When they got to the surf, Reiva's heart beat faster. She took a steadying breath. Then another.

Tolm shot her a look. "Can you handle this?"

She nodded. "Sharks don't swim too close to shore, do they?"

Tolm made a noncommittal sound. "I'm sure it'll be fine."

"Forget I asked."

They waded into the surf. The water was surprisingly warm, Reiva thought, given that the sun was hardly even turning the eastern horizon pink.

When they were to their chests in the water, Tolm offered his hand.

Reiva took it. "And you're *sure* this will work?"

"Would you like to go knock on the front door instead?"

Might as well—she took as big a breath as she could manage and dunked her head beneath the waves.

And she waited.

Something tickled her skin, but she kept her eyes shut, lest the salt water blind her. The tickling sensation spread—until she felt a pocket of air form.

"Done," said Tolm.

Reiva let her breath out with a heavy sigh.

The collection of weapons helped weigh them down, but Reiva still had to fight the impulse to float to the surface. Well, it was close enough that she could straighten up and breach the water—but the sandbar in front of her led to a drop off where that would no longer be an option.

The bubble Tolm had formed around their heads only had so much air, so Tolm regularly had to form bubbles at the surface, then bring them down to replenish their air supply. When Reiva had asked why he couldn't just create a funnel, he told her that spent air was heavier than fresh air—it was the same reason wells could become dangerous once they were dug past a certain depth. Not enough breathable air could get down to the diggers, and they suffocated.

Given the dim light and the sheer unlikelihood of anyone thinking much of bubbles forming near the surface though, they didn't think they would have to worry about being spotted.

So, they began to swim. Reiva was responsible for most of the propulsion, given Tolm's concentration on ensuring they could breathe.

Reiva didn't have a map, of course, so she judged their approach based on the curving of the shallows. As they went, they passed by a sort of underwater garden—rocks (or were they plants?) of vibrant pinks and blues and greens lay along the ocean floor, and flocks of fish darted in and amongst them.

Reiva couldn't imagine that a whole world of life existed beneath the waves—she had always thought it was just endless sand and endless water. Maybe being a fish wasn't so boring after all.

When the topography changed—a great formation of mossy rock appearing to their left, they knew they had reached the edge of the cove.

Here, Reiva's muscles tensed. Her nerves tingled, ready for the split second reactions combat would demand of her. The weight of her focus around her neck was a welcome comfort.

They swam around the rock until the mouth of the cove opened to them.

It was dark—frighteningly dark, and Reiva had to fight off mental images of ghoulish sharks gliding through the surrounding gloom— but they could see what they needed to see.

Above them was a dock—they swam under it, taking advantage of the cover it provided. Alongside the dock was the hulking body of the pirates' ship, the *Brinemaiden.*

That meant this was the main cove. There was a smaller adjoining segment of the hideaway where the smaller pleasure craft was stowed. They were after this one, so that was good luck for them —the layout Scobo the pirate had given them was holding true.

"Ready?" Reiva asked. When Tolm said so, she took a deep breath and let go of his hand, kicking for the surface.

To Tolm's credit, he managed to split the bubble and keep it around her head all the way to the top. When she lifted her head out of the water, she peered around. She couldn't hear anyone walking on the dock above her, but she thought she could make out some sounds from further into the complex.

After scanning the area, she held out two fingers underwater.

That would signal Tolm that she couldn't see any pirates. Then she held out four fingers, signaling that she didn't see any hostages.

A few moments later, Tolm surfaced beside her.

"Last chance to turn back," he muttered.

Reiva shook her head. "Let's raise hell."

She stretched her arms toward to dock overhead, and then Tolm raised one of his hands. The water around Reiva congealed, hugging to her legs and waist, and began to rise.

Reiva grabbed hold of the dock as soon as it was in reach, and the water quietly drained away, still under Tolm's careful control. As she clambered onto the dock, Tolm lifted himself up similarly.

Reiva nodded her appreciation. "You've got a lot of tricks."

"If I didn't join my father as a fisherman, I would have become a magician."

She stared. "Really?"

"It's an honorable profession in Mizkhar."

"No wonder you wanted to go back."

Together they scampered along the dock, every creak of wood sounding impossibly loud in Reiva's ears.

The dock adjoined to a rocky interior, rough and slippery underfoot. Fighting on it would be dangerous under normal circumstances, but as Tolm set foot on the rock, he made a subtle parting motion, and the water curled away to the edges.

There were two passages—down the left, Reiva could hear snoring, down the right, she heard voices.

She motioned her intent to go right, with a question for whether Tolm would follow.

He indicated he would go left.

Reiva nodded.

Her Art had more destructive potential—it made more sense for her to go after the wakened pirates. Tolm could slit throats while they slept.

She gave him a brief salute, which he returned, and they parted.

Reiva crept along the corridor. Based on the description they had received two days ago from the pirate on the beach, this would lead to where the hostages were being kept.

Unfortunately, the voices echoing down the corridor were distinctly not Lazarran.

The corridor had a series of sconces set along the wall for torches, but they had not been lit, which gave Reiva the advantage of darkness. As she delved further, she passed a series of doors, each a somewhat unusual shape as it had been carved to fit the profile of the cave wall. So some were shorter than her, others four times her width. Each one she snuck past, fearful of awakening any pirates still slumbering within.

According to Scobo's report, the crew was used to sleeping through shouting—so long as it was not the captain's.

The person hurling most of the yells, in this case, was a pirate with a red bandana tied around his forehead and a notched cutlass he waved to and fro as he spoke. His back was to Reiva, giving her a good view of a whole host of scars—old whip marks, from the look of them.

Alyat had once told her that few men were as cruel as those who had known cruelty themselves. The pirate was berating a legionnaire tied to a stake in the ground.

"What's this coughing?!" bellowed the pirate. "Are you *sniveling*? Crying for your mum? *I was sleeping!* We can't all laze around on our arses all day, dog. Some of us have to work—we can't all get paid from the taxpayers' purse."

The legionnaire receiving the abuse had a grim snarl on his face, which bore a mess of mottled black and blue bruises, one eye entirely swollen shut. He had no shirt, revealing even more welts and marks. Judging by the way he was breathing, Reiva feared he might have a broken rib.

"Right," growled the marine, "and you just go around stealing what you want."

The pirate practically jumped into the air. "What's this? He speaks!" The pirate delivered a vicious kick to the marine's side. "Who's the thief, eh? I never asked to be born under an Emprah, made to pay so he can have fancy silks to wipe his backside with! *That's* theft, you ask me!"

"Oi, Walca, could you stop it for ten minutes? We're *this* close to being done, and I'd rather go to sleep without me ears ringing." This speaker was lounging at a table in the corner, head propped on one fist. Another pirate, and one who clearly didn't have as much energy in him.

Walca spread his arms wide. "Do you not hear what the army man is saying? He's calling us thieves!"

"Aye, we're pirates. We take things from people. Just last week you lifted that sack of—"

"We *liberate*."

"Sure, sure. Well we're about to be liberated from our watch, so keep your britches on."

Walca marched over to the sleepy pirate. "Listen 'ere, I don't reckon it's proper for you to go on..."

Reiva set her jaw. She'd been hoping for more of an opening—the pirate at the table's attention was on Walca, but he was in a position to spy Reiva when she set foot in the room.

She'd have to be fast if she wanted to get these men free before the next watch came in.

The room's layout was simple—the two pirates were at a table along the right side wall, while the hostages were all arrayed throughout the center of the room, either tied to stakes or manacled to the wall. Since the Lazarrans were the most recent addition, they were closer to her, with civilian hostages seeming to make up the majority of those positioned toward the far side.

Reiva wanted to get people free *before* an alarm went up, if possible—and she alone couldn't take out two men without making a ruckus. On the other hand, every passing second brought greater and greater likelihood of Tolm causing an alarm.

When the seated pirate yawned, closing his eyes, she moved.

There was a stack of crates along the left side wall. Some were open, revealing them to be full of odds and ends, random things that might have been brought back from raids, but were too mundane to sell or display anywhere meaningful. These crates provided handy cover for Reiva as she slunk along the wall.

She had to step cautiously, lest one of the cutlasses thrust through her belt scrape the wall and give her away. For once, she was glad to be barefoot, padding along the rock without a sound.

The crates only took her so far though, and the nearest legionnaire was beyond arm's reach.

Reiva grimaced, peering at the two pirates. They were still engaged in their back and forth.

"Psst."

The nearest marine made a grunting sound, as though rousing from sleep. "What's the—"

"Shh!" She shot another glance at the pirates—still clear.

The marine started, looking up with wide eyes.

Reiva waved furiously at him. "Stay still."

Thankfully, he caught on quickly. He put on a convincing act, dropping his head back down and slackening his limbs.

"Can you fight? Nod or shake."

He nodded subtly.

"And could others?"

He tilted his head slightly. She took that to mean a few could.

Well, she would take what she could get.

"This will hurt for a moment," she whispered.

Carefully, she held out her hand, and with as much precision as she could manage, sent out a puff of fire.

In training, she had always thought the bigger and more powerful she could do her magic, the better. Thank the gods Alyat had forced her to learn the—truth be told, much more difficult—art of subtle control.

Well, as subtle a control as one could exert over fire.

With a faint crackle, the bonds around the marine's wrists came undone. He rubbed at where the ropes had rubbed his skin raw, still lying as if he was bound. Instantly, a change came over him—his muscles tensed, his jaw clenched. He was no longer a captive. He had been returned to the vocation he knew best: that of the warrior.

By now, a handful of other legionnaires had noticed Reiva's presence—and the freedom of their comrade. She got several meaningful looks, people nodding toward their own bindings.

She scowled. It wasn't going to be easy to get enough people loose without the guards noticing—

A horrendous shriek split the air—something more bestial than human.

The guards leapt to attention, scrambling to draw weapons. A moment later, Walca relaxed somewhat, scratching his eyebrow. "Was that Cap'n's cat?"

"Damned fleabag," muttered the sleepy pirate. "Got me heart going. Now I won't get to sleep for another—"

"TO ARMS, YOU BILGE RATS! THERE'S AN INTRUDER!" roared a ragged voice.

"And there's Cap'n."

So Tolm had made his move.

Well, nothing for it then.

Reiva sprang to her feet, tossing a cutlass to the one marine she had freed. The man caught it effortlessly, hopping to his feet.

Instantly, the pirates spun on them.

"Oi, what's this!" snapped Walca. "That's the lass Scobo saw!"

The other pirate yawned, raising his cutlass to a fighting stance. "Damn, I put a bet he made her up."

"You dumb anchor, she's one of them Adepts!"

"Is she really?"

Reiva raised her free hand. "Really."

This time, she only held back so as not to scorch any captives.

The pirates yelped, throwing themselves to either side as fire licked past them.

Reiva ran forward, handing daggers to legionnaires as she went. "Get loose! We're finishing what we came here for!"

Even among those who didn't have an immediate prospect of getting free, a battle cry went up.

Reiva charged on the guards, the legionnaire with a cutlass close behind her.

Walca had recovered first, and he flung his brawn at Reiva, hoping to overpower her by sheer force.

So the look on his face was quite priceless when Reiva, empowered by aether, met his blow unflinchingly. It was second only to the look on his face when she began to push his blade away.

"Devilry!" he cried. "Witchcraft and—"

Reiva aimed an empowered kick squarely into his gut, knocking the breath out of him. A quick follow-through with the cutlass shut him up for good.

The sleepy pirate, despite appearances, was quite a skilled swordsman—and the legionnaire was clearly not in top fighting condition. He took a few bloody gashes before Reiva swept in and they overwhelmed him.

By then, a number of legionnaires had gotten loose, and they quickly claimed the fallen pirates' weapons. Reiva did a quick head-count—six.

"This is everyone who can fight?"

"Yes," growled the legionnaire with the ugly bruise along his face. "But I assure you, Adept, we're more than capable of making up for the rest. We've got a score to settle."

"Glad to hear it—because right about now, my friend could use some backup. We'll be back for the rest of you!"

They ran through the corridor, followed by a hearty swell of cheers and quite clear admonishments to "give 'em hell."

All the doors Reiva had snuck past now lay ajar. She desperately hoped Tolm hadn't let himself get cornered—even he couldn't match this many foes on his own.

When they got to the area they had first entered, she realized her worries had been in vain.

Over a dozen pirates were standing on the dock and aboard the ship, waving their swords and hurling invectives.

But they were doing battle with a foe they couldn't touch.

Tolm had lifted himself up in a column of water, and he was striking out at the pirates from far beyond their reach. He couldn't kill them—but he had all their eyes on him.

Reiva and the legionnaires wasted no time in charging the foe.

In the surprise attack, half the pirates fell without a chance to strike back. Once their fellows realized the threat, they quickly stopped their fruitless efforts at hitting Tolm with spears and hatchets and turned to fight.

Unfortunately for them, this meant they weren't able to respond to Tolm's water whips.

A pirate lunged at Reiva, only for a tendril to swipe at his legs and send him sprawling at her feet.

Another came for her, only to get a faceful of salt water before he could strike.

Reiva handily worked through them, throwing blasts of fire to sear pirates engaged with legionnaires.

The pirates fell back to their ship, bunching up around the gangplank so that it would be multiple of them against one legionnaire at a time.

It was then that Reiva realized these pirates, though certainly formidable, really were not prepared to fight Adepts. Then again, was anyone?

They presented such a nice, massed target for her that she dropped her cutlass to blast them with flames from both hands. Taking the ship after that was a given.

"WHAT'S THIS?!" bellowed a pirate who could only be the captain. Standing back on the dock, he cut an almost theatrical figure —his beard was thick, his voice was harsh as a tempest, and most damningly, he looked absolutely *furious* at the sight of Reiva and the legionnaires aboard his ship. The scene was only completed by the man standing beside him who was head-to-toe muscle, with a vicious snarl—the bosun, Reiva guessed.

"You damn sea dogs!" snapped the captain. "Can't ye gut *one* girl and a pack of bruised-up bucketheads?!"

Tolm blasted him in the face with water. The pirate captain took a tumble, then got to his feet, hacking up water. "Why you..."

Tolm's water pillar carried him to the dock, and he jumped from it, tucked into a roll, and popped to his feet, ready to cross blades with the bosun. At the same time, Reiva jumped from the deck of the ship, landing on the dock with a perilously loud *thud*, her enhanced legs taking the impact, and lunged for the captain.

All told, the sight of two Adept Initiates bearing down seemed to be too much for the captain and bosun, who turned and ran, bellowing and spewing curses all the while.

She took off with Tolm after the pair, shouting over her shoulder for the legionnaires to clear the rest of the hideaway.

As they ran down the corridor, she saw Tolm's handiwork from before the alarm had been raised. A pirate lay in a pool of his own blood here, there a door lay ajar, with two more bodies still in their beds, never to wake again.

There was also a fluffy, well-brushed cat loping along the corridor, meowing incessantly at Reiva as she ran past.

Tolm pointed at a side passage, which she recalled led to the smaller cove with the pleasure craft. "I'll check down there!"

"I'll check outside!"

He looked at her, nodded—and for the briefest of moments, Reiva had the uncanny sense that he was trying to tell her something—and then Tolm was gone.

Reiva followed the main corridor all the way out onto the beach, where she hit the sand running, peering around for any sign of the captain and bosun.

Nothing.

Something scuffed the sand behind her, and she whirled—only to meet a fist with her nose.

Something *crunched*. Her head whipped back. She tasted blood.

Countless scraps in the Nine-knuckle House had carved the motions into her body.

Disengage.

Eyes blinded by tears, she rolled backward, feeling the double whistle of blades passing over her.

She tossed her sword aside, putting her hands up to her nose.

Broken.

Before she could let herself hesitate, she snapped it back into place, another well of tears coursing down her cheeks. She channeled aether—by now she had another headache, the sign of onsetting aether sickness. Immediately, the cool burst of energy healed the break, stifling the pain.

The dim shapes of the pirates came for her. Dashing away the tears, she threw herself into a sidelong roll, snatching up her sword as she went.

"Hold still, bitch!"

As she sprang to her feet, still blinking clear tears, she spat a glob of sand to the side. Gently pressing at her nose with bloody fingers, she drawled, "You really should have just skewered me from behind."

"Oh, but we're here to teach you a *lesson,* lass. You haven't got that tall fellow with you now."

Reiva laughed. "Well the last time I was in this situation I didn't even have a weapon—so good luck."

The captain and his mate hesitated. Looked at one another.

"Don't worry, I can go easy on you."

The pirates narrowed their eyes.

"I'll beat and cut you up slowly and give you a chance instead of burning you quickly with no chance."

Bracing herself against the worsening headache, she funneled a quick burst of aether to her legs. The captain reacted faster, swinging for her, but her sword was already there to block it. Her free hand darted forward like a viper, knuckles leading. In a vicious strike, she crushed his windpipe.

Reflexively, he dropped his cutlass, hands going for his throat. With preternatural speed and precision, she snatched the falling weapon from the air, putting both swords in a cross—just in time to lock down the bosun's blade.

He spat in her face. She answered by breathing a puff of fire—a trick she'd never had cause to use in combat, but which was not too strenuous. The bosun cursed, ducking away, and just as his legs pivoted, she snapped a kick into his knee. Buckling to the sand, he yelped.

Turning back to the captain, who had recovered enough to make a clumsy lunge for her with a dagger, she wove under his attempt at a slash. Both swords flashed, and he went down, clutching his spilled innards.

Carrying herself on the momentum of that move, she spun toward the bosun, sticking both cutlasses into him, one in the throat, one in the heart.

She took a long breath, then let it out. She had to breathe through her mouth, her nose still glommed up full of blood.

After a quick check over herself to ensure she hadn't taken injuries, she ran back into the hideaway—no rest for the weary. This time, she went down the corridor Tolm had taken. This one should have led to the secondary cove where the smaller boat was kept.

When Reiva got through the corridor, she found the cove, and she found a pirate, lying dead with a nasty slash across his throat.

But she didn't see Tolm.

And she didn't see any boat.

28

WORTHY

THE LEGIONNAIRES HAD FOUND another three pirates. It was a short fight, with only one injury among the legionnaires that merited stitches. Reiva began moving among the wounded, channeling aether to heal wounds—to what extent she was able.

Aether channeling was not a miraculous panacea; it acted by accelerating the body's healing properties to an extremely rapid pace, fueled by the invisible energy of the aether.

This meant it could do little for anyone who had come down with infections. Broken bones it could somewhat help with, but there was always the danger the break would fuse improperly and would have to be re-broken by a physician down the line, so it could properly heal.

That left a good deal of legionnaires still down for the count.

Among the civilian hostages, there was no doctor to be found. What's more, the hostages had a flu going around, likely exacerbated by the poor conditions. As such, there weren't many able hands to crew the ship in the cove.

But those marines who were able assured Reiva they could manage. She saw no reason to doubt them.

In a matter of hours, the ship was full of all the freed hostages, with a fair helping of the pirates' treasure stowed in the hold—and the captain's cat sitting proudly atop the whole heap. Reiva wasn't sure what the protocol was for figuring out what they could repatriate to rightful owners, but the mission had demanded they recover what had been stolen.

She also wasn't sure what would happen to the cat, but that was a small issue, all things considered.

The overall holdings of the pirates were too great to take in their entirety, though, which meant more ships would have to come back later. And when they did, she hoped they would take the time to recover Luo's body. In fact, she would do whatever she could to make sure they did.

"Adept?" asked a marine standing on the gangplank. "We're ready to sail."

Reiva chewed her lip. She was standing on the dock in the cove, the last one to board.

She had tried yelling into the jungle for Tolm, but as she'd expected, got no response.

He's not on the island, she told herself. *You know that.*

But it still didn't make it any stranger, or intuitively wrong, to leave the island without him.

The legionnaires seemed to look to her guidance on the matter—but she had a hunch they had surmised the same thing she had.

So it was that they shoved off and, once they hit the open water, unfurled the sails, heading due north for Lazarra and leaving the island behind. Reiva didn't look back as they got out to sea.

The pirate's ship was sizable, and the number of marine legionnaires fit to serve was precious few, but they were dedicated men—men who had received another chance at life and freedom, and they threw themselves to their tasks wholeheartedly.

They also felt an incredible debt to Reiva, which manifested as a remarkable loyalty and respect. After the first day of sailing, she gave up on trying to correct them when they addressed her as "Adept." In their eyes, she already had the red and gold around her shoulders.

Toward the end of the second day of sailing, they caught sight of another ship. A ship flying Imperial colors.

A general cheer of jubilation went up from the crew, and the news quickly passed on to those ill and injured in the hold.

They had been found.

The distant ship quickly righted its course such that it was directly headed for them. A likely sign that they had a description of the *Brinemaiden*.

Reiva stood alongside the captain—a legionnaire Reiva had 'promoted' to the role, even though she technically didn't have the authority. He was the most senior among the able-bodied marines she'd rescued and he knew how to steer a ship, so no one had complained.

He also had remarkably keen eyesight. As he shaded his face against the setting sun's light, he murmured to Reiva, "See a mantle aboard."

Reiva perked up, running to the railing and peering for the signature red of an Adept.

Sure enough, a member of the Corps was on board.

The captain made a strange sound in his throat. "Ship's moving fast."

He was a man of few words, but it only took those three to send Reiva leaning even further over the rail.

Sure enough, the ship was being pushed—almost *carried*—forward on a surging wall of water.

Reiva finally managed to laugh—a genuine laugh, not a sarcastic or ironic laugh.

She had a pretty good idea who wore that mantle.

As the ships came alongside one another, Reiva touched her fist to her heart.

Domi nearly tackled her in an embrace. "Damn the salute!" she cried. "Are you hurt? All your limbs and fingers?" She held Reiva at the shoulders as she inspected her head-to-toe.

Reiva suddenly felt rather self-conscious. "Ah, Domi, there's a protocol for—"

"Damn the protocol too—what are you *wearing*? You look... rakish." She wrinkled her nose. "It doesn't suit you. Stick to uniforms."

In spite of herself, Reiva laughed again. "I'll keep that in mind."

The captain of the galley cleared his throat.

At this point, Reiva forcibly pushed Domi aside, and she gave the salute. "Initiate Reiva, sir. Survivor of the wrecked *Valor*."

The captain's face turned from dour to absolutely grim. "How many hands?"

A knot formed in her throat as she spoke. "Of the initial crew of thirty, only thirteen survived, sir. Six able marine legionnaires are serving this ship, while the rest are a mixture of oarsmen and marines belowdecks—besides the rescued civilians. Many need medical attention."

The captain gave a wave, and immediately several of his crew made their way aboard the *Brinemaiden* and hustled for the wounded. That lifted a burden of Reiva's shoulders, but the bad news was not yet fully delivered.

"What's more," she said, fighting to keep her voice steady, "I must report that Adept Brefon, Initiate Luo, and Initiate Tolm are lost. The first two fell before my eyes, and the last is missing."

In the corner of her vision, Domi stiffened.

The captain let loose a string of oaths so vile Reiva couldn't even understand half of it. "And you are well? You can serve?" he asked, and Reiva realized he almost sounded *desperate*.

"In body, sir. I am grieving my comrades."

The captain seemed satisfied with that answer. At the very least, he wouldn't be responsible for bringing back news that all four members of the Adept Corps who had set out were lost to the Emperor.

"Well, I offer my apologies that we did not arrive faster. The

Valor's messenger hawk never returned, so she may have been lost to the storm—it took far too long for a rescue effort. My crew will relieve you, and we'll sail back to the capital together. You may take my quarters, Initiate—you've done more than your station requires."

"With all due respect, sir, I'd prefer to stay on board with my men."

The captain gave her a strange look. She almost bit her tongue. They weren't *her* men—she still wasn't of sufficient rank to say such a thing.

But then, one legionnaire behind her spoke up—the first legionnaire she had set loose in the pirate's hideaway.

"For what it's worth, sir, I know the wounded belowdecks take great comfort in knowing that Adept Reiva is aboard. She saved our lives, sir."

The captain made a noncommittal sound in the back of his throat. "So be it then. Initiate Domi, you can propel both ships?"

Reiva knew the girl well enough to see the slight strain at the edges of her smile. "Certainly, captain."

"Then let's be on our way—I'll send a messenger hawk to inform the capital."

EVEN WITH DOMI'S arcane assistance, the journey back to Lazarra took another full two days. Blessedly, no one was lost. With the medicine stores and expertise of the other ship's physician, they had stabilized those wounded marines who had been on the brink.

When the capital city came into view, Reiva almost shed a tear.

Still, as the ship rolled into port, she braced herself. She had already told the full story of what transpired on the mission about a half-dozen times—twice to Domi alone—and she was sure things were not about to change in that regard.

So she expected someone from the Sanctum to be waiting when they docked, perhaps an Orphan escort.

What she hadn't expected was for Adept Alyat to be first at the edge of the dock, his face something between fury and dread.

Reiva stepped off the deck and onto Lazarran land. "Initiate Reiva reporting, sir."

Alyat nodded slowly, in that way that told Reiva he had a million different words tumbling through his mind—not a few of them harsh. "You all right, kid?"

Reiva blinked. *That* wasn't what she had expected. 'What the hell,' maybe, or 'I thought I told you not to get into a shipwreck.'

"I'm all right, Alyat."

He nodded again. "Good. Let's get you home."

She felt a smile forming on her lips, an uneasy smile.

Damn it, damn it, no tears, don't—

Domi shoved her forward, and Alyat wrapped his arms around her.

Whatever control she had buckled. "Home sounds nice," was all she could get out before her voice failed.

Alyat gave an affirming grunt.

She took a shaky breath and stepped back, dashing away her tears with the back of her hand. She noticed that all the legionnaires were studiously—graciously—ignoring her as they carried the wounded off and began unloading the loot from the hold.

"I must report," she began, feeling another wave of emotion build, "that Adept Brefon, Initiate—"

"I read the dispatch, Reiva," Alyat said. "You can save it for later."

She nodded her thanks. She had told of their deaths far too many times already.

As things turned out, she was to tell the story not one more time, but three more times, each to the same group of people—the Circle of Peers.

These were the most senior Adepts in the Corps. They had distinguished careers ranging from the military to the political. Many of them were heavily scarred, more than one was missing a limb. When it came to bureaucrats, there was hardly a rougher bunch in the Empire.

And they were keenly interested in what had gone so catastrophically wrong that *three* members of the Corps, one of them a full Adept, had been lost.

So she told of how the storm struck, and how Adept Brefon had held back the worst of it so every last legionnaire could make it off.

She told of how Luo had taken a thrown hatchet to the back of his skull, dying instantly.

And she told of how no one had been able to find Tolm.

On this final point, the Circle was particularly interested. They asked her to describe the layout of the hideaway. They asked questions about her and Tolm's plan to assault it, and what contingencies they had in place. They asked whether Tolm may have remained behind on the island.

And eventually, they asked about the small boat docked in the little cove.

"Initiate Reiva," said Adept Dorban, one of the most senior members of the Circle. "In your opinion, is it possible that Initiate Tolm took the 'pleasure craft,' as you described it, and set out to sea?"

"I never saw the boat myself, sir, but it was described to me as unworthy of the open waters."

"Described to you by the pirate you interrogated on the beach?" asked another.

"Yes, ma'am."

"Initiate Reiva," asked Adept Sharasthi. Reiva's stomach tightened. She had always admired Sharasthi—more than that, she had seen her as an inspiration—ever since that triumphal parade she witnessed in her first year of training. "Did Initiate Tolm give you any indication that he *would* have taken the craft out if he had thought he could sail it successfully?"

Sharasthi's gray eyes were calm, inquisitive—but unyielding.

Reiva thought back to the conversation in the cave—a conversation at the end of the world, it had seemed then. A time and place where anything could be said.

Reiva shook her head, throat dry. "No ma'am. Initiate Tolm gave no such indications."

"Or," she said, "put it this way. If Initiate Tolm could have left the Corps, do you think he would have?"

That was the heart of the matter, what the Circle had been circling around and only now finally voiced.

Reiva imagined the empty cove, recalled the emotions that had struck her when she had realized. "Tolm was worthy of his place as first Initiate, ma'am. He spoke to me of his intent to earn his commission and use the fruits of his labor to the greatest extent he could."

Sharasthi nodded, and blessedly asked no further questions.

Initiate Tolm, *Ars Aquae*, was entered into the Corps' records as *Missing in Action*. If no sign of him surfaced in the next year, he would be declared deceased. Reiva had no doubt every port in the Empire would receive a notice to be on the lookout for a lone youth of Mizkhari ancestry piloting a small boat.

As it turned out, word did come back several weeks later—a merchant vessel had spotted a boat matching the pleasure craft's description not long after the incident on the island. Its meager stores had no rations or freshwater, and it was listing heavily, having taken on water.

There was no sign of any crew.

29

IMPERIAL ADEPT

THE SEVENTH COHORT of the Adept Corps graduated, at the terminus of their training, eight Adepts. Of the nine Initiates who had gone into final missions, only seven had proven worthy of receiving the Imperial commission.

Two of the graduates, however, were not present. Adept Luo received his commission posthumously. His body had been found during a subsequent expedition to the island, then immolated on a pyre. A gold-fringed mantle would be burned tonight in memorial of his service.

Adept Tolm received his commission *in absentia*. By this point, most everyone assumed he was dead—but rules were rules, and they would not revise his status to *Lost in Service* for another few months.

Which left a mere five standing before Emperor Dioclete himself, in the Palatine Throne room, the chamber from which all the Empire was governed. The grand space seemed empty, with only Dioclete, the graduating Adepts, and a select number of observers composed of the graduates' mentors and some representatives from the Circle of Peers.

But all told, five was a strong number of commissions for a cohort. Better than most years.

Reiva thought of how many had vanished since she first lined up on the field for morning drills.

They each received from Dioclete's own hands the red and gold mantle of an Adept. With it, they had all the rights, honors, privileges, and duties attendant.

First, the Emperor vested Caulo. Then Ela. Then Domi. Then Phetan.

And then, lastly, Reiva.

"Adept Reiva," he said, his voice resonant. "To you is due the highest honors possible for one of your station. You graduate your training with distinction as the premier Initiate in your Cohort, as well as a commendation for valor in combat befitting the Lazarran ideal. Receive your mantle"—he draped it around her shoulders —"and stand proud with the knowledge that the Empire awaits eagerly the future glories you shall win her."

Reiva saluted, feeling the sting of the fresh military tattoo emblazoned on her right shoulder. She spoke, as was custom, the same words the others had: "My life and blood for you, my Emperor."

Emperor Dioclete accepted her oath with a gracious inclination of the head and turned away. As he stepped, the elegant ceremonial robes swished along the mosaic floor. Reiva watched as he lowered himself into the Palatine Throne. He was over forty, but he moved with all the grace and poise of a warrior in his prime. She would not have been surprised if his body was taut with muscle beneath those robes.

She had expected a man of his stature and position to be soft with age, but no—he truly did look every bit the Lazarran ideal. He even looked true to the profile stamped on Imperial coinage.

The Emperor raised his hand. "From the seat of Lazarran Dominion, I commission you five as Imperial Adepts. As blades in my hand and vessels of my reign, go forth and serve. Honor the well-earned mantle around your shoulders and honor the spiritual mantle you carry in remembrance of all those who have served before you. You are the Empire's greatest asset. *Ave.*"

In unison, the whole room struck their fists to their chests. "*Ave Imperator!*"

THERE WAS A PARADE AFTERWARD. Not something as grand as a triumphal parade celebrating victory in war, but Lazarrans were never one to let any opportunity for celebrating their military lapse. The newly commissioned Adepts walked from the Imperial Palace through the streets, receiving praise and honor as they went. People threw laurel crowns to them, and by the end of the procession Reiva thought she had seen enough crowns to array a full legion.

She was walking in the front of the Adepts, as recipient of the highest honors. It felt...strange. She could feel the weight of a laurel on her head. She could feel the mantle hanging around her shoulders. She could hear the cheers of the crowd, see their jubilation.

But in her mind, she saw Luo dropping face-first in the river. She heard Mylla snapping at her in rage, the last conversation they would ever share. She saw Tolm give her a nod before going down that other corridor.

Tolm. He was alive. She was sure of it. After all, he had been the greatest among them. She may have received the honors, but there was no doubt in her mind that, had Tolm stayed behind, it would have been him walking in her place right now.

But he had left, and in doing so had ensured she received everything she wanted. And now that she had it—now that all the city could see what she had earned—all she could wonder was whether Tolm had truly made the right choice. Was there really something more out there? Something worth giving this up?

After the parade, there was a great feast in the Sanctum, served by the younger Initiates—a job Reiva had done many times, and each time wondered whether she would claim the seat of premier honor. When she finally sat down, her place second only to the members of the Circle of Peers, she felt her stomach flutter.

She looked down across the table, looking at the others—Phetan,

Caulo, Ela—who regarded her with respectful glances. They had said their congratulations, and had even sounded somewhat sincere. But then she looked at Domi, who practically beamed at her. She looked at Alyat, who had an expression she could only name as pride.

Yes, she was glad to be here. Not just because of what she had done, but because of what others had done for her. She could not have been here in this spot were it not for Alyat and Domi's commitment to aiding her.

Tolm's as well, for that manner. She silently raised her cup to him in gratitude, and she hoped he had found what he was after as well. How strange that after so many years of thinking only one of them could get what they were after, it turned out they would both find what they sought in the aftermath of one of the bloodiest field missions in living memory?

There was much congratulating and toasting throughout the night, and Reiva had to channel aether more than once to burn off the effects of all the wine she was receiving. Apparently, the servers had been told not to take no for an answer when it came to filling the graduates' cups.

Afterwards, once she had shaken the last hand and accepted the last congratulatory remark, she retired to a room—*her* room.

She still was not of sufficient rank in the Corps to have a permanent residence in the Sanctum—that came after several years of service—but whenever she was in Lazarra, she would have a place all to herself. Her chest of personal belongings, meager as they were, had already been moved from the dormitory. She stripped off her formal attire and changed into a set of civilians' clothes. Then she counted out a handful of coins and set out into the night.

As an Adept, she was no longer bound by curfews, so she received a nod from the Orphans at the gate, and the way was opened.

The streets were quiet by now, those still awake either collapsed in their beds or reveling in the taverns. Reiva was grateful for it. She had had enough attention for one day. That was why she'd left her mantle—the precious gold-fringed mantle she had struggled seven years for—behind. Now that she was a commissioned Adept, she was no longer bound by the requirement to wear it off-duty.

Technically, she was still expected to wear it, as a matter of decorum and honor, but folks always looked the other way when you had just received your commission, as a matter of tradition. One brief moment of peace and privacy before the true life of service began.

She didn't want to think of that now. She wanted to look back.

So she made her way to the docks.

Standing at the edge of the sea, pitch black under the night sky, save the shimmering of reflected starlight and the moon's glow, she retrieved the coins. One by one, she took them and tossed them into the water.

Mylla.

Drop.

Luo.

Drop.

Brefon.

Drop.

Levin and Artha.

Drop, drop.

On she went, naming them to herself in an act of quiet remembrance and respect. Some of them were people she knew well, others only briefly. Some she knew to be dead, others she had no idea.

All of them had played some role in getting her to where she was now.

And so she came to the last coin. She held it between thumb and forefinger, staring at the black waters below.

She thought of her mother, who had sold her in the grove for a clinking bag of silver.

The coin rested between her fingers. And she stood there, and she stood, and she sifted through memories.

"Well, look who it is."

Reiva closed her fist around the coin, turning. She smiled. "Domi."

"Personally," began the Adept of Sea, "I was hoping for some solitude down here."

"Sorry to intrude, then."

Domi waved it off. "Oh it's fine—better to get it over with now anyway."

Reiva's smile wilted. "Tomorrow, then?"

Domi nodded, taking a deep breath. She had always loved the smell of the ocean—even before she had discovered her Art. As she breathed in, she seemed to stand a little straighter. "Yep. Tomorrow. First port of call: Ouranopolis. Then down to skirt the Southlands for a while. There won't be a pirate with the stones to sail once they hear Adept Domi is on the waves."

Reiva snorted, shaking her head. "No, I'm sure they won't."

"And you? Where are they shipping you off?"

"Hyrgallia."

Domi's eyes bulged. "You'll freeze."

"I don't think I can."

"Ah, true. Well then, be careful—I'm sure more than one enterprising legionnaire will try to charm his way into your tent to take advantage of that."

"I'll be wary."

"And even if there's a nice one, he has to come to me first."

"Even *if* something like that were to happen, I don't recall signing off on that condition."

Domi threw an arm around her. "Oh Reiva, a young, innocent maiden such as yourself *needs* someone wise in the ways of the world to keep an eye out for you."

"So I'll never be rid of you," she drawled, smiling as she said it.

"Afraid not."

"Thank the gods you'll be at sea so often—otherwise, I don't know if I could breathe. But how will you manage without me to occupy your time?"

"Oh, I'm sure I'll find some interesting people to keep me busy out there—Karellans are a handsome lot, you know. Hypothetically, if I found one willing to be shared—"

"Domi."

"Just as a thought experiment I mean—"

"I'll shove you into the water here and now."

"The last time that happened, things didn't go so well for you. It took, what, three people to pin me down?"

"You always were a difficult one."

"Well, if that's truly how you feel, I'll be glad to set sail and go far away."

Reiva scoffed, throwing her arm around Domi. "I jest."

"Reiva? Joking? Someone sound the horns from the mount of the gods."

Now she stepped away, batting at Domi's arm. "I *do* tell jokes. Everyone has heard me tell jokes! Only you say I don't have a sense of humor."

"Because you get like *this*."

"Like what?"

"Mm, fiery?"

"*Ha ha*, the queen of comedy."

Domi shrugged, turning back to the sea, a melancholic grin on her face. Reiva sat down on the edge of the dock, letting her feet dangle over the water.

"So, are you still talking to Hiran?" she asked eventually.

"Hm?"

"That Orphan you were *friends* with."

"He got betrothed. Last year."

"Oh. Yes, you told me."

Domi snorted. "No, it's all right. I'm happy for him. We were never serious. It wouldn't have worked anyway, me being away all the time."

"I suppose."

For a while, they lingered in silence. Reiva began thinking of her dispatch to Hyrgallia. She'd be on her own—no supervising Adepts, only legionnaires wondering if they could rely on her. It would be of paramount importance that she prove herself a competent servant of the Emperor. Sure, today she had been inundated with praise, but

Alyat had sternly impressed on her the significance of her first mission as a full Adept.

'People will be watching you,' he had said this morning, as she was receiving her shoulder tattoo before the ceremony. *'They'll be waiting for you to slip up, ready to pounce at the slightest sign you're fragile or incompetent. The first year of service has the highest mortality rate.'*

She fixed her gaze on the distant, faint line dividing sea and sky.

'There are already rumors going around that it's a fine coincidence you were the only survivor on that mission. It wouldn't be the first time foul play had transpired for the sake of first place.'

Well, she knew the truth. And she would prove to all the world that she deserved every last shred of honor they had dressed her with.

Standing up, she turned her back on the ocean. "I'm going back to get some sleep. It was a long day."

Domi pulled her into a tight hug. "It was." She held Reiva at arm's length. "I know you heard it plenty, but congratulations."

"Thank you. And not just for this, I mean...for everything. You pushed me along."

"Yes, you do owe me quite a lot."

Reiva snorted, disengaging from the other Adept. "Well, when we're in Lazarra at the same time, I'll buy you a drink. How long do you think it'll take to pay off my debt?"

"Oh, a lifetime. But I can tolerate that sort of friendship."

"Glad to hear it. Farewell then, Adept Domi."

"Farewell, Adept Reiva."

She walked away from the docks, making her way back to the Sanctum. She still carried the final coin, but she paid it no mind. Instead, Reiva turned all her thoughts and senses to drinking in the nocturnal weight of the city around her. A city she had come to as a slave, a city she now walked as its champion.

She was an Imperial Adept, and no one could take that from her.

EPILOGUE

MONTHS LATER…

Tjanef threw his net into the water. It was a warm morning, which he was grateful for.

He would be more grateful if his nets were full before the sun rose too high, but he wasn't particularly in a rush.

After all, he had his life back.

Another fishing boat came alongside his. "Tjanef!" called Hasut from the rudder. "You're up early."

He smiled. "Iset woke me up baking fig cakes. You want to try one?"

The man laughed heartily. "You know I would."

Yes, Tjanef had his life back and then some.

It had been tricky, piloting that little boat out of sight of the island. His Art of Water could not move as fast as the *Ars Thalassan*, but he hadn't been the number one Initiate in his cohort for no reason. There hadn't been food or water on board, but he had been able to separate out drinkable water from the sea. He'd even caught a fish by lifting a sphere of water out of the sea, the creature trapped within.

As soon as he had spotted the merchant ship and discerned it was heading for him, he had slipped underwater. And there he had stayed, holding onto the bottom of the merchant vessel by sticking a knife into its hull, pulling bubbles of air down from the surface. When night had fallen, he'd snuck aboard and stolen some food, then slipped out of sight before dawn. His luck was good, as the guards aboard the ship weren't particularly alert. What's more, they were even headed to Mizkhar.

Yes, his luck had been very good.

Once he'd made it onto dry land, it was almost too simple—he spoke the language, after all. It wasn't even much of a lie to say he had escaped from a pirate ship. His plight stirred a traveling mapmaker's sympathies, and when the man learned Tjanef was literate in not just Mizkhari but Karellan *and* Lazarran, he had readily taken him along.

The trickiest part was getting Iset out of his old village without anyone recognizing him, but it had been many years. She had known him right away, though—and that brought a smile to his face even now, so many months later.

He had used a false name for much of his travels, but now that he and Iset had eloped to this little fishing village, he had gone back to using his birth name. Tjanef. He never tired of hearing people call him so.

The people of the village had been wary of the outsiders, but once they saw Tjanef's skill with the net, and once they tasted Iset's baking, they welcomed them like old family. People had already begun saying she was probably third cousins with Madam Mertyre the apothecary, anyway, so in a sense they *were* old family.

That was how things were in Mizkhar.

As it turned out, Tjanef's luck was good yet again. He had his nets full at the end of the day, and he brought them in with a light joy in his chest.

Then, as he delivered his catch to the harbormaster—an honest man who always paid a fair price—he heard something that made his ears prick up.

"—Adept in Talynis! A fire-maker!"

Tjanef turned. There was a group of fishermen crowded around the speaker—a young man by the name of Baufre. He often brought news from the wider world, which he gabbed off of passing travelers and merchants. Normally Tjanef never paid him much mind—he'd had enough of the wider world.

But today he joined the crowd. "What's all this about?" he asked.

Hasut chuckled. "Well well well—even Tjanef is interested! You never liked stories about Adepts, I thought."

Tjanef forced a smile. "Even I get curious. So tell me, Baufre, what's the news?"

The young man was practically bursting with excitement as he opened his mouth. "A fire-maker Adept in Talynis! They say she has started a war!"

It couldn't have been Reiva. The Adept Corps never sent an Adept to the land of their birth—it presented far too great a risk.

But then again, how many female Adepts with the Art of Fire were alive?

Only one.

His mind flew down the road, to his home. He thought of the threshold, beyond which his wife was preparing for him to return so they could eat dinner. He thought of the bed where they spent their nights.

He thought of the false brick, right beside his pillow, which contained his arcane focus.

"Tell me more, Baufre. Tell me about this war."

ACKNOWLEDGMENTS

It is an Acknowledgments section cliché (among those of us who lead such interesting lives that we read Acknowledgments sections) to note that producing a book takes far more than one person—but it's true. *Adept Initiate* would be more rough, less intense, and (worst of all) just okay, were it not for the help I received.

My parents both dedicated a great deal of time, focus, and eyestrain to reading (and re-reading) this book for the sake of plot, character, and typographical errors. My dad, as per usual, was the first to start and finish the beta version; my mom told me *Adept Initiate* is "pure storytelling." And of course, my brother says it's "pretty cool" that I write. Higher praise can hardly be found, in my estimation.

Thank you to my beta readers—especially Mom, Dad, Austin, Matt, and Isaac—for quick turnarounds on a book dropped out of nowhere during a hectic time. It can be hard to know whether something you've written is actually good until someone texts, "I was supposed to start my day a few hours ago but made the mistake of opening your book."

Matt—who, true to form, only does something if he can over-do it—merits special acclaim for declining to offer feedback in a brief email, instead giving me a two hour FaceTime call. He offered invaluable feedback on Reiva's bicultural identity, the experience of integrating into a different society, and losing one's language—not to mention critical comments about the emotional arc of the book and character relationships.

Gratitude to the fine folks on the Artists Turning Pro chat server, who kindly don't mention how I post word count goals at 4AM and kindly give me a kick when I'm falling behind. Special mention on that last point goes to Cade, who more than once got me to put my money where my mouth is when it came to key deadlines.

Last but not least, my appreciation to you, the reader, for giving *Adept Initiate* your time and attention. I hope you enjoyed the ride and decide to stick around for what's coming next.

ABOUT THE AUTHOR

Nathan Tudor has researched ancient religion at Oxford, traveled the seven continents, and mastered the art of speaking in the third person. His debut novel *The Empire's Lion* tells an epic story filled with action, identity, and the struggle to do what is right in an upside-down world.

When he's not writing or reading, Nathan can be found debating matters of no particular consequence with his friends, falling down research rabbit holes, and fiddling with a hand-crank coffee grinder that's been stuck for the last few months.

Allegations that he hired an alchemist to give him the tread of a cat and the ears of a fox are categorically false.

Allegations that nathantudor.com is the best place to find him online? The reader may judge.

ALSO BY NATHAN TUDOR

The Imperial Adept

The Empire's Lion

The most-up-to-date version of this bibliography can be found at nathantudor.com